'Boils with ~~clever p~~ ... acked with gripping twists and turns, *Guess Who* is an inventive, entertaining locked room mystery that kept me utterly hooked' **Adam Hamdy**

'An ingenious twisty mystery in a totally unique setting' **Claire McGowan**

'An impressive debut and a sign of great things to come' **James Oswald**

'*Guess Who* is a fresh take on the locked room murder mystery. The plotting is intricate, the characters well drawn, and the pace never lets up as it drives headlong to the surprising end' **David C. Taylor**

'One hotel room. Six strangers. One corpse. Good fun' **Cavan Scott**

'Phenomenal. An utterly compelling and fiendishly clever read – it blew my mind ten times over' **Francesca Dorricott**

'Chris McGeorge has a knack for conjuring up the biggest of mysteries in the tightest of spaces. Dark and claustrophobic in all the right places' **Robert Scragg**

Praise for Chris McGeorge

Chris McGeorge studied MA Creative Writing (Crime/Thriller) at City University London where he wrote his first novel as his thesis. His interests are broad – spanning film, books, theatre and video games. He is a member of the Northern Crime Syndicate, a supergroup of writers from Northern England. He lives in County Durham with his partner and many, many animals.

Chris can be found on Twitter at: @crmcgeorge

By Chris McGeorge

Guess Who
Now You See Me
Inside Out

Half-Past Tomorrow

CHRIS McGEORGE

ORION

First published in Great Britain in 2021 by Orion Fiction,
an imprint of The Orion Publishing Group Ltd.,
Carmelite House, 50 Victoria Embankment
London EC4Y 0DZ

An Hachette UK Company

1 3 5 7 9 10 8 6 4 2

A CIP catalogue record for this book is
available from the British Library.

ISBN (Paperback) 978 1 4091 8759 2
ISBN (eBook) 978 1 4091 8760 8

Typeset by Input Data Services Ltd, Somerset

Printed and bound in Great Britain by Clays Ltd, Elcograf S.p.A.

MIX
Paper from
responsible sources
FSC® C104740

www.orionbooks.co.uk

for those who've found their way out of the dark

'We'll meet half-past tomorrow
Beneath a joker's dream.
We'll forgive the world it's unjust fun
And say what we really mean'

From HALF-PAST TOMORROW, CHUTNEY
AND THE BOYS (from the album Half-Past
Tomorrow, *1978)*

00.00

Colm MacArthur
Royal Navy – Operation Kingmaker
  (*Mine Countermeasures*)
50 miles off the Persian Gulf
Friday 12 October 2012
1.12 a.m. . . .

Colm MacArthur felt like he could sleep for a week. And, currently, that sleep was threatening to force him into unconsciousness. His eyelids felt heavy – slivers of a strong material he had to strain to hold up. The cool wind of the Gulf sea seemed to be the only thing keeping him awake, as his willpower and a long-expired sense of duty failed. The jet-black night stretched in front of him – the kind of night where you would question every life decision that had led you to this point – this point right here.

The day had been strenuous and filled with menial tasks that alone seemed worthless, but it was promised that they did help the vessel as a whole. He had mopped floors, tidied, washed the dishes – all jobs that the Royal Navy pamphlet had skirted over. All that had got

1

him through was the guarantee of a peaceful night.

So when his friend Gabe Steadman had volunteered them both for nightwatch, Colm could have thrown him overboard. Gabe had convinced Colm though – they needed to curry some favour and hopefully get back to something more exciting, after their high-stakes euchre game below deck had been uncovered.

HMS *Aevum*, the ship he had been calling home for the past year, was quiet, still, in a black, silent night. The only real sound apart from the wind was a slow lapping of water, as the current figured its way around the immovable vessel. Not enough to hold Colm's interest, let alone inspire consciousness.

Colm and Gabe had split the ship, and Colm was in charge of walking the port side, and he had barely managed one lap of the lengthy deck in the three hours (and counting) they'd been on shift. Now, he was leaning over a railing, looking down at the dark water below, and he didn't know how long he had been there. He would be in a lot of trouble if any of his superiors saw him, but they were all fast asleep below decks, and Colm didn't really think the ship was at risk of anything. The War on Terror was over – they had won. Both Gabe and Colm had seen it from the sidelines, mostly, but they still had some scars to show for it. Now, they were the clean-up crew – their years of experience somewhat squandered.

It sounded like Gabe was a little more enthusiastic about his job, however. If he listened really hard, he could almost hear Gabe's footfalls on the deck, gently going up and down, up and down, in about fifteen-minute cycles.

As if he had summoned them, Gabe's footsteps passed by him, on the other side of the captain's cabin as Colm straightened up, deciding he should start moving again before the cold wind jostled him along. He stretched, did his coat up tighter and started to walk.

Then Colm thought he heard Gabe stop — say something.

He stopped, listened. 'Gabe?'

Nothing.

Must've imagined it.

Colm had been silently a little worried about Gabe for a while now. The two of them had grown up together, back in the North East — a world away. He knew Gabe's history, and he knew he never wanted to join up. But for a while, he had been OK. Five years in fact. He had sucked it up, and got on with it. But now, the shadows were back in his face, the falter in his voice. He still carried on, but something had returned within him. And that worried Colm.

But maybe he was just imagining it — being overly analytical. In reality, Gabe probably was better in the Navy than himself. Maybe everything he thought of his friend were mere projections of himself. You wouldn't accuse a puddle, a reflection. Was he unhappy here?

Right now, absolutely. The night shift was Colm's least favourite activity, because it was so horrendously dull. The ship wasn't moving, and it wasn't likely you would spot a mine — they weren't exactly conspicuous.

Colm's eyelids drooped again. The wind played across his face, almost willing him to sleep. He leaned on the railing, letting it take his weight. And he felt himself slipping away, down and down into—

A loud splash. From the other side of the ship. Real.

Colm's eyes shot open. 'Gabe?' he shouted. The footfalls were gone.

Maybe something just fell.

But how? Everything was tied down; it was a quiet night (much like the one Colm wanted to sleep through) – and the ship was stationary.

'Gabe?'

Another splash. Smaller.

Something was wrong.

Colm straightened up. His mind was full of ridiculous notions – pirates mainly, sharks less so.

Where was Gabe?

Colm started to walk around the side of the cabin, crossing the unspoken line into Gabe's jurisdiction. He looked down the long span of the ship – nothing, no one. No pirates. But also – no Gabe.

Something was very wrong.

He turned to look up the other end, the wind picking up and adding a chill to the air. It took far too long for his brain to make sense of what he saw. 'Gabe – what . . .?'

Gabe was sitting on the railing, his legs over the side of the ship. He was holding something – something big and heavy, with chains wrapped around it. One of the chains snaked down to his ankle.

Gabe looked at him, in his full Navy uniform. Despite his shaved head, which reflected the moonlight, and his old and tired eyes – he looked at Colm as his younger self. 'Wasn't meant to be,' Gabe said. And he let go of the thing in his hand, a metal block as heavy as Colm's eyelids had been. And Gabe was pulled down, over the side. Shivering icy horror in the still night. A loud splash. And then another.

Colm launched forward. 'Gabe!' He inhabited the air that his friend had a second before. He looked down into the sea. And he saw his friend looking up at him as he was dragged to the depths. It looked like Gabe was smiling.

And Colm MacArthur never had a good night's sleep again.

01.00

The Past in the Static

01.01

Shirley Steadman
Chester-Le-Street, North East of England
Tuesday 9 February 2021
7.05 p.m.

'Ooh, ain't you a sight for sore eyes, lass?' old Harold said, as Shirley walked up to his bed with her badge and her clipboard. Harold had been in hospital the last three times she had visited the ward, and had developed a fondness for her, as she had him. She was not actually sure what was wrong with him, despite his arm, but he always seemed to have trouble speaking. It made him out of breath, as though he'd had a lifetime of walking uphill. 'You look younger every time I see ya.'

'Harold,' Shirley said, smiling and tapping her clipboard. 'I'm barely younger than you.'

'Mebbes, me bonny lass. But ya divant look a dey over twenny,' he chuckled through his thick accent. Twenty years living here and she still had trouble with some words.

'That's enough, you,' Shirley replied, with the air of

authority she had cultivated when raising her children, and clicked her pen. 'What'll it be today?'

'Hmmm . . .' Harold pretended to muse. He would probably have been comically scratching his chin if his arm wasn't stuck in a sling. 'Wey a bit o' Bowie, o' course. Giss us the one boot the spacemen.' His memory also wasn't the best. But Shirley couldn't really hold that against him – neither was hers. 'How's it go agen?'

Shirley nodded and wrote 'Harold' and 'Space Oddity' down on the paper on the clipboard. 'Ground control to Major Tom?'

'Aye, that one,' Harold said, who then gave a quick rendition of the chorus.

Shirley smiled and let him finish. 'Who's it dedicated to?' she asked.

'Wey you, of course.' Harold chortled.

'Harold!' Shirley tutted.

'Oo alreet then. Guess it berra be ta me wife.'

'That's better,' Shirley said, writing in the dedication box on the form. 'Do you want help getting the head-phones on so you can listen?'

'Aye if ya can.'

Shirley went around the bed, careful to avoid any wires or important equipment. The small TV unit was against the back wall, discarded. She took it and swung it around over Harold's bed. She detached the small pair of headphones, like the ones handed out on aeroplanes, and put them on Harold's head. Then she switched the unit to radio mode and went to channel 5. 'There you go. I'll be on from about eight fifteen.'

'Yer a diamond, lass,' Harold said, winking at her.

Shirley smiled back, slightly worried that she had just seen that Harold was on a fresh IV. That hadn't been there last week. Something was wrong with him, and it wasn't just a broken arm.

She said her goodbyes and left the room.

The patients of Ward 14 had really outdone themselves. Usually they weren't very receptive – the Ward was Orthopaedics and often had elderly patients or people who were really in no fit state to listen to a request on the radio. But today they had wanted a relative smorgasbord of requests. Shirley actually didn't know how she was going to fit them all into the show, or make them flow into each other. Sure, the old favourites were being played – an elderly man with a leg suspended in a sling wanted 'My Way' dedicated to his wife, a young woman wanted 'Wannabe' by the Spice Girls for her daughter and a woman about Shirley's age wanted Vera Lynn, which was very nice but also incredibly typecast. But there were also some oddball choices – a song about a JCB digger which she didn't know existed, some rap by Childish Gambino (a name she had heard before but never listened to) and something by (she hoped she had written it down right) Wise Kalifer. She was sure some of these songs would have expletives in, but they had the radio edits, so it didn't really matter.

Shirley finished her tour of the ward in the traditional way, by stopping by the nurses' station and asking if they wanted anything played. The nurses, all now younger than her daughter, thought amongst themselves and decided on 'I Gotta Get Out of This Place'. Shirley smiled and laughed, as though this were the first time she had heard that request, and wrote it down on her clipboard. She thanked the nurses and left the ward, making her way slowly to the lifts. She paused in front of them, her finger hovering next to the call button. She retracted her finger, remembering what Marsha had said in their embroidery group about her joints seizing up because she never did any exercise. She wasn't going to have that, so she took the stairs instead.

Down the last corridor, a group of nurses passed her, and to her dismay, she saw a flash of ginger hair amongst them. It was Callie. She tried to keep her head down, but as they passed, their eyes met. Shirley felt the stab of guilt that always came with Callie's gaze. Shirley hoped that Callie felt warmth come with hers. Why did they always have to meet like this? It always seemed to happen. She knew Callie worked here, but someone upstairs had to have it in for her. She used to let it ruin her night – thought that she deserved it, and in some way she still did, but she pushed the guilt down inside and forged onward.

She got back to the studio a little out of breath, her legs throbbing, promising pain tomorrow, which was almost the opposite of seizing up, so she guessed that was fine. As she input the passcode and got into the small box room, down a forgotten hospital corridor, she heard Ken Vox's familiar voice coming from Studio One.

In the packed room, a designer/magician had managed to get a small area with chairs and a computer, a cupboard full of old vinyl records, and two soundproof studios. Shirley made her way to Studio Two, by way of clicking the kettle on. She sat down in the small space, in front of a large, expansive radio deck with hundreds of sliders and knobs – of which every hospital radio member only used about five.

She looked through the window that was between the studios into Studio One. It was empty of course. Ken Vox hadn't been part of the Chester-Le-Street Hospital Radio team for going on two years now. He had been picked up by Metro Radio, a 'real' station. But, due to a loophole, the hospital was still allowed to play his old shows. So they just played them over and over, until volunteers came in to take over and do live shows.

There used to be a big team on Tuesday nights – now it was just Shirley. She didn't particularly mind.

She flicked the computer on and started searching for the requests. Fifteen minutes and a cup of tea later, they were all sorted (Wise Kalifer appeared to correctly be Wiz Khalifa and many of the songs seemed to be rather inappropriate) and put into the computer program. She sent the playlist through to Studio One, ready for her to go on. All that was left before she went live was to find one song that wasn't on the system but they would have on vinyl. She had forty minutes to do this, so turned the kettle on again, and went into the cupboard.

Vinyl records, stacked on shelves, lined every surface, save for the far end, which was piled up with old radio equipment. Given that the records were so thin, they were alphabetised with small scraps of paper poking out to denote a new letter. You had to pull out a record to know where you were within that letter, so there was still a fair amount of guesswork involved. Shirley started pulling out records in the C area, reaching up to the top shelf.

She was looking for a record by the rock band Charlie. She had never heard of them and the man who requested it, his neck in a brace, had delighted in giving her a small potted history. Formed in the seventies, a UK band with four members, ten albums, still going today (apparently). It was the kind of information which she wouldn't retain – wouldn't have, even in her memory's heyday – but also the reason why she did this job. She loved how people could hold on so dearly to something that had never touched her life in the slightest. It was a constant reminder about how big the world really was.

After a few false records, she finally found Charlie's title album which the system said had the song that she needed. She reached up and pulled the record out, satisfied. She rested it on a lower shelf, and pulled the next record out halfway so she knew where to put it back for later.

As she did, she stopped for a second. The next record along – *Half-Past Tomorrow*. Chutney and the Boys. The familiar cover art of the sphinx in Egypt but with seventies shades on – Chutney and her boys standing on it in various places, rocking out with guitars. She hadn't seen it in a long time.

She stood back, realising that her body was shaking slightly. The memories, the ones she would never ever lose, came flooding back. Gabe as a child rocking out just like Chutney, bouncing on his bed, a broom in place of a guitar. 'Half-Past Tomorrow', his favourite song, playing over and over and over – ironically the only slow song on the album, and very unworthy of an upbeat routine.

Gabe.

How would things be different if . . .?

The kettle whistled.

And Shirley blinked the immovable past away.

She made a cup of tea, put the Charlie record over next to the computer in the lobby area, and realised she still had too much time. Ken Vox was gruffly talking about something, showcasing that rugged charm that had landed him a real radio job. She had time to do something that made her feel better.

She went into the cupboard again, but this time went to the back, where the stack of old equipment was piled up. She removed a box from the top, as she did almost every other week. She took it and her mug of tea into Studio Two, propped the box on the desk and opened it. Inside there was an old radio set, far bigger than anything that would be seen maybe even in the last century.

Turning it on, she hooked it up to the studio desk so she could hear it better. Immediately, a harsh static filled the studio – the kind of white noise that wasn't possible on radios nowadays. She immediately felt an intense feeling of warmth, nostalgia and longing – the kind of feeling that almost wrenched your consciousness out of the present moment and propelled you back to happier times. In all of Shirley's seventy years, she had never felt

15

a noise so comforting as the static between radio stations.

She turned the knob to change the frequency and voices started fading in and out. Tyneside on 93.5, BBC Newcastle on 95.4, Metro Radio, among many more. The stations stacked up as she continued on her journey. Once she got to the end of the dial, she switched over to the AM band and started afresh. This was an altogether quieter track – AM stations were shutting down, and the ones that were around were often just different frequencies of BBC stations. But she wasn't looking for a station – she was looking for a fine patch of static.

She found one. And she put on the sweaty pair of over-ear headphones connected to the desk. And sat back – closing her eyes.

When you had lived as long as Shirley had, you had to take comfort in the little things. And this was her little thing. Peace and quiet for the half an hour between gathering requests and the live show, where she could just sit and listen to the static and not exist for a moment. She cleared her mind – no Bob, no Deena and the kids, no Gabe – just the noise.

On the cold nights, in this studio alone, in her head, it was so easy to live in the past. Seven decades of living, seven decades of decisions, seven decades of mistakes and fumbles and poor judgement – it could crush someone. Her body was betraying her – those stairs she climbed were going to put her out of commission till (probably) next week, her bones ached and felt like glass, sometimes it hurt just to breathe. It was harder to get up in the morning, and it was harder to sleep at night. In pure

evolutionary terms, she had lived too long. She had out-
lived her usefulness to the species. She was in overtime.

It was important to her not to live in the past. But that
didn't mean she couldn't do just that.

'. . . future . . .'

A voice? She opened her eyes and looked at the old
radio. Something in the static? Maybe just a wobbly frequency – these old radios were temperamental.

Shirley straightened up – ignoring a twinge in her
back – and looked at which frequency she was on. 66.2
AM. No radio stations anywhere near it. Maybe just
imagination then.

'. . . then . . .'

Same voice.

Shirley put on her glasses from around her neck. She
ever-so-slowly turned the dial. 66.1. Nothing. 66.0.
Nothing. So she turned the other way. 66.3. '. . . was off
to the . . .' The voice louder. More concrete. 66.4. '. . . in
Newcastle. The hounds are running and so are we.'

66.4. That was it. A radio station off the map. Pirate.
One that had never been there before.

She smiled. Pirate radio was an interesting concept.
A radio station made by an individual or a small group
using independent equipment to broadcast a transmis-
sion. The idea was older than she was, and that was
saying something. The signal must've been coming from
nearby – pirate radio often did. The signal was weak as
it was, even with the hospital radio's equipment which
could amplify the old radio. The voice was wavering,
warbled, and fluctuating in volume. The voice was also

17

strange, as though it were being disguised, fed through a computer. Shirley's interest was piqued.

She pressed the headphones further to her ears. 'Looks like it's time for the news! There's nowhere better to come to for news about Chester-Le-Street and the local area than 66.40 Mallet AM.'

Mallet AM. What a wonderful name. And it had a news segment too. This almost seemed like a legitimate radio station. It was a great effort. Whoever was playing around was doing a good job. Was this a man or woman, lonely and bored, just having a bit of fun? Or maybe a group of children experimenting? Whoever it was, she was glad she could be here to hear it.

'Today is the tenth of February,' the voice continued, 'and let's get into it. A pretty light news day today, nothing much going on. Chester Park has been seeing a rise in dog fouling in recent weeks, so Park Manager Art Fowler has put up signs to keep dogs off various patches of grass. The sign was promptly urinated on by Fiona Smith's dachshund Rodney. It is uncertain whether Art Fowler has noticed the staunch lambasting of rules yet – but, rest assured, we will have more as it develops.'

Shirley laughed and clapped her hands. This was just like a real news show. Such fun. It was exactly what she needed – this radio station was priceless.

'Houses in Chester-Le-Street are being sold at a premium to try to prove to local authorities not to bulldoze several vacant properties up near the hospital. After the dark times of last year, many businesses have been affected – and the housing market is no exception. After

18

many rushed and reportedly heated meetings at the local civic centre, MP Ralph Harver has struck a deal with private company Havanna Housings to cut costs and attract new people to the local area. It seems as though it is working now the housing market has bounced back. So much so in fact that it seems Chester-Le-Street Leisure Centre may be in jeopardy of closure and demolition.

'Here at Mallet AM, we have reached out to Harver to see how likely it is that the Leisure Centre will suffer the same fate as many of our local recreational venues. It is clear that this would be a terrible blow to the community, especially for young families, people who work at the Leisure Centre, and avid swimmers. We will update as the situation develops.'

Shirley frowned. She hadn't heard that Chester Baths (the local lingo for the blocky old building down between the bottom of Front Street and the park) was threatened with closure. She remembered taking the kids there, and seeing them sloshing around in the kiddie pool, with mesh butterflies hanging from the ceiling, cartoon animals with exaggerated smiles painted on the walls and the air thick with chlorine. It would be sad to see it go, if indeed the demolition came to fruition.

The host continued: 'And, lastly, Seb Starith, the proprietor of Starith's Bakery at the top of Front Street, suffered a nasty fall at 12.17 p.m. when he fell off his ladder while attempting to put up a new sign on the front of the bakery. He fell three feet and is reported to have bruised his coccyx. He was admitted to Chester-Le-Street Hospital for a check-up and remains there at least overnight. It is unconfirmed whether he has broken anything else, although sources say he has. Again, we will bring you more as this develops.'

This was odd. Shirley had not heard anything about this, and she was down Front Street that afternoon. No one at the embroidery group in the Parish Centre had said anything, and those women were hotbeds of gossip, especially Marsha. What was more, Shirley had walked past the bakery and not seen any commotion.

'The bakery continues to be run by Starith's granddaughter and she is keen to keep business to usual hours.'

Maybe that was the answer. Shirley had gone past about three-ish. Probably poor Seb had already been brought to this very hospital, and his granddaughter had already started up again. She hadn't looked in so that was probably what had happened.

'We will be back tomorrow at the same time with more news, but for now let's switch gears and go in for another hour of some sultry royalty-free music. Here we go.' And after a few seconds of silence, some crackly up-beat music came through the headphones – sickly-sweet like the music you would hear in a hotel lift.

Shirley listened for a minute or two, hoping for more but knowing the voice was gone, and then took the headphones off.

66.40 Mallet AM. What a chuckle. And a relatively professional outfit. Whoever was in charge, the one be-hind the microphone, really had a knack for it. He or she would be an asset on the radio team – they clearly knew their way around equipment more than most of the volunteers. A pirate radio station in this day and age – how novel. She had to remember to tell Deena when she came to visit.

She took a piece of paper and wrote the frequency down. And only then did she check her watch.

Drat! She had less than five minutes. She had been so consumed in her discovery that she had forgotten all about the show. She quickly rushed around, gathering up her request forms, the Charlie record and her cold cup of tea. She opened the door to Studio One and got comfortable in the hot seat. Ken Vox was doing his outro, and she had to be ready to fade down on him and up on her.

She ran through her usual introduction in her head. The date, the day, a humorous fun fact she had happened upon that week, and then straight into Ward 14's finest selections. She did like to think that somewhere she might have fans – although the mere notion of constant listeners in a hospital where the clientele changed hourly, let alone weekly, was a bit ridiculous. But she still liked to think it – and this opening salvo was what her fans would expect.

She already had her fun fact lined up: *Did you know that the scientific term for brain freeze is sphenopalatine ganglioneuralgia?* She had had to recite that four or five times in the mirror to get it to stick.

So she was ready. Except . . .

She brought the computer up and checked the date.

And then a bizarre thought clicked in to place. The

thing that had been wrong with the Mallet AM new segment. The voice on the pirate station had said he was reading the news for the tenth of February.

But, and this was a decidedly queer thing, it was the ninth.

01.02

Shirley's bungalow was less than a mile from the hospital in between Front Street and a district of densely packed houses known locally as the Avenues. Shirley lived on the outskirts, but that was too close for Deena, who had warned her against taking the bungalow. The Avenues were known to be rough, but Shirley didn't care. She had just needed to get out of the grand house Bob had bought in Houghton-Le-Spring, and she had ended up rattling around in alone, and downsize to a more suitable home.

When she got through the door, Moggins greeted her with a yowl and a purr. Moggins was a seven-year-old Norwegian Forest cat, white with tabby markings. Deena had got him for Shirley as a housewarming present, and represented her daughter's constant desire to look after her. Shirley didn't hold it against Moggins, although she had always thought of herself more of a dog person, but the intent had not been best received.

'Hello, dear,' she said to the cat, as it came up and

23

rubbed against her ankles. 'I suppose you want your supper.' It was the only time Moggins showed any real affection for his housemate, and that was fine. Shirley appreciated the independence afforded to both of them. Refreshing after Bob.

She chuckled to herself as she took off her shoes, slipped into her moccasins and made her way down the hallway to the kitchen. Everything in the bungalow was small, short, not unlike the hospital cupboard known as the radio station. The kitchen was compact, the living room homely, the one bedroom tight, and the bathroom sufficient. The two hallways were the only spaces in which she found herself having to move far, and even then it was minuscule compared to the distance she had to trek in the old house.

And no stairs was a constant blessing, particularly when she had bruised her hip tripping and slamming into one of the kitchen counters. If she had been in the old place, Deena probably would have fretted so much she would've moved her whole family in. But as it happened, in this little place, she was allowed to recover herself, with Moggins as her only healthcare professional.

She turned the kitchen light on. Two sides of the room were lined with cupboards and appliances. An oven, a washing machine, a dishwasher, a sink. Nothing too fancy. The rest of the room was a small dining area, where she kept her ironing board, and a small kitchen table by the window with two chairs. It wasn't much at all, but it was home, and it may've been her old ways, but she felt most comfortable in the kitchen.

She always liked doing something, and although she had succumbed of late to the allures of daytime television and the very British act of 'putting your feet up', she still felt most alive when 'doing'. That was why she had so many activities on her weekly schedule – hospital radio, embroidery, and volunteering at the local RSPCA shop, punctuated with social lunches and sometimes babysitting the grandchildren. It was as though she were screaming at the man upstairs that she wasn't quite done yet. And although she was a pensioner, and she may not do anything else vital enough to write in a history book, she could still do some good.

Shirley nodded to herself as she went into the cupboard and got out one of Moggins' favourite sachets of food. Salmon and beef. An awful concoction in theory, but even she had to admit it smelled quite good.

Moggins jumped up on the counter as she squeezed the sachet into his bowl.

'There you go, sir. Don't eat it all at once.'

Although it looked as though Moggins had set about doing just that.

She turned the kettle on and adjusted the thermostat. Getting old could just as well be called getting cold. She heard the heating flame come on in the quiet bungalow.

Peace.

'Hello, Shirley.'

Behind her. In the room. She didn't jump. Not anymore. In fact, she did the opposite – she froze. Her heart leapt. That familiar voice. The voice she knew best in the world. The voice she heard in her dreams.

She turned around. He was there, sitting at the table – a picture of how he would've looked now. Shaved head. Stubble. Wrinkles showing how much he smiled when he was alive. 'Hello, Gabe.' And she couldn't help but smile herself as her eyes filled with tears.

She quickly got ahold of herself and turned back to the kettle, taking another mug out of the cupboard – Gabe's *Doctor Who* mug in the shape of the TARDIS – and making a fresh tea. She took both of the mugs to the kitchen table and placed one in front of him.

Moggins ran out of the room, no doubt not understanding what was happening, not understanding who Shirley was talking to. Shirley didn't know if she understood either. All she knew was that about a year ago, Gabe had started to come and . . . 'visit' as she liked to call it. Sometimes she would be pottering around the bungalow, and all of a sudden he would be there. And she knew . . . she knew it wasn't . . . real . . . but that didn't mean it wasn't . . . It was complicated.

She sat down. 'You're here.'

Gabe looked at her – not smiling, but not frowning. He looked into her. 'Why do you do this?' He sounded exactly like . . . well, like himself.

'What?' she said.

'Make me a cup of tea? Every time.' The only thing was that he sometimes hesitated when he spoke, as if Shirley's subconscious was working out how her son would say the things he would say.

'I'm old now, son,' Shirley replied. 'Isn't that what old people do? They make their guests a cup of tea.'

It was true. Her life was measured in hot beverages.

'I suppose it is,' Gabe said, almost dreamlike. 'But you know I don't drink it. I can't.'

Shirley sobbed. She reached in her pocket for a hanky but couldn't find one. There were fresh ones in the drawer beside the kitchen sink, but she didn't want to turn away in case he left. Sometimes he did that – she went out of the room and when she came back, he had disappeared. She didn't know the rules of what was happening, but, to be safe, she kept him in her sights. 'Just habit, I suppose.'

'How have you been, Shirley?' Gabe asked.

'Can you call me Mum?'

'Do you want me to call you Mum?'

'Not unless you want to.'

'Shirley,' Gabe said, pausing, as though he'd been through this a thousand times. He had. 'I can only do what you think me to do. You know how this works. I will call you Mum if you think I should.'

Shirley thought for a second. As she always did. This was well-worn territory. But she thought that she might feel differently, but she found that her answer was the same. 'No. Don't.'

'Why?' His voice serene, calm. Maybe even at peace.

Shirley smiled through the tears. 'I didn't earn it.'

Gabe didn't react, merely regarding his steaming cup of tea. 'OK then. So how are you, Shirley?'

'Something did happen today, at the radio station. I've told you that I do hospital radio, haven't I?'

Gabe nodded.

'Well, I was playing with an old radio after I had finished preparing for my requests show. And I found this very odd, but very impressive, pirate radio station. Mallet AM, it was called. And this computery voice was presenting shows. Just a lot of music, I think. But I happened to tune into it when the news was coming on. And, in retrospect, it was rather odd. The presenter got the date wrong, so it was almost comical. As though it was reading news from tomorrow. Although obviously it was just a mistake. A simple mistake – which was odd because the rest was so professional. It was almost like I was listening to a real radio station.'

'Fascinating,' Gabe said, monotone.

'You don't think so.'

'I think what you think. If this is important to you, it's important to me.'

'It's just a queer little thing is all,' Shirley said. And she wished, not for the first time, that she was talking to the real Gabe. Not this . . . shell. 'I'm impressed more than anything. I do hope it is live again the next time I go to the station. I wish I knew who ran it – it must be close, as pirate stations can't have much reach. I just wish I could contact them, and let them know how much I enjoyed it.'

'But you didn't recognise the voice?'

'I said, it was disguised in some way.'

'But you didn't recognise any mannerisms? A dialect maybe?'

That was an odd thing for him to say. 'What are you trying to tell me?' Shirley asked.

Gabe blinked. 'What are you trying to tell yourself?'

'Oh, I don't know,' Shirley said, throwing her hands up and chortling. 'I'm at a loss.'

Gabe chortled too. 'Then I am as well.'

They both laughed, and Shirley sipped her tea, and Gabe looked at his. Until finally she calmed down and she decided to address the elephant in the room. 'What is happening here?'

Gabe remained silent.

'You aren't here. You can't be here.'

Nothing.

Shirley felt emotional again, and suddenly very tired. It had been a long day, and she decided that, when talking with oneself, over a table with two mugs of tea, one shouldn't mince words. 'Am I going mad? Has my brain finally given up the ghost?'

Gabe just stared. 'Do you think you're going mad?'

'No.'

'Then maybe you're not.'

'Maybe?'

'Maybe you have just conjured me because you need someone to talk to.'

'Oh, I am perfectly happy with the amount of social interaction I have right now, thank you very much. I have Deena calling me every other day, trying to convince me that it's for her benefit. I have the girls at embroidery who drive me up the wall. And I also have Moggins with me.'

'Where is he now?' Gabe asked – he had never liked cats, or rather cats had never liked him. That was why they had never had one when he and Deena were growing up. Cats were allergic to him, even when he was a baby. She would take him for a walk in the stroller, and any they came across would arch their backs and hiss. When he grew older, he would try to touch them and stroke them, but they would have none of it, darting away before he could get to them. He was too heavy-handed, and daunting. And as he became a teenager, the cats' hatred for him became shared.

'He doesn't like it when I talk to someone who's not there,' Shirley said.

Gabe nodded. 'Fair enough.'

Shirley took a sip of tea. 'Can I get you anything? I can make you a bacon and banana sandwich. I keep buying bacon and bananas even though I don't eat them. Just in case I ever need to make one. I probably shouldn't even be having bread with my cholesterol. Deena would have a fit. But I buy them. Because that is what I've always done. And that's what I'll do until I drop. Just you see.' She trailed off and then added, 'Just you see' again for some reason.

Gabe was offering nothing, doing much the same as he had when he was really here. If he had just offered her more, let her know what was happening, maybe he would still be alive. She could have helped him.

It was so bizarre. It was as if he were actually in the room sitting across from her. She had tried to touch him a few times, put her hand on his, but he always moved away. Her mind protecting itself. She couldn't believe her imagination was so vivid that it was able to conjure up a perfect image of her son. Every tiny detail was accounted for. If she stared enough, she could see the small risen scar on his forehead that he got leaning on a tabletop that wasn't screwed down at school. She could see his beard dandruff that he had never been able to get rid of, no matter how many treatments he put on it. She could see the abnormal ridges of his upper ears that made him look vaguely elf-like – and made him an easy target at school for ridicule.

And there was more – his smell was there. His musty aftershave that he always seemed to bathe in, that never failed to succumb to a slight scent of body odour. Gabe always ran hot, so always seemed to be a little sweaty. Glistening. And that smell was there – now.

And his clothing – dressed up in the old Metallica T-shirt and ripped jeans he used to wear every single day just to spite his clean-freak father.

It was such a perfect vision of Gabe Steadman that it felt decidedly eerie. What was that phrase? Ah yes, the 'uncanny valley'. This version of her son was awfully uncanny.

'What?' he said. His voice – exactly as she remembered it, if a little deeper, older.

She was staring. She was seeing, hearing, smelling her son as he would be now, today, in 2021. A year he would never see.

The first time Gabe had appeared at the kitchen table, Shirley had spent most of the time screaming and crumpled in the corner of the room. Gabe had just sat there – looking at her with nothing in his eyes. Her mind had

not fully rendered him yet. She screamed so much that her neighbour came around to see what was happening — even though her bungalow was detached and his house was almost 100 metres away. She kept him on the front porch, and when she had returned to the kitchen, Gabe had disappeared. She chalked it up to getting old, and something happening in her body that was not optimal.

But then he came back, again and again and again. And eventually she stopped screaming and crying, and she began to talk.

That was a year ago. And here they were.

'What?' Gabe said again.

'It's nothing,' Shirley replied. But she didn't know if it really was.

'You said you were wondering why I was here?' Gabe said. 'Maybe you have something to say.'

Shirley thought for a moment. What could she say? But the more she thought, the more she realised that was the wrong question. She had so much to say that she couldn't even begin to put it into coherent sentences. But she had to try. Shirley found her eyes filling up with tears again. 'Maybe it's because I want to say sorry. I'm so sorry, Gabe. If I had known . . . If I had even thought for a second . . . I should never have let him send you away. I knew you hated that place, but I never knew how much. And I'm just so desperately sorry. And I have to live with that every single day. That is my penance. To bury an empty box where my son's body should be. I'm paying for it. I'm paying for my silence. But that will never change the fact that you should be here right now, you should really be sitting across from me. You should be able to pick up that mug and drink your tea, and I should be able to make you a bacon and banana sandwich that you can eat. But you can't. I can't. And I'll always have to live with that.'

Gabe didn't react as she poured her heart out – in fact, he slightly tilted his head like a dog getting distracted by a noise. He let her wear herself out, and watched as she spluttered into the last of her tea. It was cold – what she deserved. When she finally got ahold of herself, Gabe cleared his throat. 'You know that you say that speech every single time I appear? Almost to the word.'

This jostled her. 'I . . . I do?' She had no recollection of ever saying that before – in fact, it was hard to remember anything that happened when she saw Gabe. All she could focus on was him.

'I wasn't talking about me, when I said you needed to say something.'

'I don't understand,' Shirley said.

Gabe appeared to be thinking about something – looking like he was choosing whether to bring something, or someone, up. What was he trying to tell her? What was she trying to tell herself? 'I'm talking about Callie.'

And there it was. Callie.

'I don't – I can't . . .' Shirley was stammering. 'You don't know . . .'

'Yes I do,' Gabe said.

Shirley got up. She had to get a hanky. She was a mess. And, in some way, she didn't want to sit there anymore. She didn't want to talk to a ghost, even if it was her son. She didn't need her mind to try to heal her right now. She wrenched herself over to the kitchen drawers, turning her back on Gabe. She got a hanky – a pink polka-dotted square of fabric – and blew her nose. 'That's better,' she said and turned back to the table.

Gabe was gone.

She stood there for a moment. And then, wiping her nose again, gathered up the mugs, pouring Gabe's tea down the sink and turning the dishwasher on.

A miaow from the doorway made her look down. Moggins was there, staring up at her.

'Don't say a word,' Shirley said. 'I know.'

It's stupid, Shirley thought.

'Come on, let's go to bed.' And as she went out of the room, she turned off the light because Moggins wouldn't.

01.03

Chester-Le-Street
Wednesday 10 February 2021
4.40 p.m.

The next day, Shirley's bungalow was abuzz with activity, much unlike the night before. Deena and her family had dropped in (unannounced as always), and the kids were tearing around the place participating in some kind of never-ending race. Shirley and Deena were sitting at the kitchen table – her daughter in the exact same place where the spectre of her son had been. They seemed to be sitting at the lap line – as every time Maisie and Kenneth went past, they gave a whoop.

Maisie, their oldest at ten, was shaping into a formidable young woman. She was arrogant, headstrong, reminding Shirley intensely of Deena. It was clear that instead of this racing game she would prefer to be sitting in the corner playing on her phone, which Shirley had harshly disapproved of. So instead she was entertaining her brother, Kenneth. Kenneth was six years old and very much still a child. He was grinning as he lapped his sister, putting his full energy into this race as though his life depended on it.

Deena had attempted to stop the event, incredibly unsuccessfully, and Shirley had merely allowed them to do whatever they wanted. Back in her day, she would have shouted at them, as she had at Deena. Children needed a healthy amount of discipline, as well as the occasional leeway. This would have been a discipline moment, but it wasn't her place.

Deena and Shirley were having a cup of tea. Again, here were cups of tea ruling a life. But maybe that didn't matter – tea was good, and something to do.

'So I told them that if I didn't get a similar pay rise that I would have to find somewhere else to work,' Deena said. Like her mother, she hadn't taken the Geordie accent. She had been nine years old when they moved up to the North East and her accent was already embedded in her. It was slightly odd as Gabe, thirteen in the move, actually did pick up words, but Deena had always been more introverted as a child, and didn't have as much exposure. Deena spoke as Shirley did – a Southern twang that was more akin to a BBC newsreader than the people of their home. 'I have a young family. I have mouths to feed and I just can't deal with that kind of gender bias. I can't believe we're still dealing with that kind of misogyny! You know?'

Shirley was still thinking about what Gabe had said the night before. Could she be telling herself that she had to build bridges with Callie? How would she even start going about that? They hadn't talked since Gabe was sent away. That was 2009. What? Twelve years ago. That was a hell of a wall she had to climb, a wall she'd built up herself.

'Mum.'

Shirley realised Deena was staring. 'I'm sorry, what? Oh, pay and men being better. I mean, not better, but . . . You know you can't change the world all the time, Dee. Sometimes you have to just deal with what you get.'

'Wow,' Deena said, flatly. 'My mother, ladies and gentleman. A real strong woman.'

'I didn't mean that quite so . . . I'm sorry, I'm distracted,' Shirley stuttered.

'No kidding,' Deena said, 'what's wrong?'

Shirley looked down at her hands. They were still gently throbbing with pain. They had kept her up half the night and, in the morning, she had had to soak them in a bowl of warm water to loosen them up so she could do even the most menial of tasks. But she couldn't tell Deena about that. She would make her go to the doctor and, no doubt, she would just get some more medication to add to the menagerie of pills of all different colours and sizes that she already took. 'I just had trouble sleeping last night,' she settled on.

This seemed to be OK for Deena, who picked up their empty teacups and went to the sink.

Shirley pulled herself up from her chair, and almost collided with Maisie, who came careening around the corner.

Shirley braced for a bump, but none came, as her

37

granddaughter stopped just in time. 'Sorry, Gramma,' Maisie cooed.

'It's OK,' Shirley said, patting her on the head, 'but slow down, you're doing so many laps you're going to burn a track in my carpet.'

Maisie laughed and sidestepped her, launching off again just as fast as before.

Shirley sighed and joined Deena, who was opening the dishwasher. It was still full from the night before. 'I can do that!' she protested.

'It's OK, Mum,' Deena said, already starting to unload it. 'Really it is. I don't like the idea of you constantly having to bend down anyway.'

Shirley scoffed. 'Well, if you'd just let me wash the dishes in the sink like everyone else, there wouldn't be an issue. I didn't want a dishwasher, remember.'

Deena straightened up, regarded her with judgemental eyes. She put the plates she had retrieved down on the counter. When had the balance of power shifted so much? Once upon a time, those eyes were Shirley's, and Deena was the one feeling like a naughty girl. 'Leaning over a sink isn't good either. Remember what Doctor Illyah said?'

'I should never have let you come with me to that.'

'There's no shame in wanting . . .' Deena stopped mid-sentence. She reached into the dishwasher tray, and pulled out a mug. Gabe's TARDIS mug. 'Mum.'

Shirley couldn't help looking away. 'What?'

'You never use his mug,' said Deena, 'unless . . .'

Shirley said nothing. Why was this happening? She

38

didn't need this many visits – this many intrusions. She was perfectly fine on her own. Her and Moggins, against the world.

'Mum.'

'What?' she said defiantly.

Now Deena's tone softened. No, not just softened. It was a tone of genuine concern. 'Did you see him again?'

Shirley met her eyes. 'Why is this so—'

'Did you see him again?'

Shirley shrugged, and went back to the table, sitting down in as much of a flump as her aching bones could manage. 'I may have seen him when I came home from the radio.'

Deena came and sat down too. One sweeping, fluid motion that oozed youth. 'Did you talk to him?'

'Of course I did.'

'Mother!' Like many people, Deena only called her Mother when she was really angry. She called her Mother with startling regularity these days. 'We talked about this. You agreed that you weren't going to engage. You said you would—'

'Shut my eyes, count to ten, and repeat until he goes away, I know,' Shirley said, 'but I can't, Deena. When he's here, I feel better. I feel a little more whole. I have someone to talk to . . . who's not a fluffy cat. I can't close my eyes on him. He is my son.'

'No,' Deena said, definitively. This was so effortless for her that it made Shirley's stomach turn. 'No, it's not. It is just your mind playing tricks because you are living in this place alone. It's just because you're . . . well . . .'

Shirley laughed. 'You can say it, daughter. I'm old. Yes, the cat is out the bag. I'm seventy years old and you think I'm losing it.'

Deena seemed to switch gears. 'I mean, what are the alternatives, Mum? That this thing is a ghost.'

'That *thing* is your brother. And no, I know what he is, and yes, it is my issue, but I don't understand why it has to be a bad thing.'

'It's a bad thing because it's not real. Do you want me to call Doctor Illyah?'

'Don't you fucking dare,' Shirley said. 'Illyah's not a failsafe for you to use every time I say something that fractures your fucking world view.'

Deena was taken aback. 'We're dropping f-bombs now in front of my kids? That was two in ten seconds. That something my ghost brother taught you?' Deena never liked her swearing.

'He doesn't teach me things. We talk. I talk.'

'About what?'

Shirley realised that she didn't really know. 'Things,' she mused, 'my day. Like last night at the radio.' She had had to talk to someone about Mallet AM. And Moggins wouldn't have been very receptive. So she'd told Gabe. Simple as that.

'Why don't you talk to me?' Deena said, sadly. 'Because I've been here an hour now, and you haven't told me anything about your day or the radio or anything. Why not communicate with the child who is still alive?'

Shirley opened her mouth to do just that. She could tell Deena about yesterday, about the requests she took, all about the show, and, most importantly, all about Mallet AM. She could discuss in-depth what she thought of the station, how she wished to find the man or woman and compliment her, how they could have a good career in radio. She could tell her about the bizarre mix-up with the dates – and did she know that Chester Baths might be closing down? But she didn't. Because Deena would do what she always did – she would overanalyse, she would talk over her, and she would take all the fun out of it. So instead Shirley just said, 'I didn't ask you to come.'

Deena just looked at her and sighed. 'Fucking nice, Mum.'

As she was about to say something else, Deena's husband, Tom, barrelled into the room, in his overalls, carrying his unreasonably large toolbox. He put it down on the kitchen counter a little too hard, making Shirley worry for the marble beneath.

Deena's husband was a giant, standing at 6 foot 7, and having the mass to go along with it. He was half muscular, half fat, working in construction and having equal amounts of time sitting around and carrying large quantities of nondescript 'things'. Of course, like everyone, he had gained a little weight during the dark year.

'Not sure about that attic 'atch, Shirl. Seems wedged shut some'ow. Nothin' I did could shift it.' Her loft hatch had been stuck shut for years now – maybe longer. She never used the loft, and hadn't had any reason to go up there. But recently she had been hearing birds up in the loft and she wanted to make sure that they could get out and any young were safe. 'I could ger some of me lads to come and jimmy it open for you?'

'No,' Shirley said, equally not wanting a fuss and not wanting to meet Tom's hulking construction friends. 'The birds have found a way in – no doubt they'll find their way out. And whatever else is up there should stay up there. Just Bob's stuff and some of Gabe's. His clothes and records and such. Nothing I need.'

'OK,' Tom nodded, eyeing a fresh cup of tea and immediately assuming it was his without asking. Shirley supposed that tenacity was what Deena was attracted to at the outset. Personally, she felt he was a gigantic pain in the derriere. He slurped his – or rather her - tea. 'But if you change ya mind, I can get me guys ova 'ere asap.'

'Thank you, Tom,' Shirley replied, knowing she would never take up the offer. 'I'll keep that in mind.' Although keeping things in mind was hardly her strong suit anymore. Things kept slipping away, whether she intended to keep them or not. Her life was trying to remember what that actor had been in before.

Deena ran a hand down her blouse, straightening the creases. She was obviously going to the office after this. 'Gather up the kids, Tom. We're going.'

'But I'm hungry,' Tom said.

'Then we'll stop somewhere,' Deena said, catching Maisie as she came flying into the kitchen.

The girl protested, saying she wanted to stay at Gramma's, but eventually conceded. Deena was a force to be reckoned with after all. Shirley had brought her up a little too well – of course, Bob had had nothing to do with it – and now she was on the receiving end too.

Tom didn't bother to say anything else, just catching Kenneth when the little boy came toddling in.

'Awwww,' Kenneth said, as Tom picked him up – his little chunky legs pedalling through the air.

Tom picked up his toolbox again, and shared a little look with Shirley that showed he was thinking much the same.

Deena definitely noticed but let it go, offering one final sad look at Shirley, before leading Maisie out into the hall. Tom followed and Shirley stopped in the kitchen doorway, noticing Moggins watching from the table where she put her keys and bag. The family went down the hall, and were almost leaving when—

'Oh, I almost forgot,' Tom called, pausing in the hallway, with Kenneth in his arms. 'Shirley, you migh' gerra kick outta this. I was on lunch break going down Front Street, and I pass the bakery, Starith's place. Seb's up on a big ol' ladda trying to put this massive sign up. Anyways, two seconds later, there's a strong wind, and he gaas arse ova' elbow. Hit the ground preddy hard.'

'What?' Shirley said, a sinking feeling in her chest. Starith fell off a ladder. The radio station.

'Saw him waddlin' up to the 'ospital like he'd broke his buttocks,' Tom said, chuckling.

'Tom!' Deena hissed. 'Why would Mum get a kick out of that?'

Tom looked guilty, an image offset by Kenneth's chubby face grinning from ear to ear beside him. 'I jus' though' cos Shirley's workin' up there.'

43

Mallet AM.

'And that means she'd find it funny?'

How could it have predicted something like that?

'I divant knaa, do I? It were just hospital related.'

Deena shook her head.

'Tom,' Shirley projected, over her daughter's head. 'What time was this?' What had the radio station said? The voice? Seb Starith fell off a ladder while trying to put up a sign. But what time had it said. Twelve something . . .

'Errr . . . well, I was on lunch, so 'bout 12.15 something like that.'

That was exactly when it had said it would happen.

'Are you OK, Mum?' Deena said. 'You look like you've seen a ghost.'

Shirley saw Deena's concern, and put all thoughts of Starith and the radio station out of her mind. 'No, no ghost. Not this time,' Shirley smiled, an expression that now seemed foreign on her face.

And she ushered them out and conceded that of course she would take Deena's calls with slightly more gusto, and of course she would try not to open a dialogue with Gabe – and of course she was lying about all of that. But she was thinking about something else now. As the Steadman-Wrights bundled into their car and pulled away, there was only one thing on her mind.

Mallet AM. And just how the presenter knew about what would happen a day in advance. She needed to know for sure.

01.04

Starith's Bakery still had its old sign up when she walked past it, going down to the bank. It was a cliché that old people always had to go to the bank, but she was a little surprised to find that it was true. What was the alternative? Put her trust in these new-fangled applications on smartphones? It seemed every day that there was something in the news about a hack or a fraud or a theft. No thank you – all she needed was good old in-person banking.

And, of course, there was also another aspect to the old cliché, one which Shirley would never have thought of before becoming one of the aforementioned old people herself. When you were young, and working, or starting a family, or just enjoying life, you had a reason to get up in the morning. When you were old, firstly, it was harder to get up. Your bones had got used to lying down and resting, and they didn't appreciate a rude awakening. But when you were up, finally and resolutely, you

45

had to find something to do. Otherwise what was the point in going through all the rigmarole of getting up?

The bank was halfway down Front Street, so Shirley had made her way there after *Morning Coffee* finished.

She had barely been able to sleep a solid hour. Sleep was usually a little more of a luxury in old age, but now even more so. For the first time in a long time, her brain was too noisy. She ran over and over what Mallet AM had reported – Starith's Bakery, Seb Starith had fallen around lunchtime. The voice had said a specific time – why hadn't she written it down? Well . . . that was simple. Because she had thought it had happened on the actual day it was mentioned and she would never need such useless information.

What was happening here? She had heard as clear as day the presenter tell the news of the tenth, on the ninth. And now it seemed the news had come true. Someone somewhere knew that Seb Starith was going to take a tumble. Was it real? Or was it just a lucky guess? – the old guy was a prime candidate for falling off a ladder, wasn't he? No, she knew that there would be answers at the bakery. But she just had to wait.

So after thinking about that, she had started to think of her children. The bullheadedness of Deena, who couldn't fail to be an annoyance, but whose heart was well and truly in the right place. She was too harsh on her. And then to Gabe, who had not appeared that night. Was it really destructive, what she was doing, what she was entertaining?

Her brain went around and around and around, and

46

even when Moggins had climbed under the duvet and settled himself on her bare feet, becoming a sentient foot warmer, and she had started to drift off, Callie's face would come to her out of the darkness. How would she ever begin to approach her – after all this time? How could she ever begin to express how bad she felt every time she saw her – in the hallways of the hospital, out on the street, in her head?

Eventually she had tired herself out, and she must have gone to sleep, because she'd woken up at her usual waking time of 5 a.m., with the familiar throbbing pain in her hands and Moggins sitting on her chest, staring into her face, with the kind of accusation that only a cat was capable of – that she was letting him starve to death.

She couldn't focus on *Morning Coffee* in the slightest, thinking about the kind of physics and time mechanics that wouldn't be out of place in one of the time-travel programmes Gabe loved so much. Which was utterly ridiculous – she had more or less decided that the Mallet AM newscast must have been a coincidence. There was a voice inside her – one that had Deena's tone – that said she was only fixated on this because she had nothing else to do.

And it was true. Her weekly embroidery was done and she didn't have to get ready for the meeting – which was scheduled to take place in her living room – until to-morrow. This day was entirely and horrifyingly empty.

So why not fill it with a little investigation? That, even if it came to nothing, would be a nice way to fill the time. So instead of her usual timetable of *Resident*

47

Detective followed by a switch to BBC One in time for *Homes Under the Hammer,* she'd gathered up her things and trekked out.

She paid her council tax at the bank in a line of older people likely doing the same thing and then made her way back up Front Street to the bakery. Front Street was Chester-Le-Street's high street essentially (one of the first things you had to learn when living here was all the addresses with 'Street' in the name) and shops lined a road going down a moderate hill. Shops used to be a variety of small businesses, chains and restaurants, but nowadays they were mostly charity shops, banks, hair-dressers and travel agents. Even the pubs had started to close down. Any business that wasn't one of the key four contingents was usually shut down. It was sad to see a high street die, but it was obvious that the internet (and not to mention the dark year) had taken its toll.

That's why it was important for Shirley to support the few local businesses there were left. Shirley always used the butcher's at the top of the street, which was much better quality than buying at the supermarket, and she must get back to using the bakery more – spurred on by sympathy for Starith's bruised coccyx.

The hill that lay between the bakery and herself seemed to be getting steeper by the day, as though it were growing and arching up, flexing itself, just to spite her. She passed the library, wanting to stop and catch her breath but knowing if she did she probably wouldn't be able to start again. Aging – this was the hill that Shirley was now dying on. Apt really.

She got to the bakery in the next few minutes – just past Argos and tucked in between two fried chicken takeaways. The old rusted and sun-damaged sign hung above two large windows showcasing all kinds of baked goods. She could have browsed the window alone for ages, but she tore her eyes from the tiger loaves and mountains of Danish pastries and stepped inside.

A bell above the door tinkled as it was jostled. She hadn't been inside the bakery in a few months, although she had always been rather partial to Seb Starith's Stollen Slices, which he sold year round. Every time she went past, she felt the yearn for them, not unlike the yearn for a young love. Although now, as she walked up to the counter, she couldn't see them.

There was no one else in the baker's, and there was no one behind the counter either. After a moment of Shirley just standing there and wondering whether they were actually open, a young woman dressed in baker's whites, her brown hair up in an unflattering hairnet, with flour on her cheeks, poked her head around the door to the back.

'Oh, sorry,' she said, out of breath, 'I was wrangling some baguettes out the back. You wouldn't happen to know how to make baguettes, would you?' This was Vallery Starith, Seb's granddaughter, who Shirley had seen grow up (from afar) before her eyes. She remembered when she used to frequent the bakery daily, back when she would use any excuse to get out the house, to get away from . . . Anyway, Vallery used to sit on the counter, a plump, pretty toddler, and play with whatever Seb would give her. He used to give her stray bits of dough – until she ingested them all – and then he would give her rolling pins and pastry brushes. 'This business is all a bit odd, isn't it. There's massive machines out there, just to make gingerbread. And I thought particle physics was hard.'

'It's often the jobs that look the easiest that are the hardest,' Shirley said, taking one hand and leaning on the counter. She should have brought her cane – a prop she never liked to use but had to start admitting that she did indeed need sometimes. Truth was, she usually just forgot about it.

Vallery nodded and then seemed to click who she was talking to. 'Oh, I'm sorry. It's Shirley, isn't it? Shirley . . .' She trailed off.

'Shirley Steadman,' she said, rescuing Vallery. And then, realising she hadn't thought up any tactics here, added, 'I heard about what happened to dear old Seb. I'm so sorry.'

'Yes,' Vallery replied, dusting off her hands in mid-air, leaving a cloud of flour, and coming to rest on the other side of the counter. 'Well, if you will try and haul a heavy sign up a rickety ladder, I guess you get what you bargained for. I was in the back, and even I heard the noise.'

'The fall?' asked Shirley.

'Pfft no. Him complaining,' Vallery said. 'Surprised you didn't hear it over in Houghton-Le-Spring.'

Shirley was going to let it go, but couldn't. 'Actually,

I live up towards the Avenues now, in a nice little bungalow.'

'Oh? Must be a squash in there with Bob.'

'Oh no, we're no longer together. We grew apart. Well, that and he's dead.' *And a monster*, Shirley added in her mind. But she had to steer the conversation back to what she needed, like trying to turn a ship with just the sail and the wind. 'So what have the doctors said?'

'He'll be up and about in no time,' Vallery said, rolling her eyes. 'He has a bruised coccyx and a few ripped muscles, which can't really be treated, so he just has to rest for a month. He's only allowed to move for the bathroom. Which is fairly bad when you run a bakery. So, until then, I'm here doing what I can. The loaves are easy enough, but some of the stuff I can't even begin to fathom. It's like a whole series of *Bake Off*, but I have to make every single thing in one day. I'm not cut out for this.'

'I'm sure you're doing a fabulous job,' Shirley said, seeing the uncertainty in her face. She didn't believe in herself, and Shirley knew what that felt like all too well. Her marriage had practically been built on that principle. 'He wouldn't have left you in charge if he didn't think you could hack it.'

'He didn't leave me in charge. I'm the only one who volunteered,' Vallery replied, clearly a little miffed. 'Now I'm starting to realise why no one else did. There's not so much as a pamphlet back there to explain any of the machinery.'

Shirley felt the conversation getting away from her.

How did people do this? – she had watched enough *Vera* and *Midsomer Murders* and *Death in Paradise,* she should have this down. 'Out of curiosity, what time did this accident happen?' Great – all the subtleness of a geriatric bull in a china shop.

'Why would that matter?' Vallery asked. A valid question.

'Oh . . .' Why? Why? Why? '. . . I was just passing by yesterday and it seemed all was right as rain, that's all. Seems I missed quite a show.'

This seemed enough. 'You sure did. It was around midday, I think. Yes, it was, because Grandad had me making the afternoon bagels. He says bagels only sell in the afternoons. Who am I to argue with him? Man's been working in this little place for almost forty years. So yeah, midday. We caught a little bit of it on CCTV. You want to see it? I'm thinking about sending it into *You've Been Framed!*'

Shirley needed to see it – that recording would have the time down to the second. But she still didn't trust Vallery's jokey nature. She didn't know if she was actually unironically getting offered to view it. So she said, 'Oh, I don't know. I don't think poor Seb would like me to see it. I knew him when he was the town's tough guy. He'd be terribly embarrassed knowing I'd seen it.'

Vallery's face lit up. 'Then I insist.' She rummaged around below the counter and brought up her phone. 'I downloaded it to my phone in case Grandad deleted it. You know, on account of it being majorly embarrassing.'

She tapped the screen a few times, and then turned it around to show Shirley.

Shirley took her glasses from around her neck and put them on.

On the screen was a black and white image. It was at an odd angle, and it was hard at first to make out exactly what it was. The edge of the shop was visible, the camera pointing down the street. As Shirley watched, Seb's head popped into view. He was a scrawny moustachioed old man, looking even older up close and in high definition. Shirley noted the time in the corner – in digital numbers: 12.15 p.m. Something stirred in Shirley's memory – of what Mallet AM had said. This was lining up, wasn't it?

She decided to keep her full attention on what was happening. In the corner of the screen, over Seb's shoulder, Shirley could see pedestrians walking up and down Front Street. Only one man was watching Seb in the foreground muddling about on the ladder. The man, across the street, outside the RSPCA charity shop, had a brown trench coat on, and a flat cap and was watching Seb with an expression Shirley couldn't make out in the fuzzy image – although she expected it was an expression of bizarre wonder.

Seb, meanwhile, pulled an electric screwdriver into frame with his hand and he was trying to reach up out-of-frame to screwdrive something – probably the old sign.

The time ticked to 12.16.

Seb stumbled – it looked like he was going to go over, and then he looked down, stabilised himself. 'Watch out down below,' he chuckled. He took the screwdriver again and reached it over his head. What an idiot – he must have thought himself quite the thrill-seeker going up there all by himself!

'Here it comes,' Vallery said, who had obviously committed the clip to (even audio) memory.

Someone went by, walking up the street. Seb staggered again, his hands shot to the ladder. The electric screwdriver went falling out of frame. And then something else. The new sign started falling, directly down on Seb. With one final 'Oh, bugger,' Seb went crashing out of frame. After an almighty thump, what followed was a string of expletives, some of which Shirley had never heard before.

'The new sign split in two,' Vallery said, chuckling.

To be fair, it was amusing. So much so, that Shirley almost forgot to look at the time. But she did. And that same sinking feeling she felt when she had first heard of poor Seb washed over her again.

The time had just clicked over to 12.17.

And there it was. In that moment, she heard the presenter as clear as day in her head say '. . . at 12.17 . . .'. How was this possible? How could Mallet AM get this event right, to the minute? She had to . . . She didn't know what . . . She had to listen again. She had to go back and listen to Mallet AM again. Because if this was true, what else could be?

'Are you OK?' Vallery asked, putting the phone back behind the counter. 'Usually there's a bit more laughing when I show people.'

Shirley found it in herself to smile. It was like trying to raise a drawbridge with her bare hands. 'I'm fine.' She turned to go.

'Wait,' Vallery said, 'didn't you come in here to buy something? I recommend anything but the baguettes. Or the pastry swirls. Or the—'

'Sorry,' Shirley muttered, 'I completely forgot what I wanted. I'll come back when I remember.'

'OK,' Vallery looked unconvinced.

Shirley didn't really care. She had to get out of here – the bakery was starting to feel very claustrophobic. She couldn't listen to anything else Vallery was saying, she just stumbled out of the place, passing a man who was on his way in. He held the door open for her before barging in.

Out on the street, Shirley got clear of the bakery windows and rested herself against the next shop sill. She breathed in and out – people passing her like it was nothing – just another old person taking a break. But Shirley's mind was racing, and every lap led back to Mallet AM. They knew about Seb, no doubt they knew about the Baths too, and that other thing about the park and the fouling sign – well, that was more than likely accurate too. What was Mallet AM? Who ran it? And where, if anywhere, could they get their information? No, that was stupid, there was no information. When Shirley heard what had happened to Seb, it hadn't happened yet. It was information that was impossible to know, because there was none to know.

What was this? Was it possible that Mallet AM . . .

No, no, stupid . . . But what was the alternative? Was it possible that Mallet AM reported the future?

Shirley looked around to see that, indeed, no one was paying attention to her. And she broke out into a smile. She had to find out what Mallet AM was. And as she took off for home, she realised she hadn't felt so alive in a long time.

01.05

Shirley got back into her bungalow, with a fresh sense of energy. The Front Street hill had tried its best to take it out of her, but the rush of adrenaline prevailed, pulsing in her blood. She had to find out what was really happening here – and she thought that maybe she was the only one who had discovered Mallet AM. What were the chances that anyone else had stumbled upon it? A pirate radio station with a weak signal. It wasn't likely.

Moggins was there to greet her when she opened the front door, and watched as she strode past him, nonplussed. She went into the living room and over to the cabinet in which was Bob's old high-fi stereo. It was the only thing of his that she'd kept as it could play CDs, tapes and, most importantly, vinyl records. But it could also do the radio.

She opened the cabinet and turned the hi-fi to the radio setting. Radio 4 instantly filled the room. She turned it to AM and started turning the dial. She had written down the frequency but, for some reason, that was the one thing that was stuck in her memory. She felt a certain trepidation as she made her way past many stations – the radio grabbing small parts of speech and music – towards the 60s.

'What are you doing?' Gabe asked. She didn't have to look – she knew he was sitting in her favourite chair behind her.

'You tell me,' she said, still focusing on the radio.

Gabe sighed behind her. 'You're hung up on this radio station. What was it? Mallam FM.'

'Mallet AM. I thought you were in my head.'

'I am. But that doesn't mean I have to be complicit in whatever this is.' Gabe sounded worried – like he didn't believe it. Did that mean she didn't either?

She got to the 60s.

She held her breath.

66.4.

Static. It wasn't there.

She checked either side of the frequency. Nothing. She checked even further either side. White noise, strong and overbearing. Almost mocking.

She carried on fiddling – turning the dial even slower, and when that didn't work, fast. Still nothing. She turned to FM, then back to AM, tried again. She spent five minutes trying everything.

A tut from behind her.

She looked around to see Gabe staring at her – his arms crossed. 'Shirley, it's not there.'

Shirley left the radio on – but came to sink on the sofa in front of the TV. 'I don't understand.'

'There are many factors here, and you're not seeing them,' Gabe said. 'When did you become so impulsive?'

'It happened sometime between growing old and your father dying.' Shirley laughed miserably. 'What am I not seeing?'

'Work through it,' Gabe said.

Shirley thought – really thought – for the first time since leaving the bakery. She had been so swept up in the sheer thrill of it all, the very idea, there were things that she hadn't even considered. 'It's a pirate station, most likely run by one person.'

Gabe nodded. She was on the right track.

'There's no way that the station runs 24/7,' Shirley said.

'Bingo.'

'We can assume that it's probably live around the time I found it. So the best time to try to find it again would be between seven and eight.'

'Anything else?'

Shirley thought again. 'It might be a question of location. It's likely that the signal doesn't have much strength, being an independently run frequency. The hospital could be closer to where the station broadcasts.'

'That could be it. Or . . .'

'Or . . .' Shirley trailed off. She was lost. There was an 'or'? But then it came to her. 'Or when I hooked up that old radio to the radio deck it made it stronger, so it could pick up frequencies that maybe my radio couldn't pick up.'

'Yes,' Gabe said. 'So you have two variables.' Gabe uncrossed his arms and put them on the arms of the chair just like he used to when he was alive. It was crazy how many small details she added to him, even when she was focusing on something else. 'So what are you going to do now?'

Shirley straightened up and leant forward, smiling, the fire coming back. 'I need to go back to the hospital. Tonight. That's the most likely time I'm going to find Mallet AM again.'

Gabe smiled. 'Yes.'

Shirley wondered who was on hospital radio tonight. It was Thursday – fuck. It was the worst possible night. Thursday was known as the youngsters' night – where the managers put together all the younger volunteers so they didn't clash with the older ones. The age gap was hideous, and the youngsters always had different ways of doing things.

It had been a fight to even get youngsters to come to the hospital radio, and the managers were really resistant to the idea. But at the AGM a few years ago, they conceded that they had to allow people from eighteen up into the studio, regardless of personal bias. Sometimes ageism cut both ways – it was important to remember that. And the managers were some stubborn bastards. Their compromise was to let three youngsters loose on a Thursday night on a trial basis. Lemmy, Carl, and Krystal had a combined age of 56, and Shirley didn't agree with their ways. Their shows were loud and obnoxious, their request gathering informal yet persistent. But they got results. And Shirley, like all the other older volunteers, had just resolved to stay out their way.

She hadn't seen any of the youngsters since the last meeting, and she had to concede that she wasn't feeling great about it. It would be like walking into the lions' den. No, it would be liking walking into her own work-place where three lions had taken over. But she had to go if she wanted to find Mallet AM again. And she didn't want to miss another day – of possible news.

'Quite a quandary,' Gabe said. 'You're thinking about going in of course.'

'Of course,' Shirley replied. That fire, that pulsing energy – still there. She had to find it again. She'd walk into the den if there were a million lions there. 'I just need to think up some kind of story about why I'm there.'

'That's not the hard part,' Gabe said, resolutely.

'What is?'

'The hard part is having to wait five hours to go.'

Shirley knew he was right. And, indeed, she already felt restless. She got up and turned the radio off. Then she didn't really know what to do with herself. So she put the kettle on. And when she'd finished her cup of tea, she put it on again.

Gabe left at some point. She didn't know when. She was too busy thinking.

She left the kettle boiling and went to the cupboard in the hallway, finding the laptop that Deena had given her for her birthday. She had got used to it – she wasn't a technophobe at all (she used all the technology at the radio after all) – but she just found that she didn't use it much. She'd spent the vast majority of her life without the need for computers and the internet and constant barrages of information, and she found that she preferred her simpler life.

Now, though, she opened the laptop, sitting at the kitchen table and going to the internet. She had fast Wi-Fi for Netflix on the telly and before long she was on Google.

She searched '66.40 MALLET AM'.

Nothing. At all. Not even one search result.

She deleted it, and searched 'RADIO STATION PREDICT FUTURE NORTH EAST ENGLAND'.

The top two results were the only relevant ones. The others had words of the search crossed out. She clicked the top link. 'RADIO STATION PREDICTS RAFFLE WINNER' at northeastnews.com. It was a fluff newspaper piece about some child who appeared on radio in 2015 guessing the prize of a raffle. Totally worthless.

Shirley sighed, backed out and then clicked the second link – 'RADIO STATION PREDICTS DEATHS'. She found herself at a webpage that looked very old even by her standards. A clipart banner at the top of the page proclaimed 'THE ENIGMA FILES'. The rest of the page was segmented into boxes not unlike a newspaper. Unfortunately, most of these elements were missing. It seemed that something had gone wrong with the site, as there were error codes and icons of broken links everywhere.

The title of what she wanted was there, but under it

was nothing. Or, more accurately, a string of computer jargon and gobbledegook in typewriter font. Shirley quickly scanned the article nonetheless but couldn't make out anything that made any sense.

She almost closed the page before getting to the end of the nonsense language, but as her eyes got to the final line, she stopped.

```
4044=4=====45555___FFFFFFFVVVV<<<<VV@
ED@ff)£%%%RRRACABFT::::::::::????///<<< 66.40 III@)
(%^*)637 61927F%%%%%## #*()@$%^&"""hhhgiydv
0__
```

Nestled in the code and repeated characters, highlighted and popping out instantly to her, the frequency – 66.40. Could be a coincidence – easily. Could just be part of the nonsense. But Shirley couldn't help but seize onto it. Maybe whoever had written this article, which presumably had been legible at one point, knew about Mallet AM. Someone to talk to, someone to confide in.

She clicked around the website, finding similar overwhelming pages of jargon. But, eventually, she found a link that was intact, titled 'CONTACT US'. She clicked it, and was greeted with a black screen with one solitary blue link at the top.

An email address – theenigmafiles@rito.com.

She clicked it and was taken to her email, with the Enigma Files address in the 'recipients' field.

She started writing. She wrote everything that had happened. She wrote about finding the radio station.

She wrote about Starith. She wrote about what she had seen and how she had seen it. She wrote about what she thought, and her excitements, her fears, and her trepidation.

It took her an hour.

And when she was done, and she found that she had to scroll up about ten substantial paragraphs, she realised she'd written a letter and not an email. Emails were meant to be snappy, slightly less personal, and she couldn't be telling this complete stranger so much personal information.

With a little reluctance, she highlighted the whole text and deleted it.

Short and snappy. Something to make this person take notice. Enigma. Maybe whoever was at the other end would respond to some mysticism.

Fighting every instinct she had, she typed – I know about 66.40 AM. It is real. I have proof. Please respond. Shirley.

In the subject field, she typed one word – MALLET – and hit send.

And she shut the computer. And resolved to check tomorrow. Maybe it would amount to nothing. That website looked like it had been abandoned. Maybe the email address was too.

In the absence of any confidant, she had her own investigation to start.

01.06

It seemed wrong to be in the hospital on a Thursday evening. Usually Shirley was sitting at home, in front of *The One Show*, with Moggins on her lap, finishing up her embroidery ready for the Friday meeting. Instead, she was scanning her ID card and making her way down the familiar corridor to the radio cupboard.

She had checked her email before coming out, but there was no response to her message. She had expected no less, but hadn't been able to stop a little optimism creeping in. She just wanted someone to talk to – like many people her age. Unlike most people her age, however, she had something burning to say.

She got to the studio door, hearing the loud voices of the youngsters inside. She suppressed a sigh and punched in the keycode. Inside, Lemmy, Carl and Krystal were standing in the tiny area in a little huddle. At the sound of the door, they each looked around with an identical guilty expression on their faces.

65

'Shirley,' Krystal said, backing away from the huddle. 'What brings you here? You haven't been reassigned to Thursday, have you?' The panic in the air was palpable.

Shirley let them sweat for a moment. 'No.' The three of them couldn't hide their relief. 'I just came to use some of the equipment.'

'Oh,' Lemmy said, thankfully. The lanky eighteen-year-old was dressed all in black with a floppy fringe. She believed he was what the kids called 'emo'. In addition to having a silly name, his style was beyond Shirley. Lucky that Gabe or Deena had never ended up like that — but no, she never would have let them anyway.

'What were you doing?' Shirley said, seeing that Carl had a fist suspended in the middle of the group with three straws poking out of it. Carl was probably the most presentable one of the bunch and the only one with whom she felt she could withstand a conversation.

'We were . . .' Lemmy started to say, looking like he had no intention of finishing the sentence.

Krystal smiled. Her popstar look was dazzling, colourful and obscenely grating. 'We were just drawing straws to see who had to go and get requests.'

Shirley raised her eyebrows as the door shut behind her. 'Going to get requests is meant to be one of the highlights of the job. Talking to the patients, offering them some human contact.' Getting requests was arguably Shirley's favourite bit. She liked going around and meeting people, offering a conversation that wasn't with a nurse or a doctor. Some patients didn't get visitors, so

Shirley was the only friendly and non-professional face they saw all day. She wasn't really surprised this was lost on the youngsters though.

'Oh . . .' Lemmy muttered, like he'd never thought of that.

'We know,' Carl said. 'Right, guys? We just can't decide who should do the early show, so we leave it up to chance.'

'Fine,' Shirley snapped, sidestepping them and going into the cupboard. 'Far be it from me to interrupt such a well-oiled machine.'

She could practically feel the eye-rolls as she went to get the old radio, just as she had forty-eight hours before. She wondered if Mallet AM had had a news programme last night what would it have revealed?

As she came out of the cupboard, she heard Carl and Krystal exclaiming and saw Lemmy holding up the long straw.

'Fuck,' Krystal said, and then saw Shirley, 'I mean, fuck yeah, I get to go talk to sick people.'

Shirley frowned at her, and seeing as she was right next to the wall where the clipboards hung, she handed one each to Carl and Krystal. 'Good luck out there, don't catch anything.'

Carl and Krystal stared and silently made their way out of the room. As they moved in the confined space, a strange herbal smell wafted around. Marijuana. They couldn't be smoking in here – there were smoke detectors everywhere – so they had to be doing it outside, which meant she couldn't really do anything about it. If some nurse or doctor caught them out there, they were on their own.

Lemmy was a hive of activity as the door clicked behind the other two. He went into his black backpack and brought out an iPod, a small stack of CDs and a bunch of cables.

Shirley left him to it, as he rushed into Studio One. She went into Studio Two and set up the radio. She put the canned headphones on, and started searching through the channels.

Out of the corner of her eye, through the window into Studio One, Lemmy was starting the early show, and although it was meant to be soundproof, she could hear a steady bassline. She had never listened to one of Lemmy's shows, but she expected it contained one hundred per cent more laser beam sound effects than hers. She predicted it would be a tireless experience with minimal talk and maximum head-banging. The patients of the hospital should beware – they had no idea what was about to hit them.

She realised that she was sighing more than usual. She didn't want to act like an old grandma, but it seemed that she was. These young people just had such a different way of doing things. And even more than that, they had such a different way of living. It was like they were a different species.

Shirley focused on her task, finding the frequency that Mallet AM was on before – 66.40. Slowly, out of the static, sickly-sweet stock music started to emerge. She turned the dial slowly until it was clearer. She felt it was even stronger than when she'd heard it before, as if it was justifying its existence to her and damning her for doubting it.

The music filled her ears and made her feel like she was in a lift in some fancy American hotel. She turned down the volume as she looked at the clock: 7.08 p.m. She thought back to two days ago – she would still be gathering requests around now. She thought she got back just after twenty past. Searching everything wouldn't have taken more than five minutes, which meant the news had probably been on at 7.30 p.m.

She settled back in the uncomfortable desk chair. There had been a whole item on the agenda last meeting to discuss replacing them. She didn't really know what there had been to discuss – these chairs had been here since before her time. She had joined up in 2008, just after Gabe went away on tour and sitting around the house with Bob made her feel sick. Since then, she, and the chairs, had never missed a week.

Her phone buzzed in her bag. She could tell because the vibration was so strong it vibrated even the fabric. The man in the shop had turned it up so she would 'never miss a call even if your hearing's bad'. She'd bitten her tongue.

She took her phone out – it was Deena. Her finger hovered over the green button, but wouldn't press it. Why was she calling? Just to check in? She wasn't a child. Dee didn't need to know what her mother was doing every second of the day. Shirley was off on her own adventure. She pressed decline. And tried to stop the feeling of guilt that immediately sprang up. She put her phone back in her bag, and resolved not to take it out again.

Through the window, Lemmy was having a solo dance party, his fringe in constant motion as he banged his head to the bassline. Shirley tutted.

She zoned out for a minute, listening to the faint quaint music and resting her head on the back of the chair. Her excitement made her feel young again. She felt like she had energy, so much energy. She had tutted at Lemmy, but she almost wanted to get up and dance with him. She felt like she had to do something, move around. But all she could do was sit and wait.

She tried to remember the last time she felt like this. And she was a little shocked and a little disgusted with herself to realise that it was just after Bob had died. She had been under a cloud for so long – so repressed and silenced – that after he was gone, she almost felt like her life had begun again. It wasn't nice to think of how glad she was that someone had died but that didn't change the fact that she was.

The chair wasn't comfy, but something about the music almost lulled her to sleep. After the troubled nights she had had since finding this radio station, she almost felt she deserved a bit of peace by its hand. She closed her eyes.

The music pulled her under.

Under.

Under.

And time passed.

Clink. Clink. Clink.

She opened her eyes. Her body had started to shut down, move into sleep mode. And now she had to wrench it back. She straightened up with some difficulty, and started.

Lemmy was looking through the window at her with one wide eye. He had rapped on the glass between them. Relief blossomed on his face. And he shouted, 'I thought you were dead.'

Cheeky fucker. Shirley shook her head. Still alive. She held Lemmy's gaze until he got uncomfortable and went back to his show. And then she remembered what exactly she was doing. The music in the headphones had changed. It was now a folk track with actual vocals. She turned the volume up and checked the time: 7.28 p.m. She never thought she'd think it, but thank God for Lemmy. Although she probably would have woken up if the voice came on.

Shirley listened to the music. It wasn't bad. Some song about a creature in a pond who'd grant you a wish if you brought it a beating heart – average folk fare, kitschy with a touch of darkness. It might have been something she'd listen to, if it wasn't keeping her from the presenter she hoped was going to pop up in a minute. Eventually, the song started to fade out, fading and fading and fading until silence.

No.

No. There was supposed to be . . .

'And that was "Down By The Wishing Pond",' the presenter said. Shirley almost whooped with joy but didn't want to miss anything. She held her breath to make sure she didn't. '. . . From local band The Oil Mongers. Who knew, huh? Talent like that right on our doorstep! This is Mallet AM, hello to you all, whether you're returning listeners or brand spanking new! And whoever you are . . .' it was like the presenter was talking directly to her. '. . . you're just in time for the news. It is 7.30 p.m. on Friday the twelfth of February.'

Shirley breathed out. News for the twelfth; it was the eleventh. This hadn't been some fever dream, this was real. Now she had to find something to prove that this wasn't just an elaborate coincidence.

'We have three items up on the docket tonight, as always. So let's just jump right in to it. First up, we have a report on The Lambton Arms, which seemed to be at threat of closing the bar forever after the dark year hit it hard. Thankfully, though, it seems that the business has bounced back because proprietor Damon Moran is reporting record sales as the pub's reopening has driven more customers to sample the quintessential pub experience than ever before. I for one am ecstatic that our local will not be closing, and I'm sure you are too.'

Shirley sighed. That item was very general – it wasn't really anything she could prove was real or technically 'tomorrow's news'. She had seen the crowds around The Lambton Arms – it wasn't exactly monumental to predict that they were doing well. Two items left – maybe there would be something better.

Unfortunately, the next item wasn't. 'Squabbles still continue over whether or not the Metro Centre is going to be sold. The Centre, once the largest shopping centre in Europe, has had its future up in the air for a while now. The dark year obviously did not help as it remained closed for the majority of an entire year, bringing in no profits and no punters. However, the future doesn't seem as bleak as it looks like a private benefactor may be interested in purchasing it. Little is known about this individual or entity but they are said to want to preserve the Centre exactly as it is, with it still being a beacon of North East commerce.'

Again, just an item of pure conjecture. There was nothing to grab onto. No Seb falling off a ladder. Just something like you would see on the actual news. Full of fluff.

Two down and one to go – Shirley literally crossed her fingers for something tangible.

The presenter continued, and gave her exactly what she wanted – 'Lastly, it seems that milkman Roy Farrow has suffered a whole caseload of spilt milk as he drove his milk float into a post box in the early hours of the day. At 6.52 a.m., Farrow was making his way down Benthal Street at the top of the town. He wasn't looking where he was going. At the same time, a pedestrian was crossing the street. Farrow looked up at the last second and had to wrench his truck to the left, colliding with the nearby post box. Both Farrow and the pedestrian, whose identity was unconfirmed, were unharmed, although the same can't be said for Farrow's van, as well as its cargo. The whole incident took less than a minute, and unfortunately woke up half the street. Farrow was understandably embarrassed. A tow truck came to remove the milk float later in the day. Residents of Benthal Street will have to wait until tomorrow for their milk orders.'

Shirley couldn't believe it. Not only was this something she could confirm, but it was going to happen only a few streets away from her bungalow.

'And that is the news for the twelfth of February. Happy Friday everyone! So let's get back to the music. Here's some . . .'

The voice continued, but Shirley had what she needed. She took the headphones off and sat back. Well, she hadn't imagined it all. It was real. Totally real. It seemed Roy Farrow potentially wasn't going to have a fantastic day tomorrow. She had to be there to see if it happened. If it didn't, then she could forget the whole thing, she could just see Mallet AM as a neat station, which was having a little joke. If it did happen, then the presenter either had some bizarre kind of information or . . . Shirley couldn't believe she was thinking this but . . . Or he could predict the future.

She picked up the radio and left Studio Two. Carl and Krystal were back – Carl at the computer looking up requests and Krystal playing around with something on her phone. They were both talking and not paying much attention to what they were doing. As Shirley shut the door, they quietened down – Carl wheeling round to go back to the computer.

Shirley ignored them.

'You find what you were looking for?' Krystal said, a little foggily.

The weed smell had grown stronger, and Shirley

74

thought that the request gathering had probably included a smoke break.

'Yes, thank you,' Shirley said, pointedly, disappearing into the cupboard to put the radio back. 'How are the requests?'

'Pile of shite,' But seeing Shirley's face reappear, Carl added, 'but we'll make them work. A few nice dedications.'

'Can I see the list?' Shirley commanded, and Carl handed her his clipboard. She looked down the list of songs written in Carl's crabbed handwriting. Pile of shite was generous, although she never would have said it out loud. Carl and Krystal had also somehow managed to get half the number of requests she usually did alone. They really were slacking off, but they were volunteers, so you couldn't reasonably get angry. Even though she did. 'You find them all?' she said, handing the clipboard back.

'Yep,' Carl chirped, in a tone that indicated Shirley should be impressed. 'They're all in the system, so it was pretty easy.'

'Good,' Shirley said.

'We're just waiting for Lemmy to finish up, then we'll go live,' Krystal said. 'We've already got all the links and everything ready to go.' It was clear they were trying too hard now.

She wasn't going to bring it up, but the sucking up annoyed her. 'Is that weed I smell on both of you?'

Carl and Krystal's eyes grew cartoonishly large, which only accentuated how puffy and red they were.

'Would hate to tell the managers,' Shirley said. 'It might not surprise you, but all of us old people know each other.' Shirley offered a sickly smile.

Carl offered a tentative one back. 'Won't happen again.'

Shirley nodded.

Krystal slowly stood up. 'Do you want to listen in to the show? Carl and Krystal's Requests?' She grinned.

Shirley didn't. 'No, thank you.' And with that, she left the station.

Listen in? She couldn't think of anything worse.

01.07

It was still dark, with only a little light peeking from the horizon. Rain was threatening to break through the clouds on a windy Friday morning. It wasn't exactly the type of weather Shirley wanted to be out in. She had got up early even for her, showered, soaked her hands so they actually worked, fed Moggins, who was confused by everything that was happening recently, and then made her way to the front door.

She stuck her head out at 6 a.m. – fifty-two minutes until, if Mallet AM was to be right again, Roy Farrow would take a swerve into a post box to avoid a pedestrian. Seeing the weather, she stuck her head out again at 6.05 a.m., now donned with a woolly hat and a second coat, over her first. She just hoped the rain in the clouds wouldn't turn to snow. That would be her worst nightmare.

She knew Benthal Street was a few streets back from her. She was only one street away from the main road that went from Chester-Le-Street up to Waldridge, going past the primary school and, further up, the secondary academy. Benthal Street was deeper, and even closer to the Avenues. She stepped down her garden, picking up her cane that was always propped against her front wall. She usually left it behind — a weird act of defiance for no one except herself and Old Father Time. But the icy wind already threatened to seize up her joints and sweep her off her feet, so she thought that just this once she would need all the help she could get.

She started up the street, checking the doorsteps of every bungalow along the way. No milk. He hadn't come yet. So she was ahead of him at least. Although he was in a van and she was on two rickety legs well past their warranty. She hurried her pace. She cut through an alleyway, going further away from the main road. She didn't know exactly where she was going, but she had lived in this area for so long that she refused to check a map. And sure enough, after the second alley she cut through, she came across a street sign saying Benthal Street. It was on a brick waist-high wall, in a little courtyard with a withered-looking rock garden and a bench, and it pointed up a long street.

Benthal Street was very unassuming — much like her own. In fact, it was almost identical, although the bungalows had an extra storey. There was no indication of what was about to happen, and why would there be? Shirley, for some reason, had almost expected a masked observer. Mallet AM making sure what was meant to happen happened. Something silly like that.

The street was empty, of course – it was six in the morning. She could hear movement somewhere – probably a dog or a person putting out a bin, but otherwise the street was deathly silent. She started to slowly walk along it but didn't have to go far – she found a post box on a corner next to another alleyway. This had to be it.

She checked her watch – 6.42 a.m. Wait, what? It had really taken her that long to walk here. Oh God, it was getting worse.

She couldn't think about that now – she had ten minutes. In ten minutes, she would know if Mallet AM was for real – or if it was all just an oddity – a blip in time maybe. Gabe would have liked the way she was thinking.

Ten minutes. And she had to find somewhere to go – she couldn't just stand out here in the middle of the street. She made her way back to the bench and sat down, her legs instantly thanking her. She could see the post box perfectly. To the onlooker, she would just be an old lady who had stopped to catch her breath, not a potential witness to an incredibly small-scale tragedy – maybe a tragedy if you liked the simple joy of an upright post box.

A van started to make its way down the street towards her, and she perked up. But as it came closer, she saw it was just a delivery van. It slowly came to a stop right next to her, blocking her view. Shit.

A man, barely older than the youngsters she had left behind at the radio the night before, in a high-visibility jacket got out the driver's side. He opened the back of his van and rummaged around in there for what felt like an age. Finally, he re-emerged with a small parcel and went to the nearest door. He knocked, waited for a minute, and knocked again. It was clear no one was awake. He scratched his neck, and then knocked again.

She cleared her throat. 'Excuse me, sir.'

The man jumped out of his skin. He hadn't noticed her. He stepped towards her. 'Yes?'

'Could you please hurry up?'

He looked apologetic and then seized on something. 'Are you the neighbour? Could you take this parcel in for them?'

'Oh no,' she laughed, 'I don't live around here.'

The man looked at her very confused. 'Oookaay.' He opened his mouth, most likely to ask just what she was doing sitting on the street at six in the morning, but apparently thought better of it, and just rummaged around in his pocket for a red slip, putting it through the letter box. 'Have a good day.'

Shirley waved him off, dismissing him, and he got in his van and finally drove away.

It was now 6.48. Four minutes until the accident was due to happen. And as Shirley looked away from her watch, she heard something. The rev of an engine, rather old and hauling a cargo. Much like herself. It was a few streets away, but as she listened, it started getting louder, until she saw a white van with an open back appear up the street.

The van stopped every few feet, and a figure popped

out and put something on the doorsteps. Milk bottles. This had to be Roy Farrow.

So Mallet AM was right in predicting when Farrow would be here, just like it seemed to have predicted when Seb Starith was going to go up a ladder. But was an accident going to happen again?

Shirley suddenly had an urge to walk up to Farrow and maybe warn him about what was potentially going to happen. She had a moment where she realised that what she assumed she would see when she arrived on the street − Mallet AM's silent watcher − was actually here. It was her. It was a little morose to just sit here and watch an accident unfold − especially one she'd been warned of in advance. She'd practically bought tickets for the front row.

But she had to know. She had to know if Mallet AM was the real deal. And the presenter had clearly stated that there were no casualties. No one was going to get hurt − absolutely no one. As long as Mallet AM was correct. And if it was wrong, nothing would happen anyway. She quite simply had to let this play out to know for sure.

Roy Farrow continued his way down the street, stopping at almost every house. Comically, he didn't seem to do any of the houses in bulk, he literally stopped at every one. It took him ages. If he didn't hurry up, there was no way he was going to get up enough speed to lose control.

For the first time − really − Shirley started to doubt that the truck would crash.

But then, all of a sudden, when Roy had united a bottle with a doorstep and got back in the truck, he put his foot to the pedal. Maybe the rest of the street didn't get milk, because the truck was whizzing down towards her. She glanced at her watch – 6.51 a.m., no, it just clicked over to 6.52. If it was happening, it was going to happen now.

And when Shirley looked up again, she saw how it was going to be. A person was appearing from the alleyway, a woman all wrapped up in a coat, scarf and hat, walking with intent. She had earmuffs on, with the primary purpose to warm her ears, but doubtless with the unfortunate side effect of muffling her hearing. She couldn't hear the truck coming.

The van advanced, and Shirley saw Roy Farrow in the driver's seat looking down at something, not at the road – the idiot. The woman wasn't looking either – Shirley couldn't even see her face, she was so hunched over in her coat. She started to cross the road.

Shirley shot up, ignoring the jolt of pain in her legs. Screw the silent observer – Roy Farrow was going to hit the woman. Maybe Mallet AM was only half-right. It had predicted the milk truck, it had predicted the pedestrian, but maybe it was wrong about one thing – maybe it wasn't going to end without a casualty.

Shirley launched forward using her cane to steady herself. But she saw quickly that she wasn't going to be anywhere near quick enough. The van was careening along and the woman was in the middle of the street.

'Hey!' Shirley shouted, but the wind carried it away.

By coincidence, Roy Farrow did look up then, and although Shirley couldn't really see before, she saw the shock in his face then. The woman was carrying on – if any side was favoured, she was on the right. Shirley watched as Farrow acted fast, wrenching the steering wheel to the left.

The woman finally noticed the danger she was in, and dove to the right. The float went sailing on to the pavement. It was only another ten yards until it crashed into the post box, the front of the truck folding around it and a great crash filling the silence. As soon as it was there, it was gone – followed only by a pop as the front seat's airbags triggered – far too late.

Lights started clicking on along the street in the morning gloom as Shirley battled the wind, getting herself up the street. It had actually happened. It had happened exactly the way Mallet AM said it would. This was real – Mallet AM was reporting things that would happen a day in advance.

But she couldn't think about that right now. 'Are you all right?' she called, to the smoking front of the truck. She couldn't see Farrow through the white but could hear a low moaning.

She was almost at the van, when a man in a dressing gown poked his head out of his door. 'What the hell's going on?'

'The milk float crashed,' Shirley said, out of breath. 'I think you better call 999.'

The man nodded and disappeared.

She hobbled on and looked into the cab. Roy Farrow was sitting there, unharmed, his hands still on the steering wheel, with his face white as a sheet. He was staring straight ahead as though he were still driving.

'Are you OK?' Shirley asked.

She had to repeat it three times before he even acknowledged that she was there. He slowly turned his head to look at her. 'The woman,' he croaked.

Shirley looked around. The woman was gone, had probably wanted to get as far away from here as possible, given how close that was. 'She's OK. You didn't hit her.'

'Thank God,' he said, 'I thought I was really gonna.'

'I know, but you didn't. Are you hurt at all?'

'No,' Roy said. 'The milk?'

Shirley didn't know what he was talking about at first. And then she stepped back to survey the damage at the back of the truck. It looked like every single bottle had smashed. Every crate was just full of a jumble of glass, with milk seeping out onto the pavement.

Mallet AM had even predicted that too.

'Don't worry about the milk, OK?'

Shirley stayed with Roy until the ambulance arrived, and the milk stopped leaking out of the back of the truck. The paramedics checked him over, and said he was fine, although given his age, he should go to the hospital to get assessed. Roy shrugged the suggestion off angrily. He had more than recovered from the shock. 'I need to sort out all this mess!' he barked, gesticulating to the still smoking van.

Shirley looked around to see that most of the street was now up, and watching them. Windows were twitching, blinds were rising, and some front doors were open. A young woman with a plump baby was staring out of her window. A child in school uniform was unapologetically gawking as his dad got the car ready. A man in a brown trench coat and a flat cap was watching from the top of the street.

Wait . . .

A man in a . . .

But Shirley was distracted as the paramedics fussed around the truck and when she looked back the man was gone, taking with him the thread of thought she had been trying to seize.

Shirley took her leave as the paramedics asked Farrow if he thought anything was broken and he replied, slightly pathetically, asking if they could save the milk. Soon after, she left Farrow to his problems, as a text heralded one of her own. It was from Marsha. In all the Mallet AM excitement, she had totally forgotten about the embroidery afternoon that she was hosting. Marsha was asking if Shirley was sure she couldn't bring anything? Shirley replied curtly, saying she didn't need any help, secretly hoping that the aggressive taps she had taken to type out the message were interpreted. But Marsha had indeed reminded her to take her leave.

Walking away from the hissing milk truck was like walking away from a dream – a dream she had been forewarned of. There were too many questions – what was Mallet AM? Who was the presenter? Where did it broadcast from? And then on to the big ones – how was this happening? How did Mallet AM know the news before it was going to happen? Could whoever was behind it really see the future?

Was something like that possible? She would have said, just a few days ago, an outright 'no', probably along with a snort of derision, and a quick escape from whoever had posed the question. But now – now she had heard what she'd heard, seen what she'd seen? She couldn't be so sure anymore.

She wondered what the possibility was of getting two events, with all the details and thousands of variables, exactly right. One hundred per cent spot on. Even one event with the small intricacies lined up was odd. Seb Starith and his bakery ladder escapade would probably have been enough for most to believe wholeheartedly. But she had needed a second sign, and boy, had she got it, at the expense of poor Roy Farrow and the hard work of half a dozen cows.

But still there was something holding her back.

As she hobbled down the alley, back to her bungalow, she wished Gabe would take walks with her, so she had someone to talk to – puzzle this out. But she had never seen Gabe outside of the house, and she supposed he wouldn't have anything really to say anyway. What was there to say?

Gabe, the real Gabe, would have loved this. He loved *Doctor Who* and anything else devoted to the concept of time, and the bending of it. His favourite topic was Physics in school, and he even had a few books on the subject.

She wondered if she still had them? Yes, she thought, she must, in the spare room in a box of Gabe's stuff. Maybe they would be useful – at least they couldn't hurt.

Gabe would have loved the concept too – a radio station that told the future. What a riot. And in some ways, she felt that pull too. It was a riot! It was fantastical! But the logical part of her brain had to ask the pertinent questions.

This was the real world. Things like this didn't happen.

Until they did, the fun part of her brain thought.

No, but they really didn't happen. This was the stuff of a science fiction movie – if, and that was a big IF, it was true. There was a lingering remnant of a thought that this may all just be some elaborate hoax.

But a hoax for whom? And to what end? To her knowledge, no one else had found Mallet AM – so for her? What would be the reason for pulling a fast one on her? There wasn't anything in it, no monetary gain to be had – short of the presenter asking for her credit card details next time she listened. A hoax that wrecked a milk truck, and bruised an old man's coccyx. Really, in this day and age, who had the time?

No, her gut instinct, although her gut had been patchy before (indeed she had some medication to prove it), was telling her that this was at least earnest. This was real and it was happening. There was nothing to imagine, or misconstrue.

So, as she rounded the corner into her street and started towards her bungalow, she realised that this came down to a simple question. One that she would have to think on for a long time.

Could she really believe that someone could see the future?

01.08

The sandwiches were made and the tea was brewed, in the nice china that she kept for special occasions – well, that and Marsha Thompson coming over. Shirley felt like she had been buttering bread ever since she'd got back home, but, in reality, she had been intensely thinking. So much so, in fact, that when she was done buttering, she realised she had coated every slice of bread in the house. Therefore, the sandwiches were piled high on the china serving plate that had been a wedding gift from some now long-estranged friend, and they averaged out to around six triangles per person. She expected to be eating salmon and cucumber sandwiches well into next week.

The embroidery girls were in the front room, while she attempted to balance the sandwich plate and the plate with a Marks and Spencer lemon tart on it. Gabe watched her wobble from the safety of the corner of the room, propped against the wall. She shot him a scathing look

– if only he could help. What she wouldn't give to see Marsha getting served afternoon tea by a ghost waiter.

Shirley gave up, and put the tart down, resolving to come back for it, and took the sandwiches in. The living room was loud and full of life for once. Shirley had had to bring the kitchen chairs in to accommodate everyone. They were all gathered around the telly, with a recording of *The Chase* on low volume as per Marsha's instruction. The group was four little old ladies and one, comparatively, young single mum.

Sandy was the young mother, twenty-nine to be exact, who appeared one day about a year ago at the Parish Centre, with her own kits and needles. She was seeking refuge from her baby, only demanding a few hours away with some like-minded women. They let her in with welcome arms, although Marsha did have to reconfigure her ageist attitude to anyone over twenty years younger than her.

Shirley found Sandy to be a breath of fresh air – an independent, youthful woman who had a good heart. Shirley even got Sandy involved with hospital radio and she now ran the requests show on Saturday nights. She loved it when Sandy brought her son, Rex, to see them. He was a podgy two-year-old, and she had seen him grow up before her eyes. Shirley wouldn't have said it to anyone, but she preferred Rex's company to either of her own grandchildren. Sandy often brought Rex to the group, although she hadn't today. She was sitting there, looking over-tired and stressed, but intensely happy. Shirley liked her like that.

The other four – Marsha, Edna, Deirdre and Colleen – were exactly the stereotypes that one of advanced age complained about – living caricatures almost. Shirley sometimes had a hard time connecting with them, as their lives seemed so respectively dull – and that reminded her that hers was as well. Their conversation often was too – Edna's husband had gone back in for hip surgery, Colleen's neighbours were being too loud again or Deirdre's hearing aid was acting up and only picking up vowels and incredibly enunciated consonants. This was all capped off by the group's self-imposed ringleader.

Marsha Thompson was the kind of old battleaxe that could command an army, let alone a small town's craft gathering, and although it was Shirley's house, Marsha was clearly in control. She was eighty-five years of age and wasn't afraid of reminding you, especially if you were younger than her. And, obviously, most people were.

As Shirley put the sandwiches down on the coffee table that she had had great difficulty moving into the centre of the room, Marsha grabbed the plate and moved it to where she thought it should be. That was fine with Shirley, but when she had done three more laps back and forth, bringing the tart, the cups of tea and some small plates and cutlery, Marsha looked up at her expectantly as if there was more.

Shirley made a point to keep eye contact as she sat down in her chair and crossed her legs, picking up a sandwich with one hand and retrieving her embroidery from the arm of the chair with the other. She tried to banish all thoughts of Mallet AM and supernatural concepts like future predictions to attempt to catch up with the conversation.

Turned out it wasn't hard.

'That Bradley Walsh is lovely, isn't he?' Colleen was saying, trying to embroider and watch the television at the same time. 'Have you seen that clip of him where he can't stop laughing?'

'You talk about that every week, Col,' Marsha snapped, far too forcefully for the situation. 'And the answer is yes. And yes. He is rather lovely.'

Shirley didn't say anything. Marsha reminded her very much of Bob. She was abusive, rude, commanding. But there was something about her – something that made you want to impress her. Even Shirley felt it – and she had sussed the old woman out a long time ago.

Marsha plucked a sandwich from the top of the pile, and put it on a plate. She removed the top slice of bread and looked at the filling inside, and seemed to deem it acceptable.

Colleen shut up and resumed her dual tasks in silence.

An awkward silence enveloped the room, punctuated with Bradley Walsh asking something about Beethoven, not the composer but the dog movies.

'How is everyone?' Shirley said, trying to break an unbreakable tension.

There was a rumbling of not much in particular and then nothing else.

Shirley looked at Sandy and caught her eye. 'Uh, I'm good thanks,' Sandy said. 'Sandy's good, everyone.'

'What are you doing currently?'

'Oh, I'm embroidering a patch on to Anthony's work shirt,' Sandy replied. 'See,' she held it up. She had a little neon-coloured patch on the left arm of a putridly boring blue shirt. 'It says Have a Great Day.' She smiled at everyone.

Edna peered through her glasses 'So are you doing that so he can look at it and remind himself to have a great day, or to tell people around him that he hopes they have a great day?'

'Huh?' Sandy withdrew her offering and looked at it for a long time. 'I guess a little of both?' She stared out into space as though her entire world view had been turned on its head. Sandy's big heart was not matched by the size of her brain, but she was adorable and harmless.

Edna held up her embroidery and proclaimed loudly, 'I'm stitching a canary.' Edna had been part of the group for at least as long as Shirley had, and she had never embroidered anything but canaries. Even when the group had scored a guest speaker to give them a masterclass in the art, and they were given the task of embroidering a Hawaiian beach as a landscape, that beach was infested with holidaying canaries.

Marsha tutted loudly, so the attention came all the way back to her, and Marsha directed that onto Shirley as though she were a mirror reflecting a sunbeam. 'What I would like to know is what is wrong with Ms. Steadman? Your weekly task seems very slap-dash, which is a first for you, and you seem to be embroidering nothing but a straight line.'

Shirley looked down to see that she was doing just that. 'It's . . . um . . . it's a very rigid snake.'

Colleen snorted with laughter, although whether it was at Shirley or a well-timed Bradley Walsh retort, she didn't know.

'What's wrong, host?' Marsha said, in a tone that barely veiled her enjoyment at this.

'I just . . .' Shirley started, thinking the age-old excuse would probably work . . . 'haven't been sleeping too well, that's all. My hands ache when I lie down.'

Even Marsha had to murmur in agreement at that.

'Everything hurts when I lie down,' Colleen said, 'sometimes I think I'll never get up again.' She cackled, as though it were a joke, but she was the frailest out of the lot of them and not getting up was probably a real possibility. Maybe that was why she laughed – to try to make her fears into a joke.

'Here, I've got a solution,' Edna said, 'I do this every night. You run two flannels under the hot tap for about five minutes and then you wrap them around your hands when you go to bed. It's like a hot-water bottle for your digits.'

Shirley had to take her hat off to Edna, that actually sounded like a great idea. She opened her mouth to ask more, but Edna was already off on another topic, as though she'd forgotten about the cure for their ailment.

'Have you all heard about Sebastian Starith?' Edna said, trying to thread a needle by holding the needle and thread right in front of her face. Edna regaled them with what happened at Starith's Bakery and, astoundingly, most of the details were correct. Edna often told stories in radically different ways to how they actually took place. Sometimes she even added the odd canary.

Shirley listened intently, but didn't comment until she was finished her tale. When asked if she had heard directly from Edna, she said, 'Oh, I just heard about it on the news.'

The girls looked at Shirley. 'It wasn't on the news.'

'Oh,' Shirley murmured. She was, of course, referencing Mallet AM, forgetting it wasn't an actual news programme. 'I must have been mistaken.'

That was good enough for the others.

'I can do you one better,' said Colleen. 'Have you heard about what happened to the milkman?'

There was a chorus of 'No's. The news obviously hadn't spread yet. Colleen told them about what happened that morning on Benthal Street, as relayed through her friend who lived there. Shirley tensed when Colleen referenced an old woman who rushed to the van to make sure Farrow was all right.

'Who was that?' Marsha said.

Shirley looked away. She didn't know why she didn't want them to know, but she definitely did not.

'Don't know,' Colleen said, 'it was probably one of Farrow's old girls. You know what they say about him down the bridge club. And he is the milkman after all. Gets around, you know what I mean.'

Shirley rolled her eyes, and decided to collect up the empty cups.

'You're not going to tell them?' Gabe said, still in the corner, as she went into the kitchen.

Shirley put the cups down, and turned to him. 'What?' she whispered. She had to keep her voice down, as their gracious host talking to herself would be incredibly valuable ammo for Marsha.

'You don't want to tell them that you were there when Farrow crashed into that post box?' Gabe mused. 'Sounds like a good talking point to me.'

'How am I going to explain that?' Shirley huffed. 'Marsha's practically a gossip generator. I don't want everyone in Chester-Le-Street to know I was there.'

'It was an accident,' Gabe said, shrugging. 'And it was an accident that happened three streets over from here. I think it's feasible that you were there.'

'At six in the morning?'

'I don't know, do I? Say you were walking Moggins or something?'

Shirley gave him a look, a look she had given the real Gabe plenty of times – a look to stop kidding around. She filled the kettle and clicked it on again. It was going to be a long socially drowned afternoon.

Many cups of tea later, and more ITV than she'd watched in many years, the group started to wrap up. Marsha heralded the ending, by simply going to the loo and coming back in her coat and bag. Edna and Colleen followed, while Sandy stayed back and asked if Shirley needed help tidying up. Shirley waved her away, appreciating the sentiment but equally not needing it.

She was very happy they were leaving. Her thoughts had been begging to be left to wander, and her body was starting to will itself to bed. They all lined up in the hallway, to be seen off by the host.

Edna and Colleen went first, happily saying goodbye and thank you for letting them in her home. She just smiled and hugged them. On the way out, Colleen remarked that next week was her turn to host, which was definitely going to be interesting. Colleen lived up near Pelaw, next to the Church of England school. Shirley wasn't quite sure how she was going to get up that big hill, but she would climb that when it came to it. The two of them went out into the night, tittering and chatting with each other, thicker thieves than any of the others could hope to be.

Marsha was next and she clutched Shirley by both arms surprisingly strongly. She looked Shirley deep in her eyes. And shook her head. 'I asked you if you needed me to bring anything! Don't be afraid to ask for help.' She was out the door before Shirley had the chance to respond, which was just as well. Shirley wanted to grab her and shout in her face how long she'd taken buttering that fucking bread, and how awkward that coffee table was to move with bad knees. And she hated that a little part of her was disappointed Marsha hadn't said something nice.

Jesus Christ.

Lastly, Sandy came up to her, with her oversized bag, and smiled, hugging her. 'I do have a favour to ask, but do tell me if you can't do it.'

'Of course,' Shirley said. There wasn't much she wouldn't do for Sandy.

'I'm going to have trouble getting to the hospital for tomorrow night. Rex is going through a tough spot — I think he's teething or something.' Shirley could've commented on this, but was too interested and hopeful for what Sandy was going to say next. 'I really don't think I should leave him right now. My mother has him at the moment, and she's good with him, but I really can't see my partner dealing very well. He doesn't like it when Rex interrupts his silent yoga.'

'A problem, I suppose, with a young child,' Shirley said.

'Yeeahhh,' Sandy said, long and drawn out, 'so I was wondering if, because it seems like you never have anything on, and you're all alone and stuff, you could possibly take over for me tomorrow. I promise I'll never ask you to do this again and if you need me to take one of your . . .'

'Consider it done,' Shirley cut in. She could hardly contain her elation. It was all lining up — again. 'I'm happy to help.' And never a truer word was spoken.

Sandy looked as happy as if she didn't have a teething toddler, but rather tickets to *Hamilton* or something. She enveloped Shirley in a hug and rocked her around. 'Thank you!' and then she held Shirley and said 'Aww!' for some reason. 'You have a lovely home,' she added.

'Thank you,' Shirley said, 'and don't you worry about tomorrow night.' Saturday was only Sandy, so Shirley would have the run of the place to do what she wanted. All she needed though, was Studio Two, that old radio, that desk, and some canned headphones. 66.40 Mallet AM, with one faithful listener.

'Yay,' Sandy said, giving her one last hug for good measure. She gathered up her things, shrugging her coat on, which was just as comically large as her bag. It made her look like an Inuit, but then maybe if Shirley had had something like that this morning, her bones wouldn't have seized up so much. 'Bye,' Sandy sang. She practically skipped out of the door, waving all the way.

Shirley looked after her, watching her shut the front gate behind her. Shirley waved her off. She was really something, and the meeting had gone well enough. Well, there was always the wanting to kill Marsha thing, but you got used to that. And it was interesting to hear Colleen and Edna's perspective on events that felt, for Shirley, almost years old. It made them seem even more real – because, of course, they were.

This was really happening.

Edna and Colleen and Marsha and Sandy were real. The group was real. Her life before was real. But Mallet AM was just as real as any of them.

Shirley shut the front door, locked and bolted it. She was alone again. She had practically got a ticket to Mallet AM's next broadcast put in her lap. It was almost as if something, some grand plan, wanted her to listen to it. And maybe that was the case. If Mallet AM could be real, why not that?

Moggins came and curled around her ankles, glad that everyone had gone and he could finally have some peace and quiet. If not for her knees, Shirley would have bent down and given him a pet and told him that she was thinking exactly the same thing. She was exhausted and rightly so, it was 7.45 p.m. and she had been up for a long time. She didn't have the energy to do this anymore.

She thought about turning the radio on and searching for Mallet AM, but she couldn't summon up the drive to do it. She had probably missed the news, and if she hadn't, she would inevitably find an item that needed investigation, action and brainpower. She couldn't know the future everyday – it wasn't her job. But that didn't mean she wasn't excited to see what tomorrow – and subsequently, she guessed, the day after tomorrow – brought.

Tomorrow was tomorrow and today, she decided to go to bed, read a few chapters of *The Kite Runner* and then try Edna's hot-water wraps around her hands, because they really sounded great. Moggins meowed as if in agreement.

She finished the night by taking the excess sandwiches back into the kitchen. As predicted, there were about twenty left. The tart, however, was gone. She left the washing-up on the counter – not even wanting to bother with the dishwasher tonight. Finally, she did her nightly ritual, making a Horlicks, going into her medicine cabinet and taking her nightly pills. She now took seven at night. She took one by one with a glass of water while the Horlicks was heating up.

And then she remembered – the email. She hadn't checked it.

She got her laptop and turned it on, stirring the Horlicks while it started up. As she got to her email, the optimism she'd had before was gone.

But now there was a new email – a response. A response from The Enigma Files.

The mug of hot liquid almost slipped out of her fragile hands, as she went to clap them together, forgetting both her age and that her hands were occupied. She set her mug down and clicked the email.

Luckily, it was far less cryptic than the website it hailed from. In fact, it was warm and inviting.

I'm listening. Maybe we can compare notes. I'm at 19 Quillback Terrace, Newcastle. Any day except Tuesday. Any time except 4–6 p.m. AND NOT BEFORE 11 A.M.
– Arnie

Arnie. This Arnie might have some information. And it looked like he wanted her to meet him at his house. The alarm bells were ringing, but she was trying to think over them. This was a bad idea – an awful idea really. You didn't just meet someone you met on the internet – and she hadn't even really MET this Arnie.

But what if his intentions were exactly as they appeared? And he could help.

No. It was too much of a risk.

She left the email to fester in her inbox – maybe she would use it later, but for now, the risk was too great.

She had to remember herself. And just knowing that there was someone else out there was probably enough, wasn't it?

She got up, laughing off a feeling that she had escaped something. She almost felt a thrill like jumping out of a bear trap just before it snapped shut, even though she had merely been sitting at her table. She had to trust her instincts.

Breathing out slowly, she turned off the kitchen light, and went to bed, with Moggins hot on her heels, and her dead son nowhere to be seen.

01.09

Chester-Le-Street
Saturday 13 February 2021
6.30 p.m.

The radio station was a mess. Friday night was the night when the managers were in, doing their own shows. You'd think that would mean that the studio would be impeccable when left, but it was the exact opposite. The request clipboards were strewn everywhere, with slips piled up on the desk. Records were out and not put back in the proper order, and the old radio Shirley was going to use was on the chair for some reason. It was a total pigsty, and she had no one to complain to.

She hadn't slept much again. She had lain awake with her hands wrapped in slowly cooling cloths and wondered what she had missed on the Mallet AM news. What would it have revealed about the day ahead? It was impossible to know – she couldn't see the future. But she had a direct line to someone who could. There was a tremendous kind of power in that.

And when her thoughts had drifted from that line, they fell on the email from Enigma. Was it a mistake to ignore it? That thrill she'd felt at leaving it — maybe it was the wrong move. Or maybe not. Again, as of right now, impossible to know.

All day, she'd had a new pain. There was a small stabbing in her chest, next to her heart — like she was constantly getting prodded with a sword with thousands of blades. As the day had progressed, the sword dug in more and more. By the evening when she was due to start getting ready to go out to the radio, the pain was almost overwhelming. But she didn't let it consume her. She had been just pottering around the house all day, cleaning and thinking. She had had nothing else to do except feel it. It would have been so much worse if she just stayed home.

That, and she couldn't stay home. She had missed one Mallet AM broadcast, and it had kept her up all night, wondering what she could have learned. She needed this. It was something new, something exciting. She had to carry on, and get to the bottom of what this was. The pain was wanting her to slow down, but, however much it hurt, she had to continue. What was the old saying? Plenty of time to sleep when you're dead. She hadn't really understood why people said that until now.

Maybe this thing — this radio station — was the last great thing she was ever going to experience. A wonder of the North East of England. One that, it seemed, only she knew about. She felt like she was sharing a beautiful secret with the presenter — the voice on the other end. And half-seven every day was the time for them to enter the confessional.

She put down her bag and started to tidy up. She moved the old radio into Studio Two and hooked it up all ready. She put the headphones on and tuned in. Mallet AM was playing exactly the same music that it always did. She had plenty of time.

She checked the chart on the bulletin board to see which ward was up for requests tonight. Ward 11, general. She guessed that she'd see the usual mix of old and young people with various ailments given that the ward was pretty much a dumping ground for anyone who didn't fit into a specific medical category. She picked up a clipboard and wrote Ward 11 at the top of one of the forms, before making her way out of the studio.

The hospital was very quiet compared to a weekday. There were fewer nurses and doctors in the corridors, there was no real sound in the hallways, and even in the ward when she got there, there weren't as many beds full — a relief after the events of the dark year. The hospital tried to get as many patients out on the weekends as possible, as there wasn't any possibility of them seeing their assigned doctors.

Even with the clientele that were unlucky enough to be in hospital over the weekend, Ward 11 was much worse than Ward 14 had been in terms of variety. Everyone seemed to want golden oldies, which, contrary to popular belief, not every old person enjoyed. Any young people on the ward didn't want to talk to her, and the older people wanted to talk to her too much. And, of course, it was all capped off by another uninspired choice from the nurses. This time they wanted

'Shove This Jay-Oh-Bee' by Canibus and Biz Markie. She laughed of course.

Mallet AM was the only thing on her mind. What would it divulge today – and would she believe it? Yes, she thought she probably would – whatever it was. She had to get back to the station and get these requests ready before the news programme went live. She was pretty sure all of the songs requested were in the system, so it shouldn't be too difficult.

She left the ward, using the hand sanitiser station as she did. It was remarkable how many people ignored it when coming and going, even after the dark year. Maybe she should talk about it on the requests show.

Or maybe she shouldn't – this was Sandy's audience, and she didn't know how Sandy usually ran things. She would have loved to have listened to one of Sandy's shows, but she had no idea how to access the archives – the only thing available to normal volunteers was Ken Vox's entire back catalogue. They were specifically told that if something went wrong, just stick on some Ken Vox.

Sandy might have a specific style that her listeners were used to, and it probably wasn't being lectured about hand sanitiser. She could save it for her show next week. She wrote it on a virtual Post-it and stuck it in her brain, although she knew that that Post-it was likely to lose its stickiness and waft away into the nothingness.

Shirley emerged into the first-floor corridor and started making her way towards the lifts. The pain she had been feeling all day had mysteriously disappeared, and she couldn't help but feel it was gearing up for something, although her breath was ragged. Or more likely, she was just too busy to think about it. No, Mallet AM called now.

She got to the lifts and put her finger to the call button. And then, as always, Marsha came into her head again. That thing she'd said almost a month ago now. 'If you can't stand a flight of stairs, you might as well just fade away.'

'Fuck you, Marsha,' she muttered under her breath.

And went to the stairs instead.

Her breath was still a little ragged, so she took every step with a little hesitance. But soon she was halfway up. And then something happened. Suddenly she felt incredibly dizzy. She gripped on to the handrail, and found that her hands were shaking. She should stop, go back down. But she found she couldn't. She couldn't move her legs.

Her heart was starting to beat louder and louder, and a steady warmth was spreading through her chest. She had to get off these stairs, whatever was happening. And now she was really thinking 'Fuck you, Marsha'.

Going upwards seemed easier — less chance of falling. She moved her hand up the railing and pulled herself up. Her head swirled — like she was going around on the teacups at Disney — but she was also here standing still. The absolute antithesis of both these concepts wrapped around her, threatening to drag her down. But she kept pulling herself up, one step at a time, until the beats of her heart were all that were left.

She got to the top of the stairs and tried to smile. She couldn't. She couldn't really do anything. The beats were now stabs of pain, every one like a punch in the chest. Her legs gave way and she collapsed to the floor. Her vision became blurred. And she thought that maybe this was it.

Just when things were starting to get interesting.

Beat, beat, beat. Punch, punch, punch. That last one caught her off-guard. She wailed. And reached out with her hands, feeling for the floor.

She couldn't leave this place – this life, not in the stairwell of Chester-Le-Street Hospital. But that meant maybe she'd have to swallow her pride. She took the last of her strength and, between deafening beats of her heart, she yelled, 'Help!'

She couldn't hear if it worked. There was nothing in her ears except pulsing blood.

'Help.'

Her vision started to go dark. But before it did, she saw a change in colours in the blur. Black. Blue. Light blue. And a flash of red. 'Shirley? Shirley, oh God.'

Shirley opened her mouth. And her heart felt like it exploded. And that was it.

Plenty of time to sleep when you're dead.

Maybe it was her bedtime.

01.10

A steady beeping sound. Shirley opened her eyes, and the scene slowly tried its best to reveal itself to her. Blurry shapes turned to real objects, uncomfortable colours became vibrant and a face came into view. Callie? It was Callie? But what . . . where was she?

Shirley tried to get up, and Callie launched forward and stopped her. She was in a familiar place, but at an unfamiliar angle. She was lying down – in a hospital room. Her entire body throbbed with pain, and tubes were coming out of her arm. Next to her was a machine – the beeping – measuring her heart rate. There were two things poking up her nostrils – she'd seen them on many patients before. 'No, no, no . . .'

'Keep calm,' the soothing voice of Callie came to meet her panic. 'It's all right. You're all right. Everything is all right.' Even without the nurse's uniform, Shirley would still be able to tell she worked here. She talked with a friendly, soft tone, that betrayed how many times she had done it before. She sat there, beside the bed that now could be called Shirley's, as beautiful as ever. Her autumn-leaf red hair was tied up in a bun, revealing her freckled youthful face. How old must she be now? Early thirties? Mid-thirties? She was always younger than Gabe. She didn't look a day older than the last time Shirley had seen her — and she meant really seen her — not just bump into her in the hospital corridor. That day in the conservatory in Houghton-Le-Spring, when Gabe and Callie were going through the ultimate rough patch, was oddly melodic, colourful. A simpler time.

'Callie,' Shirley rasped, not knowing if it was a question or a statement. Her throat was so dry.

It seemed the younger woman didn't know either, because she just nodded, and said sadly, 'Yes, it's me.'

Shirley wrenched her head off the staticky pillow and looked above her. The whiteboard above the bed now had her name on it. The name of her doctor had been left blank, as had what was actually wrong with her. 'What happened?'

'We're not sure yet,' Callie said. 'I found you in the stairway, collapsed. I heard you shouting for help from the corridor, and I knew your voice straight away. I called in everyone I could and we got you here.'

'Where is here?' She could use a drink.

Callie read her mind, producing a cup with a long straw from the bedside table. She held it up to Shirley as she took the straw in her mouth and had a long drink. The water was lukewarm, but that was OK. It coated her throat and brought some life back to her.

'You're in the hospital. In a room off Ward 11.'

Ward 11. Back again. So they didn't think anything was severely wrong then.

But then Callie said, 'It was the easiest ward we could get you to. And moving you around might do more harm than anything else. So here's just as good as anywhere.'

'Wait . . .' Shirley started to remember something. Why had she been so eager to be here today? The radio station. The radio. The old radio. Her path of thinking snaked around and finally found its prey. 'What time is it?'

'Uh . . .' Callie looked at her watch. 'It's ten past ten.'

Callie carried on talking, but Shirley wasn't listening. She had missed the news broadcast. What could have been on there? What future was bearing down on Chester-Le-Street? She would never know.

'. . . so I'm afraid you're here overnight,' Callie was saying.

'What?' Shirley snapped, a little too harshly. Firstly, Callie had no idea about Mallet AM or why the time of seven thirty (and very much not ten past ten) was important. And, secondly, it wasn't Callie's fault she had missed the daily broadcast, it was hers. Or rather, it was her body's fault.

She felt like she had been waiting for Mallet AM, something to make the rest of her life seem worthwhile. Now it had finally come along, but was it too late. Her own body was betraying her — and she couldn't keep up with young people. Hell, she couldn't even keep up

111

with Edna or Colleen and they were five years older than her. She wasn't looking forward to seeing what she'd have to cope with now.

'I was saying,' Callie started, 'due to the time of night, there isn't a doctor available right now to look at your charts, and since it seems like you have at least recovered a bit, the staff on the ward seem happy with monitoring you overnight and then a doctor is going to come and see you tomorrow.'

'No, no, no!' Shirley said, this time entirely as harshly as she meant. 'I am not staying here overnight. I have to get home. I have a cat. And tomorrow's Sunday – what kind of a doctor is going to come in on Sunday? I mean, don't be so ridiculous.'

'There's that Shirley I remember,' Callie said, smiling. 'I've sorted out the doctor. And I can pop in on the way home and feed your cat. And I'll come back tomorrow and see you.'

'I am not staying here.'

'You have to, Shirley.'

'No, I am not.'

'I'm sorry, but yes you are. You have to sort this out, before it kills you.'

Shirley grumbled. It seemed like Callie had it all figured out. But suddenly, Shirley realised what was so wrong in the room. Callie. It was Callie. She was here talking to Callie – the woman she had been so afraid to talk to for so long, the woman she had to apologise to the most. The Shirley she remembered, said Callie. The Shirley that Callie and Gabe had needed, and didn't show up when she was needed. Not the Shirley who saw her son off to his death.

'Callie,' Shirley started, but her eyes filled with tears, and her hands started to shake.

Callie took her hands, seemingly knowing exactly what she was thinking. 'It's OK. It's OK. I'm here.' There was a time when Shirley and Callie were thick as thieves. Ever since Gabe brought her home, as his first ever girl-friend, the two women had just clicked. They used to sit at the kitchen table and talk and gossip and Shirley would feel some kind of release.

Bob never allowed house guests. Or, rather, that wasn't exactly true. Bob had cultivated a home atmos-phere that made Shirley never want to invite anyone to her home. He never outright said that she was not to bring anyone home, because he didn't have to. That was his genius really, as if anyone had ever found him out, he could fall back on the fact he'd never said a word. Shirley isolated herself – which was true. But Bob was over her shoulder.

So when Gabe brought Callie to her, she couldn't be-lieve her luck. Callie was eighteen years old at the time, and she could reclaim her stolen youth. Shirley had met Bob at sixteen – they were childhood sweethearts. Back then, Bob was as controlling as ever, but he hid it behind a charming, endearing and warm exterior. He still had that exterior, but he didn't show it to Shirley anymore. With Callie, Shirley could have a friend, a lifeline, some way to live, however vicariously. Callie seemed to just get her, and the feeling was mutual.

113

'It's OK,' Callie said.

'You would have done anything for Gabriel,' Shirley cried.

'And I still would,' Callie said, strongly.

'I should have done anything for him too. You looked out for him more than I ever did,' Shirley cried.

Callie hugged her as best she could, with all the wires and hospital rubbish surrounding her. 'It wasn't your fault. No one blames you for what happened. I certainly don't.'

And there it was. Shirley had been so afraid for so long that Callie held her accountable – that was why she had kept away from her for all these years, turned away whenever she was coming, kept her head down when they passed each other in the corridor. But now she realised maybe she wasn't afraid of what Callie thought of her. Maybe she was just afraid of what she thought of herself. Maybe if Callie forgave her, she would have to think about forgiving herself.

'I miss him,' said Shirley.

'I do too,' Callie replied into her shoulder. 'I do too.'

And she hugged Shirley until Shirley had stopped crying. And as she sat back down on the chair, Shirley saw that Callie had been crying too.

'You should get going,' Shirley said, 'it's late.'

'Ah, pfft,' Callie waved it away, 'all I've got at home is a chicken pot pie for one, and re-runs of *Shetland*. I'd rather sit here, truth be told. Besides, we have so much to catch up on.'

And so they did. Shirley told Callie what had been

going on with her and then Callie told her what had been going on with her. Callie had trained to be a registered nurse, and was doing a PhD in nursing part-time. She still lived in Chester-Le-Street, but when her mother and father had died a few years ago, she moved up towards Waldridge. It sounded like she wasn't actually that far from Shirley. Her mother had got cancer and died in 2015. Her dad followed soon after, dying, Callie said, of a broken heart. They left behind a sizeable inheritance for Callie and she was able to sell the old pokey family home and get something bigger.

In her personal life, Callie liked her independence. She didn't mention any boyfriends, or partners, or children. She lived alone, without even any pets. But she still looked so, so happy. Some people were just like that. Shirley wondered if Callie had needed a break in relationships after Gabe.

Then Shirley started talking about what had been happening recently – although she left out the frequent visits from her dead son. She had planned on stopping at Mallet AM, but to her surprise, she continued eagerly. She told Callie about the first time she had found it, Seb Starith and his ladder, Roy Farrow and his post box, and how she confirmed both events.

Callie sat there and listened intently, not betraying what she thought until Shirley was done. 'Hmmm,' she said, 'that's an interesting story.'

'It's not a story, it's real.'

'No, yeah, I believe you totally. I'm just trying to wrap my head around this.' Callie thought for a moment.

115

'And you're saying both events happened exactly like they were reported?'

'Yes,' Shirley said. 'Down to the very minute. Down to the tiniest detail. Seb Starith fell off the ladder exactly when he was supposed to. A woman walked out in front of the milk truck, causing Roy Farrow to swerve into a post box exactly as it was meant to.'

Callie sighed thoughtfully. 'This has to be some kind of trick. An extremely elaborate coincidence maybe. Or someone having you on.'

'I've thought all about that,' Shirley said, and she had never said anything truer. The thoughts had gone around and around in her head. They had kept her up at night, distracted her during the day. 'I just don't think it's possible.'

'So what's the alternative?' Callie asked. 'That this radio station tells you the future?'

Shirley didn't even have to think, 'Yes.'

Callie scoffed. Shirley didn't blame her. 'I don't know . . .'

'I can show you,' Shirley said, 'the news is on at 7.30 every evening. I can take you to the hospital radio station and let you listen.'

Callie didn't seem convinced, but she nodded nonetheless. 'OK, let's make a deal.' And Shirley understood why she was playing along, even before she said it. 'If you promise to stay put here until tomorrow, then I promise when you get discharged we can go and listen to this Jimmy Mallet radio station. On the proviso that your condition isn't anything incredibly serious.'

'OK. But the station has nothing to do with Jimmy Mallet. It's just called Mallet AM.'

'I wonder if that has significance?' Callie mused. Which was odd as, surprisingly, Shirley hadn't considered that before. She had thought of everything except the name. Maybe it was the name of the presenter, maybe it had something to do with the predictions? Maybe . . .

She couldn't think about it now. So she said, 'I accept your offer. As long as you, in turn, promise that my little incident stays between us. You can't tell Deena.'

Callie held up her hands and smiled. 'Already done. Why do you think she's not here right now? I sorted it so the hospital won't contact her.'

Shirley felt an outpouring of emotion for this young woman – who, by all accounts, should be a stranger. But, through Gabe, they had become intertwined. Just another thing to be thankful to her son for.

Callie bent over her bed and took her hand again. 'It'll all be OK,' she said, and looking at her pretty face, and the genuine emotion, made Shirley believe that it would be. 'I'll be back tomorrow.'

Shirley nodded, and sniffed. 'OK.'

Callie nodded back, reassuringly, and asked permission to go into Shirley's bag and get her house keys. Then, after some instructions about what Moggins liked for supper (half a sachet of food, broken up by a spoon, and some dry kibbles with a smidge of warm water mixed in), she left Shirley alone.

The room was uninviting, cold. The bed was lumpy

and hard. A nurse came in ten minutes after Callie left and took some notes by the ECG machine, then she turned off the infernal beeping. She asked if Shirley wanted the light off, and she said yes, but could the nurse swing over the television and radio set. The nurse did so and left the room.

Shirley tapped on the screen of the little plastic set. It came to life, with a pixelated version of the Chester-Le-Street hospital logo. She tutted, never believing that she was going to have to do this malarkey for herself. She picked up the phone that was part of the set, and dialled the number she had memorised before she'd even completed her hospital radio induction.

'Hi, can I activate this set please?' She had to give her surname and her postcode, but she declined giving her card details to get virtual credit. You needed credits to watch television but she wasn't interested in any of that. She just wanted the radio.

She hung up the phone and had to wait a few minutes before the logo on the screen dissolved into a menu. She pressed the radio button, taking the little pair of plastic over-ear headphones and putting them over her head. They were very uncomfortable.

The voice of Ken Vox flooded her ears. His smarmy voice had always been grating to her – it wasn't because he had gone on to greater pastures, she couldn't care less about that. It was because he was always so full of himself. Right now, he was regaling his audience with the story of how he was at a wedding and the singer cancelled, so he stepped up and sang a full five-hour set. She had heard that story so many times that she could probably tell it better than him. He was just so self-centred, pompously plump. She always liked to think that her work at the radio was important, but when Ken was here, he had taken it to a different level. When he did a show, he thought he was broadcasting to the world. He even had a name for his fans – Voxxers. And again, this was at a hospital radio station, where it was highly unlikely he would get the same listener for more than two or three weeks.

Shirley took great pleasure in turning Vox off. The radio menu came up, showing the pre-tuned stations. The usual – Radio 1, Radio 2, Radio 3, Metro, Sun FM, et cetera. She switched over to manual mode and tried to find Mallet AM. She wasn't hoping for much – the signal had to be incredibly weak, the same system was powering every machine on the ward, and Mallet AM wasn't strong as it was.

She punched the plastic buttons, and it took over a minute for her to get to 66.4. All she heard was static, but then . . . A sliver of music fought through the fuzz. It was the usual lift music and mixed with the static it created an awful mix. But something about it was soothing, familiar. It was like she was at home.

She hadn't slept anywhere except the bedroom in her bungalow ever since moving in, unless you counted the odd forty winks in the afternoon in the living room in front of *Countdown*. She had never spent a night in the hospital, not once. When Bob had had his first stroke, he stayed overnight, but she had gone home, revelling in the freedom. That night, she had slept like a baby, and was sad when he came home the next day.

She wasn't used to how oddly quiet it was. Quiet but not empty – there was an atmosphere that felt electric – as though things may kick off at any moment. So Shirley thought she'd need all the help she could get, and kept her headphones on.

She found the bed remote and pressed the button to slowly move the head of the bed down. When she had got it into a relatively comfortable position, she awkwardly shuffled the pillows around, and lay back. The lift music stopped, and two minutes later it started again. The static went in and out, sometimes growing stronger, sometimes wafting away. Like waves on a beach.

She closed her eyes. Today had not gone her way. She hoped that the people she had collected requests from on this very ward weren't upset that the requests show hadn't run properly. She would apologise next time she did a show, but there was no guarantee anyone who she had met tonight would be there. It was more for herself. She was also worried that she'd let Sandy down – but she knew the young mum would be mortified to see her now and forgive her without a second thought.

She tried to stop thinking, focusing on the static and the music. It wasn't worth worrying about what had happened in the stairwell, it wasn't worth worrying about what futures she missed, it wasn't worth worrying about how Moggins would react when a strange human came to give him his midnight snack. It wasn't worth worrying. Period.

So she rested.

And soon, the resting turned to sleeping.

It was good until . . .

She dreamed of the previous day, an alternate past, where she ushered the embroidery girls out early and tuned in her radio in the front room. She sat in her chair and listened to Mallet AM's news with the ghost of Gabe in the corner and Moggins on her lap. It was all mundane until the final item – 'And lastly, tonight, Saturday 13 February 2021 at 7.04 p.m., we have some sombre news. Shirley Steadman, 70-year-old hospital radio volunteer, collapsed at the hospital after attempting to ascend a flight of stairs. It is uncertain what actually happened, but Steadman remains in hospital, and the outlook is not good.'

The dream ended in darkness and uncertainty.

01.11

Valentine's Day. Didn't mean much to Shirley anymore. Just a day when other people took stock, remembered to say they loved each other. The ward was abuzz with visitors, some with balloons and presents. They all passed her open door.

She had woken at four thirty in the morning, unable to go back to sleep. The headphones had slipped off her head in the middle of the night and now all she could hear was the deafening silence of the ward. Someone had obviously come in, in the middle of the night, as the door to her private room stood ajar. She could see out into the dark corridor and sometimes she caught the silhouette of a nurse walking past.

Minutes felt like hours, and hours felt like days. Being in hospital was one of the worst experiences she'd ever had. It was such an empty existence. All she could do was lie there. There was an odd smell in the air – slightly medical but also slightly foody. The concoction was an assault on her nostrils. Her ears buzzed with tinnitus due to the lack of anything to focus on.

Finally, at half five, a nurse had come in to read her ECG machine. Seeing that she was awake, she had made her do a questionnaire about how she felt. There was no option for 'bored out of my fucking skull'. The nurse made some stale toast with some flavourless jam, and a cardboardy cup of tea. Shirley ate and drank as enthusiastically as the situation required.

Given that her prevailing emotion was boredom, she almost forgot why she was actually here. She felt absolutely fine. She pulled the stupid pipes out of her nose – she didn't need them, they weren't doing anything anyway. She started to wish she hadn't shouted out when she was collapsing. Maybe she would have just lost consciousness for a moment and then she would have woken up on the stairway floor and she could have just gone about her business.

But there was one saving grace to this whole situation – she had reconnected with Callie and that was priceless. Not only that, but she had confided in someone else about Mallet AM, and although she wasn't sure Callie even believed her, it was nice to have someone to talk to about it.

Shirley knew that it was going to be a long day, even before she experienced the year-long morning. Any hope of seeing the doctor first thing was dashed when a nurse came and said Sunday rounds were in the afternoon. She said it chirpily, like it wasn't the worst news she'd ever heard, which made Shirley want to whack her with her cane. She wished she had her cane with her or the strength to wield it. But the hospital seemed to be sucking the energy out of her. She felt glued to the bed — as though the tubes in her arm (which she only realised were connected to an IV when the nurse reached around the back of her bed to change the bag) were pumping her full of poison, instead of fluids to keep her alert.

At lunchtime, one of the nurses came to take the needle out of her arm and take the IV away, which she thought was a good sign. However, when the nurse appeared, Shirley was mortified. It was the nurse she had seen the night before — the nurse who had laughed as she'd suggested 'Shove This Jay-Oh-Bee' as a request. She removed the bag and the needle without even looking at Shirley, and then finally, as if by accident, the nurse's gaze wandered onto her face. She looked confused, glancing around as if she was being pranked.

'Were you . . .?' the nurse stumbled over her words. 'Weren't you . . .?'

Shirley just allowed the nurse to be confused. It was a slow day and she needed at least a little bit of entertainment. Eventually the nurse just backed away. Shirley laughed. It was the little things.

After a horrendous lunch of pasta something, the doctor finally appeared. He was younger than Gabe was when he died. Everyone seemed to be getting younger and younger these days and getting into higher and higher positions. Give it a few decades and the country would be run by toddlers if this rate was going to keep up. (Some people would argue that it already was.)

Sometimes Shirley was glad that she would be dead before she saw the carnage.

The doctor was a tall, relatively lanky, bookish-looking man with rectangular glasses and a rather plucky disposition. He clearly wanted to prove himself to his older peers, but that didn't translate into anything particularly great for her. He was flustered, and confused at first, as he'd clearly been rushing around.

Callie appeared before he started to give his news, bad or good, and it took Shirley too long to realise that Callie must have asked to be called when the doctor came. She sat in the chair beside Shirley's bed and held her hand – her soft, smooth hand in Shirley's wrinkled, coarse one. There was something in Callie's face – a worry that wasn't there before. Shirley didn't want to think what it was about.

'I'm Doctor Graham Turner,' said Doctor Graham Turner, having to slide his glasses up his nose given how much he was sweating. 'I'll be your, uh, doctor. According to all the tests we have run, it seems what you experienced last night was a mild heart event.'

'Heart event? What is that?' Shirley asked.

Callie looked around at her and smiled sadly. 'I believe what Doctor Turner means is a heart attack.'

'Yes,' Doctor Turner said, 'that is what I meant unfortunately. It was lucky that it wasn't very severe, but this means that the chance of you having another event . . . uh, attack . . . is more likely. You are going to have to make some lifestyle changes to lower the risk.'

'Lifestyle changes?' Shirley repeated. 'What does that

mean? I don't smoke, I don't really drink. What is there to do?'

Callie turned and told her, 'Maybe you just need to start taking it a little slower.'

'Yes,' the doctor said, 'take the lift, not the stairs.' (*Really, really fuck you, Marsha,* Shirley thought). 'Maybe cut down on your activities slightly. You are entering a complicated stage of life and—'

'Excuse me,' Shirley said, 'what stage of life would that be?'

'Uh . . ..' The young doctor seemed to realise he was on thin ice, but went on anyway. 'The last one.'

Shirley tutted loudly and gave him a disapproving glare.

'Can I have a look at her charts?' Callie said, standing up. 'I'm a nurse here. Callie Brennan.'

The doctor handed the file over without a word and Callie started reading, furrowing her brow. He continued to dig himself into the hole he'd made, 'It is important, at your age, to realise your limitations, and if it means taking a step back from some of your activities, then there is no shame in that. The nurses were telling me you volunteer here?'

So that nurse had finally realised where she knew Shirley from. 'Yes, I work on the hospital radio.'

The doctor looked confused. 'We have a hospital radio?'

'Yes, and I'm not giving it up. Over my dead body.'

'I'm not saying you have to, maybe you just have to configure it a bit.'

'I'll configure you, you—'

'OK,' Callie said, pressing the chart into the doctor's chest, 'let's all calm down and take a minute. Doctor Turner is just here to help, however unhelpful he may appear. He's telling the truth, it looks like you had a small heart attack, probably just brought on by taking the stairs instead of the lift. Little changes like that can really help to lower the probability of having another attack.'

'Yes, that is very true,' Doctor Turner seized on this. 'I do have some literature that I could pop back and give you if you would like to take a look at it.'

Shirley raised her eyebrows. 'Literature about stopping doing things. That'll be fun.'

The doctor side-eyed Callie, looking like he wanted some help, but Callie didn't seem like she was going to give it. So he forged ahead. 'In addition, we do have some medication we'd like you to . . .'

'Ah-ha,' Shirley said loudly, 'there it is. Just add the pills to the pile and get out. I have haemorrhoids older than you.'

Callie gave Shirley a scathing but comical look as she ushered the doctor out, but he wanted the final word, 'If you want, I can also prescribe some haemorrhoid cream . . .'

'It was clearly a joke,' she heard Callie say, just before the door closed.

Well really? So what if she had a small heart attack. People had heart attacks, and they were fine. She didn't want to stop doing things. Hospital radio was her favourite time of the week, and she had to get up and go out to places to feel any semblance of being alive. What was the alternative? Just lie in a bed like this, and wait to die.

And she especially couldn't stop now. Not when she had found Mallet AM. If anything, now was the time to speed up. Hopefully the pills would help, because she'd rather have a fatal heart attack than even entertain the idea of 'slowing down'.

She grumped to herself until Callie came back ten minutes later. 'OK,' she sighed, 'well, I didn't get much more out of him, but you are free to go whenever you like.'

'Thank goodness,' Shirley said. She instantly started getting up.

'No, wait a second,' Callie smiled awkwardly. 'There's that old Shirley again. We do need to acknowledge how serious this was.'

'It was serious,' Shirley acknowledged.

'No, not just like that,' Callie said, 'we need to discuss this.'

'Can we discuss this somewhere else?'

Callie conceded, 'Yeah, I guess.'

'Good. I'm fucking starving.'

01.12

Chester-Le-Street
Sunday 14 February 2021
5.30 p.m.

Leaving the hospital wasn't quite as easy as just walking out. Even with Callie there speeding things along, it took an hour and a half to get all the paperwork done and then wait for Shirley's prescription of new 'heart' medication.

Throughout all the bureaucracy, Shirley had one prevailing thought – that Deena would kill her if she ever found out she had spent a night in hospital without telling her. In her mind, Deena could never know about this little episode. She would wrap her up in cotton wool, she would come round more and more – or, even worse, she would put her in a home. Deena had threatened that once before – when Shirley had had a fall. She hadn't talked to her daughter for a month. The very idea of going into a home was repugnant to her.

When they finally left the hospital, Shirley's stomach was hurting almost as much as the heart attack she'd experienced, so they found themselves at The Watering

Hole, the franchise pub at the top of Front Street. The hospital was just over the road, so it would be fairly quick, even with her rapidly decreasing walking speed, to get back in time for the Mallet AM broadcast. Even so, as Shirley sat in the window looking at the blocky hospital building, she couldn't help but keep checking her watch.

'Fish and chips for both of us on the way,' Callie said, as she brought over the drinks. She put a beer in front of herself, a glass of lemonade in front of Shirley.

'I asked for a glass of dry white wine.'

'Yeah,' Callie said, 'it's on its way. They're just getting a new bottle from the back.'

Shirley laughed. 'You scared me there. I thought you were going all nurse on me.

'No,' Callie replied, although she didn't return the laugh, 'the odd glass of wine is fine. But you do need to slow down a bit, Shirley. If you don't do it for yourself, then do it for us, the people who care about you.'

Shirley almost choked up at the thought that Callie was now back as someone who cared about her. All those years avoiding her had been wasted. She could have been Callie's friend all along, all because she was scared. 'I don't think I know how to slow down. After Bob passed, it seemed like I had so much to catch up on. I was done just sitting there and taking shit, you know?'

Callie nodded, and sat back as the waitress brought over Shirley's glass of dry white wine. Shirley took it greedily and had a sip. Not the best, but not the worst. 'I

130

understand. But you're not as young as you used to be. And I know hearing that from me, or Doctor Idiot – who totally tried to ask me out by the way – is infuriating. But it's true. If you carry on like this, you will die before your time. And you can't leave me again.'

She ignored this. 'What did you see on that chart?' Shirley asked, narrowing her eyes.

'Nothing that the meds he gave you won't fix. Along with his advised, but ill-considered, change of lifestyle. Just say you'll consider it.'

Shirley sighed. 'I'll consider it.' She looked at her watch. 'How was Moggins?'

Callie stabbed a chip and ate it. 'He was fine. Hissed a bit at me. Do you leave the TV on for him?'

'No.'

'Oh, it's just you left the TV on.'

'Did I?' Shirley said. She tried to think back to when she left the day before. She didn't think she'd left it on. She never would have done something like that back in the day. But she must have. Maybe there was something about her growing old and forgetful.

Callie saw it in her face. 'You see, there's no shame in forgetting little things like this. Maybe it's your time to stop and smell the flowers, as it were. Slow down.'

Shirley considered it. 'Maybe. But you don't know about this radio station. It's spell-binding. When you hear it, you'll want to run a marathon too.'

'Oh,' Callie said, like she'd forgotten about what they had talked about the previous day, 'Mallet FM.'

'AM.'

'What's the difference?'

'It's two different frequency bands,' Shirley said. 'I forgot how young you were.'

'Shirley, I'm thirty-five,' Callie said strongly.

Shirley baulked. She suddenly felt dizzy even thinking how much time had passed. Callie was thirty-five years old. She had been barely eighteen the first time Shirley had set eyes on her. Now, she was a woman. Gabe would be thirty-seven next month – that didn't even bear thinking about. Everyone was getting older – including herself. She practically had one foot in the grave. Maybe there was something in what that dickhead doctor and Callie were saying.

But she couldn't let herself think that way, still. 'Just wait until you hear the news, that's all. You'll understand.'

They didn't talk much more over dinner. The fish and chips definitely filled a hole, after the ghastly hospital food, but Shirley still had to force herself to eat. All she wanted was to get into the studio and tune that old radio in. So when they were finally done, and the time ticked to 6.45 p.m., Shirley could barely contain herself.

Callie noticed as they left the pub, letting Shirley lead her back to the hospital. 'What's got in to you? You do realise you had a heart attack yesterday?'

'Yes, yes,' Shirley said, as she waited to cross the road. 'Why won't you stop mentioning that?'

'Uh, maybe because it was a heart attack. There's usually a recovery period – you should be resting. Shouldn't we just get you home?'

Shirley turned to her – ignoring that the pedestrian light had gone green. 'You don't understand.'

A man behind them grunted in disdain as he had to go around them to cross the road.

'What?' Callie asked softly and genuinely.

'You don't understand . . .' but what was the end to that sentence. What was this interest, this obsession? Was it wholly for the oddity of it, the possibility of finding something in life that for once was inexplicable? Was it that it was just hers, she had found it first, and she could decide whether to unleash the secret out into the world? Or was it solely because, for a long time, she had been bored – completely and utterly bored – and this was something so radical that it upset her status quo? Was it just that she finally had a purpose – she finally had something to do? 'You don't understand how important this is to me.' She settled on that – a mix of all the options. Yes, that was good.

Callie glanced around, presumably to make sure she wasn't blocking anyone else, and then she stepped closer to Shirley. 'No,' she said, quietly, 'I'm afraid I don't.'

'You just need to listen to it.'

'I don't know if I do.'

And there it was. 'You think I'm making this up? You think I imagined everything?'

'I think you definitely believe what is happening,' Callie said, clearly picking her words very carefully. 'But listen to what you're saying. A radio station that reports news a day in advance – do you blame me for

133

being a little dubious at least? Things like this are science fiction. They don't happen in the real world.'

Shirley conceded that she couldn't exactly blame Callie. She hadn't been along for the ride so far, she hadn't seen first-hand everything come true. She hoped that Callie would tonight. 'Can you just keep an open mind?'

'I don't know,' Callie admitted.

'You promised to come and listen. You asked me to stay at the hospital, and get the tests, and stay and get my diagnosis. You asked me to do that for you. Can you do this for me?'

This got her. Callie shook her head, but said, 'Of course. Yes. I'm sorry.'

Shirley smiled her thanks and pressed the crossing button on the traffic lights again.

The hospital was even quieter than it had been the day before. Sunday evening was well and truly the witching hour for hospitals. Nothing really happened – no consultations, no rounds, no one even on reception. Of course, in the next building, where A and E was, there would still be plenty going on, but this was the entrance for the wards and offices.

Shirley led Callie through the empty corridors and took them to the third floor, making sure to highlight that she was taking the lift. Callie rolled her eyes, but laughed, and seemed thankful Shirley was actually listening. Shirley scanned her volunteer's badge and led Callie down the poky, narrow corridor to the radio station.

Most doors were closed, but they went past one that was ajar, with a ghost of a light on behind it, and the clickety-clack of a keyboard. A doctor, even more out of place right now than they were.

'Who works here?' Callie whispered, as they went past the open door.

Shirley realised that she had just assumed they were doctors, but didn't actually know. To her, this was just the corridor to the station. 'I'm not actually sure. Don't you know?'

'I didn't even know this corridor was here.'

Shirley got to the station door, input the code, and beckoned Callie inside.

The station was exactly as she had left it. The quieter day in the hospital extended here as well. There were no live shows or request shows on Sundays. This was something Shirley had staunchly come up against at the last AGM, as she remarked passionately that there were still plenty of patients in wards on Sundays, so why should the radio not run. The managers didn't seem keen though, saying that they didn't even have enough volunteers to run six days a week, let alone seven. Shirley rebutted that if the four managers split up their lads' night on the Friday evening, there'd be more than enough. That didn't go down well. At least no one being in on a Sunday worked to her advantage now.

Shirley took off her coat and hung it up, picking her way around the room – sidestepping the chairs, dodging the desk and negotiating the piles of folders to Studio Two.

She glanced back to see Callie, looking around slightly dismayed. 'I was expecting something a little bigger, less cupboard-like.'

Shirley scoffed. 'It actually was a cupboard, before they made it into the hospital radio. It was all the trust could afford.'

'I see,' Callie said, 'you've really been up here all this time?'

'Yes,' Shirley replied, 'you get used to it. Tiny living's the trend now, right?'

'Yeah, but not tiny operating a radio station.'

Shirley shrugged. 'We're in this one, Studio Two.'

Now Callie's expression turned to an impressed one, as she really saw what was in the space, how much they fit in there. She started to make her way to Shirley, looking around at everything as she did. 'Huh?' she said.

Shirley smiled. 'See?' She went into the studio, with the old radio still wired up to the deck just like she had left it. The headphones were there, where she had discarded them. She unplugged them, and switched the volume control to speaker. The normal Mallet AM lift music filled the studio.

Callie poked her head around the door.

'This is it,' Shirley said.

Callie nodded. Shirley let her go into the studio taking the swivel chair, and she went to bring another chair in. By the time she got back, the music had ended, and there was a folk song on instead. Shirley could already tell it was from the same band that she had heard last time she'd tuned in.

'Catchy tune,' Callie said, and it was. This time, they were singing about a relationship and how they'd rather be working, doing hard labour. Shirley believed it was what the kids called a 'diss track'.

Callie shuffled over as Shirley put her chair in the small space between the deck and the wall of the studio. With Callie in here too, it was even more of a tight squeeze than usual.

'This is crazy,' Callie said, her knees bunched up to the radio desk. 'How do you work like this?'

'I'm lucky. There's usually at least two people in every night, but I'm the only one who comes in on a Tuesday nowadays. My partner was poached, although I don't know if you can say poached when he got an actual job.'

'Who was your partner?'

Shirley said nothing, just pressed a few buttons, tapping into the audio of Studio One and a new voice appeared over the folk music. A voice that was all too familiar.

Callie's face lit up. 'Is that Ken Vox?'

Ken Vox was regaling the audience with how he once had a meeting in a high-rise in London and was the first to pull the fire alarm when he noticed flames coming from the break room, and how if he hadn't pulled it, the whole building might have burned down, with who knew how many casualties.

Shirley opened her mouth to say something pissy, but behind Vox's annoying voice, the folk music started to fade out. She cut the audio from Studio One – Callie wouldn't hear the end of Vox's story, but that was OK

– Shirley could tell her the end, she'd heard it a thousand times.

She turned up the volume on Mallet AM.

The folk song started to become inaudible. And then there was silence.

The usual slice of nothing before the presenter spoke.

Shirley looked at Callie. 'Are you ready?'

Callie looked unsure. She was obviously looking for something to prove that this wasn't what Shirley thought it was. But now she was on the precipice, actually here, and that wasn't lost on her. This was either real or fake, and it would be proven either way in the next few minutes.

She nodded.

01.13

Shirley looked at Callie, with purpose, as the presenter's voice came over the studio speakers. 'And that was the local band The Oil Barons with "Some Kinda Nothing". How fabulous was that, guys!'

Callie was just sitting back listening. Why wouldn't she? Right now, Mallet AM just sounded like any other radio station. Apart from one little thing – the presenter's voice.

'He sounds like a computer,' Callie said.

'He's masking his voice, I think,' Shirley said, and Callie nodded.

'Well, it's almost exactly seven thirty, so it looks like now's the perfect time for the news. How prompt are we? This is Monday the fifteenth February, this is Mallet AM and here are the headlines that matter in Chester-Le-Street today.'

'See, it's tomorrow's news,' Shirley whispered and

139

Callie nodded, holding up a hand. She was listening intently now.

'First up, we have an update on something we mentioned a few days ago. The Chester-Le-Street Leisure Centre debacle. Unfortunately, it does look like the writing is on the wall for Chester Baths, as the premises is due to close this week. The plans to demolish the centre are already underway, with the pool being drained as early as next week. The news is a shocking blow to the community as the centre has been a staple of the town for over fifty years. Local authorities have released a statement saying that the demolition of the centre will free up land for over forty new housing units, and bring in more young families to Chester-Le-Street. Quite how those young families are going to teach their children to swim is a matter up for debate. As always, we have reached out to the MP's office to see what they say. I wouldn't hold your breath though.'

Callie shrugged. 'I've heard about this already. It's not even news to me, let alone news for tomorrow.'

'It's always like this,' Shirley whispered, almost defensively. 'It's like they lull you in. There's usually two items that aren't really predicting much, then it hits you with something big.'

'Well, I'd hardly call a ladder accident and a milk truck crash *big*, but I get your point.'

'Item two for tonight saw Creamy Creamy Ice Cream open its doors today, at the bottom of Front Street. At 10 a.m. on the dot, local entrepreneur Matthew Tharigold and general manager Tiffany Laidlow greeted the first ever customer to their American-style ice cream diner. As the morning progressed, it seemed that business was booming. Due to the isolation of the dark year, and the real need for some good ice cream in Chester-Le-Street, it seems Creamy Creamy Ice Cream has weathered a perfect storm. The future looks bright for the new venture despite the awful name, and Matthew Tharigold has well and truly announced his arrival in the region. We'll be keeping an eye on him!'

'See,' Shirley said, 'just a general thing. Nothing to predict, but nothing to clarify either. Creamy Creamy Ice Cream has been known to be opening tomorrow for ages. I saw it in the *Advertiser*.'

Callie didn't look convinced by any of this. But as long as Mallet AM continued its traditions, this was the item they were listening for.

And Shirley got what she wanted. Although as the presenter spoke, in his garbled computer voice, she wished she hadn't. 'In the final item, we have some very sad and shocking news. Terror has come to Chester-Le-Street, as local man Frank Peterson was found murdered in his home in South Street.'

The ground seemed to have dropped out from under her. Shirley felt that if she moved even slightly, she would slip off the chair and fall into the void for eternity. An intense cold rushed through her. Murder? This couldn't be . . .

She chanced a look at Callie. The young woman was just sitting there listening as before. Their eyes met, and Callie must have seen the fear in Shirley's eyes. She opened her mouth to say something, but Shirley harshly shushed her.

The cold digital voice continued. 'Unfortunately, we must say again, this is a matter of murder, the likes of which Chester-Le-Street hasn't seen in a long time. South Street was the location for a cold and terrifying crime to take place. At 3.57 p.m., on this bright and unexceptional day, a shadowy figure entered the small terraced home of Frank Peterson and brutally killed him. Always a loner, Frank Peterson, thirty-six, was discovered by his neighbour two hours later, when his cat was seen pawing and mewing at the front door. The front door was left unlocked, and Peterson was in his kitchen lifeless on the floor. It appeared that he was strangled to death. There was no evidence of the perpetrator at all, which means this is going to be a tough case to solve. A murderer is at large in our beloved town of Chester-Le-Street. Frank Peterson is survived by his mother, father, brother and sister.'

Shirley couldn't believe what she was hearing. She was finding it hard to breathe, but it wasn't because of a heart attack this time. She couldn't process this. And the fact that Callie didn't seem affected, even slightly, made it all the more worse.

'And that is the very sad end to the news for Monday the fifteenth of February 2021. Such a great loss. Up next on the schedule is the daily poop joke.'

Shirley turned the volume down. And just sat there. She didn't know what to say.

Callie breathed out loudly – not quite a sigh. 'So that was what you wanted me to hear.'

'Yes.'

'I . . . don't know what that was.' Callie looked truly lost, as Shirley was. There was nothing to say, but there was also everything. The room was icy cold but also burning hot. Absolutes were now called into question, as though the very fabric of Shirley's reality was breaking, ripped apart, stretched too thin. But Shirley was more affected than Callie, it seemed, as her friend leaned forward and said, 'But I do know one thing.'

Shirley looked at her. She knew what Callie was going to say before she said it.

'What that man said, that's not real. That is not going to happen.'

Shirley didn't know what to do. She left the studio, took the kettle and went to fill it up down the corridor. It was just something to fill her time with, something easy and known to occupy her. But when she went back, she had to face it.

Callie was out of the studio now too. She was leaning against the back wall and on her phone. 'No records of any deaths, let alone murders, in Chester-Le-Street today. So it's not that they got the date wrong.'

Shirley said nothing, her mind on fire. A man was going to die. There was absolutely no reason for her to believe it wasn't going to happen. At 3.59 tomorrow afternoon, someone was going to invade Frank Peterson's home and strangle him to death. Just like Seb Starith fell off that ladder. And just like Roy Farrow crashed his milk truck into that post box. She has seen first-hand the power of Mallet AM. Right now, it didn't matter how it was possible, how the presenter could see the future, all that mattered was a man's life.

'You're not seeing,' said Shirley, handing Callie a cup of tea.

Callie took it and sighed. 'Is there any way to verify anything that man said? Anything to make me slightly believe this a bit more. Because for me, this could be entirely fictional. The first two things he talked about – the Leisure Centre and the ice cream parlour – there was nothing there – he didn't talk specifics, any notable events, anything to prove that he hadn't just read about them on some website. That ice cream parlour's had a sign up for about a week, saying exactly when it's opening. Chester Baths closing has been on the cards for what seems like ever, especially after last year.'

'Have you heard about the last item before? Any signs for that one?' Shirley asked.

'Shirley, I'm trying to wrap my head around this, OK.'

Shirley stopped. Callie was right. Shirley herself had taken a lot of time to 'wrap her head around it' too.

'Have we ever heard of a Frank Peterson before? Is there any way we can place him in South Street without knocking on doors?'

Shirley clicked her fingers – a foolish move that she'd pay for in pain later. 'South Street is Pelaw, right?'

'Yeah, I think so.'

'Colleen lives up there somewhere. My embroidery friend,' Shirley said, going into her bag and getting out her phone. 'Wait a minute.' She rang Colleen. Luckily, the phone signal went through – it was always pretty spotty in the studio. Sadly, Colleen wasn't there. She left a message lightly and conversationally, asking whether she knew a Frank Peterson, and to be polite, saying she was looking forward to going to her house next week for the embroidery meeting.

When she hung up, Callie was busy on her phone. 'Any luck?'

'No, what are you doing?'

'I read about this thing where you could check housing registries to track people down. Wait, here we go.' She was quiet for a moment, tapping her phone with a swiftness that had long left Shirley's fingers. 'Frank Peterson. We just have to input the name, and pay fifteen pounds.'

'I'll get my card.'

'No,' Callie said, holding up her free hand. 'It's already done. They'll email us the results.' Shirley couldn't fathom it. But a few seconds later, Callie's phone pinged. She looked at it, studied it briefly and held it out to Shirley. Shirley read the entire page – a housing listing for a Frank Peterson that lived at 11 South Street. He had bought the terraced two-storey house in 2014. It was crazy how easily that information was just freely available.

This was why Shirley wasn't on social media and didn't bank online. But it seemed like it didn't matter – she was on the housing registry, so she was online, without opting in or anything. Bob would be rolling in his grave (the only saving grace).

Callie took the phone back. 'So there is a Frank Peterson who lives in South Street. But you saw how easy that was. The presenter could have just done the same thing. He could have just picked this guy and decided to pretend something is going to happen to him.'

Shirley stopped herself from snapping. 'You're forgetting the two instances that he – if he is a he – has been right before. I saw the CCTV at the bakery and I was there at the post box. I know it's crazy, but they were real.'

'Yeah,' Callie said diplomatically. 'But they were just small accidents, weren't they? Nothing in the grand scheme of things. They're the type of things that happen every day. Maybe not tiny things in those people's lives, but tiny in the sense of the town, let alone the world. Is it possible that these things just happen?'

'What are you saying?'

Callie looked like she almost didn't want to say it. 'Coincidences.'

'Callie! Every single detail was right.'

'OK,' Callie said, 'OK. There's two avenues here – either you believe that these events are incredibly elaborate coincidences and this person just got lucky . . . or these things are actually foreseen and this person can see the future.'

'Why is it so hard for you to believe it's the second one?' Shirley said.

'If you believe the second,' Callie replied, 'why is it so hard for you to believe it might be the first?'

And Shirley knew she had her on that one. She was

silent and just sipped her tea for a while, while Callie went back to her phone. It all came down to which option was less unlikely. But Shirley's gut told her that she was right – that the even more fantastical option was correct. And, anyway, even if the first option was right – surely she owed it to this man, this stranger, to check that the second wasn't true.

After a few minutes of sips and taps, she had to break the silence. 'I'm going to the police. First thing tomorrow, I'm going to the police. I'm going to tell them everything about Mallet AM, the news, the murder. They have to know.'

'What are you going to tell them, Shirley? That a man who's alive and well has been murdered? That you're aware he's going to be murdered at 4 p.m.? Because some disembodied voice told you so.'

'Really?! You're being facetious. A man on the radio is not a disembodied voice!'

Callie stopped. 'OK. I'm sorry. I just – I like to think I have a handle on stuff, you know. This just doesn't fit into my world view.'

'Will you come with me to the police station, Callie? If you're with me, they may not think that I'm just a crazy old woman.'

'I can't, Shirley. I have work. Thirteen hours tomorrow. All day. I should be getting ready for bed right now. And you should be resting. You've just had a flipping heart attack.'

'A *small* heart attack.' Shirley couldn't believe what she was hearing. 'And a man's life is hanging in the balance.'

'Allegedly,' Callie said, almost apologetically.

'Fine – *allegedly*, a man's life is hanging in the balance. *Allegedly,* a man's life will end tomorrow. We have the power to do everything we can to stop it. And you're saying you have to go to work.' Things were getting heated. Shirley didn't want to fight with Callie, but she wasn't seeing the priorities here.

Callie sadly shrugged. 'Yes. I have to work. I have people's lives to save here. I do my small part every single day. Maybe I don't save *alleged* people from *alleged* strangers, but I do my bit.'

'Yes,' Shirley said, 'you do.'

Callie smiled and walked up to her, putting a hand on her shoulder. 'There's absolutely nothing I can do to stop you is there?'

They both chuckled. 'Not a fucking thing,' Shirley said.

Callie sat on the desk, laughing. 'What if this is all an elaborate ruse to wipe out Shirley Steadman by making her overexert herself?'

'I think I was doing a pretty good job of that by myself, thank you very much!'

Callie rested her head on Shirley's shoulder. It wasn't until then that Shirley realised how much she'd missed her. 'If you want, I can take you to the police station at 8 a.m. Just before I start. But I won't have time to go in with you.'

Shirley knew that this was the best she was going to get. So she nodded, 'OK.'

'I'm sorry,' Callie said. 'If it was any other day . . .'

'No. It's fine,' Shirley interrupted. Callie wasn't convinced – it was written all over her face. And why should she believe it? It was insane. And anyone else who heard the theories, and even heard the radio station, would probably laugh uncontrollably or run as far away from Shirley as possible. However annoyed she felt at Callie, she had to remember she was lucky that the woman was still there. 'That'd be great.'

They finished their tea in silence, an unspoken agreement that neither of them were going to get their way entirely, and a compromise was the only way to go. Shirley washed the mugs in the kitchen down the corridor and then put them back on the filing cabinet where the tea station was, and slipped her coat on.

As they left, and passed the open door again, the clickety-clacking of a keyboard was still going on behind it. How oblivious that doctor was of anything that had gone on just down the hall. Shirley wished she was too.

'If you told me twenty-five or twenty-six hours ago, this was how today was going to go, I wouldn't have believed you,' Callie said, as they left the narrow corridor and got back into the main hospital.

Neither would Shirley. So much had happened.

'It's a weird old world,' Shirley settled on.

'If you're even half right about this radio thing,' Callie said, 'it's gonna be a hell of a lot weirder than I think I'll be able to process.'

'For all our sakes, I hope you're right.' And Shirley actually did hope. This wasn't about coccyx injuries or gallons of spilt milk anymore, this was serious. And

Shirley wished it would be Callie's way – a coincidence.

But she knew that it couldn't be. And as they left the hospital, and Callie gave her a lift home, she had a startling revelation that she wasn't able to put into words until she walked up her garden path and put her key in her door.

This wasn't a power trip but . . . she was the only one. Maybe in the whole of Chester-Le-Street. Maybe in the whole world. And she wished with all her heart that she wasn't. But that didn't change the fact that she was. She was the only one who could save Frank Peterson's life.

01.14

Chester-Le-Street
Monday 15 February 2021
1.17 a.m.

Sleep wouldn't have come, even if she'd tried. Shirley couldn't even start to think about doing her nightly routine – feed Moggins, go around and make sure all the lights and the plugs were turned off, lock the front door and the back door, make up a bowl of piping-hot water and soak two flannels in it, start the thirty-minute process of getting changed into her pyjamas and putting her old clothes in the washing hamper, and cleaning her teeth and washing her face. All before actually lying there and realising that sleep was going to dodge her once again.

No. Not tonight. The only item on the list she had completed was feeding the cat, who would have stood on the kitchen counter and mewed until she did it anyway. She sat at the kitchen table and thought about everything and thought about nothing. And as she thought, or didn't think, she took it upon herself to perform another item on the list – lock the doors.

Gabe was sitting at the kitchen table when she got back. 'What was that for?'

Shirley sat down and put her head in her hands. 'There's a murderer out there.'

'Technically not a murderer yet,' said Gabe.

'You're the second person to say that,' Shirley replied.

No one understood. No one could possibly understand – unless they had seen. She couldn't explain it, because it was utterly inexplicable. She was alone. Unless . . .

Her eyes were drawn out of the room, to the cupboard in the hall, where her laptop was kept. Arnie at The Enigma Files. Maybe he could help. But he was still a faceless figure, a stranger at the end of a phone line. There was every possibility that he could be trusted even less than whoever was about to murder Frank Peterson.

But her eyes were still drawn to the cupboard door. As if just staring was writing an email back agreeing to meet.

No. Deena would say it was a bad idea. And, for once, she would be right.

So Shirley snapped her gaze away, and attempted to distract herself. 'I didn't tell you that I reconnected with Callie.'

'Callie?' Gabe said, in a tone that almost betrayed genuine shock. Just how she thought he'd say it.

'Yes,' Shirley said, 'it was stupid really. Turned out I'd been avoiding her. Not the other way around. Strange what we do to ourselves, isn't it? How we isolate and protect, but sometimes it turns out you weren't really protecting yourself from anything. There were no enemies at the gates.'

'You should write that down, that's not bad.'

Shirley tried a smile, but found she couldn't. 'Are you sure I can't make you a bacon and banana sandwich?'

'If it makes you feel better,' Gabe said.

So she did. She fried the bacon, she cut the bananas up and buttered the bread, assembling the sandwich with decades of experience. Gabe had first come across the unusual combination when he was seven years old, and it had been his favourite sandwich ever since. She tried it once and guessed Gabe liking it so much had something to do with the warmth of the bacon, making the banana go all gooey. She didn't understand the appeal herself, though.

She finished and put it in front of Gabe.

Gabe just stared at it. He looked hungry. But he didn't go to pick it up. Of course, he couldn't. 'It looks good,' he said, almost longingly. At least that was how she took it.

'I don't know what to do,' Shirley said.

'Do what you think is right, like you always do. It's not easy, it never was.'

Shirley picked up the sandwich plate and put it on the side. 'But how do I save him?' She looked back at the table.

Gabe was gone.

She sighed.

For the rest of the night, she sat in the living room,

watching BBC1, which was showing children's programmes with a sign language interpreter in the corner. She tried to do some embroidery but couldn't because her hands were hurting too much. So she made up her washing-up bowl with hot water and got the flannels from the bathroom. She sat back down in the living room with her hands in the flannels and watched a signed version of *Balamory* and tried not to think too hard about the next day.

Right now, Frank Peterson would be sleeping. He wouldn't know that when he woke up, he would have the last breakfast he'd ever eat, he'd watch the last *Morning Coffee* he ever would, he'd feed his cat for the last time. But equally he didn't know that there was someone out there fighting his corner, someone that would do everything to try to save his life.

Shirley knew no one would believe her. Even Callie didn't really. There was no chance a policeman would. She'd have to do her best to convince them. She liked to think she was pretty persuasive, but this was a whole new level. Tomorrow, or technically today, her skill would be put to the test, with the largest stakes imaginable.

Balamory became re-runs of *Teletubbies* and sleep still seemed to elude her. She replaced her flannels, and then said fuck it and brought the bowl of water to the living room and dunked her hands in once more. She watched the sign language interpreter on the television, moving her hands with rapid, confident movements. She wished she was back in time to when she could do things like

154

that. If she had found Mallet AM even five years ago, she would have been more able to intervene. But, as it was, she had to face her limitations.

She watched the woman do magic tricks with her hands, communicating in a language she didn't understand. Watching her move was almost rhythmic, soothing. It was such a simple job (she meant in concept, rather than execution), translating something for a whole new audience to enjoy. It was nice.

Moggins came in and looked at her lap, busy with the bowl of water. He stuck his nose up at it, then proceeded to wash his bits then curl up and go to sleep. He had no idea what was going through her mind, had no idea about anything in particular. A nice life – the kind of life she had before all this.

How much could things change in such a short space of time? It was remarkable really. And how much could things change within oneself? She felt invigorated, driven. After Bob had died, she'd resolved to become more proactive, and she had. But she'd also fallen into the usual ruts that everyone did – the same routine, the same familiar faces, the same fruitless conversations. She felt that, in some ways, she had lost herself. This thing, whatever it was, had revived her. So maybe Mallet AM was a blessing and a curse.

She doubted Frank Peterson would see it that way though.

She looked at her watch – 2.46 a.m. She needed to try to get some rest. She had to stop thinking – clear her mind. She focused on the sign interpreter – translating

Tinky Winky as he made some Tubby Custard. He finished and served it all to the other Teletubbies. Shirley's mind baulked — trying to force her back to Mallet AM. But she relented, watching the screen.

Moggins started to purr in his sleep. He was having a nice dream.

Shirley hoped she would too, although that wasn't likely. She pressed the button on the side of the chair and reclined it. She put the bowl of now lukewarm water on the table beside her. She hadn't set any alarms for the morning, but somehow she didn't think that would be a problem.

She put her head back, watching the translator out of the corner of her eye. And as the Teletubbies watched a clip of a girl at her dance class and then proclaimed 'Again! Again!' she fell into a restless sleep.

A sleep filled with nightmares of stranglers and soothsayers.

01.15

Chester-Le-Street
Monday 15 February 2021
7.31 a.m.

Callie picked her up at seven thirty, calling her from the road. Shirley came out and locked the house. The street was deathly quiet, as though the world was holding its breath — waiting to see what the day would bring. Shirley may be the only one who actually knew what it would bring, because she doubted Callie believed it, and if Shirley had her way, it wouldn't go how Mallet AM had predicted. She was going to stop it — prove Mallet AM wrong for once. Yes, that sounded good.

As she walked up the path, she decided to take her cane for support. It was going to be a long day.

'Are you ready?' Callie asked, faltering as though she was going to ask 'How did you sleep?' but, seeing Shirley's weathered face, didn't need to.

'I'm ready,' Shirley replied, sitting in the passenger seat and putting her cane between her legs.

They barely said another two words to each other as Callie drove through the town. Chester-Le-Street Police

Station was on Newcastle Road, just beyond Front Street, moving up Birtley way. Shirley had never been in there, but she knew it well as it was next to what used to be the old civic centre, where she used to have to trek to pay her council tax.

Callie dropped her off as close to the entrance as she could get, and with a few more apologies that she didn't have time to come in with her, she left Shirley to it. Shirley watched her go, and when the car disappeared around the corner, she knew she could put it off no longer. She went in.

Inside, was an empty, small and dark reception. A waiting area with plastic chairs and a selection of magazines was in the corner. Black walls and grey carpets made the whole place feel dreary and there was a slight smell of damp. It looked more like a place where a crime would be committed than a place where you would report one. Along the far wall was a window letting in at least a little light. It showed an office beyond it – with a single police officer, a middle-aged balding man, working at one of the desks. There was the low sound of pop music coming from a radio on the window ledge in the office. Radios – they were everywhere.

Shirley walked up to the window. 'Hello?'

The police officer didn't even look up.

'Hello?'

Nothing.

She started to get annoyed and rapped on the glass. 'Excuse me!'

The police officer looked up, seemingly surprised to

158

see someone so early. He glanced at the clock on the wall and went back to his paperwork.

Shirley couldn't believe it. She banged on the glass again. 'Excuse me! I'm standing right here!' she shouted, adding, 'For fuck's sake,' under her breath.

The police officer looked up again, visibly gave the greatest sigh she'd ever seen (one that the sign language interpreter from the night before wouldn't have needed to translate) and walked up to the window. 'Ye cannit pay your bills here, lass. That were the civic centre next door, but it's moved now.' That seemed enough for him as he turned away to go back to his desk.

But Shirley shouted, 'Wait!' This got the police officer back. 'I'm not here for bills, I'm here for the police station.'

'Oh, well 'fraid we're not open for enquiries for another forty-five minutes, lass. Come back at eight thirty.'

'What the hell do you mean? Not open for enquiries.'

'I mean, we're not open for enquiries, simple as that.'

Shirley scoffed. What a cheek! 'I'm here for something important.'

The police officer shrugged, 'If it's that important, it'll still be important at half eight. Now, if you'll excuse me, this is my me time, OK. An hour before everything starts, away from the wife and kids, I sit at my desk, put on some Tay-Tay, and do my paperwork.'

'This is about a murder!'

The officer stopped. He couldn't ignore that word – one of the words that had to stop every police officer in their path. He came back to the window. 'Excuse me?'

'This is about a murder, simple as that,' she said, sarcastically.

'OK, two seconds,' the officer said, going under the desk and rummaging around. He came back up with a clipboard – it must have been the murder clipboard.

Shirley realised that her new friend was chewing gum and for some reason that annoyed her more than anything else. A man was going to get murdered and this guy was chewing gum.

'OK, so you want to report a murder,' he said, in a tone that sounded more like Shirley was booking a holiday than trying to alert the police of a crime.

'Yes. Please.'

'Why didn't you call 999?' he asked.

'Well, um . . .' Shirley stumbled over her words and she realised her error. She hadn't thought of what she was going to say. She just expected the police would help her because . . . well, they were the police. This subject was their territory. But now, faced with explaining it, she was out of her depth. The wrong words could be disastrous – but the right ones still eluded her. 'The murder hasn't actually happened yet.'

The police officer looked at her, worried. It actually made him more alert, which was the opposite reaction to what she was expecting. 'Who is planning to commit a murder? Wait, are you planning to commit a murder?'

'No, that's not it. I don't know who's going to do it.' She had to make him see. 'I just know the victim is a man called Frank Peterson. He lives up near the Church of

England school in Pelaw – 11 South Street. He is going to be murdered just before 4 p.m.'

The police officer stopped writing, scratched behind his ear with his pen. 'What are you talking about, lass?'

'Frank Peterson is going to be murdered!' Shirley shouted. She was glad no one else was around, she was coming across as just a shade off crazy.

'Yes, lass. I got that bit. I've written it down. But you've gotta start explainin' yasell. How do ya know about this?'

'Well,' Shirley said, 'I um . . . I heard it on the radio.'

'You . . .' the officer paused, looking like he was trying to process what she had said. 'I'm sorry, can you run that by me again?'

'I heard it on the radio. There's this radio station that—'

'The radio? So this has already been reported? So this happened yesterday? I haven't heard of a murder.'

'No. Please just listen to me, there's this radio station that I found, it's called Mallet AM.' She was getting flustered under the officer's stare. 'M A L L E T. If you want to write it down.' She noted that he didn't write it down. 'It reports things a day before they happen. Seb Starith fell off his ladder – you may have heard about that. And, um, the milk truck, up near the Avenues. Roy Farrow swerved into a post box because a woman walked out in front of him from an alleyway. Mallet AM reported those two events the night before they happened. And I saw them happen. And now it has reported that Frank Peterson is going to be murdered at 3.57 p.m.'

161

The officer looked at her like she was a magical creature, but there was something else there. It was something she was used to as an older person, and an older woman in particular – it was pity. Pity at the old guard who had decided to stick around long past their time. Well, she wasn't ready to relinquish control just yet. 'Can you just run me through this slower. A radio station . . .'

'. . . That reports things before they happen. Yes.'

'Like murders?' There was a new little spark in the officer's voice. He couldn't help letting out a little snigger.

This made Shirley snap. 'What is your name, young man?'

'Sorry, sorry,' he said, still doing what he was allegedly sorry for. 'My name's Dave.'

'Dave,' she gave the name as much venom as she could as it left her tongue, 'if you don't believe me, tune in to the station yourself.'

Dave looked at her and threw his hands up. 'Sure. Why not?'

For the first time in the conversation, Shirley actually felt a little bit of hope. 'OK, it's 66.40 AM. Remember – AM.'

Dave sighed and put down his clipboard, going over to the window and playing with the buttons on the radio. He turned the knob and the pop music disappeared. All that came in its place was static. Overwhelming static.

'66.40 AM,' Shirley reminded him.

'This is 66.40 AM,' Dave said, flippantly.

'Just wait a moment, sometimes it takes a while to come through.'

'Nothing is coming through,' Dave said, and to her annoyance, he walked away from the radio back to her. 'Lass, I don't know what to tell you, no crime has been committed here. And just cos you have some kind of sixth sense that this Fred Peterfield . . .'

'Frank Peterson!' Facetious fuck.

'Beg ya pardon, Frank Peterson, is going to be killed, that doesn't mean we can do anything. We don't operate on hunches, or crystal balls, or whatever. We deal with facts.'

Shirley slammed her hand down on the desk. 'I am telling you there is going to be a murder! You could save a man's life.'

'How?' Dave said, matter-of-factly. 'You haven't really given me anything. The radio station you claim to have heard it on doesn't exist . . .'

'No,' Shirley shouted. 'No. It's probably just because the signal's weaker this side of town. You can hear it if you're up at the hospital.'

'The signal's weak? That's convenient.'

'Don't,' Shirley hissed. 'Don't talk to me like I'm crazy.'

'Look,' Dave said, with that pity soaked into his voice, 'you really think you're the first old person to come in with stories like this. You sit and you watch a bit too much *Murder She Wrote* or whatever, and you start seeing conspiracies and murders everywhere. We waste a lot of paper on you people.'

'You people?' Shirley snarled.

'Yes, you people,' Dave said, confidently. He probably wouldn't have been so confident if there wasn't a glass window between them. 'I hate to tell ya, but I highly doubt this "radio" station is real.'

'Someone heard it with me!' Shirley said, annoyed at how defensive she sounded. This is why she had wanted Callie to come with her – to combat the prejudices someone her age would face with something like this.

'Mm-hm,' Dave cooed. 'I bet you talk to people that aren't there too.'

'I . . .' Well, he might have her there. Gabe was pretty much a mainstay in the house now. It seemed like he was appearing of late with startling regularity.

'There you go,' Dave said. 'So why am I supposed to believe that you heard this voice on the radio when you're hearing voices in your head. Did your voice tell you I won the lottery? Please say yes.'

'Fuck you,' Shirley said.

'OK, lass, I'm going to have to ask you to leave, you can't swear at an officer.'

'You're a glorified receptionist!'

This silenced Dave for a second. It appeared she'd struck a nerve. She saw a flash in his face – a flash of a man disgruntled with his job, a boy who had a dream to become a police officer and finally got there but had been shackled to a desk, far from the movie version of the job he longed for. No wonder he was a jaded fuck. That didn't make Shirley hate him any less though. 'You're going to have to leave now.'

'Oh, I'm gone. I'll do this myself,' Shirley said, gripping her cane and backing up.

'Don't harass people or I'll have to arrest you.'

'You don't even have the power to arrest a photocopier.'

'Nice one. Go back to your knitting.'

'You!' hissed Shirley, giving him the evil eye of an elder. She thrust her cane at him, as if it had the power to curse the pompous man. He treated her like an old fogey, she was happy to fit the role. 'You should be ashamed of yourself.'

'I regularly am. But that has nothing to do with this,' Dave said, shrugging again – which seemed to be his signature move – and walked away.

Shirley couldn't stay there anymore, or she may have actually done something worth being arrested for. With one final scathing look at Dave's back – hoping her stare was so piercing he felt it in the back of his head, she walked out of the police station, taking care to slam the main door behind her.

Outside, the wind was picking up, and the sun was starting to rise over the far rooftops. There was a chill in the air – almost solid as it buffeted into her, threatening to knock her fragile frame over. She had lost so much mass in the last few years. Back in the day, she had been slim but at least firm. Now she felt like a glass ornament – the kind you didn't like to handle, always on the verge of breaking, barely worth putting up just to see it topple down. The wind attempted to pull her over as if laughing at her. It was shaping up to be another freezing February day.

Shirley didn't quite know what she was going to do now. What was there to do? Callie was at work, Deena had no idea what was going on, and Gabe couldn't help her. What would Gabe say in this situation? – this time not thinking of the real-life Gabe as much as the one she had constructed in her mind. So, she guessed, she was really asking herself. Through the guise of Gabe, thinking was clearer. And she came to a realisation, proclaimed in his voice. It was clear. Dave the Police Officer had made it crystal.

She was on her own.

01.16

South Street was another hill — and this hill was about twice as steep as Front Street. Shirley had found her way to the base of the hill, walking at a steady pace on two legs and one cane. Early-morning dog walkers passed her and people getting in their cars going to work. The flat journey from the police station to the hill took twenty minutes. Any people going her way overtook her, proving she couldn't even walk fast on flat ground. When she finally got to, what might as well have been, the mountain, it was already half-eight.

Time was slipping away, and she had to get to South Street.

She started up the hill. Instantly, she found it hard to wrench her cane upwards, and even harder to move her feet that way. She just focused on the task of breathing and coping with the immense weight she felt she was dragging behind her. The sensation was odd — she felt like a husky dragging a sleigh, but looking back there was nothing at all.

As she continued upwards, she thought she should not look back again. The movement made her feel dizzy and want to stop still. If she did that, though, she thought she'd lose her footing, and go tumbling down. All they'd find at the bottom would be a pile of bones that looked vaguely human.

Halfway up, she had to stop. Thankfully, there was a bench, and she sat there and recouped some energy. She felt a pain in her chest – luckily, on the opposite side to her heart. Not that that helped with the pain. She wondered what Doctor Idiot would think, if he could see her now. Would he feel some personal pain at not being able to stop her, that maybe if he was a better doctor he could have got through to her how serious her situation was, or would he just think she was a silly bint? She guessed it didn't matter – and in some ways she wouldn't wish him to feel bad. This was all her doing – she had decided to flaunt the rules, she had decided to push it to the limit, ignore her shortcomings. But if she was going to die scaling this behemoth, she just hoped Death would stay its blade for a day, so she could try to save someone else's life first.

Dying by saving someone else? Didn't sound like a bad way to go.

This got her moving again, and as she thought, it was even harder now she'd paused. Her joints had stiffened in the cold air, and the wind felt stronger the higher up she got. She began to resent all the cars passing by her, travelling upwards – and what was more she envied every person inside of them.

At one point, she thought someone was going to offer her a ride, and she was equally pleased and mortified. However, it was just someone pulling over to pick some-one up. When the person being picked up crossed the pavement to the car, they took a glance at Shirley and she thought she saw something between confusion and sadness. She showed a flash of disgruntled discontent back.

When Shirley finally got to the top of the hill, she looked at her watch and wished she hadn't. It was half-ten. It had taken her two hours to go maybe a mile. What was happening to her? She was getting worse.

Shirley checked a street sign as she went past – Arch-er's Street. She had seen a map the night before, when Callie showed her the housing registration. She knew South Street was just a street away. She had made it – however long it had taken. And she still had plenty of time to save Frank Peterson.

As she cut down a narrow street, and saw the sign for South Street, she wondered about her plan of attack. What was she going to do? Frank Peterson was due to meet his end at 3.57 p.m. She was almost drowning in time but didn't know what to do with it. She supposed the first thing to do was try to tell Frank Peterson what his destiny was. So they could both tell destiny to fuck off.

South Street was a densely packed street of two-storey terraced houses – probably rented – on one side, and semi-detached bigger ones on the other. It was like a class divide exemplified, and the poorer people had a front-row seat for the more affluent. Shirley walked along the street looking for house numbers. Not many of them had any indication of what number they were, but luckily every so often there was a number. And eventually, Shirley came to one, near the end of the street, that had a 10 on it.

She went to the house next door to number 10 and lightly knocked on the door. What was she going to say? She had absolutely no idea. She guessed she would just explain as well as she could, tell the whole truth and nothing but the truth. It seemed like she was going to have some more time to wonder, however, as no one answered the door.

She stepped back and looked up at the top window. The curtains were drawn, although, as she looked, she saw a figure pull them slightly aside, look down at her and then pull them back. She knocked on the door again, thinking that maybe the person was coming down to see her. But that didn't happen. Whoever had peered out at her must have decided she wasn't worth coming to meet. She knocked one last time for good measure, but it was very clear that her knocks weren't going to be answered.

She sighed. What now? It was ten forty-five. Maybe Mr Peterson was having a lie-in.

She spent the next hour walking around the neighbourhood, looking for anything odd, out of the ordinary. Of course, she found nothing. It was not like a murderer advertised when they were going to appear, and it wasn't likely they were even around yet. Unless they lived here. Which, if true, meant she wouldn't know who it was until it happened.

She got back to 11 South Street about eleven forty-five and knocked on the door again. There was still no answer. She looked up at the window again – the curtains still closed. Maybe Frank Peterson wasn't there – maybe he'd gone out for the day. Maybe he'd already broken Mallet AM's prediction. She could only hope.

She stepped further back – having to go into the road, trying to see if there was any movement of the curtains. Nothing, no twitching. So he was either asleep or—

'Hello stranger,' a familiar voice chirruped.

'Shit,' Shirley muttered before turning with a big smile on her face. 'Hi, Colleen, how are you?'

Colleen was slowly making her way down the street, pulled along by her two chihuahuas. When the two big-eared, big-eyed dogs saw Shirley, they started showing their teeth and barking. Apparently they didn't like old ladies. Which must have been a challenge, living with Colleen.

'What are you doing round my neck of the woods, pet?' Colleen asked, coming up to her. She hugged Shirley as best she could with two leads in her hands. The chihuahuas sat there and growled at her. 'It's lovely to see you. Here, this is Daisy and Maisy.'

'Which one is which?' Shirley said, not really caring.

'Oh, who knows,' Colleen laughed, 'I get them mixed up all the time.' One of the chihuahuas was long-haired and white, the other was short-haired and sandy. It

171

didn't seem possible to mistake them for one another. 'What are you doing all the way up here in Pelaw? A bit far from home for you, ain't it?'

'Yes, well,' Shirley grunted. 'Umm, sometimes I like a walk.' Her knees gave out a throb of pain as if to say *Are you fucking serious?*

'Wait,' Colleen said, seeming to realise which house Shirley was outside of. 'This isn't about Frank Peterson, is it? I wondered what your answerphone message was about yesterday.'

'Do you know him?' Shirley asked.

Colleen started to talk, but the chihuahuas were getting impatient. They pulled on their leads, yapping, so Colleen asked if Shirley wanted to walk with them. Shirley couldn't imagine anything worse, but said yes anyway. If Colleen knew anything that could help her protect Frank Peterson she had to know it. So she walked with her. 'Frank Peterson is not someone I would have thought you'd be associating with. How do you know him?'

'I don't really,' Shirley said. 'Do you know him?'

'Well, I know of him,' she said, reining in the dogs' leads as another dog walker passed. 'He's a bit infamous around these parts. Bit of a bad neighbour, I think.'

'Bad how?'

'Things like being too noisy, not taking his bin in when he needs to, rubbish strewn everywhere out the back in the alley. The normal sort of stuff. Apparently, he drinks like a sailor all day every day. He used to work at the local quarry but got laid off during the dark year.

He's currently drinking through his severance package but likes to pretend to everyone that he's still working. Oh, and his cat.' *Cat*. Mallet AM had mentioned the cat pawing at the door, which alerted the neighbours to the murder. The first detail was falling into place. 'His cat is treated like a king and only has eyes for Frank. It hisses and tries to scat anyone else who comes along. Even tried to go for my poor Daisy once. Or was it Maisy?'

One of the chihuahuas arched their backs and started squeezing out a poo in the middle of the street. It looked up at Shirley and stared her in the face with its big marble eyes for the entire process. It was creepy. Shirley liked dogs from a distance but didn't quite see the appeal of owning one. There was something about having to be bossed around by an animal that rubbed her the wrong way. Cats could look after themselves for the most part – Moggins only needed feeding twice a day and she didn't have to pick anything up when it came out the other end.

'Would you be a dear?' Colleen said, holding out a bag to her. Shirley had to stop herself saying the first thing that came into her head – *Fuck right off!* She was mortified – she had come here to stop a murder, not pick up dog shit. But Colleen looked so feeble, and her back was indeed bad, so Shirley did it. She handed the full bag to her friend, who tied it up and started swinging it from her fingers as they walked along.

Shirley decided she was definitely a cat person.

'Does Frank have any enemies?' Shirley asked, wanting to get back on track.

'Enemies?' Colleen squeaked, surprised. 'Well, no one likes the bastard, but I wouldn't really say he has any enemies. People just really feel a bit sorry for him, they get annoyed by him sure, but enemies? No. Not as far as I'm aware. How do you know him?'

'Oh,' Shirley said. She didn't really know what to say – had never been great at lying. That had been one of the reasons why Bob had been able to get to her so much – because she always told him the truth. And he could weaponise that. 'I . . . um . . .' What could she say? She couldn't tell Colleen the truth. The old girl was too loose-lipped, and fantastical – she'd probably believe Shirley, but not in the way that would help her at all. 'I met someone who knew him at the hospital when I was on the rounds for requests. They gave me a message for him.' Not a bad lie.

Colleen seemed happy enough with it. 'Well, I wouldn't expect to see him before one o'clock at least. He's always sleeping off a hangover.'

Shirley walked with Colleen a little more. Conversation moved to embroidery and Colleen's hosting duties in a few days' time. Colleen seemed to think Shirley's hosting was a phenomenal success, a feeling that she wished had been shared with Marsha. Shirley knew one thing – Marsha would eviscerate Colleen, judging everything from her home to her ratty chihuahuas, to the brand of tea she presented.

Shirley left Colleen and the dogs when they started walking towards the hill that Shirley now felt intimately acquainted with. She couldn't face even looking at it,

let alone going down it and up again. She said her goodbyes, one to Colleen and, since her friend was expectant,
two little byes to the dogs, and made her way back to
South Street.

It was 1.15 p.m. when she got to number 11.

Shirley knocked on the door, every knock feeling like
she was hitting diamond. When no one answered for a
minute, she hit the door even harder. She'd be feeling
that for a week – maybe more. But it was worth it.

Finally, a man who looked far older than he actually
was, towering but stout, with a long beard and varifocals,
stuck his head around the door. He had a red pudgy nose
peppered with purple veins, betraying years of alcohol
abuse. He regarded her and croaked, 'What do ye wann?
I'm watchin' me stories, ye knaw.' As he talked, she saw
a row of black, crooked teeth, and smelled a day's worth
of beer already consumed. Colleen wasn't wrong – he
was already drunk.

'Are you Frank Peterson?' Shirley said.

'Oo's askin?' So yes, then.

'I'm a . . . concerned citizen.'

'Ooh fer fuck's sake, for the last fuckin' time, I'm not
turning the music down at night. I work my fuckin' arse
off all day at the quarry, and when I come home, if I
wanna blast music, I should be fuckin' well allowed to.'
The outburst made him short of breath.

Shirley saw where the man was wrong. If he worked
all day at the quarry, what was he doing here right now,
at 1.15.

'Sir,' Shirley said, and that shut Frank up. He

obviously had never been called 'sir' before. 'I'm not here about the music. I'm here about your well-being.'

'My well-bein'? What the fuck are you talking about?'

Clearly no one had ever cared about his well-being either.

'I have reason to believe someone might make an attempt on your life. Today.'

'An attempt on my life? I'm not following ya, lass,' Frank said, snorting and swallowing what sounded like a mouth full of mucus. He disappeared for a second and came back with a can of beer. She didn't know why anyone would try to kill Frank Peterson, give it a year and he'd probably have killed himself.

'Someone is going to try to kill you,' Shirley shrieked.

Frank looked at her with glazed eyes, and then erupted in gruff chunky laughter. He doubled over and laughed so much, he coughed up a lungful of snot and spat it out on his doorstep. Shirley just stood there, having no idea what could possibly be so funny. This man was going to die, and he couldn't care less. 'That's a bloody good one. I ain't laughed like tha' in a good long while. Why are you really botherin' us?' He burped in her face. Charming. Frank Peterson really knew how to put the moves on someone.

'I literally just said,' Shirley reaffirmed. 'Someone is going to kill you.'

Frank proceeded to crack up again. 'You are really sommat else, lass. I mean, really?' He upended the beer can into his mouth, crunched it in his fist and then threw it over his shoulder. It clattered somewhere down the hall. Shirley wondered how many cans were back there. 'Cheers for giving us a good laff, but I got plenty of important stuff to be deing.' Frank started to disappear. Shirley bet the important stuff he wanted to do came in an eighteen can crate.

'Wait,' Shirley said, her hand shooting out to the door. It sang with pain as it collided with it. 'Do you know anyone who would want to kill you?'

Frank snarled his black grimy teeth. 'Who's gonna wanna murder me? What a fucking waste of a good murder. Get the fuck off my doorstep.' And with that, he slammed the door in Shirley's face as though she were the murderer herself

Shirley couldn't believe it. She was trying to save him, and she got a door shut on her. She almost had a thought to leave him and his murderer to it. But that moment passed and, instead, she decided to sit across the street on a brick wall and wait.

So she did just that. She sat staring at 11 South Street for what felt like hours, and it was. The street was very quiet – apart from people putting out blue-topped recycling bins every once in a while. The wall was very uncomfortable – the bricks poking into her derriere. Just another thing that would ache tomorrow. If she stopped this murder, she would allow herself to sleep for a week.

She still hoped that she, and Mallet AM, would be wrong – that the spell of the radio station would be broken. Coincidence, Callie had said. That word had never felt so warm.

At two-thirty, a man from number 10 put his recycling

bin out. He stared at Shirley all the time, and she met his gaze. He then got his phone out and started to tell someone, covertly but also obviously, about how he thought the TV licence people were here. He got in his car and drove away.

In the car's place, Shirley saw a tabby short-haired mongrel cat sauntering up the road. She knew that this was Frank Peterson's cat, even before it saw Shirley and hissed. Shirley had never been hissed at by a cat before, thinking she had some kind of unspoken affinity with them, and was surprised at how offended she felt.

As she predicted, the cantankerous cat stopped at number 11 and tapped on the front door with a confident paw. After a few minutes, Frank opened the door. 'How ey, Big Mac.' As the cat slipped in, Frank glanced up and did a double take. 'What the fuck are you doing sittin' there? Leave me alone.'

'I can't,' Shirley said. 'I have to protect you.'

'Get the fuck out of here, or I'm gonna call the white coats to come get ya, you loony bitch.'

Shirley was stunned into silence, but she just turned her nose up at him, crossing her arms and sitting firm.

Frank chuckled, and went back inside, muttering something about how he would've wished his 'fuckin guardian angel' would've been 'young 'n' fit'.

Shirley decided to ignore the last bit as the time slid to 3 p.m. Within the hour, she would know one hundred per cent if Mallet AM could tell the future, but right now she was acting as if there was no doubt. Any potential murderer would, hopefully, be put off by seeing a random seventy-year-old woman sitting outside the house of their victim.

But as the hour started to pass, Shirley realised there was a flaw in her plan. There was a back door too – why wouldn't the murderer use that? Suddenly, everything unravelled. Seeing as these were terraced houses, she would have to walk halfway down the street to get to an alleyway to cut through to the back of the houses. Even if she could run, which she couldn't – running was something other people did – she wouldn't be able to cover both entrances.

As quickly as she could, which wasn't very quick at all, she made her way around the back. There was a larger alleyway, for cars, with bricked backyards for every house. She had no way of knowing which one was number 11 as they all looked the same and she couldn't see over the walls.

For the first time, her confidence was knocked. She looked at her watch. 3.15 p.m. What was Frank Peterson doing now – drinking in front of the telly? Which dominoes would lead him to the kitchen where his body would later be found? A fresh can of beer perhaps? Or maybe he'd spill his current one and need a cloth to mop it up? Maybe he would even hear a noise, maybe the murderer would knock something over, and Frank would go to investigate? But all that would be waiting there for him would be death. He would be strangled to death – the life draining out of his face, the shortness of breath he had because of his constant drinking acting against him – the drink contributing to his death. What would the murderer do – where would he or she leave? Front or back?

Shirley made her way back to the front – seeing as it was easier to know which house to focus on. There was nothing suspicious around back anyhow. It was 3.35 p.m. Just over twenty minutes. She had to try again.

She hammered on the door, her fists practically numb at this point.

Frank Peterson only opened the door a crack, but did it violently, as though he had stormed up to the door. 'Oh, for fuck's sake.'

'Mr Peterson, please. I am only trying to help. I have reason to believe you are going to die in the next twenty minutes.'

'Well, ain't that nice. Piss off. Or I'll call the police.'

Shirley seized on that. 'You know what, yes. Yes. Yes. That's a great idea. Call the police. Call the police right now.'

'You are fuckin' barmy, you, ain't ya? Jeessus.' Frank seemed a lot drunker than the last time she'd seen him, even though that hadn't been long. He was slurring his words, and his intimidating frame wasn't as effective when it was swaying side to side. 'Last time I'm gonna tell ya, leave me alone.' He slammed the door. It was the last time he was going to tell her – one way or the other.

She knew he wouldn't call the police, and even if he did, he probably wouldn't be taken seriously. Even on the phone, the handler would probably smell the alcohol on his breath.

As Shirley crossed the street again, a great roar came,

along with a beeping and whooshing sound. Shirley looked to see a recycling truck stopping at the first house down the street. Those trucks made a lot of noise, no doubt perfect to cover up a murder. The truck started slowly to come down the road, but so did someone else.

A man in a woolly hat, and one of the face masks from the dark year, was walking down the street. He was stopping often and looking at every house. Shirley stiffened – in her mind, there was no doubt. This was him. This was the murderer. Miraculously and crazily, he hadn't seen her – as he got to number 11.

The murderer looked up at the house and then he got out his phone, as if to check something. He read the screen, looked down the street and then continued along the road. He was going to go round the back, she just knew. But he wasn't going to kill Frank, she was going to stop him.

He walked fast, and she had to keep up. Her entire body was screaming with pain, but she pressed on. If it was her or Frank Peterson, she guessed she would throw in the towel – let someone else have a chance. Even if that person was Frank Peterson.

The murderer walked all the way to the bottom of the street, where there was an outcrop of trees and bushes. There didn't look to be a way to get to the back of the houses there, so she wasn't sure what he was doing. Instead he went into the outcrop, where there was a small, well-worn path, over a ridge. Maybe he knew another way.

Shirley got to the outcrop about a minute after the

man did. It was 3.55 p.m. He was going to have to be fast and so was she. She got out her phone, and dialled in 999 ready. She looked around – the recycling truck was still slowly roaring down the street, lumbering along like a geriatric dragon. The cover under which a horrific crime was going to take place.

She thrust herself through the outcrop with the help of her cane and emerged out the other side. She saw the murderer and . . . her stomach dropped.

On the other side of the outcrop was another street, a busier one, running perpendicular to South Street. On the other side of the road was the primary Church of England school. Her 'murderer' was standing outside the school gates, glancing at his phone every so often, and waiting. As she watched, a young boy came out of the gates carrying a guitar case.

'Fuck,' Shirley muttered under her breath, as the child and man met, and the man ruffled the boy's hair. They started up the street together.

But if he wasn't the murderer . . .

No. No. No.

It was 3.56 p.m.

Shirley turned around and launched herself back through the outcrop. She landed back in South Street, crunching on one leg as her cane went flying. 'Arrrr,' she huffed, suppressing a stronger howl of pain. She staggered to get her cane, as the recycling truck reached the end of the street.

'You alreet, pet?' She looked up to see one of the men in fluorescent jackets.

'I'm fine,' she hissed, with so much venom that the man immediately backed off, returning to his job at hand.

She steadied herself. The truck was blocking her view of 11 South Street. She quickly hobbled past it, ignoring the fact her left leg felt like it was twisted the wrong way. She got clear of the truck and saw . . .

No.

The cat. Big Mac. The little pretentious fuck. He was there on the front step. Meowing and pawing at the door. No, how was he outside again? Frank Peterson must have let him out the back. The cat must have decided he wanted to get back in and come around the front. He was sitting there, looking pissed off. The door looked like it was open slightly, but too heavy to swing open with the cat's paltry pats.

It was just as Mallet AM said.

No, no, no.

Shirley looked left and right to see that no one was paying attention to her. The recycling truck was backing up, creating the deafening noise that may just have masked a murder. Who was she kidding, it was happening exactly as it was reported. All she could do now was hope – hope that it was different.

She crossed the road and went to the front door. She knocked but knew no one would answer. Instead it just opened. Big Mac meowed his thanks and went inside, and with another glance at the street – so did she.

The hallway she found herself in was very small and packed. It reminded her of the hospital radio. There was a quaint little entrance area with a coat and shoe rack, and then a staircase up to the second floor, alongside two doorways, one facing her – the other on the side wall. There were beer cans strewn everywhere – not really in piles, more distributed

'Hello,' Shirley said. It was crazy how much she wanted to hear the voice of the man she'd never met before today, a man she had found to be rather repulsive and rude – it was crazy how much she wanted Frank Peterson to be OK.

But she knew – this house was cold. This house had just had something ripped from it – something denied.

Big Mac strode ahead of her, pushing open the door. She followed.

A small cramped kitchen – dirty. A full sink and cup-boards open, with filthy plates in them that looked like they hadn't been used in years. Everywhere, there were cans, both empty and full – on the counters, piled up on the floor. It was clear Frank Peterson drank more than he ate. However long this had been his life, it had been too long. She was surprised he could stand up.

But as Shirley looked over to the kitchen table and down to the cat, she knew that Frank Peterson wouldn't be standing up ever again.

Big Mac was sitting there, lapping up the contents of a dropped can of beer. Beyond the podgy feline, Shirley saw an arm outstretched and lifeless. She took a deep breath, knowing what she was going to see, and stepped around the kitchen table.

She tried to prepare herself, but nothing could have prepared her for the pure horror of it. Her hand shot to her mouth to stifle a scream.

Frank Peterson was lying there, his limbs splayed out as though he were a dropped marionette, lying in a sea of cans. His eyes were open and wide – looking up at her lifelessly. There was no question that he was dead. His neck was exposed and bruised – the purple blossomed from the last moments he was alive.

She had failed. This man was dead – and she might as well have killed him herself. If she hadn't followed that man – who just turned out to be a father getting his son from school – she might have seen something, anything. But, as it happened, this man died for nothing. She didn't see a thing.

Shirley fumbled for her phone, with the number still programmed in from when she had made her fatal mistake. '999. Ambulance please.' Then she realised that that wouldn't do much good. 'No . . . Police. And ambulance maybe. But Police.'

'Yes,' the operator said.

And after a click, a new voice came over the phone, 'Police. What is your emergency?'

Shirley sobbed. 'There's . . . I think . . . Someone's been killed.'

'Who has been killed, ma'am?'

'Fr-Frank Peterson. 11 South Street, Pelaw. He's . . . I think he's been strangled.' There was no question about it. The marks on his neck, the bulging of his eyes, the protruding chest that looked like it was holding a breath

185

that would never be taken. 'Please hurry. The murderer could still be here.'

'Where are you now, ma'am?'

'I'm in his house. I'm in his kitchen. He's here . . . he's on the floor. He's dead.' Shirley backed up, and almost tripped on a full can of beer in amongst the sea of empties.

She couldn't look at him anymore. The dead man, who she had talked to just a few minutes ago. If she had been more persuasive, if she had raised more of a stink, he might have called the police on her – scared the murderer off. Her failure was as stark as Frank Peterson's deathly stare.

'OK, ma'am, you are going to need to get out of the house and wait for the police.'

'Yes.'

'What relation are you to the victim, ma'am?'

'I . . .' This wasn't an odd question, it was just one she hadn't thought of. She needed to think of something that put her at the scene. 'I'm just a neighbour. The cat was making a fuss and I saw the door was open.' A lie, followed by an untruth. Mallet AM had made her a liar to the police.

'OK, ma'am. Just wait a second and I'll . . .'

The voice continued, but Shirley didn't hear it. Something caught her eye, out of the kitchen window. The window looked out into the small yard, so there shouldn't have been anyone walking past. So why had she just seen someone, out of the corner of her eye?

And that figure snagged in her memory. Because it

had been wearing a brown trench coat, and a flat cap. The person. The person she had seen on the CCTV outside of Starith's bakery and the person she had seen at the scene of Farrow's accident. In the yard.

Was it possible that this figure had killed Frank Peterson?

Was it possible that this figure was dangerous?

Yes.

'Police are on their way, ma'am. If you could stay on the line and—'

Shirley hung up. She went to the kitchen window and looked out into the minuscule backyard. The back gate stood ajar. The figure had gone, fled. She had to catch up. She was the only one who could bring this person to justice. Whether or not he actually killed Frank Peterson, he'd know. Because, like Shirley, the figure had been watching – watching all along. Watching the future unfold.

She left the kitchen, taking one look back at the kitchen table. She could only see Frank Peterson's arm. Big Mac was sitting there, having lapped up all the beer. He stared up at her, and she interpreted it as a question. She knew it wasn't, couldn't be, but she heard it anyway – 'Why didn't you save my master, female human? Where am I going to get my beer now?'

Shirley staggered out into the back alley, shutting the gate behind her. She looked around to see a figure, *the* figure, disappearing left into an alley at the end of the street – the ends of his trench coat carried backwards by the wind. Shirley found her footing and strode after him, as quickly as she could – her head pulsing with the pain from her legs. In her mind, there was nothing else to do but to catch up with the figure.

And she got to the alleyway as quickly as possible, and as slowly as she'd feared, as the pain shuttered her vision, making things blurry and dreamlike. And all there was was forward. Following the figure until—

BLLLLAAAARRRRPPP. Her world snapped back to vividness. And Shirley launched backwards. A black BMW roared past; the driver screaming obscenities at her.

She looked around to see the alleyway had brought her out to the main road. She wheeled around, her eyes trying to seek out the figure. But the only people she could see were two children playing football on a field opposite and a young family with a pushchair. The figure was gone – how could that be? It was as if he had evaporated into thin air.

Sirens started up in the distance and Shirley found herself standing there wondering what to do. She had failed. Totally and utterly. And her thoughts drifted back to Mallet AM and snagged on a thread. *Found by a neighbour*, it had said. Because of the cat knocking on the door. She was the neighbour. In her own small way, she had done her bit to secure the promised future.

Mallet AM had seen her.

And if it had seen her, it had seen the figure in the trench coat too.

01.17

Shirley walked. She didn't know where. She didn't know how far. But when she looked up, she realised she hadn't gone very far at all. She was standing outside of the school. And sirens were growing louder. She didn't want to be there when the police arrived – she had no aversion to talking to them – even after her experience earlier, but she knew she would be drowned in red tape – when she needed to be out and about, on the streets, finding Frank Peterson's killer.

Every corner she turned, she half-expected to run into the man in the trench coat and flat cap. He had definitely seen her. If he had killed Peterson, he'd want to make sure she didn't tell anyone else.

But whatever connection to the scenario the figure had, it still didn't change the two things that were in her mind. Firstly, there was no doubt. The radio station reported the future, just as she had always suspected. Now, it was irrefutable though. Three times the station

189

had been right – and the last time was a murder. Would the station continue – and what would it say? She had to tell people, she had to do the opposite of what she had been doing. She had been keeping it a secret, delighting in the fact it was just hers. She should have been shouting it from the rooftops, warning people. If Frank Peterson had heard the newscast for himself, would it have been different? Or would he still have nearly laughed himself into a coma, drinking himself silly and thus, however uncooperatively, accepting his fate? She guessed she would never know. But she could stop it from happening again.

And she would. Wouldn't she? She tried to feel confident, but found she couldn't. This wasn't a job for someone like her, someone as old as her – not really. Maybe if she'd have been able to be quicker, keep up with the man she believed to be the murderer, cover more ground quickly – things would be different.

The second thing was that she now knew she needed help. The scenario had changed – lives were at risk. She had to accept that she couldn't do it alone. She was old, a lot feebler than she would like to admit, and even her mind was starting to slow down. She needed someone else. And there was one lifeline she had discovered, but dared not try yet. Now it was time.

Before the killer caught up with her.

As if to confirm her fears, a car pulled up to her, as the sirens grew louder and louder. At first, Shirley thought it was the police coming to arrest her – after all, she was the only one who was definitely at the murder scene – but she saw it wasn't a police car. A shiver went through her entire body. This was the murderer. He had seen her go into Frank Peterson's house, he knew she knew, and he was going to kill her too. Mallet AM hadn't reported what happened after the murder. She – and, to the same extent, the murderer – was flying blind. Anything could happen.

The car's window rolled down slowly. She would see the murderer if she looked around. Just waiting to get her. He would grab her and she'd never be heard of again. She wouldn't be able to fight him off, all the energy was gone from her body. Even if the fight remained, she wouldn't be able to do anything. She would succumb. And her long life would end because of her curiosity and insistence at being the goody two shoes.

A shadowy figure appeared beyond the descending window. There was no doubt in her mind that this was it—

'Shirley,' a familiar voice called.

Relief flooded in. She looked into the car, and asked with a gushing, thankful voice, 'Callie?'

Callie looked a lot different from when she had left Shirley at the police station, as Shirley probably did. There were dark bags under her eyes, and her light make-up seemed to have slipped slightly so it wasn't quite as perfect. Her hair was still tied back in a bun, but it seemed to have been readjusted, and looked more scraped back than before. Instead of the spritely youthful air she gave off, there was one of tiredness and heaviness. 'Shirley, I found you. Get in,' Callie said.

So she did. And as soon as she had buckled her seat belt, the emotion overwhelmed her and tears started to fall down her face. The crying came and didn't stop. Callie put a hand on her shoulder, no doubt would have hugged her if she could. But it didn't help. She just carried on, and through it all she told Callie about everything that had happened that day, ending with going into the house and seeing Frank Peterson dead. Callie just listened quietly, with an increasingly morbid look on her face. 'I've not seen a dead body since . . .'

'Yes,' Callie said.

Callie didn't need her to finish, but she did anyway. 'I've not seen a dead body since Bob.'

'I know,' Callie said, going into the glovebox and pulling out a pack of tissues. She gave them to Shirley. 'Just relax now. It's all over.'

Shirley tried but couldn't get Frank Peterson's dead stare out of her head. She blew her nose, wiped her eyes and felt a molecule better. 'Why are you here?' Shirley asked, trying not to sound as annoyed as she could have been. She really wasn't – she was just happy to see Callie.

'I just couldn't stop thinking about what we heard on the radio,' Callie said, 'and more, I couldn't stop thinking about you out here on your own. Putting yourself in danger. I was thinking about it so much, I almost made a mistake administering some medication, so I knew I had to leave. I made my excuses and came to get you. I heard the sirens. Did it . . .?'

'It happened . . .' Shirley croaked, her mouth dry. 'It happened exactly as the radio said. Frank Peterson was strangled, at 3.57 p.m. And I was the "neighbour" who came and found him. Mallet AM is real – I told you – do you believe me now?'

Callie looked down, like she couldn't meet Shirley's eyes. 'Yes. Yes, I believe you,' she said. 'I should have believed you in the first place. I'm sorry. If I'd been here, maybe I could have done something, maybe I could have—'

'No, don't you see? It would have always happened. Because Mallet AM can see the future. It would have seen me. Just as it would have seen you. It happened exactly as it was reported. The presenter would have known I tried to stop it.'

'But you were there because you heard it on the radio,' Callie said. 'That's a paradox, isn't it called? Gabe used to talk about those kind of things – something that only happens because of something else – locking one possibility off. Or something. We can change it. We can stop these things from happening. I think. I wished I paid more attention when he was talking about that stuff now, but at the time I just thought it was a pile of shite.'

Shirley thought for a moment. A paradox. She hadn't even considered that. Callie was right – Mallet AM couldn't have seen Shirley because the future he saw couldn't have had her in it. Because she heard it from here. Shirley went round and round thinking of it – which came first, her trying to stop the murder or Mallet AM seeing it. It was so complicated. When did her life become science fiction? – all about time and variables and possible futures. Gabe would have been able to

193

make sense of it. She wished he was here. Would he be proud of her – or would he see futility in what she was doing?

'And from now on, I'm with you,' Callie said, taking her hand over the gearstick. She gripped it hard. 'I should have been with you from the start.'

Through everything, Shirley managed a smile.

'OK, let's get you home,' Callie said.

'No,' Shirley said, 'I'm not going home.'

'What? You need rest.'

'I need to go somewhere first.'

'Shirley!'

'I'll find my way there with or without you,' Shirley said, wiping her face with finality. 'There's someone who I think might be able to help.'

Callie sighed, and stared ahead for a moment. Then she seemed to realise the pointlessness of standing against Shirley. 'OK. Where are we going?'

'Newcastle,' Shirley said.

Callie raised an eyebrow, but said nothing. She just started the engine. 'Whereabouts?'

'I'll have to get into my email. Can I use your phone?'

Callie handed Shirley her smartphone, as she pulled away from the kerb.

01.18

Newcastle was busy for a Monday afternoon, hustling and bustling with shoppers and workers. Shirley and Callie were not part of them. As everyone made their way up the street, towards Eldon Square and the main shopping precincts, the two of them made their way down towards the station.

Although Callie had driven them here, she had still taken some convincing to continue on. 'I don't know about this,' she said, when Shirley had explained all about the mysterious website, the emails and everything else to do with The Enigma Files, 'this sounds very dodgy. And this guy could just be full of shit.'

'Maybe he could,' Shirley said, 'but isn't it worth a try? He might be able to help.'

Callie nodded. 'Yes, but that's assuming he's not a creep who's just trying to lure you to his house.'

Well, the thought had crossed her mind, hadn't it? After all, there was no reason to believe this Arnie character even knew about Mallet AM. The only evidence was a random number on a webpage filled with random characters. All the other evidence had been provided by herself. But she couldn't let Callie know that she was just as wary. So she simply said, 'Please trust me.'

And Callie said she did. So they continued, on the condition that Callie stop and get Shirley a coffee. 'You've had a shock. You need to keep your sugar levels up. You're probably still running on adrenaline. When that runs out, you're going to crash. Hard.' So Shirley drank her first ever caramel latte – extra sugar.

They had parked at The Gate and Callie put Arnie's address in her phone. It wasn't far away. Callie had to slow her walking speed to match Shirley's. She knew because every so often she would get two or three steps ahead, remember to slow down, and then smile at Shirley as if in apology. It was not meant to be but it was a little patronising, although there was no alternative.

As they got to the station, Callie looked at her phone and led them down a side street to a row of mismatched houses which were obviously hidden away by some town planner. She looked up and down the street, and then went to the nearest front door. 'I think it's this one.'

Shirley let herself be led down the path, as Callie knocked on the door. First, they waited. And then they waited some more. And then there was a tremendous clatter behind the door, before it opened. A middle-aged woman stood there – she looked exhausted with dark bags under her eyes, her pale blonde hair was tied up in a messy bun with multiple strands breaking loose, and her white T-shirt was stained with something that looked like green paint. She didn't say anything – she just stared at them.

Shirley stepped forward. 'Hello there. Um, we're looking for Arnie?'

The woman still said nothing. But she did roll her eyes, let out a long sigh and turn away from them. 'ARNIE, THERE'S SOME NUTJOBS HERE FOR YA,' she shouted into the house, and slammed the door shut.

Shirley and Callie looked at each other, and after a moment, and another loud clatter, the door opened again to reveal a tall, slender man in an open shirt with a Metallica T-shirt underneath. He was clean-shaven and had uniform short hair. He looked entirely normal, much unlike the images of an internet psychopath that Shirley (and undoubtably Callie) had conjured in her mind. 'Hello,' he said, with a smile.

'Hello,' Shirley replied, 'we're looking for Arnie?'

'That's me,' Arnie said, 'ah, you must be Shirley Steadman, right?'

Shirley froze. 'How the hell do you know my name?'

'Quite simple really. I traced your IP address by extracting the residual datacodes from the email you sent and hacking into the underground mainframe to reveal your identity,' he explained, laughing at Shirley and Callie's looks of fear. 'That and you sent the email from an email address titled shirleysteadman1951@quill. com.'

Shirley and Callie let out a simultaneous thankful sigh.

'Just a little joke,' Arnie said. 'I make them too often. My wife says anyway. And you are . . .?' He looked at Callie.

Callie looked like she had no intention of responding, so Shirley introduced her.

Arnie took Callie's hand from her side and shook it. 'Nice to meet you, Callie. I'm Arnie Enigma.'

'Arnie Enigma,' Callie said, 'is that your real name?'

Arnie snorted. 'Of course not. But then I know that a dumb name like Callie isn't yours.'

Callie raised an eyebrow. 'No . . . it is.'

Arnie looked baffled. 'Oh . . . right. You may want an alias. You look like an Electra or a Banshee. You want me to brainstorm some names?'

'Arnie,' Shirley said, slightly impatiently, 'we're here because of 66.40 AM. Mallet AM.'

Any troubling notion that Arnie didn't know what she was talking about left her when she saw the twinkle in his eye. And Arnie cut out the waffle. 'Oh, of course,' Arnie said, 'sorry, please come in.' Thankfully, Arnie shut up and guided them both down a narrow hallway and then to a flight of stairs. Instead of going up them, however, he went to a doorway in the side of them. Another staircase led down into a dark and dingy basement. 'This way,' he said, happily, his tone in stark contrast to their surroundings.

Callie went down the steps into the basement first, with a glance at Shirley that said 'If I die . . .' Shirley followed close behind.

Arnie switched on the light, a bare bulb in the centre

of the cramped basement. The surroundings weren't unlike Gabe's hideaway in the attic, except the walls were
actual walls and the clutter was astronomical. Framing
everything was a wide desk that covered two walls, with
an iMac computer, and a familiar-looking whiteboard
above it with similar scratchings. If this man was like
Gabe, he was playing it very well.

Arnie marched around the space with ease, stepping
through every pile of papers and heap of rubbish. Callie
just stayed at the foot of the stairs, moving aside so
Shirley could join her. The young woman seemed similarly perplexed by it all, but she also looked incredibly
out of place in her uniform – she might as well have been
in a clown costume. She was looking around and sighing,
clearly still not believing that this was worth their time.
'Someone's got an ego,' Callie muttered, and Shirley followed her gaze to above the whiteboard, where there
was a shiny large sign that read THE ENIGMA FILES,
and smaller under it THE ONLY TRUE FUTURE.

Arnie started fussing about, trying to clean up the
room. He moved stacks of papers from one messy corner
to another. And then back again. 'I'm sorry,' he said,
'I'm not very good at hosting. I don't do it much. Would
either of you like a drink?'

'We'd really just prefer to know what you know
about the radio station,' Callie blurted, bluntly.

'Of course,' Arnie said, 'I'm sorry. Sometimes I get a
little flustered. Um . . . I prepared something . . . um . . .'
Arnie sat down in a leather desk chair and reached under
his desk. He pulled out a big file, as plump as himself,

with papers sticking out of it everywhere. He dusted it off and held it out to Shirley. 'This is my scrapbook. I've been working on it for decades. Since I was in short pants, you know. You need an extensive history of these people. People who can see the future. Some people call them soothsayers, some people call them fortune tellers – hell, there's a thousand different names in a hundred different languages. I've collected a lot of information here.'

Shirley took the scrapbook.

But Callie clicked her tongue. 'Is this all just off the internet because I wouldn't believe any of that stuff?'

'No, no, no, no,' Arnie said, clearly thinking she would be impressed if she looked through it. 'This isn't just "The Simpsons Predict 9/11 and Trump" or "Paul the Octopus Predicts the World Cup". This is the serious shit, OK. Everything in this scrapbook will blow your mind wide open. I'm not saying all of it is true, far from it. But I'm saying there's no way everything in here can be fake.'

'Hearsay,' said Callie.

'Maybe, but compelling hearsay. Think about it, it's not so uncommon. Tesla predicted self-driving cars, and things like Wi-Fi and smartphones. Vannevar Bush practically predicted the internet and modern computers. Pulling all that stuff out of nowhere, out of their imaginations, or maybe some sixth sense. Kubrick and Arthur C. Clarke predicted iPads in *2001: A Space Odyssey*. You remember, that tablet thing?'

Shirley flipped through the scrapbook as Arnie talked.

There were masses of newspaper articles. She happened upon one that looked very old and faded, titled 'What May Happen in the Next Hundred Years' by a man named John Watkins. It was dated 1900.

'This is all well and good, but these aren't really telling the future,' Shirley said.

Arnie jumped up from his chair excitedly. 'I knew you'd be good. Yes, you are right. These predictions are more just thoughts from minds that were ahead of their time. Tesla, and Bush and Watkins, and others were more . . . let's say, just extremely prepared. If that makes sense. No, what these people do is actually see something in their mind's eye that they are simply not prepared for. They're almost the antithesis of the geniuses. These people, I call them Aevums, they have no idea what they're doing. They don't even necessarily want the gift they have. They just see things. They're blessed by the sight. They may see something they couldn't even fathom, someone they've never met before, a name they don't recognise.

'The most famous of them was obviously Nostradamus. You've heard of him, right? The media pulls him out every so often. He saw so much that it's practically impossible to deny that he had the sight. He predicted things like the Great Fire of London, Adolf Hitler's rise in Europe, John F. Kennedy's assassination, for God's sake. The Twin Towers. It's all in the books. Have you read Nostradamus?'

Shirley shook her head and Callie bluntly said, 'No.'

Arnie didn't even stop, 'Some say Nostradamus saw

the dark year. In one of his works, you can clearly see that he foresaw it. Wait, I have it here somewhere.' Arnie dashed around the room and finally found a book. He flipped through it crazily. 'Yes. Century 2. Quatrain 53. "The great plague of the maritime city/ Will not cease until there be avenged of death/ Of the just blood, condemned for a price without crime/ Of the great lady outraged by pretence." Huh, huh?'

'Yeah, I don't know,' Callie said. 'How is that anything, really?'

Arnie slammed the book shut, and looked at her a little perturbed. 'Some people just can't accept it, that's OK.'

'Do we know how these predictions work?' Shirley said.

'Not really,' Arnie conceded, 'and without finding someone who is willing to talk to me about it, I'll never really know. That's why I'm so interested in 66.40 AM. And that's why I spent an astronomical amount of money extending the signal of my radio receiver to Chester-Le-Street.'

'How long have you been listening to Mallet AM?' Shirley asked.

Arnie scratched his cheek and said, 'It's not quite as simple as that.' Arnie took the scrapbook, riffled through it to a certain page before handing it, open, back to Shirley. 'This is a timeline of the presenter's, um, enterprises.'

Shirley looked down to see a crude diagram – a line with dates across it and lines coming off it with bubbles of handwritten information.

'I first became aware of 66.40 AM on the fifteenth of November 2018 when I was going around the internet, researching something else entirely, I think it was someone who predicted the Standedge Five case, and I happened upon this radio station in Diggle, Huddersfield. Someone posted about it on Facebook — a radio station which was reporting things. But the date stated was the next day's. From then, there was a station just outside of Glasgow, one in Kirkby Stephen, one in Stony Heap near Witton Gilbert and one in Darlington. Never around for long, and always under different names, but always the frequency 66.40 AM.

'But here's the kicker — every prediction that the presenter made was wrong. Totally crazy-town banana-pants wrong. Some were so wrong, they were laughable. The presenter would predict someone would get hit by a train, and instead they'd go on holiday. He would say a man would get stabbed and instead he'd win the lottery. He would say someone would lose their child when they didn't even have one. In fact, it seemed that sometimes the exact opposite of what the presenter said was true.'

Shirley had too many questions but settled on one. 'But everything he's said on Mallet AM has been correct. A person has died today in the exact way he's said. How is it happening?'

Arnie was nodding — did he already know Frank Peterson was dead? Or was he just playing it off? 'I think it was probable that he was just cultivating his gift. Sometimes it seems this "sight" comes to people later in life and they have to work at it to understand it. The presenter may have been one of these people and decided to use his gift for good.'

Shirley looked at Callie. She was shaking her head.

If Arnie saw it, he didn't pay attention. 'Every wrong prediction that he put out there, it was just another stepping stone for him to unlock his true . . . I'm going to say, power, but I'm afraid she's going to hit me.'

'She won't,' said Shirley, although she wasn't sure.

'Just one thing,' Callie said, holding a finger up to stop him, 'what else do you believe in?'

'What do you mean?' laughed Arnie.

'I mean, you strike me as someone who believes the earth is flat, and the country is run by lizard people, and the moon landing was fake, and stuff like that.'

'No,' Arnie said. 'This? This stuff is real. I promise you.'

They talked for another hour – Arnie revealing all he knew about Mallet AM. He and Shirley compared notes. She suggested that it seemed localised to the upper end of Chester-Le-Street – Arnie furiously snatching back his scrapbook and making a note of it. Arnie offered some more specifics – the station always came online at 5.15 p.m. every day and went offline at 10.00 p.m. Most of the broadcast was just music, with the news being the only notable thing shared.

They both mused over who they thought the presenter was. Shirley had a hard time imagining the presenter as a real person, but he had to be. A real person with a real life. Arnie had a more solid picture – 'I feel like he's a man, probably quite young. Thinks of himself as some kind of superhero. Using his gift for the betterment of mankind. He probably doesn't have many attachments, and he may have a professional background. The production is pretty seamless for pirate radio.' And on he went. Arnie was clearly passionate about this stuff. And Shirley found herself warming to him.

Callie, meanwhile, let them talk but didn't participate. She stood there, clearly listening but having nothing to contribute herself. The only time she even looked like she was going to cut in was when Shirley told Arnie about Frank Peterson and almost started crying. But she didn't.

Arnie asked them both to stay for dinner, but Shirley declined, accepting Callie's look of gratitude. They resolved to keep in touch, 'See – just a nice man,' Shirley said triumphantly in Callie's ear, as Arnie escorted them back up the stairs.

He opened the front door, and Callie was through it before he could say anything.

'Oh, one second please . . .' Arnie said, and Shirley turned on the doorstep to see him disappear back the way they came. He went into a small cupboard near the front door. Shirley could see a bevy of coats hung up there – principally a . . .

She felt like she'd plunged into icy water. Her legs threatened to buckle.

Arnie reappeared, carrying a small scrap of paper. Shirley couldn't even meet his gaze. He held out his hand. 'Here's all my contact information. Easier than having to email through the site.'

Shirley didn't move. Callie had to take the scrap of paper and thank Arnie, if only out of politeness.

Shirley didn't remember much of the journey home, or what she and Callie talked about – she was operating on some kind of autopilot.

But, inside, she could only think of one thing.

The thing she saw hanging up in Arnie Enigma's coat cupboard.

There on the hook – a brown trench coat. And perched above it, a blue flat cap.

01.19

How long had she been sitting at the kitchen table? The cup of tea in front of her was freezing cold, and so was the air around her. There had been no movement, no kinetic energy in the room, for what seemed like days – even though it had only been hours. Wait, had it even been that?

Gabe was there, sitting at the table across from her. He looked like he was waiting for his cup of tea, although he couldn't drink it. Since seeing Callie, Shirley seemed to see the age in Gabe. He looked old – just as he would be. He looked at Shirley with eyes that had seen the world, and rejected it – eyes that had ended up at the bottom of the sea. 'Do you want to talk about it?' Gabe said, in a husky voice, older than she had heard before.

'There's nothing to talk about,' Shirley snapped.

'Right,' Gabe said, unconvinced. 'So explain those.' He looked next to him, at the mountain of bacon and banana sandwiches that Shirley had made. She'd gone through a whole extra loaf of bread, as well as using the pieces she'd stress-buttered the other day.

'You looked hungry,' Shirley replied, defensively, not admitting that she had had to find something to do. She had needed to keep her brain occupied, or it would drift back to Frank Peterson's blank expression and dead eyes. Was this her life now, having to be filled with dull repetitive tasks to escape the images etched all over her memory? How many bacon-banana sandwiches was enough to erase the sight of that body? 'Please eat.'

She would have given anything to see Gabe pick up a sandwich and bite into it, but she knew he wouldn't. He wasn't there, and no matter how hard she willed him into existence, he wasn't going to enjoy his meal. Why did she continue to kid herself? That was easy – because she was afraid Gabe would disappear.

Shirley glanced at the clock.

Gabe read her mind. Of course he did. 'Are you going to listen tonight?'

Shirley didn't say anything – didn't know what there was to be said. And the more the seconds passed, the more she knew the stark truth.

Gabe said it out loud, 'Or are you afraid what it's going to say?'

And there it was. She felt like she had an obligation to listen, but she couldn't bring herself to. When this had all started, she thought it was a bit of fun. It felt like years ago, but was less than a week, and now she wished she had never found 66.40 AM. If she had seen the future, seen herself playing with that old radio on

Tuesday night, what would she have done? Would she have stopped herself?

And now – what now? The future was already written. What did the presenter see for her? Was she meant to listen, or wasn't she? What was the point of anything if it had practically already happened – if someone had seen it, it must have.

So she listens. What if Mallet AM reported something she didn't want to hear. What if it reported another murder? Was she meant to launch herself out there again, try to stop it all over? How many days did she have left like this – how many murders could she try to stop until she killed herself?

So she doesn't listen. She sits here with her dead son. She gives in to fear. Again. Just like she always had once upon a time. She'd told herself she'd never let fear control her again. And she'd never let the shadow come home again.

The trench coat. Arnie Enigma would be listening. Would he be carrying out Mallet AM's justice? Or was he merely a casual observer? If he was so innocent, why hadn't he told Shirley he was there at the scene of Frank Peterson's murder – at the scenes of all the futures?

'It's all going wrong, Gabe,' she said as she crossed over to the kitchen counter and filled the kettle. 'Mallet AM is not what I thought it was. I thought it was going to be a force for good, something to look forward to, to put your faith in. But it happens that it's like everything else in this world – it's a curse.'

'A curse?' Gabe said.

Shirley replied, shakily, 'Yes. A curse and a shadow.' Hadn't she suffered enough? But even though time had tried its best to heal over the cracks – he was still here.

Not Gabe.

Bob.

Bob was the shadow she lived in. His small, plump frame always managed to tower over her. Being dead wasn't enough. She still felt like he would appear. Sometimes, when she awoke in the middle of the night, which happened too much, she would temporarily forget that he was dead. In those times, her eyes would fill with tears and she would break out into uncontrollable sobs. She'd be back to where she was – scared and silent.

Sometimes when she got in the house, even though she'd moved, she'd expect to hear the television – the horse racing – and the shouting coming from the living room. Or, even worse, the silent stare reflecting in the light of the screen.

But there was no one there. Bob was gone. And she was now supposed to be a more confident, outspoken woman. The man had robbed her of the best years of her life, and she had been forced to sit there and watch him do it. He had taken her freedom, her voice, and what was worse, he had taken her son.

She thought back to that day too often. The day everything changed. The day that Gabe was set on the path that would lead to his death. He was so brave – and it was thrown back in his face. He had sat his parents down at the kitchen table, told them that he had something to tell them and then he did. And it didn't bother

her, it didn't make her love him any less. If anything, it made her know that he was confident enough to follow his heart – to stand up for what he was. In that moment, more than any other, she knew that her second-born would be all right, he would be able to forge ahead into the world alone, without the need of his aides, known affectionately as parents. He would be OK. (And this was a feeling that Shirley constantly came back to – the last really truly happy moment of her life. And the desolation of grief that came after.)

All this positive energy had died as the two of them – the mother and the child – had looked to the husband, father. Shirley had never seen such ugliness in a human being and thought she never would again. For can there be a shade uglier than a man resenting his son? Behind Bob's eyes were thunderstorms of hatred masked with the lightning of mirth and regret, and she could've got lost in there, on a high sea, trying to weather the storm. But he'd got up, the kitchen chair scraping back ripping into a piercing shriek.

She saw it all in Gabe's face now. The past written in wrinkles. She saw the following few months after his dramatic speech in the lines on his forehead. The time that he told Callie in the conservatory, and how supportive she was. The time he told Deena and she loved him more. But Gabe would never get the acceptance he really craved, and Shirley knew what it felt like. Bob was a bigger, meaner Marsha. You craved acceptance from people like that. And Gabe didn't get it.

Bob had left the house that day, and Shirley had

hoped against hope that he would never return. She hoped for herself, for Deena, for Gabe. But he did come back, smelling of stale cigarettes and beer. And slowly, across the silent days, he formulated a plan. He sat Gabe down at the table which should have symbolised their unity and tore everything apart. He forced Gabe into the seat, shouted at Shirley to get him a beer, and showed his son the paperwork. 'Royal Navy. Sorted me out when I was a lad. They'll sort you out too. They'll teach you discipline. They'll teach you what it means to be a man. They'll beat it out of you, if they have to.' Bob had smiled at this notion, and Shirley had to hold back from gagging. She wanted to step in, to protect her son, but she couldn't. She was mentally frozen in place. A silent onlooker.

Gabe said he didn't want to go. Bob said it wasn't a discussion. For Gabe to stay, and he had to as he had nowhere else to go, he had to submit to the master of the house. And who was going to stop Bob? Shirley? Maybe she would have, once upon a time. But her courage had been beaten and beaten again and again into line.

Then Bob had started shouting. About how much he did for his family. About how much he did for his household. And Shirley had winced at every pointed remark, feeling it in her soul. Bob slammed down his beer with every single sentence so it frothed over and flooded the table, dripping over the sides, but he didn't care – he wouldn't be the one cleaning it up after all. Gabe was trying to stay strong, but Shirley knew well enough Bob would win in the end. Bob always won in the end.

He ended his tirade by getting up and getting his coat. Thank God he was going out – no doubt to the working men's club – but he left with one remark that would shatter Gabe forever. 'You'll get it ripped out. Or you're dead to me. Because I am not having a poof for a son.'

The rest didn't need to be said. Shirley remembered seeing Gabe off. Towards the end, there was so much conflict. Shirley and Gabe went through the same emotions – Gabe had to leave, but maybe it would be better for him. And sometimes Shirley wished she was going too. She had felt the same when Deena had left for university. But it was stronger this time. Bob had become hostile at the smallest thing, almost physically violent – a line he had never crossed before. He lived in the safety of the threat – but now he was constantly a hair away from carrying it out. He never talked to Gabe, never even looked at him. He only talked to Shirley when he wanted something, or wanted to let off some steam – which was almost constantly. He didn't let her leave the house – except to buy him beer and food. He didn't relent until Gabe was gone.

'Someone else's problem now,' he'd muttered, as they drove away – left their son in the wind. If she'd been stronger, at that point, she would have driven the car into the ocean, condemned them both to the depths. Maybe then their son wouldn't have ended up there.

She almost heard Bob's voice now, 'What the fuck are you doing? Get me a fucking beer and stop sounding like a pussy.' She looked around hurriedly. She suddenly had the incredible fear that her mind – the same mind that had conjured Gabe – would rake up a mental image of Bob too. But he wasn't there. Just his shadow.

'You should listen,' Gabe said.

'To him?' Shirley said, in disbelief.

'What? No. To the radio.'

Oh. Shirley put her head in her hands. She had to stop living in the past. She had to let this go. And she would never be able to with the figment sitting across from her. 'Gabe,' she whispered, hardly able to make it louder. Tears started running down her face. 'I think I need to go on alone.'

'What do you mean?' Gabe said.

This was never going to work. Deena was right. It was damaging. She had to finally let Gabe go, once and for all. If she was going to be able to keep her mind clear, deal with this new thing, this new stage in her life, she needed to have release. 'I need you to stop coming here.'

Gabe smiled a denial. 'I'm here because of you, Shirley. I don't have any say in the matter.'

'Can you not just call me Mum?' Shirley hissed, sobbing. 'One time.'

Gabe shook his head. 'That's not how it works. You know that. Stop this silliness, make another sandwich if it will make you feel better, put on the radio maybe. See what tomorrow has in store.'

She didn't want to send him away. She could see that in Gabe's face. But she had to. 'No, Gabe. I need—'

The front door opened, closed in a slam.

Shirley and Gabe regarded each other.

Gabe was acting odd, a new emotion taking over his face. She hadn't seen it on him for a long time. He looked frightened – an expression that he had worn often growing up with his father. And a look that he wore every day after the conversation that would take him away from her.

Maybe this Gabe was frightened because she was? Because she knew exactly who had just let themselves in. And she knew the absolute hurricane of grief that was coming to meet her.

Shirley wiped her face with a hanky.

Sure enough, a shout came from the hall, approaching. Dee appeared through the front room. 'Why the hell didn't you tell me that you spent the night in the . . .' She trailed off. She just stood there. '. . . Hospital,' she whispered so quietly that Shirley might have imagined it. Deena went white.

She was probably wondering what Shirley was doing sitting in the kitchen talking to herself. But that wasn't entirely it – there was something else. There was something very, very wrong.

Deena dropped the keys she had in her hand.

Shirley got up and Gabe did too, standing next to her. Shirley was staring at Deena. Her daughter had started to move her lips but nothing was coming out, and it looked like she was trembling. She wasn't looking at Shirley, she was looking next to her, to . . .

'Who the fuck are you?' Dee said, in a voice that wasn't her own. It was cold, and robotic, but also violently angry. A voice that had seen a ghost.

'What?' Shirley said. She couldn't think. She couldn't . . .

'WHO THE FUCK ARE YOU?' Deena shrieked.

Shirley looked to her side, to Gabe. And then back at her daughter. She could almost see Gabe's reflection in Deena's eyes. 'You can . . . You can . . .' she was gasping like a beached fish. 'You can see him?' Any thought of what had been happening over the last week left her, because she was focusing on what was happening right in front of her. Mallet AM was nothing anymore.

'Get the fuck away from her. Get the fuck away from her right now,' Deena roared, rummaging in her bag, and pulling out a can of something that looked like mace. 'Get away from my mother.'

Shirley slid her eyes sideways, trying to catch him out of the corner of her eye. He was still there – Gabe. He looked worried, but not scared anymore. He was just motionless. 'This is Gabe,' Shirley said, because that was all that was in her head.

'It can't be Gabe, Mum,' Deena broke her line of sight with him to tell her. And then it was back. 'You. I don't know who you think you are, coming in here, but this is over.' She threw the mace at him with force, as she brought out her phone.

The mace can hit Gabe in the chest. Really. It hit him in the chest. It collided with him, stopped and fell to the floor. Shirley looked at his chest and then up at him. Gabe was sighing, and suddenly a smile broke out on his face. He looked insane, aggressively evil. She had never seen Gabe with that face. She wouldn't have been able to imagine it.

Because this wasn't her imagination. The ghost she'd been talking to for over a year was not a ghost at all.

'999. Police. There is an intruder in my mother's house,' Deena was barking into the phone. 'Yes. Yes. Yes, I can see him right now. Yes, he may be violent. 28 Yharnam Crescent. Please God just get here as quickly as you can.'

'Gabe?' Shirley whispered harshly to her spectre, the one that she had seemed to will into existence.

'Hello, Shirley,' Gabe said, grinning. The smile may not have been familiar, but the voice was. He reached around her, to the stack of bacon and banana sandwiches. 'Well, might as well. You went to all that trouble,' he said, his voice slick with contempt as he swallowed one triangle almost whole. 'And I am so very hungry.'

He was real. And he was Gabe. Her Gabe.

She felt the ground fall out from under her, and she fell back into darkness.

02.00

The Present, Retold

00.00 (Redux)

Colm MacArthur
Monday 15 February 2021
4.48 p.m.

He slammed the door to Route One, backing himself up against it and having to fight not to collapse with relief. He had run all the way. Must have been miles.

His favourite Chester-Le-Street bar was starting to warm up for the evening, with the music a little louder than usual, and the place a little more occupied. However, Colm's sudden and loud appearance was still enough to get everyone to stop their conversations and look around at him.

Every soul in this bar would know he had just arrived. It would be ingrained in their memory. Ol' Colm making his grand entrance. Even the faces he didn't know (of which there actually were a few) would recall the grizzled, hairy, sweaty brute barrelling in.

He wasn't exactly being smart about this. But the bar called to him — it always did. And he needed a drink. Hell, if there was anyone in the universe who needed a drink right now, it was him. He took off his outer layers and hung them up by the door.

He was physically shaking. His skin was simultaneously burning hot and icy cold – it was odd how those two states felt the same. His lungs were pulling in air and unable to expel it fast enough, giving him the feeling that he was constantly in motion while being completely still. He existed between everything.

The rabble of faces in the dark bar soon lost interest, going back to their gossip, and their drinks, and their floaty worries, and Colm did his best to casually sidle up to the bright red bar he knew so well. He found his home, and his balance, on the same stool he had sat on ever since he had first found this place.

'Rough day, Colm?' Margaret said, coming over. She was the proprietor of the place and was older than the décor suggested. Sometimes he thought of her as his mother figure, even though his mother was still very much alive.

Colm was surprised to find out that he could speak, even if the noises he made did come out in thick chunky rasps. 'I need my usual.'

'Usual classy or usual cheap?'

Colm got out his wallet and opened it. He already knew he wouldn't find much in there. How had all that money gone already? 'Cheap.'

Margaret pulled him a pint, regarding him all the time she did with the cold judgemental eye of a matriarch. Colm found himself shrinking under her gaze; could she see what was troubling him? What he'd just run away from?

He tried to act casual — running his hand across his scraggly beard, which had seemed to grow since he had last checked. When had he last checked? He couldn't remember.

Margaret placed the pint in front of him. 'Didn't think you'd be in so early today. Thought you might be drinking up at Caliente's place.'

'What?' Colm said, shaking so much he couldn't pick up his glass. 'No. I haven't seen him all day.' Such a bald-faced lie, it was obvious.

Margaret looked like she was going to say something, but didn't. She just left him to it.

So, like most days, he drank. His fourth drink was the one that really hit the spot, and it didn't take him long to get there. His fears and worries were dropping away with every swig — the police wouldn't be taking this long to catch up if they were on his tail, even if someone had just seen him and called them. He had got away somehow — the sight of . . . He didn't want to think of it . . . scaring six hours' worth of hard drinking out of him. He'd kept his wits about him and he'd got out of there. There was an intelligent human left somewhere inside him.

But he had to think about it. He had so many questions. And front and centre was: why was *she* there? Of all the people he had expected to see, she was practically the last person on Earth he would have been able to think of.

She couldn't have . . . No. Impossible.

Wasn't it?

Colm stayed in the bar for the rest of the day and most of the night, and by the time the regulars started coming in and his friends started sitting with him, he had almost forgotten what had got him so worked up. There were peaks and troughs, of course – one friend remarked 'Where's Caliente?' and he had to run to the bathroom to throw up everything he'd drunk thus far – but the warm, temporary happiness of the beer was impossible to ignore. There was peace in letting it overwhelm him.

And when the last-orders bell rang – a gong in Route One – Colm's day was a long-forgotten illusion, let alone the trauma of his past, let alone the Navy and Gabe, and his father, and his entire goddamn fucked-up existence. And with one last pint, he sealed it away forever.

Forever was tonight. He knew it wasn't really forever – when he woke up in the morning, everything would be back. His problems would still be there. The images seared into his brain from the day would return. And he'd still have to face his reflection in the mirror.

But he found it hard to care.

He ordered one last drink, having to persuade Margaret he'd be able to pay her for it tomorrow, with the limited vocabulary of a drunkard. But she relented as always – she had a soft spot for him for some reason.

He drank that last beer too quickly and got the hiccups. He got up off his stool and immediately found his world buckling and swaying like a fairground pirate ship. He was able to get to the door though – he was a pro at this.

'See you later, Colm,' Margaret said and Colm whirled

round. 'And if you see Caliente, tell him we miss him.'

Caliente — the images threatened to come back. They called him Caliente because that was the brand of whiskey he liked. But Frank Peterson liked that Colm just called him by his name. Colm wouldn't be doing that again though. Because Frank was dead.

You're in some deep shit, boy, Frank would've said.

'Colm?' Margaret said.

Colm snapped out of it, drowned his memories under hours of alcohol, managed a smile, waved goodbye to his friends in turn, and left for his lonely flat with the two cases of beer he had stashed under his bed firmly in his mind.

Before he left, however, he retrieved his coat. And his cap.

02.01

Shirley's eyes shot open. 'Gabe,' she shouted into the dark.

She was on the settee, which had been made up with the pillow and duvet from her bed. She had had a flannel placed on her forehead – which now lay in her lap. Someone had put her here. But why? What had happened? She remembered Mallet AM and Frank Peterson and his face. Was that why she had been put here? She had fainted – she knew that.

And then it hit her.

Gabe.

No . . .

Bang.

A noise coming from the hallway, far away but also very close. She felt like her reality was wrong – truth and lies were fluid, constantly interchanging with each other. Everything was so fucked up, she could even imagine that it was all a dream. Mallet AM, the news, Gabe,

226

everything. Her life was unravelling. First, the radio station becoming science fiction, and now her dead son coming back from the dead.

She hadn't been imagining. All that time when she had been seeing Gabe, he'd been real. She thought he was confined to the bungalow because she didn't want to be seen talking to herself, but he was real, and that was why she never saw him out of the house. She thought her mind was trying to see him as he would have been now, but he was real, and that was why he looked older than she remembered him. He did always look thirsty when she made him a cup of tea and hungry when she made him a bacon and banana sandwich. He had been taking advantage of his mother – a little old lady who probably couldn't hear when he whooshed himself away behind her back, or couldn't smell that he was real, or couldn't see his tiny details betraying that he was real. She supposed he was right on that front.

Gabe was real.

She thought that anything could happen now.

Bang.

Maybe that noise was Bob in the hallway, kicking the shit out of a wall because Shirley hadn't made him tea yet. She could almost see him, having just come in from the pub. He would be six beers deep and countless cigarettes and his smell would be starting to flood the house. She would have to start his tea – usually chicken pot pie after a bender – and carry on, the last ten years of her life being nothing but a welcomed dream.

No, that would be too easy. That's how fucked up her life was now, she was almost pining for the good old days of subjugation and emotional abuse. But that was what had kept her in that prison.

Shirley sat up, wrenching her body out of the relative warmth of the duvet. The house was cold and dark – the only light the reading lamp someone had put on in the corner of the living room. Gabe was not here, nowhere in the house – she knew that instantly.

There was a miaow, and she saw that Moggins was sitting across from her, on Bob's chair. He regarded her with his glistening eyes, unable to comprehend what was going on. But, in his small way, he had tried to warn her. He had never come in the room when Gabe was around and, every so often, Shirley found him hissing in the hallway at nothing in particular. Because he knew Gabe was alive. Gabe had been here – all this time. She had thought he was her ghost – especially for her. But it turned out he was real. She felt scared, confused about why her son wouldn't be straight with her – why he would allow her to grieve him for so long? But she also couldn't help feeling so unbelievably happy, a soaring joy that she hadn't felt in years. Because her son – however much he had deceived her, however much he had played her – was alive.

She pulled herself up onto unsteady feet, using the side of the settee. She wished she had her cane, but it was outside, propped against the wall. Her legs couldn't hold her, and she staggered, almost falling over the coffee table. If she hadn't put her arms out, she would have gone arse over elbow. The mug on the table flew off and clattered by the television.

Bang.

There was movement beyond her vision. Anything not close to her was blurry, and as she strained to look, she saw a door open and a figure come into view. It rushed over. 'Mum,' Deena said, catching Shirley by the arm and bringing her back to a standing position, 'you shouldn't be up.' Deena's make-up had run all over her face, and she had done a half-hearted job at wiping it off. She had been crying – a lot. Her eyes were flecked with blood-red veins. 'You've had a shock, you fainted. We don't know if you broke anything in the fall yet.'

'Gabe – where's Gabe?' Her voice was cracked and broken. *She* was cracked and broken.

Deena hesitated a moment – and then pulled her mother into a hug. 'The police took him away. They're holding him until they can get a better idea of what is going on. Do you – I have to ask . . .' She released her from the hug and looked into her eyes. 'Did you know that Gabe . . .?'

'Was alive?' Shirley said incredulously. 'Of course I didn't.'

Deena nodded, apologetically. 'I know. Of course. I just had to . . . You know.'

'I kept trying to tell you that I was seeing him . . .'

'I know.'

'You made me think I was crazy.'

Deena let out a fresh sob. 'I know. I know. I'm so sorry,

Mum. I should have listened to you – really listened to you. But it just sounded so . . . You know.'

Shirley scoffed, 'Because I'm old and barmy.'

'No!'

Bang.

Shirley looked towards the hallway. The banging was definitely coming from just beyond the living room. 'What the fuck is that noise?'

Deena wiped her eyes, and sniffed. 'It's . . . Tom. Tom figured it out. You told me you'd never seen Gabe outside these walls, right?'

Shirley shrugged. 'What does that have to do with that infernal racket?' And she tried to sidestep Deena and go to the door, but as she moved, she instantly felt dizzy.

'Use this,' Deena said, pressing her cane into her hand. She must have retrieved it from the front garden. Shirley was grateful but tried not to show it on her face. She just started hobbling to the door, with Deena close behind her. 'You asked Tom to do it, remember.'

'Do what? You're not making any sense,' Shirley barked, as she got to the door. Not much was making sense anymore.

Deena started to say something, but Shirley opened the door and went out into the hall. Artificial light flooded her vision, and she had to blink away a hazy blinding yellow. Then she saw the cause of the banging.

Tom was there – his towering, bulky frame just down the hall, past the kitchen door, holding something heavy.

It looked a bit like a battering ram, but he was holding it vertically, thrusting it into the ceiling. Bang.

'What the hell is going on?' Shirley shouted, and Tom jumped out of his skin, nearly dropping the battering ram on his foot.

'Fuckin' 'ell,' Tom said, as he bent his knees, regaining his grip on the battering ram and gearing up for another thrust.

Deena appeared at Shirley's side. 'We thought that maybe Gabe was living here, since this is the only place he's been seen. And then Tom remembered. The one place he could be that you didn't go to . . .' She wanted to go on, but Shirley held up a hand. Deena didn't need to say any more. Shirley knew what she was getting at.

And as if her knowledge was the key to this particular lock, Tom thrust the battering ram upwards and the attic hatch finally gave way. It shot up into the dark, into the attic – a place she hadn't been in years.

'Where's your ladder?' Deena asked.

Shirley told her where to find it, as she experienced another rush to the head. She rested against the wall, while Deena and Tom ran around, positioning the ladder under the hatch. Tom put one foot on the bottom step.

'No,' Shirley screeched, and they both jumped, before turning to her. 'It's my house. I'm going up first.' She launched herself forward and tried to ascend the ladder before Deena or Tom could say a word, but she didn't get very far. Trying to get up the ladder was harder than she thought, and she could only manage the first step. The steps were metal and hard and cut into her feet.

'Let me help you,' Tom said, and offered a shoulder. With Tom's help, she could manage to get herself up and finally she got through the hatch, finding her footing. She emerged into a red-hot, stuffy, pitch-black expanse. Last time she had been up here had been not long after she'd moved in, when she directed people to put things here she didn't need from the old house in Houghton-Le-Spring. Bob's stuff mainly, all the stuff she didn't throw out that she thought may have some value one day – his record collection, his old stacks of newspapers with key events in them, his motorcycle jackets. Even with everything up here, it was pretty empty. Or at least, it was supposed to be.

She turned on the attic light – and instantly wished she hadn't. The space had been transformed into a den – Gabe's den. All the boxes and piles of stuff were pushed to the sides of the space in stacks, making almost three walls. In the corner of this 'makeshift room' was a single mattress with a ragged pillow and a blanket that used to be a throw over Shirley's settee – it had disappeared about a year ago. Next to the mattress was a short stack of books, which Shirley recognised as Gabe's collection of science books from when he was a child. One was actually open on the mattress and looked like he was currently giving it some bedtime reading.

Along the back 'wall' was a free-standing railing, like one would see in a department store, with a selection of Gabe's old clothing on it. There was a reason Shirley only ever saw him in clothing she recognised and it had nothing to do with her memory. Below the railing was a bucket, which faintly smelled – and Shirley didn't really want to think what that was for.

'Holy shit.' Deena's voice, from behind her. She must have come up to see for herself. Shirley didn't pay any attention. She just moved her head to the left.

And what she saw was too much to process.

It was a long desk, with a broken, stained desk chair swivelled around the wrong way, looking at her. Above the desk was a whiteboard, covered with Gabe's unmistakable untidy scrawls. But that wasn't what caught her attention. She stepped forward to the desk – pushed the chair out of the way. What she saw was very familiar to her, and the whole picture came to her in pieces.

It was a radio deck – just like the ones she used at the hospital. A deck with so many knobs and sliders, you needed a manual to even know how to turn it on. The deck was connected to a monitor, turned on, that showed the exact same software she used when she was broadcasting. There was a pair of headphones plugged in, and Shirley had to stop herself from picking them up. She looked at the monitor, and knew without listening that nothing was playing. Next to the monitor, two more machines were plugged into the deck. One she knew well enough – a microphone. The other was a weird-looking thing that, if she had to guess, was some kind of signal amplifier. Propped up by the monitor was a smaller screen showing a black and white image that seemed to be cutting in and out – it was a view of the hallway, her hallway, from a corner of the ceiling. It was pointed at the front door.

'What the hell?' Tom had joined them now. Deena was quietly weeping somewhere behind Shirley. And Tom let out a string of expletives. She didn't have time for them. She had to figure this out. 'Must have put the breeze-blocks over the hatch, so you couldn't get up here when he was here,' Tom said, matter-of-factly.

The final piece of the puzzle came when she turned her attention to the whiteboard. She had to focus to read Gabe's handwriting after all these years. He had a doctor's handwriting – absolutely atrocious. His 'a's looked like 'e's, which looked a bit like his 'y's, and there was so much more wrong. First, she focused on the larger writing – lines going off them. There were three names, in big letters. One said – wait . . .

One said SEB STARITH.

Another said ROY FARROW.

She didn't want to look at the last one. So she looked at the smaller writing in bubbles. Phrases like 'Falls off ladder', 'Milk truck crashes into post box', 'Captured by CCTV' and 'Woman walks in front of truck'. At the edge of the whiteboard was a hand-drawn list titled OBSERVATIONS, with dates and times listed below.

It was obvious now. Somehow, Gabe was the presenter of Mallet AM. He was the one she had been listening to all along. The station was operating out of her own bungalow. It made sense – it was close to the hospital, which was why she had been able to pick it up so clearly, but why it wasn't even faint at the police station. How did Gabe get the knowledge to set all this up? And how did he know what was going to happen? And she started to think as she turned her attention to the last name.

The last of the large writing said FRANK PETERSON.

She felt sick. There were two avenues her mind could go down. It would be so easy for her to fall back into science fiction, into believing that someone could see the future. It would be so easy to believe that Gabe was still the boy she remembered. But things were different now. And she lived in the real world – and she should have been looking at the whole situation that way to begin with.

So she turned to Deena and Tom, and kept it together as she said drily and truthfully, 'I think Gabe's in real trouble.'

02.02

Shirley had spent the night combing through the entire attic, looking for anything that could either prove or disprove her theories. Deena had tried to persuade her to rest, but she wasn't having any of it. Tom, surprisingly, came to Shirley's defence, to his detriment, as the two of them were having an argument down in the hall when Shirley came across a notebook that had all of Gabe's scribblings in. It seemed to be something of a diary, but instead it was called Observations. The rest of it seemed to be written in some kind of code. Shirley had looked up at the whiteboard – the dates and times. She took the first one – 09/10/13 23.16 and tried to find it in the book. She found it, but was none the wiser – Gabe had written 'Noose, World, Mikey'. Was this like a dream journal or something? She almost wished she could ask Arnie Enigma if he had that down in his scrapbook, but she couldn't trust him. She had flicked through the diary and tried to find anything about Starith, Farrow or

Peterson, but it was all just goobledegook. She was going to keep it anyway.

She had tried to use the computer, finding a mouse and keyboard hooked up below the desk. She had pulled them up and put them on it, using them to try to click around in the computer program she knew so well. But every time she tried to click, an exclamation sound alerted that she couldn't. A pop-up box just said 'ACCESS DENIED'. When she had tried to use the keyboard, the same thing happened.

She had turned over the entire rest of the attic, but found nothing else of worth. Instead, she put the diary on top of the stack of Gabe's science books and tried to pick them up. She couldn't, so she had to call Tom to come and get them and carry them downstairs. Shirley had resolved to stay up and start reading them – she had to get into Gabe's head, she had to understand his delusion.

When she was finally done, she realised that part of the reason she had been so meticulous about everything was that now she would have to talk to Deena.

And she did. She had sat Deena down and explained everything that had been happening the past few days. She didn't leave anything out – even the small heart attack (and at that point in the story, Deena almost looked like she was going to explode) – and when she was done, Deena just sat there. It was clear she didn't believe all of it, but that didn't matter.

'What do we do now?' Deena had said.

'I don't know,' Shirley had replied.

'You really think it's Gabe? That that man is Gabe?'

Shirley had passed Deena the diary she found in the attic. 'This is in Gabe's handwriting.'

'Coincidence,' Deena had said, putting it on the table without even looking at it.

Shirley had sighed. She couldn't blame Deena. She didn't even really know herself.

After a rough minute's silence, Deena had said. 'Well, we have to tell the police.'

Shirley had agreed, to start with, but then said 'No.' When Deena threw her hands up and asked why, Shirley said levelly, 'Because if we tell them, they won't let me see him first.'

So that was how Deena, Tom and Shirley ended up in a car outside the police station at 8.30 a.m. Deena was still expressing how much of a bad idea this was, as she had been all night. She seemed to have a knack for saying exactly the same thing in a thousand different ways. And she was saying it yet again, as well as outright refusing to take part in this and support her mother by going in, when Shirley looked at her watch, saw it was time, and got out.

'Mum, please, think about this,' Deena said through the open passenger window.

'He's my son,' Shirley snapped at her. 'I need to know why.'

'You really think that's Gabe in there, don't you?' Deena said.

Shirley turned and didn't answer. She didn't know the answer to that question, but she knew it lay inside.

Deena had said they were holding Gabe in an interview room while officers worked to actually understand what was going on.

When she went inside and asked a receptionist, who thankfully was not her friend Dave, to see Gabe, she was ushered into an interview room herself and told to wait. After a few minutes, a suited middle-aged detective came in, with a dazed expression and half a cup of fast-food restaurant coffee.

'Ms Steadman, hello,' he said, shaking her hand. 'I was going to ask you to come in this morning anyway, and then here you are.' He smiled and took out a notebook, putting it on the table between them. He started writing in it, even though she hadn't said anything yet. 'I'm DI Mike Fletchinder. Please call me Fletch. I'd just like to ask you a few questions about this whole situation so I can get a handle on what is really going on.'

Over the next half an hour, DI Fletchinder asked her about everything that had been happening. Shirley told him, actually happy to tell someone who was an un-known, a third party. She wondered if Fletch believed it – that she thought her dead son, who was actually very much alive, was just an illusion conjured up by her own fractured psyche. Fletch didn't seem to think it so radi-cal, as he just quietly scratched in his notebook. Shirley skirted around the issue of Mallet AM and Arnie Enigma and Frank Peterson, not lying but not telling the whole truth either. She lived in the happy middle, forging her own path through the past.

When she was done, DI Fletchinder very obviously

drew a line under everything in his notebook, and looked up, sighing. 'OK, I'm going to let you in to see him.'

'Can I ask?' Shirley said. 'That is definitely my son in there?'

Fletchinder gave a little sigh. He didn't know. 'You'll be able to tell that more than us. But from what he's told us so far, it's an interesting story at the very least. And you'll be able to get more out of him. I think you deserve some answers here, but you have to promise to share them with us. He's more likely to talk to you than any of us – sounds like you've had a lot of conversations in the past, but those conversations were on the wrong foot. He's your son – I don't need to tell you what to do. I'll give you twenty minutes in there.'

'Thank you, DI Fletchinder,' Shirley said.

'Fletch, please.'

'Fletch. Thank you, Fletch.'

DI Fletchinder sighed again and leant in. 'I will tell you this though. Later today, we're going to have to let him go.'

'What?' Shirley said sharply. It took her by surprise.

But as Fletchinder spoke, what he said made more sense. 'He's a squatter. The police acted and they got him out the property. He hasn't been violent to you at all, in the almost-year he has been there. In fact, all it seems that he does is sit and talk, and probably uses your toilet and eats your food when you're not there. He took advantage of you, yes, but he didn't commit any other crime.'

Yeah, he had her there. This would be the time to tell him about Mallet AM, and her feeling – no, conviction, that Gabe killed Frank Peterson. But if she told Fletchinder now, he might stop her from seeing him, and she needed answers first.

'Now,' Fletchinder continued, 'if it is confirmed that this man is your son, there is the pseudocide – sorry, the faking of his death – that is going to take some more looking into. I don't believe that it's technically illegal to do it, but he may have committed other crimes in the process. That and he is no longer a citizen of the United Kingdom, because he actually doesn't exist.' Fletchinder stabbed his temple with the end of his pen. 'It may not surprise you to learn I've never actually worked a pseudocide case before. I'm kinda flying blind here.'

'But if he has committed a crime,' Shirley affirmed, 'you're just releasing him?'

'We can't hold people just because we think they may have committed a crime,' Fletchinder explained, 'we need evidence – facts. I need time to build the case. We'll let him go, yes, but we'll be keeping tabs on him. We'll ask him not to leave the North East and, more importantly, we'll tell him he can't come back to your house. In the meantime, I'll be working to get a full picture. But you may also be able to help with that.'

'Yes,' Shirley said.

'Let's talk again later,' Fletchinder smiled, pocketing his notebook and getting up. 'And then you can talk to me about that thing you're not telling me.'

Shirley got up too, apprehensively. He was good, but

he didn't know exactly what she was hiding. She was hiding it for good reason. Yes, she thought Gabe might have done it. But maybe he had a good explanation for everything. Maybe Mallet AM had a source — where somehow someone knew of Frank Peterson's murder. She didn't know what to say, so she just said again, 'Thank you, DI Fletchinder.'

She followed him out of the room, listening to his stipulations about what would happen when she went into the next interview room — the room with her simultaneously alive and dead son. *Schrodinger's son*, she thought. All of the stipulations were pretty standard, and Fletchinder took out a bunch of keys and unlocked the door, reminding her that she had twenty minutes and no more. Shirley nodded and Fletchinder added, just before opening the door, 'Remember, don't get too close.'

He opened the door and Shirley took a deep breath. She went inside, with Fletchinder shutting the door behind her.

She tried to walk into the room as confidently as possible, but it was hard on unsteady feet. It was exactly the same as the interview room she had just left. A small room with a large table in the centre.

Gabe was sitting there, head down. His hands were shackled to the table with metal handcuffs that were glinting in the light of the single bulb hanging in the centre of the room. His hands were crossed in front of his face and he either didn't or chose not to hear her come in.

And she knew – she just knew. This was Gabe.

She felt sick – she actually almost retched. This was so fucked up. How did this happen?

'Gabe?' Shirley said.

He looked up. Something that definitely was in her head was how different he was. He had far more stubble than he did when he usually appeared. He obviously shaved when he was at Shirley's house. His eyes were also dancing with life, giving him a crazed look that she had never seen on him when he sat at the kitchen table. He looked like Gabe, yes, but far less like him than he had when Shirley had believed he was in her head. 'Hello, Shirley.' He sounded far less sure of himself as well. Maybe a night in this room had broken him.

'You can't call me Mum. Not even now?' Shirley sobbed.

Gabe sadly smiled and said, 'That's not how it works.'

Shirley would still believe she was conjuring him up if he hadn't been acknowledged by so many others.

And there was no doubt that this was her real son. The entire situation rushed up to meet her – attempted to overwhelm. Gabe was alive, he was right here – sitting in front of her. She had so many things to say, but all she could do was sink into the chair across from him and gasp. There wasn't enough air in the world for her.

'Why are you shocked?' Gabe said softly. 'Isn't you happy to see me?' That was an odd sentence. It was like he knew what to say and picked the wrong word. That wasn't like Gabe – he was always so articulate and well-spoken. Maybe this wasn't Gabe – just someone with his face. 'You saw me all the time for so long. I'm here now.'

Shirley didn't know which question would win the race to her mouth first. So when she said, 'How did you do it? Why did you do it? Why would you let me think you were dead?' it turned out it was a tie.

Gabe looked confused. 'Which question do . . . you want me to answer first?' His speech was soft, unconfident, fractured. What was wrong with him?

'How?'

Gabe seemed like that was the one he wanted to answer. He was almost proud as he talked about the plan, that night in 2012, dropping into the water, unlocking the shackles and floating to the surface. 'I was dead, and I'd never . . . never felt more alive. I knew, knew, knew I had to keep swimming if I was going to stay alive. I had to make my way back to the co-ordinates I had . . . memor . . . memorised. There I had a boat, small small motorboat to get back to the mainland. Then, in Iraq, I got a fake Iraqi passport, and started to make my way wherever I wanted. I lived there for a few years. Then I crossed to Syria, which was a wild couple of months. Then I chartered a flight to Austria and lived in the Austrian . . . um . . . pointy . . . yes, mountains for a few years. I wanted to stay there forever – but I couldn't find as much work as I wanted. The money started to run out and I knew without proper identification I was screwed. So, I did what everyone does. I found my way home.

'I stayed away for the longest time. Spent a while travelling England. Then I had to sleep on the avenues, the roads, I mean – the streets, yes. So I knew I would have

244

to squat somewhere. Then I saw, in the paper, an obit . . . oblong . . . habitual . . . obituu . . .'

'An obituary?' Shirley said sadly, and Gabe nodded. 'You saw your father was dead?' And there it was. Just another thing that Bob was responsible for. Even in death, he was still pulling the strings. He was still the wolf at the door.

'I knew I could . . . To come home. I hitched to Houghton-Le-Spring and found out you had sold the house. I was glad – that place, that place was full of of of . . .'

'Bad memories?' said Shirley, rescuing him.

'Yes,' Gabe said thankfully, slapping his forehead with a palm. His hand just reached and he had to duck to receive the slap. 'So I had to find you again. It took a while with no . . . pounds and no . . . contacts. But I found a guy in a pub who was willing to help. He . . . found you straight away. So I came to Chester-Le-Street and I found the bungalow. And as I watched, you came out and went off somewhere. With your cane.

'That's when I . . . Got it . . . Realised . . . too much time had passed. You had moved in, you had grown older . . . without me. I wanted to talk you, talk you about my everything. In my head, I would come . . . house . . . and it would just be like old times. But I knew that couldn't happen. So I broke in . . . I started to think about how I could be part of you . . . your life without you knowledge that I was there. That was when I found the attic . . . and I found a way to talk to you. Accidental.

'The first time you saw me . . . Do you remember?'

'You were at the kitchen table,' Shirley said. 'Just sitting there. Like nothing had ever happened. You looked older, not just physically but mentally, you were my Gabe but you weren't. I thought my mind had just made you look like you were to punish me in some way, to show me what you'd become. But it was so much worse than that – it was actually what you'd become.'

Gabe shook his head. 'Not what I mean . . . meant. I thought you were out. I'd been eating a sandwich. I thought you walked in . . . saw it . . . saw me. I thought it was done. My happy . . . little . . . existing . . . was over. But you didn't scream. You almost . . . seemed . . . happy.'

Shirley could feel the tears coming. She harshly sniffed them away. 'Of course I was happy. You're my son. I'm sitting here right now, happy beyond belief that you're alive.' *And sick to my stomach at the same time*, she thought, but didn't say that bit. 'No matter what has happened, or is happening.'

'I was happy too. I knew I could . . . make-believe. I was better when I was pretending, pretending to be Gabe. It seemed like all the . . . the . . . the . . . smoke, no, steam, no, fog, yes fog . . . went away. I was the old Gabe again, which I had to be for you.'

'What happened to you?' Shirley said. 'Why are you like this? Your speech?'

Gabe shrugged. 'Can't think . . . don't know. I came out the water like this. Sometimes words get stuck in my . . . in the back of my throat. So I like to pretend. I pretend to be Gabe . . .'

'You are Gabe.' Shirley tried to touch his hands, but without even a thought, he launched back – his wrists getting caught by the cuffs, the only reason he didn't end up falling back off his chair. Her motherly instinct to protect her own child was returning – thick and strong. Maybe she should have been more shocked – her son, she had grieved for, back from the dead? Shirley would have thought so herself. But in the cold moment, love was all she had in her heart.

Then Gabe brought her back down to Earth. 'Maybe I am Gabe, but I am more.'

Shirley stopped. 'More?' This was what she was fearing, the shift in the conversation that had to happen. Surprisingly though, Gabe had done it instead of her. 'Do you pretend to be a presenter too?'

Gabe looked a little perturbed. 'You've been up in the . . . upstairs?'

'The attic, yes.'

Gabe nodded. 'When I'm the presenter, I can talk normally. I'm Mallet when I can be. Pretend.'

Shirley went into her bag, and placed Gabe's notebook on the table. She noted his reaction, or more accurately, lack of one. 'What is Mallet AM, Gabe? You're pretending you can look into the future? What for, what reason is there to do that? And then, when your predictions don't come true . . . what then? You make sure they do.'

This got to Gabe. He looked incredibly angry in a flash. He slammed his hands down on the table. 'No, no, no, no, NO. Shirley. No. I have . . . I have . . . I have . . . See . . . See . . . No.'

Shirley tried to calm him down. 'OK. OK, Gabe. Take a deep breath. You're all right. Just you need to tell me what Mallet AM is. You persuaded me to carry on listening. And I did. You need to take me back to the beginning.'

Gabe breathed in and out. Shirley could almost see in his eyes how he was travelling back in time. Shirley expected him to launch into a grand story, but instead he said simply, 'I have the sight.'

'What does that even mean?' Shirley said incredulously.

And finally the story began, 'It started on the . . . boat. I saw how . . . I dreamed how . . . I was going to do it. How I was going to die myself. I wanted to, after Dad. I wanted to kill myself, more than anything. I did everything for that man, and he threw it back in my face. He threw it back at me like I was . . . not anything . . . nothing to him.'

Shirley allowed herself some tears then. She would have tried to touch Gabe again, if she wasn't afraid of the reaction. 'I'm so sorry, Gabe. It was my fault. I should have done more, more to protect you. But I didn't, I couldn't. I was stuck.'

Gabe was shaking his head. She was worried what that meant, before he said, 'It wasn't you. You didn't send me behind . . . back . . . AWAY. He did. When I heard he died . . . I saw his obituary . . . why do you think I read it . . . I always kept searching for it. On library computers. One day . . . I finally saw it. I was so happy, I thought it was crazy . . . how happy I could be that someone d-d-died. I liked to think I was a good person, but he made me something else.

'But I was talking about the sight . . .' Gabe said, changing the subject. Shirley was glad. The more he talked about Bob, the more her heart broke. 'The sight started when I knew how I was going to do it. And I did it. And when I came out of the water, it grew stronger. I started to dream about real people – but people I didn't . . . ken. KNOW. Things happening to people. But to-morrow. A day in advance. I can see a day in advance. I know it sounds craze, I know it sounds stupid, but I need you to truth me . . . I can see the future.'

Shirley watched him as he said it. He really believed it – honesty and wholly. Was his delusion really so strong that he could believe something that wouldn't be out of place in the shows he watched as a kid? 'Gabe, that can't happen. That is not a thing that can happen. Don't you see that?'

Gabe looked confused. 'But you believed? You believe it. You told me.'

Shirley chuckled at her son's hubris. 'I believed it when it was ladders toppling over and milk trucks crashing. I even believed it when it was the threat of a man dying. I tried to help him. But when Frank Peterson died – it made it so much more real. This isn't some fan-tasy, it's the real world, Gabe. Remember, that's where you are – you may have successfully faked your own death, which is fantasy in its own right, but at least that is in the realm of possibility. Cognition can be changed, altered. Telling the future is impossible.

'Did you see me when you had your premonition about Frank Peterson? Did you see me standing in his kitchen, over his body, with his bloody cat drinking a puddle of beer. Did you see a man in a trench coat and a flat cap peering in at me? I doubt you did, did you?' Gabe just sat and listened. He didn't even shake his head. Shirley may have thought she was getting through to him if she didn't know her son better. He was stubborn, proud, and the look on his face was a familiar one. 'And I think, that whatever has happened to you, whatever happened to your brain . . . it won't let you accept that you can't tell the future. So when whatever voice told you Frank Peterson was going to die, you couldn't handle it. So you went out and you made sure it happened just the way you said it did.'

Gabe snarled, 'No, no, no, no.' He slapped his forehead repeatedly and then slammed the desk. 'I can see. I have the sight. I tell people, I report it. Because people need to know. Know what is coming.'

Shirley shook her head — wished she could believe Gabe. 'No, Gabe. I'm sorry, but no. I think you killed Frank Peterson because you were scared that you couldn't tell the future.'

'I DIDN'T DO IT,' he shouted, trying to stand up, but the handcuffs pulled him back down into his chair. For the first time, Shirley was afraid of her son. Judging by his expression, he was a little afraid of himself too. 'I didn't do it,' he said, softer. 'I need you to . . . believe me. I can show you.'

'Go on then,' Shirley said. It was really very simple.

'What's going to happen tomorrow?'

Gabe said nothing.

'What's going to happen tomorrow?'

Still nothing. And this time he looked away too.

Shirley shouted, 'What's going to happen tomorrow, Gabe?'

Gabe whipped his head back to her and hissed, 'I can't tell you that.'

'Convenient, isn't it?'

'No,' Gabe said, matching her volume, 'I can't tell you that, because it doesn't do that way. HAPPEN. Doesn't happen.'

'What do you mean?'

Gabe laughed. 'You have to see, time is a . . . a . . . You think time is a line, but it's more like a . . . a . . . a . . .' He slapped his forehead, clearly annoyed he couldn't find the word. 'A scattergraph. If two points, no worry where they are, line up on the same . . . line. I have seen. Seen a day in advance for so long.'

'Then why can't you tell me about tomorrow?'

'That's what I'm trying to say you. I can't tell you about tomorrow because today has already happened. And how it happened was not me telling you about to-morrow. And I can't change things. This is just today – retold.'

Shirley saw what he meant, but it still sounded like an excuse. And she was tired of hearing them. She took the diary back and put it in her bag, getting up. 'I should tell the police what you did.'

'No,' Gabe said, panicked. 'If you do that, the police

251

will look . . . find . . . focus on me, they will let the real killer go way. GET AWAY. You have to give my way a chance.'

Shirley looked down at him. Gabe – sitting there, living and breathing. The old Gabe would never kill anyone – he didn't have it in him. But the new Gabe had already killed someone – himself. Didn't that show a level of violence? A level which could be replicated. There was no doubt that Gabe believed the shit he was spouting, but she couldn't. But, as she got to the door and looked back on his poor frame sitting there, was there any chance? She was his mother, and if that wasn't a free card for a benefit of the doubt, she didn't know what was. 'OK,' she said, 'I'll tell the police in one day. Tomorrow morning. You have one day to do what you like.' Gabe looked nervous. 'After all, it's all already happened, right?' She left Gabe to his handcuffs and his table, and stepped outside.

Fletch was there, waiting. Shirley hoped that he wasn't listening in, but his first remark put paid to her concerns. 'Did he say anything useful?' and then he saw her face. 'Are you OK?'

Shirley touched her face, and wiped away tears. She had been crying. She didn't realise quite how much. 'I'm fine. It's just a shock, you know.' She wasn't lying. With the whole Mallet AM situation to hide behind, she had forgotten how utterly crazy Gabe's presence was. Other people could see him now too, because he was really there. 'From now on, he's going to fully co-operate with the police.'

'He told you that?'

'No,' Shirley said, taking her cane and starting to walk away, 'it's just a prediction.'

Fletchinder didn't follow her, in fact she thought she heard him going into Gabe's interview room. She wondered what they would talk about, but realised that she had too much to think about without that. Gabe had been genuine and adamant when she had said she was going to tell them he killed Frank Peterson. What did he say? – that would focus the police on him when they should be finding the real killer. He'd said it so strongly, when he struggled to say everything else.

She walked past the front desk to leave and then stopped. She went up to the desk. 'Excuse me.' She asked about the death of Frank Peterson. She said she'd seen it on the news – and she hoped to God that it had actually been reported by real news outlets and not just Mallet AM.

Thankfully, the officer didn't skip a beat. 'We're look-ing into the death of Frank Peterson, yes of course. We have a number of leads, which obviously I can't disclose. May I ask why you want to know?'

'My friend lived near him,' Shirley said, 'just old lady gossip.' Now she was just straight-up lying to the police. Great. But she suffered so much shit for being an old lady, it was actually refreshing for once to use it to her advantage.

'Who's your friend?' the officer asked, getting ready to write it down.

'Colleen Adams,' she said, apologising to Colleen in her head.

The officer seemed to get that too. 'It's OK. We just need some background. Guy kept himself to himself a lot. Hard to find people to talk about him. Tell your friend not to worry.'

Shirley nodded. She went to leave, but as she walked up to the door, it opened and Dave the Police Officer marched in – the officer that had known she was talking about Frank Peterson's murder before it happened. She held her breath and kept her head down, but Dave was on his phone and didn't even look up. He knew someone was there, as he held the door open, but he was so fixated on whatever was happening on his little screen that she'd be amazed if he even saw her feet as she crossed him and left the station.

'Yo,' she heard Dave say to the officer at the desk, 'any luck finding that person of interest I met yesterday?' The door shut and Shirley couldn't hear the rest of the conversation. She almost laughed – Dave was talking about her and if he had just looked up, he would have seen her. Modern technology.

'No,' the officer at the desk said. 'But we've identified the suspect.'

And Shirley's hand shot out and clutched the door to keep it ajar. She had to know the name.

But she wasn't ready for it.

'Suspect's a wash-up called Colm MacArthur.'

A name she hadn't heard in a long time.

02.03

Shirley couldn't stomach another car ride with Deena and Tom. She went out to see them and stood by Deena's window and told her she was going to walk home.

'Mum, what happened in there?' Deena said, rolling her window down.

'I'll talk to you later,' Shirley said, starting to walk away.

'You can't walk all the way home. You've just had a heart attack,' Deena called after her.

And Shirley knew that her daughter would have got out of the car and forced her to come with them if Tom hadn't muttered, 'Let her walk if she wants.' Tom to the rescue again, and the sacrificial victim to Deena's ire as she turned her anger on him. As Deena started to say something, Shirley thankfully got out of earshot.

She walked up the street, away from the police station. She had so much to think about, none of it good, and she thought the pain she would start to feel halfway

255

there, probably as she was just approaching the Front Street hill, would be a nice accompaniment to her mental pain.

She started to ascend the hill, thinking each stab of pain was more than deserved. What a mess this was becoming. How did it all get so complicated so quickly? Two weeks ago, she was just a normal old lady. But two weeks ago she also had a dead son and extremely limited reasons to leave the house.

Gabe was here. And he was caught up in all of this. So was she. And Callie. And Arnie Enigma.

And now . . . Colm. How did he figure into the puzzle that was Mallet AM? She hadn't seen Colm for years – last time must have been when she spotted him going into a pub in town maybe five years ago. They hadn't talked and he hadn't seen her. But now he was back in her life, or at least his name was. As a suspect in Frank Peterson's murder.

But the biggest suspect was Gabe himself.

She tried to clear her mind – just focus on walking. Hoping for some clarity.

It took Shirley just over two and a half hours to get home. It would take an able-bodied person less than half that. But she did stop along the way, at Starith's bakery – not on business, but pleasure. A strange man was behind the counter, someone she hadn't seen before. Obviously they had had to get someone else in, while Starith recovered from his fall. She bought some tiger bread, and as she was leaving, she received a call from Deena. She was surprised it had taken her this long.

Deena was none too happy about being left in the car park, and even less happy when Shirley gave answers she described as 'aloof' and 'flippant'. She wanted the entire story on Gabe and Shirley couldn't bring herself to repeat everything he told her. She had ended the call by saying that if Deena wanted to know, she should go and see Gabe herself. And then she'd hung up.

As she'd got to the top of Front Street, and passed Chester-Le-Street Hospital — a place that seemed part of her so long ago (even though it was merely a few days) — she realised that, to an outside party, it would appear that herself and Deena hated each other. It wasn't that — they had a strained relationship, true, but it was a strain built on love. No matter how much they wound each other up, there was a mutual understanding that each only ever wanted the best for the other. Even though Deena did piss her the fuck off a lot of the time, and she was sure the feeling was mutual.

For a more traditional and by-the-numbers mother-child relationship, herself and Gabe used to get on like a house on fire. They used to play in the garden when he was a child, she used to listen to his problems when he was a teen and he used to listen to hers when they were adults. They used to talk on the phone all the time. And then it all changed.

Shirley used to stay up at an unreasonable time when Gabe was halfway around the world, just on the off-chance that he would call. Most times he wouldn't, he was busy after all. But sometimes he did — and they would sit there and talk until Shirley saw the sunrise, and heard the horrible sounds of Bob stirring in the up-stairs bedroom.

She remembered getting the call about Gabe. She had stayed up as usual, hoping for a call – she had to tell Gabe about the new woman at embroidery – someone who in years to come would become her friend – Edna, and her unreasonable love of canaries. She was also slightly apprehensive to find out about Gabe's sleeping. The last time they had talked, Gabe had revealed that he hadn't had a full night's sleep in about a month. He'd been plagued with hyper-realistic dreams and night-mares that he had trouble distinguishing from reality. Shirley had been troubled by this, mostly because she knew what the lack of a good's night sleep could bring (she'd been experiencing it for years), but also because she couldn't do anything to help. Gabe might as well have been on another planet and her only connection to that planet was a voice through a speaker.

She had picked up the phone on the first ring, expect-ing to hear his voice. Instead though, there came a plain, almost alien tone. The man said there had been an inci-dent. As he shared his fairy tale, she broke down – she cried and wailed, so much so that a six-beer-deep Bob woke up. He clattered downstairs, effing and blinding, and he only got worse when he saw the shuddering and screaming Shirley. He snatched the phone from her and barked over the phone. And then he listened to what the plain man had to say.

Bob never cried. Bob never said a word. Bob never comforted his wife or his daughter. He just doubled down on his life – he was more vicious, more thirsty, more abusive. And that made Shirley hate him more than she ever thought possible.

The times after that were the darkest times, before Bob thankfully had a pulmonary embolism and passed away in his chair, in front of the horse racing. Communication between the two of them was gone – they didn't talk to each other except when Bob wanted something. The contents of the fridge became over fifty per cent beer. She supposed Bob was showing his grief in his own way – although grief seemed like a strong word. It was like he was just showing that things had changed.

It turned out Shirley was still giving him too much credit though. One night, after a particularly long session at the pub, Bob came home to find Shirley crying at the kitchen table – the same kitchen table that was now in her new bungalow in fact. Bob had staggered around her, getting another beer or three from the fridge. He had held them all in one hand, one slipping away and bouncing on the floor. As he'd retrieved it, his and Shirley's eyes met.

'Wha' the fuck are you crying 'bout?' he had said.

Shirley didn't say anything at first, but the crazy, drunk fire in Bob's eyes scared her into an answer. 'Why do you think I'm crying?'

'Not still fuckin' Gabe, is it?' he'd said, like it was nothing. 'I'm fuckin' glad, you know wha'? Least I can say I've got a dead son now, and not whateva the fuck 'e was. Killing 'imsel' was the bes' thin' 'e ever did'

That was the only moment in Shirley's life when she'd ever considered killing someone. The knife block was behind Bob, behind his shoulder on a shelf. She could have easily got there before him. Or if she didn't feel like chancing going past him, she could pick up her mug of tea, slam it into the table until it shattered and drive a shard of it into Bob's throat. Or, failing that, she could launch herself at him — he was stronger, but she would claw at him and punch him until his face and, most likely, her hands were a pulp.

But she didn't kill him. She didn't say anything. And a moment of possible murder became her 'could have been' moment. That moment would be one she ruminated on for years to come. It would have been worth it — and she thought she owed it to Gabe. She still did, even though now the tables had turned — Bob was dead and somehow, some way, Gabe was alive.

She thought on how odd that felt, all the way home — so much so that she didn't feel her limbs ache and didn't notice how much it felt like she was dragging more and more of herself along.

She took her cane inside, as she thought she may need it to get up now. Moggins had been sitting, poised on the second rung of the ladder. Shirley had told Tom to leave the attic hatch open with the ladder ready for her to go up and sort through some of Gabe's things. Deena made her promise that she wouldn't go up there without someone else present, which she accepted easily. It wasn't like she was going to adhere to it, but if it made her daughter feel better, it was fine enough to say.

What was that she thought earlier about how they were bitches to each other?

After giving Moggins a treat, she sat down in Bob's chair in the living room, but she couldn't settle. And finally she knew why. She spent the next hour thoroughly searching the house for anyone. Gabe had been living here for at least a year and she hadn't known and that gave her a deep feeling of unease she couldn't shake. And even though Gabe was absolutely still at the police station, and probably wouldn't return even if he wasn't, she still felt the need to check. But the house was empty – she even stuck her head through the attic hatch to look at the new room that she didn't even know she had.

She sat back in the chair, cane propped against the arm. Moggins jumped up on her lap and started to purr. She stroked him, scratching his chin just where he liked it. And she found her eyes closing.

And finally she was allowed to sleep.

02.04

A constant knocking. Loud.

Shirley's eyes opened. The first thing she noticed was that her hands were stiff – just like they usually were overnight. She forgot where she was – it was dark and cold. As she looked, she saw the shadows of the furniture in the front room. And then it all came back to her. She was sitting in Bob's chair. She had fallen asleep – a deep and long slumber with no dreams and no nightmares. Apparently, her mind thought that her real life was dreamlike enough. She felt well rested but achy. Moggins had gone from her lap – who knows how long he had been gone.

Knock. Knock. Knock.

The front door.

She took her cane and pulled herself up. She was expecting Deena, although she thought her daughter would probably just let herself in again if it was her. After the Gabe situation, Deena would probably never

262

leave her alone now. She hobbled into the hallway and got to the front door, opening it.

To her surprise, Callie was standing there, in her nurse uniform. She rushed to Shirley and hugged her. Shirley felt an amazing rush of warmth at seeing the young woman and she melted into her arms, as though she let go of all the stress she had been feeling the past few days, and Callie was holding her up. 'Is it true?' Callie said, over her shoulder.

'Yes,' Shirley gasped, 'it's true. How did you know?'

'Deena phoned me.'

'What?'

'We've been in contact this whole time. It's not important right now.'

Shirley had questions, but she had to agree. Callie took Shirley into the living room, where Shirley told her about everything. Absolutely everything. Gabe and his story. Her seeing Gabe around the house. Gabe's hideout and Mallet AM. And finally how she thought Gabe had to be a murderer, as he had seemingly gone mad.

Callie grew misty-eyed at points, but she never outright cried. She was stronger than most. She just kept listening, hanging on Shirley's every word, until Shirley was done. And then she sat back on the settee and looked deep in thought. 'I want to see him,' Callie said. It was clear that it wasn't going to be real for her until she did. And Shirley didn't blame her. This whole thing was so fucked up that one just had to see it for oneself. It was clear her real emotion was being held back for then.

'Of course you do,' Shirley said. 'He's at the police

station, but they're not keeping him for long. I don't know where he will go after that.'

'I really can't see Gabe as a killer.' Callie shook her head. 'I agree that there is no other explanation. But, still, it just doesn't seem right.'

'Something's happened to him. When he's not pretending to be someone else, he struggles for his words, like he can't get them out. I think something happened, when he was in the water.'

'And he was here all this time . . .' Callie remarked, marvelling at it. 'And Mallet AM was here too. The signal must be strong here.'

'Yes.'

'But wait, didn't you say you tried to get Mallet AM on the radio in this room once? And you couldn't find it?'

That was true. 'Yes, I did try,' Shirley said, remembering, 'but Gabe was here. He was sitting in this chair when I tried. So the radio wouldn't have been online.' It was all coming together in her mind. Gabe was definitely clever – he had the perfect set-up. But something was niggling at her – how Gabe had tried to guide her to carry on searching for Mallet AM. It was like he was proud of it – like he wanted an audience. It didn't sound like Gabe, but then he didn't sound like Gabe anymore. 'It's so odd, seeing him again. When I've been seeing him for so long. But I really see him now. I don't know, maybe I'm talking rubbish.'

'No, I understand,' Callie said. 'Can I make you a cup of tea or something?'

Shirley laughed drily. 'One thing I'm done with is fucking cups of tea. I think there's a bottle of whisky on top of the kitchen cupboards. You could get me one of those.'

Callie smiled. 'Well, I'd like to say I wasn't fishing for that but . . .' She left the sentence open-ended as she went into the kitchen and quickly came back with two crystal glasses, which Bob had won in a raffle. She placed one in front of Shirley. Shirley picked it up with hands that felt fractured. She almost joked that she would have liked a straw, but instead Callie said, 'At the start, I didn't believe he was dead. I went through all the stages of grief. Then I hated Bob, no way as much as you must have done. Then I finally let go. And I moved on. And now, now I know that he's alive, it's all coming back. Every single emotion all at once. And I know you must be feeling it so much worse than me.

'I see Gabe everywhere too. But it turns out my Gabes were actually not real and I knew it. It was so odd, when you showed me Mallet AM, when I heard him. I know he put some computer shit over his voice, but I think I somehow knew that presenter was Gabe. I know that's easy to say in hindsight, but there was something in his diction, or the way he said words, constructed sentences, that just made me know. So when Deena told me, I wasn't shocked. I was every other emotion under the sun – but not shocked. Somehow I just knew.'

'I remember sitting across from him,' Shirley said, the both of them taking a long drink from their glasses, 'and just thinking that I would trade anything, anyone, for him to be real. And it turns out he always was.'

'So even with this, even with everything – everything he's done, the whole life we have now without him, the life he has without us,' Callie said, 'your son is alive. Isn't that worth it all?'

Shirley didn't need to think. She had been thinking the answer all day, just feeling guilty for it. She let a smile escape her lips. 'Yes, it is.'

They fell into a contented silence and Shirley was almost sad when she had to interrupt it. Because she had one burning question for Callie.

'This may be a little random, but do you keep in touch with Colm MacArthur?'

Callie raised an eyebrow, and then tipped her head – not a nod or a shake. 'Yeah – I guess he should know.'

Shirley was so wrapped up in her intended line of questioning that she had to think about what Callie was saying. But, of course, she was right. Colm had a right to know that Gabe was still alive. Gabe's death had had a profound effect on him – of course it had. It was why he had started his downward spiral, and why he had been discharged from the Navy. Lord knew how unkind time had been to him since. 'Yes,' Shirley said, 'he should know.'

'We don't talk – he got a little intense after . . .' Callie trailed off. 'But I think I have his number somewhere.'

'Good, we should contact him.'

Callie opened her mouth to speak, but something happened that instantly changed the mood. There was a sound, a clicking – from far off, somewhere in the house.

And then, faint music suddenly wafted through the air. Music that sounded incredibly familiar. Shirley and Callie looked at each other, exchanging confused looks.

'Can you hear that?' Shirley asked.

Callie nodded, looking around to the hallway. 'Gabe?'

Shirley shook her head. 'I don't think so.' She pushed herself up from the chair. 'But that music is awfully familiar. I just can't place it.' It was an instrumental track. Synthetic instruments playing a chintzy tune.

Callie was up first, of course. She went to the door and was out in the hall before Shirley even reached a standing position. Once Shirley was in the hall too, Callie was standing at the foot of the ladder under the attic hatch. 'I think it's coming from up there.'

Shirley tensed. Maybe it was Gabe. Because that was where she knew the music from − it was the lift music that preceded a Mallet AM broadcast. Callie went to step on the ladder, and Shirley harshly whispered, 'Take this.' She held out her cane. Callie raised her eyebrows, shook her head and went up the ladder, sticking her head through the hatch.

After a heart-pounding few seconds, her head reappeared. 'He's not here,' she said. 'But the computer's on. It's broadcasting.'

Callie got up into the attic and helped Shirley get up too. The room was illuminated by the light of the computer monitor. It was still showing the radio programme, but now there was a steady waveform going across it. Shirley turned the attic light on, and Callie instantly gasped.

'He lived up here?'

Shirley didn't pay attention to her, couldn't. She went to the computer. She tried to click on the waveform but got the usual Access Denied notice. She found that she could access some options in the top bar, but nothing like starting or stopping the broadcast. She was truly locked out. She'd never seen anything like it at the hospital radio.

'Jesus,' Callie said, 'he must have gone mad up here alone.'

She didn't know the half of it. As Shirley continued to fiddle with the computer, the lift music started to fade out, and she saw a spike in the waveform coming up. Sure enough, the music changed, something louder. The folk music that usually came after the lift music was starting. The folk music that came before . . . But Gabe wasn't here – there couldn't be a news broadcast. Unless . . .

She couldn't see what was coming up, because she couldn't click on the programme. All they could do was wait.

'What the hell?' Callie said behind her and Shirley turned to see Callie picking up the bucket.

'I wouldn't do that,' Shirley said, but it was too late.

Callie retched and had to launch herself away.

Shirley turned back to the computer. 'I think the programme is going to go ahead.'

Callie recovered, spluttering, and then came over. 'But Gabe isn't here. That would mean it would have to be . . . But Gabe didn't know he was going to get caught, did he? So how would it be . . . ' She trailed off, evidently thinking all the ramifications which Shirley had just thought of herself.

The folk song – this time about the process of shearing sheep and how that was somehow inexplicably linked to the concept of love – started to fade out, and Shirley found herself holding her breath. There was no way – it was impossible, it had to be.

The song ended and there was the usual silence. Shirley willed it to continue – as if such a thing was possible. But then –

'And that was The Old Mill Gang with "Wool and Wishes".' Gabe's voice, recorded, garbled and scrambled by the computer. He was talking clearly and with purpose – nothing like how he talked at the police station. She knew what Callie meant – now she knew it was Gabe, it was so obvious. 'They really are a great local band. I mean, I remember when I first heard them back in 2008, I believe . . .' As he continued to talk about the band, Shirley had a thought. She navigated to the top bar on the monitor, the only place she was allowed to click, and searched through her available options. She found what she was looking for – VOICE. In a few clicks, she fixed it. '. . . Anyway that was just a quick story . . .'

'Wait, it's just Gabe's voice now,' exclaimed Callie. 'If he does sound a bit bravado-y.'

'I turned off the distortion, and the masking,' Shirley explained.

'. . . So I guess we've stalled long enough, let's get into what everyone – and by everyone, I mean one person . . .' – Shirley gasped. Did he mean her? – '. . . is waiting for: the news!' How was this happening? If Gabe reported the news now for tomorrow, it meant he knew further than a day in advance. 'It's Mallet AM, and today is Wednesday the seventeenth of February 2021.'

Tomorrow. So Gabe had set this up and pre-recorded it knowing he was going to get found out and be spending this news cast in a police interrogation room? Or was this just some kind of failsafe, if he was ever away from the desk? She had no idea, but she had to focus on what he was saying now. She glanced at Callie and saw that her concentration was matched.

'Let's see what we have up for today's news. As always, we have three items, and there's the usual mix of stuff.' It was as if she was being talked to directly. He might as well have said, 'We have two items of guff, and then one thing you actually care about.'

'First up, we have even more developments on Chester-Le-Street Leisure Centre. Tired of it yet? Because we sure are! Especially seeing that the demolition appears to be going full steam ahead. Today saw the pool getting drained. That's over 30,000 litres of water just sucked up into a big truck and taken away. That means that currently at the deep end of the swimming pool, there is an eight-foot drop. That's a long way down! Meanwhile, the kiddie pool only has a three-foot drop, but that's still a good stumble. The Leisure Centre is now cordoned off with high fences to make sure no youths get into the derelict building. I imagine an abandoned swimming pool would be a wicked spot to goof off, drink and smoke

– but, alas, it seems impenetrable.' Conjecture again. Easy stuff to start with.

'Next up, we have an explosive situation at Piroetti's Italian Restaurant. Yesterday, after the broadcast, the restaurant prematurely closed after a heated row between the married owners, Jim and Jan. The two were seen coming to blows in the car park after Jan walked out of service after a customer refused to pay for his meal as it was over two hours late. Jan was seen escorting the customer out and then refused to come back in. Jim, who is usually the head chef, went out to see her and Jan was seen giving him a slap! Someone call Gordon Ramsay. This is one real kitchen nightmare!' Easy to predict. Jim and Jan of Piroetti's were infamous for their fiery tempers. It would have been a more radical future if they weren't slapping each other in the car park tomorrow.

'And, lastly, we bring you some more shocking news.'

Shirley tensed. She needed to hear, but she would have done anything to take a young pair of legs and go running as far as she could. She knew she was about to hear her son planning to kill someone else, and she tried to prepare herself.

Unfortunately, nothing could prepare her for the words that Gabe said, 'Local legend, Marsha Thompson, 85, has passed away in the home of friend Colleen Adams.' Her world dropped from under her. Marsha . . . 'It seems that Colleen was hosting a meeting of some kind, when Marsha excused herself. She was found later on the upstairs landing dead. It is unclear at this time what exactly happened – whether she died of natural

271

causes, or was killed. Unconfirmed reports say she was murdered, possibly by a laceration to the throat. Colleen Adams and the other members of the gathering are said to be shocked. Police do not suspect any of the members of the gathering and are instead said to be looking for a male suspect. This may be victim number two of the killer known as the Chester Terror. This could indicate that we are looking at an individual who is intent on continuing to reign his vengeance over the town. Is this the start of something, or is it the end? We don't know, but we know we'll be here reporting every single step!

'Up next, we have more lovely synthetic music to try to take your mind off the bleakness of the news. This is the world-famous Track 5 from freemusic.org/funky.' Gabe stopped talking and a moment later music started. Shirley wasn't listening by that point.

She couldn't believe what she just heard. Her entire body was shaking. Marsha Thompson was going to die tomorrow at Colleen Adams' house. The embroidery meeting. She was going to die at the embroidery meeting. It was absurd – but there it was. Gabe had known it had been moved to tomorrow somehow – and he knew that Marsha was going to die. And she was almost sure that Gabe was going to do it.

The radio – Gabe – hadn't given her as much to go on as Frank Peterson, and definitely not as much as Starith or Farrow's mishaps. There was no exact time, only an exact place, and certain parameters. That would make it harder to stop but also give her less to obsess over. So maybe it would actually make it better. After all, she wasn't going to have to invent a reason to be at the scene.

But why would Gabe do this? Why would he target a defenceless old woman? Unless it was to spite her?

There were two paths forming in her mind.

One – Gabe was being clever. He was inventing a narrative to cover a murder spree. Maybe he needed it to justify it to himself. Maybe he was watching when Marsha was being an absolute bitch to her in the house last week and he found his latest mark. Why Frank Peterson then? It wasn't a cast-iron theory.

Or two – Gabe actually believed he foresaw this murder and was now convincing himself he had to carry it out. Why? Buggered if she knew. Maybe he thought something bad was going to happen if he didn't – something like the world would end or time would fracture, or anything from the pages of his science-fiction books.

Seeing Gabe that morning, hearing him speak about 'the sight' – it killed her that option two actually seemed more likely. But something was broken in her son. Something was seriously wrong.

'You know her,' Callie said, standing back from the desk and regarding Shirley, 'this Marsha Thompson?'

'Yes,' Shirley replied, 'she's a stubborn so-and-so, and I'll do you one better – I'm supposed to be at Colleen Adams' house tomorrow afternoon. It's the weekly embroidery meeting. I'm going to be there. I'm going to be there when she dies.'

'Then we can stop it,' Callie said. 'We can stop Gabe, and if it's not Gabe, we can stop whoever's going to do it.'

Shirley ran a thumb across her forehead, a stress thing she had done ever since she was a child. Callie was still in denial. 'Who else could it be, Callie? Gabe thinks he "foresaw" this, and now he's got to make sure it happens.'

'Gabe's not a murderer.'

'No, Gabe wasn't. But this new person, this new Gabe, I don't know. He did all this, didn't he? This whole radio thing. He pre-recorded the news, just so he wouldn't miss a night. He's being calculating, clever.'

'Clever would be not advertising a murder.'

Shirley started to say something but realised she didn't know what it was going to be. 'This doesn't matter right now. All that matters is we know when the next murder is going to take place.'

'You're right,' Callie said. 'The only thing we know for sure is that this crime is going to happen.'

'I have the information for tomorrow on my phone,' Shirley remembered, 'it's downstairs in my bag.'

Ten minutes, and a rather precarious trip down the attic ladder, later, they were back in the living room. Shirley looked around for her bag and finally found it, pulling out her phone, barely even registering the pain she felt when she bent down. She unlocked the screen and her heart skipped a beat. She had an answerphone message. She rang the relevant number and put it to her ear.

'Put it on speaker,' Callie said.

'How do you do that?' Shirley asked, looking at the phone screen.

'This button.' Callie pressed it.

The automated voice filled the room, saying Shirley had one new message. It began: 'Hello, Ms Steadman, it's DI Fletchinder here, from Chester-Le-Street Constabulary.'

'Shit,' said Shirley, already knowing what Fletchinder was going to say.

'I thought it best to call just to let you know we have, as I warned earlier, just had to release your son, Gabriel Steadman. We can't hold him on any official grounds, although he has been advised that if he attempts to enter your property or approach yourself, he is to be subject to further arrest. We are still looking into whether he committed any crime as a direct result of his pseudocide . . .'

'What's pseudocide?' Callie whispered.

'Faking your own death,' Shirley whispered back quickly. 'I think.'

'. . . but this process could take a while, and legally we aren't allowed to detain him. I understand this may put you in a bit of a difficult situation, but if Mr Steadman goes against police wishes and decides to contact you in any way, please let us know immediately and we can have blues and twos over there right away. I will let you know as soon as I have any more information. Speak soon.'

Shirley didn't heed the advice of the automated voice, neither saving nor deleting the message. She just hung up. 'Gabe is out.'

'Do you think he'll come here?' asked Callie. There was almost a hint of excitement in her voice, and Shirley gawked at her. Callie shrank back and Shirley felt a little guilty. Callie hadn't seen Gabe in ten years, thought he was dead for most of that – there had to be some kind of hope there. She felt sorry for her.

'He won't come here. But he'll know one thing,' Shirley said. 'He'll know I heard the broadcast. Whether he foresaw it or not. And he'll know that I'm going to be there. He'll have prepared for the fact I might try to stop him.'

Callie thought for a second. 'But he won't know I'm going to be there too.'

Shirley didn't know what to say. 'What?'

'I said, I'm with you. I'm going to help you.'

Shirley felt tears prick her eyes. But she drove them away with a sniff. She felt a little dizzy and Callie must have seen it as she caught her by the arms. 'Thank you.'

'Of course,' Callie said, smiling. 'Now, what's our first play? Do we tell the police?'

'Because they were so interested the first time? I can't rely on them, and if I try to warn them about a crime again, they might just lock me up. I nearly ran into the officer I talked to about Frank Peterson this morning. I think he's looking for me as a "person of interest".'

'So it's just us,' Callie said. 'We have time. We just need a plan.'

Shirley nodded, looking up at the clock. 'Marsha Thompson is not going to die tomorrow. We are going to stop Gabe.'

She affirmed it so definitively, she almost believed it herself.

02.05

Shirley stood with Callie on the step of Colleen's house with plates of offerings. It was a small but really rather beautiful semi-detached a few streets away from where Frank Peterson was murdered. As Callie drove up the monstrous hill that had almost bested Shirley a few days before, she'd felt a shiver of fear. Two murders in such close proximity, and both involving her, had taken a toll. But Callie had passed the entrance to South Street and the feeling passed.

Shirley had found some extra canvas and an embroidery kit for Callie – who maintained that she had no idea what she would be doing. It didn't really matter anyway. Their main focus was elsewhere. The whole thing had the air of a spy caper – and if the stakes weren't so high, she might actually be having fun.

They had spent the entire night and the day looking up any piece of information they could that would help them stop Marsha Thompson's murder. They had slept for about two hours each in shifts while the other worked. They brought up maps of the surrounding area, street view pictures of Colleen's house – covered the entrances and exits. They knew where Gabe would be coming from and where he would be going. There would be two of them this time, they would be able to cover multiple areas.

They had talked a long time about whether they should tell the embroidery group about the fate that was going to come down upon them. They had decided that they really should, but it may make things worse. If they were all hyper-alert that was fine, but it likely wouldn't happen that way. Colleen and Edna would be beside themselves, Marsha would probably want to confront death if only to say 'no' and Sandy was bit of a wild card. It was too much of a risk, it was better left to just Shirley and Callie. If it looked like Marsha was going to separate from the rest of them, either of them would quietly take her aside and let her know.

Lastly, Shirley told Callie about the trench-coat man, that she saw a similar trench coat at Arnie Enigma's house, and what she'd heard at the police station. She really had to – Callie deserved to know who they were up against. Callie couldn't believe that Colm was mixed up in this, but she had no problem believing Enigma was. 'I knew that guy was shifty,' she said, momentarily satisfied by her intuition and forgetting the task at hand.

The sun was up before they felt ready. But they *were* ready. It wasn't like Frank Peterson – nothing like it. Shirley knew what Gabe could do. And she knew how to correct it. Gabe wanted her to think that Marsha Thompson's minutes were numbered, he wanted to boast about it, glorify it. But, in the visible hubris of Mallet AM, the opposite had happened. Marsha Thompson was going to be the safest person in Chester-Le-Street today – they would make sure of it.

In Shirley's mind, there was no way Gabe was going to get away with this.

So why was she still so scared?

Callie knocked on the door. Shirley knew that Edna was already there since her white Toyota was outside. They heard Colleen's two chihuahuas before anything else. What were they called – Maisy and Daisy? She only remembered because one had the same name as Deena's oldest. The barks seemed to propel themselves out of the letter box.

Callie went to knock again, but Shirley stopped her. She knew how long it took for one of her own to get to the door.

Finally, Colleen, dressed up in a sparkly sequinned top and a long black skirt that reached her ankles but was also somehow still too short, opened the door and crooned, 'Welcome to my Casa, Shirls!'

'Hi, Colleen,' Shirley said, trying to sound as positive as possible, which was hard under the circumstances.

'Oooh,' Colleen cooed, turning her attention to Callie, 'and who's this? A newbie?'

'This is Callie,' said Shirley, 'she's just here to try it out . . . seeing as she enjoys . . . um . . . embroidery and such.'

'Yes,' Callie agreed, '. . . I just love threading a needle, and putting the needle in a hole, and then pulling it out and putting it in another hole.'

Shirley stared at her and then at Colleen.

Colleen looked like she didn't know what to say, and then, after a beat, she beamed and said genuinely, 'It is a rush, isn't it. And what do we have here?' She nodded to the large plate wrapped in cling film in Shirley's arms.

'Oh, just some bacon and banana sandwiches that I had left over from a . . . mass making.'

'Bacon and banana,' Colleen mused. 'That's an interesting combination.'

'Gabe's favourites,' Shirley said, before quickly adding, 'used to be, I mean.' She foresaw something clearly then, just like Gabe must. Having to try to explain to her aged embroidery chums about the ins and outs of Gabe's fake suicide. That would be a laugh. 'I make them when I'm stressed, so . . . here you go.'

Colleen looked at the pile – no doubt assessing just how stressed Shirley had been recently. She took the plate from Shirley and ushered them both in, by some swift thrusts of the head. 'Come in, come in.'

Colleen took them into a front room, which was practically cavernous compared to hers. The embroidery group sat across a vast expanse of a coffee table. Edna and Sandy were already busy threading and snipping away in grand armchairs that looked out of place in the otherwise surprisingly modern living room. A large flat-screen TV on the far wall framed them, which was on low volume and currently showing a carpet advert.

Marsha was notably absent – Shirley tried not to read too much into that. She was probably just running late, and definitely not already lying dead on the second floor, her saviours being too late.

Colleen showed Shirley and Callie to their own grand chairs around the coffee table, and took down their coffee orders in her phone. Unannounced, she drew attention to the fact she had just got a new phone and she could do anything on it, even write notes. 'I never need to trust my memory again!' she said, in what was probably the saddest sentence ever, before disappearing into the kitchen.

Sandy was chuckling, and Edna was looking mortified. 'Modern technology,' she grumbled.

Callie took the opportunity to introduce herself and the other two welcomed her warmly. You could say what you wanted about the embroidery group, but without Marsha, they were probably the kindest and warmest group Shirley had ever known. Minus Marsha, there wasn't the bitchy level of bureaucracy that the hospital radio had.

Shirley left Callie giving a potted history of herself and went to help Colleen with the teas and coffees. The kitchen was similarly massive, but it was cluttered with all manner of contraptions and doohickeys. Shirley really wanted to test the back door, and when Colleen had finally boiled the kettle and shown Shirley around some of her more complex machines ('this one knows exactly when you want your toast, and it flips it, *and* it keeps it warm'), she tasked Shirley with taking two mugs of brown hot liquid into the lounge and took two herself.

Before doing that, Shirley went to the back door. She held the handle, prayed it would be locked, and pressed it down. It wasn't. Of course it wasn't. Because she knew she wouldn't lock it either. They were from a different age — love thy neighbour and all that shit. Nowadays, people would rob you, rape you, murder you, just as soon as look at you. But it was hard for people like them to understand.

Shirley stuck her head out the back door, to see a small well-kept garden bursting with colour, and patio stones up to an easily hoppable gate. Shit. She went back inside and looked around for a hook with the keys on, or a ledge where the keys might be, but she saw none.

Enigma, or Colm, or Gabe could easily get in by the back door, and with everyone making a noise in the living room, it wouldn't even be difficult. She wondered if she could at least prop open the door between the kitchen and living room somehow. She picked up the drinks and got to the door without spilling them, even though it was hard to hold them steady. She silently rejoiced as she saw a fabric doorstop in the shape of a disproportionate chihuahua. She went through the door and slid it into position so the door was three-quarters open and the chihuahua's big dumb head was stopping it from closing. As long as no one closed the door again, she would have a clear line of sight from her chair to the door. If Gabe came that way, she would see him.

Shirley put the drinks on the table, guided by Colleen

to put one in front of herself and one in front of Sandy. Bradley Walsh's face was filling the television screen, indicating Colleen had found some way to watch *The Chase* without it actually being on at this time.

Colleen was busy explaining her magic trick – '*The Chase* is on ITVHub Plus, you know. It's like four pound a month and you get everything ITV. You get all the *Dinner Doorbells*, all the *Resident Detectives*, all the *Morning Coffees* – you just have to fast-forward through the news for that one. It's grand. And it's got about a thousand episodes of *The Chase*. I'll be watching Bradley Walsh until I drop!'

Edna exclaimed her delight and then mused, 'Imagine doing a thousand episodes of something? I get bored if I'm doing the same bit of embroidery for a week!'

'Well, he gets paid for it, doesn't he? And it looks like he enjoys it,' Sandy said.

'You know who I like? That Morgan Sheppard,' Edna said. 'He's a bit of all right, but you never see him on TV anymore, do you? I don't like that new one on *Resident Detectives*.'

And so the group fell into its usual rhythm of idle gossip punctuated with a small amount of embroidery talk and more answering Bradley Walsh's questions before the on-screen contestant could, until someone knocked at the door.

Colleen jumped up and quickly disappeared, leaving behind, 'That'll be Marsha.'

Shirley and Callie looked at each other, apprehensively, as they heard Colleen and Marsha talking in the porch. And then Marsha appeared in the doorway. She didn't look like she was going to die today – it was an odd thought, Shirley admitted, but she didn't. She wasn't dressed for it – though her formal jacket, skirt and pink cravat were definitely not for a casual stitching meeting at a friend's house either.

'Sorry I'm late,' barked Marsha, somehow turning an apology into an accusation aimed at the room. 'I'm having a little trouble in the digestive department.' She surveyed the entire living room, and then turned to Colleen. 'Oh, dear, I asked if I could bring anything!' The exact same bullshit she had pulled on Shirley. Shirley thought that maybe if the murderer didn't show up, she would throttle Marsha to death herself.

No, she shouldn't joke about that. But this did make a strange thought cross her mind. What if the murderer was not Gabe, and instead was one of the members of the embroidery group? They would have buckets full of motive. Each of them had had myriad times when they had to bite their tongue, Colleen looking like she was having to do that right that moment.

Marsha sat down in the only chair available with a sigh, plopping her comically large bag in her lap. 'A tea please, Colleen. I see you've all started without me.'

There was a murmur of apology as Colleen went into the kitchen. Shirley was sad to say one apology was from her. Marsha's power was alive and kicking, strong and almost physical. Shirley knew it well, and knew it would reign over the group, always, whether she stayed alive or not.

Callie looked confused, like she was trying to figure out the power dynamic – as if it wasn't totally obvious. Everyone else carried on as they always did, catering to Marsha while avoiding her harsh remarks, trying not to show the hurt they caused.

Conversation returned – Sandy talking about her family while Marsha made deft comments occasionally. When she had got out her embroidery, she was less of a pain, but she still stuck her oar in at points.

Colleen came back in with a cup of tea, closing the kitchen door. Shirley almost yelped, exclaiming against the action, but she didn't know how to justify the fact she wanted the door open.

One of Colleen's chihuahuas trotted in from somewhere and sat staring at everyone – she had no idea which one it was – and Marsha baulked. 'Allergies, allergies!' Shirley was pretty sure Marsha had talked about having dogs before, and had talked about her disdain for chihuahuas, so it was likely the 'allergies' in question were more breed-based. Colleen ushered either Maisy or Daisy out the room, before sitting down.

'So,' Marsha said, 'is anyone going to introduce me to this new presence?' Her piercing eyes fell on Callie, and Shirley felt very, very sorry for her. They had worked so hard at trying to scope out the murder scene, Shirley had totally forgotten to warn her about Marsha's rampant opening salvo for anyone who was thinking about joining the group. It was actually why more people didn't join up – their first meeting being their last. It was an unspoken acceptance among the others that Marsha liked the group small so there was less likelihood of there being any threats to her reign.

Over the next hour, two rounds of cups of tea, the food being brought out and countless episodes of *The Chase*, Martha's attention was solely on Callie. To her credit, Callie seemed to handle the cross-examination perfectly, which must have come with the territory of being a nurse. The others were talking amongst themselves, but Shirley's attention was solely on the closed door between the lounge and the kitchen.

Shirley and Callie had identified that the back door was probably going to be the point of entry for the killer. Outside, there was an alleyway, not unlike the back of the South Street houses – it was perfect for someone to sneak in. If only Colleen locked the back door. Still, as long as they kept Marsha in sight, they should be OK. If the killer was here, most likely the sight of Shirley would scare him away. And if not Shirley, then she had an ace up her sleeve. Callie. Gabe and Colm loved Callie with all their heart – they wouldn't murder someone in front of her, and Enigma would likely be so startled to see a familiar face.

Currently, Marsha didn't seem interested in going upstairs though. She was still too busy giving Callie the third degree.

'Awful business about that Frank Peterson, isn't it?' Edna suddenly said, and Shirley's ears twitched.

'I'm mortified,' said Sandy. 'I can't even sleep knowing there's a murderer on the loose.' *If only you knew what was coming*, Shirley thought — and then she felt

286

guilty. The knowledge was a burden, and they had felt they shouldn't share it. But maybe they should. Maybe the group should know.

'To think it just happened a couple of streets away,' Colleen was saying, 'and near a Church of England school too. Some people have no shame. Have you heard about it, Shirl?' Colleen's gaze betrayed nothing – had her friend already forgotten that Shirley was asking after Frank Peterson? Or that she saw Shirley practically outside his house the day of the murder? Or was she being coy with the truth – knowing that that gossip would be a bit too much?

'I did,' Shirley said, not betraying anything either. 'Nasty stuff, isn't it?' She had a flash of Frank Peterson's dead body, splayed and lifeless. Big Mac the cat sitting next to him. Frank's eyes so full of fear but so devoid of anything else. 'Nasty' was the biggest understatement in the world. 'I hope they catch the bastard.' *Or I do*, she added in her head.

There was a noise above them. Was it footsteps? Shirley and Callie looked at each other. Was he already up there?

'What was that?' Shirley barked.

'Must be the huahuas,' said Colleen, prouncing huahua *waa waa*. Sure enough, there came two shrill, high-pitched barks from upstairs, and then more skittering around. 'Yes, they're playing around. They get awfully snarly with each other, sometimes I think they don't like each other!' Colleen burst into laughter, even though what she said was actually rather sad.

If the dogs were upstairs, maybe that would help. After all, dogs were meant to warn off burglars, even chihuahuas. Marsha wouldn't exactly enjoy the dogs' presence, but maybe it would be better than getting her throat slit, when—

As if on cue, Marsha started getting up. 'Well, I'm afraid my digestive issues are cropping up again. And I'm pretty sure those bacon-banana sandwiches have turned. I mean really, Shirley?' She was right there, but then the sandwiches were a few days old. 'Where is your bathroom, Colleen?'

Shirley held her breath for some reason, before Colleen said, 'Upstairs.' Of course it was.

Marsha sighed. 'Really? Do you have a stairlift?'

Shirley could hardly believe it – the woman who told her that she should be climbing every flight of stairs for fear of fading away was asking about a stairlift? She almost said something, but realising that if something went wrong, it could be the last thing she ever said to her, she bit her tongue – just like she always did.

Colleen said chirpily that she didn't have a stairlift and Marsha sighed deeply again. 'I'm going to need someone's help getting up the stairs then . . .'

Callie was fast – Shirley was impressed. 'I can help you. And I'll wait outside for you, and help you down too.'

Marsha left an empty hole where a 'thank you' should have been, and instead said, 'Well, OK, but only because you're a nurse. And don't listen to me on the toilet.'

Callie stood up, laughed and said, 'Of course not.' She

shot a look at Shirley and she parried a similar one back. This was it — the moment that Gabe told them would happen. Yesterday. Callie almost imperceptibly raised her eyebrows to Shirley and she understood perfectly. How the hell was she going to get upstairs too?

But then the answer came. 'Colleen,' Shirley said, 'could I go and see your doggies? I really enjoyed seeing them the other day, and it wouldn't feel right if I didn't say hello.'

The other ladies stared at her for a moment, and stupidly Shirley felt like a naughty schoolgirl whose secret plan had just been discovered. But then Colleen beamed and the others went back to their work. 'Of course you can!' Colleen said happily. 'As you heard, they're bouncing around upstairs somewhere. Don't worry about snooping around. Mi casa is your casa!'

Shirley started getting up with Callie and Marsha, as Marsha muttered, 'Love that I get an audience.'

Callie and Marsha left the room, and before the lounge door shut, Shirley was out too. Callie and Marsha went up the stairs one step at a time arm in arm. Shirley trailed behind them, looking around for signs that anything was out of order. The sounds from upstairs had stopped, apart from the small footfalls of two small Mexican canines. The door to the kitchen was closed. And as they got to the top of the stairs, she saw that all the upstairs doors were closed too. But that wasn't a good thing – the killer could be hiding behind any of those doors.

Shirley and Callie stayed by the stairs as Marsha forged ahead across the landing.

What happened next was so intricate, and so fast, that Shirley had to really replay it over and over in her head to realise what happened. And even then, she only had a basic understanding of how things went so wrong so fast.

The first thing Shirley noticed was a small window at the end of the landing. The landing was so small that even from the top of the stairs, Shirley could see over the street to the pavement across from Colleen's. And even with her limited eyesight, she saw a flash of a trench coat running across the sliver of pavement the window showed her.

She stepped forward, passed Marsha, who was far slower than her, and went to the window. She was sure she had seen him – Arnie Enigma. He could be planning how to get up here. But as she got to the window, she couldn't see him anymore. If only she could see further to the right.

Then she realised there was a door to the right and it looked shut but was actually ever so slightly ajar. She opened the door and saw it was Colleen's bedroom. The two chihuahuas were wrestling on the floor, with their wide eyes turned to see who was interrupting them. Shirley barely noticed them or the chintzy décor of the bedroom as her eyes could only look out of the large bay window that showcased the entire street. Shirley gave the dogs a wide berth as she went to the window.

She was pretty sure the next thing that happened was that there was a harsh knock at the front door. 'Who could that be?' she heard Colleen say. The bedroom window looked out to the side of the house so Shirley couldn't see who was at the door. And she couldn't see Arnie Enigma anymore either. But she was sure she'd seen him.

'Yes?' Colleen from downstairs answering the door.

'Colleen Adams?' A male voice, but not one Shirley recognised.

Then the toilet flushed, and very quickly Shirley knew there was a figure behind her. She looked to the door to see Marsha standing there. She felt a flood of relief. 'Marsha, you're OK.'

From downstairs: 'My name is Officer Hawking, I have a few questions for you about the murder of Frank Peterson.'

Shit. Shirley saw what had happened, as if it was spread out in front of her. The police had got the wrong end of the stick and thought Colleen was the person of interest that was trying to get the police to pay attention to Frank Peterson.

'Of course.' Colleen sounded a little confused. She had known that Shirley was interested in Peterson. Would she put two and two together? For the sake of Marsha's life, she hoped she wouldn't remember. 'What do you want to know?'

'I think we should maybe continue this conversation down at the station, ma'am,' the police officer said.

Fuck. But at least Marsha was OK. She was standing in the doorway, but . . . was there something wrong? She was clutching her throat. And she looked at Shirley with bloodshot eyes. 'Of course I'm bloody OK.' But then

291

blood started streaming from between her fingers.

Shirley couldn't tear her eyes from the horrific image of her friend's life literally dripping from her fingers. Callie shouted something on the landing, and then there was a thundering clatter from across the landing and a loud crash of glass.

Shirley's mind was racing. How did this all happen? She screamed as Marsha fell to the floor — a red stain expanding on the carpet. 'Upstairs,' she shouted at the top of her voice. 'Upstairs! Please! Police.'

She quickly got to the door, having to step over Marsha, but she had to make sure that Callie was OK. She rounded the doorway onto the landing and saw Callie lying face down, a pool of blood blossoming out from below her. No. No. It couldn't be. She wrenched Callie over to see that she was bleeding from a deep cut on her forehead. Her eyes were closed, but her chest was moving. She was alive.

Officer Hawking was coming up the stairs. Shirley couldn't tear her eyes from Callie. So she just pointed to the bedroom. 'In there. Marsha, she's . . .'

But that was enough. The police officer moved past her.

If only they had done it differently, if only they had done *something* differently — whether it was telling everyone, telling the police, doing more research, being more vigilant, or all of the above, maybe this wouldn't have happened.

Shirley felt a gust of wind and looked up to see the window at the end of the landing had been shattered. The murderer must have jumped.

Callie was moving — she was alive. But she had a large cut on her forehead, where someone had slashed her. She pushed herself up against the wall. 'I tried to stop him,' Callie said. 'I tried . . .'

'Who was it?' Shirley asked.

'I . . . I don't know,' Callie replied, 'but I got his jacket . . . I tried to pull him back, but he got out of his jacket and just kept running.' Callie gestured beside her and indicated something Shirley had missed when she had passed her. There was a jumble of a clothing item — a fabric hoodie, purple. Shirley picked it up and held it to the light.

She knew the jacket well. It had the insignia of the band Chutney and the Boys on the back with the first line of 'Half-Past Tomorrow' embroidered on the front. She hadn't seen it for a long time.

There was no doubt about it.

It was Gabe's.

02.06

Callie sat in the back of the ambulance, in front of Colleen's house. She had refused to go to the hospital, so the paramedic was putting steri-strips on the cut on her forehead. Shirley stood with Colleen, who had a blanket around her shoulders. 'I just can't believe it,' she kept saying over and over again. 'Poor Marsha.' And there it was – Marsha may have been awful but that didn't mean she deserved to have her throat slit, especially while in the bathroom with digestive troubles.

Shirley had cried a little for her acquaintance. She knew that Marsha had no immediate family, or had, at the very least, alienated them all so much that she didn't even talk about them. She'd be surprised if any of them came to the funeral. Marsha was well-known in the town, but in a notorious kind of way. Her death would be seen as more of an oddity and footnote to the legend than a source of grief and mourning. It would be something talked about excitedly over cornflakes and

294

orange juice and then swiftly forgotten about in the day ahead. So Shirley cried for Marsha, and she actually felt she would miss her, in her own odd way.

She wondered what would happen to the embroidery group now. Marsha had been the driving force in it continuing, when the group probably would have already disbanded (especially during the dark year). She wondered if the gaggle of women would stay together now their glue was gone.

As if to confirm this, the women were each standing alone. Colleen and Shirley were hugging, but in their own worlds. Sandy and Edna were standing next to them, but not with them, their heads down, digesting the situation in their own isolated ways. Shirley hugged Colleen and told her everything would be all right, but she couldn't comfort her when her chihuahuas trotted up. One of them, Maisy or Daisy, had a globule of blood on its oversized forehead. Colleen shrieked and went inside to clean her up.

Shirley told the police everything, spurred on by the mental image of Gabe in his Chutney and the Boys hoodie deftly slicing through Marsha Thompson's throat. She asked for DI Fletchinder and when he showed up, she launched into everything, leaving no stone unturned. She told him about Gabe, Mallet AM, Gabe's delusion, and finally showed him Gabe's hoodie. She also told him about Colm MacArthur and Arnie Enigma, and how she thought she had spotted Arnie outside. Now was not the time for secrets.

Fletchinder surprisingly took it all calmly, barely

interrupting, just nodding and scratching in his note-book. Afterwards he asked her a few questions, and then said he wanted to talk to the other women. It seemed Colleen was going to get her grilling after all.

Fletchinder spoke to Callie first, asking her so many questions about the short time between Callie reaching the top of the stairs and her ending up on the floor that when Callie was done talking, Shirley felt like she had lived it herself.

Callie had gone upstairs with Marsha, noting how feeble the old woman was. She could hardly make it up the stairs without becoming out of breath and her hand starting to sweat. Marsha had told Callie — or ordered was a better description — to wait at the top of the stairs as she made her way to the bathroom. Callie had been vigilant, listening and watching for even the slightest movement. But she had no idea what was about to hap-pen. Marsha opened the bathroom door and instantly someone rushed out — Gabe in his hoodie. He didn't even think, he slashed Marsha's throat and didn't even pause, barrelling past her as she clutched her throat. That was when Callie had screamed, causing Gabe to turn. Callie said he had his hoodie so tight that she couldn't tell one hundred per cent that it was him. Her scream was the first thing to give him pause and Callie used that moment to launch at him. Gabe started running to the window, Callie grabbed his hoodie, and that was when he slashed out, caught Callie in the forehead, wrenching the knife through the air, giving her a deep cut. The movement actually made his hoodie come looser so Callie pulled it free and Gabe was free too, to run to the window and go crashing through it. All while Shirley was in the bedroom.

Fletchinder told Callie that he would probably need to interview her formally, and asked if she could give a description of the man, even though she had only seen him from behind. She described Gabe, even though she obviously couldn't bring herself to say it. Shirley fought back tears.

The police wanted a thorough statement from all of the others, and gave them the warning that there was probably more to come. After that, they had to comfort Colleen, who was absolutely beside herself. It was fair enough really – Marsha had died in her house, the old battleaxe's blood was soaking into her landing carpet.

They got home about three hours later. A police car followed, and DI Fletchinder and Officer Hawking were currently rifling through the attic space. Shirley made them all cups of tea, as Callie sat in the living room, recuperating. She heard creaks and groans from upstairs, as the bungalow adjusted itself to having so many people inside it.

This was the right thing to do, however wrong it may have felt. Gabe was dangerous, he was a murderer, and that overrode the fact that he was her son. Gabe coming back from the dead should have been an otherworldly blessing, but she was shocked to realise that that feeling was fading away fast. Maybe it would have been better if he had stayed dead.

Mallet AM remained silent: 7.30 p.m. came around

and there was nothing. There was no broadcast. Almost as if Gabe had known the police would be there. Shirley told the officers all about the station and implored them not to touch the computer. Tampering with it would disconnect it from the radio deck and probably erase any future broadcasts that Gabe had already programmed in. She knew the program well, and the computer didn't seem to have any other data on it. Officer Hawking just tried to look through it as much as he could – which he could do when he nimbly bypassed the 'ACCESS DENIED' message. When he found nothing, DI Fletchinder agreed to leave it where it was, on the proviso that someone could come back every night to check the waveform. Shirley knew that that was the best she was going to get, so left them to it.

Later, DI Fletchinder appeared in the doorway, with several full evidence bags in his hands. One had a small blocky mobile phone inside, another had some of Gabe's clothes all squashed in, another had Gabe's notebook in it. Shirley couldn't help feeling incredibly guilty – this should have happened after Frank Peterson's murder. She should have told the police everything before, and now Marsha was dead. 'We're going to analyse some of this back down at the station,' Fletchinder said, putting the bags on the kitchen counter and swapping them for his cup of tea. 'If he has any contacts, has made any calls, it'll be in his phone. We'll be able to get DNA samples from his clothes and cross-examine them with DNA from Peterson's and Adams' houses. We'll also look into this notebook and see if we can crack just what it's saying.'

'Thank you, DI Fletchinder,' Shirley said.

'Don't worry.' Fletchinder was picking up on her concern. 'We'll get to the bottom of all of this. But before we go, I need you to promise me something.'

'Yes?' Shirley said, thinking that she at least owed Fletchinder that.

Fletchinder took a long sip of tea and then put the cup down again. It was still half-full, but it was clear he was done. He looked at her long and deep. 'I need you to leave the rest of this thing to us. Don't try to engage your son, don't try to play the hero, don't listen to the radio. I appreciate what you have done so far, but regardless of who it is, there is a murderer out there, a murderer who won't think twice about taking out someone like you. So will you please promise me you're done?'

Shirley thought. Could she really accept this? She had never been one to sit back and let others do the work, especially since Bob had died. She always wanted to be the one on the frontline, doing the jobs, living the life. But she wasn't young anymore – she had to take a step back. And action hero/murder detective was not on the cards anymore. 'OK,' Shirley said, although she would have crossed her fingers while saying it if she could without her fingers feeling like they were on fire.

Fletchinder didn't look convinced, but he carried on anyway, picking up his evidence bags and calling to Hawking to follow. They bid their goodbyes and left, Shirley seeing them to the door. When she shut it, everything was quiet again. Moggins appeared from hiding away and she fed him. Callie was still asleep in the chair, her dressing having a slight red tinge to it where blood had seeped through. Shirley sat on the settee, and wondered what the hell she should do now.

What she couldn't do was think too much. If she did, she would think about how Gabe was somewhere out there in the town, most likely washing blood off his hands. What could bring him to do that, to Marsha, to Frank Peterson? Something obviously was broken inside of him, but could it be that bad? Could he really think that murdering people was fulfilling a prophecy? How did his brain work – picking victims out of some kind of celestial lottery to be offered up for slaughter? It was impossible for her, someone who lived in the very real world, to comprehend.

Now it was for the police to unravel. And she hoped by the end of it all, she could sit down with her son and dare to understand it.

'Fuck,' Shirley said.

In response, her phone started ringing. She looked around. Her phone was in her bag out in the hall. The prospect of getting up to fetch it felt like looking up at Mount Everest knowing you wouldn't stop till cresting it. But she knew she should go – what if it was important? What if it was Gabe? So she went and retrieved it.

Shirley fumbled in her bag morosely thinking that her trying to fish something out of her bag wasn't too far off a carnival game. She finally got it and pulled it out. Grand prize! The number listed on the screen was unknown. She didn't know who it could be – surely not

DI Fletchinder already. That would really be excellent policing!

She raised the phone to her ear and asked tentatively, 'Hello?'

'Hey.' A gravelly and somehow familiar voice – altered by time. 'This is Mrs S . . . I mean . . . Shirley Steadman, right?'

'Yes,' Shirley said, with trepidation. She was busy wondering where she'd heard herself called *Mrs S* before.

But she didn't have to wonder for long, as the voice announced, 'It's Colm MacArthur.'

Shirley's eyes grew wide and she looked around even though no one was currently with her. 'Colm?'

'Yes. It's me, Mrs S. I think I need help.'

02.07

Callie stayed longer than Shirley would have liked. By the time she started gathering up her things, saying she should really get home to change the dressing on her forehead, Shirley was practically vibrating with impatience to get away. But it wasn't as though she could tell Callie that she was going to meet Colm MacArthur – a man who had the potential to be dangerous.

Callie put her coat on – and then turned at the door. And she said something that was oddly relevant, given where Shirley was going. So much so it was almost as if Callie's subconscious knew. 'I've been thinking, about the jacket I snagged. From the murderer.'

'Gabe's jacket,' Shirley said, who had been barely listening but was now at full attention.

'Yeah,' Callie replied, pulling her scarf around her throat, making Shirley think of Marsha again. 'But it wasn't just Gabe's was it. Don't you remember? They had two made. Because of that awful band they loved

302

so much. And because they were blood brothers. Two identical jackets. Gabe and Colm.'

Those final words from Callie followed Shirley out into the cold night and down to the town. She couldn't remember the last time she'd been out so late, let alone to town, and she kept her wits about her as she traversed the dark streets. They were mostly deserted, but there were a few troubling gaggles of young people, who were at various points of inebriation even though it was a Wednesday night. She gave them a wide berth.

Route One was around the back of where the old Woolworths used to be – she knew because Edna, who lived nearby, always complained about the noise. And she had never believed her. But now she found herself rounding the corner to the bar, and seeing its neon garishness and hearing its thumping bassline, she realised she wasn't giving her friend enough credit. The bar was veritably alive – every fresh thump of noise a tangible heartbeat. As Shirley walked up to the door, she had the distinct feeling of walking up to a maniacal beast with open jaws ready to swallow her whole.

This wasn't a place for her.

But she walked through the door nonetheless.

Inside, Route One was far less intimidating. Its outer shell seemed to be just a front, all she saw as she paused in the doorway was a quiet midweek bar with unjustifiably loud music. There were maybe fifty people there maximum, and given the place was incredibly expansive, it looked sparsely populated. The low light cast an eerie glow, with people looking like they were being consumed by darkness. There were a few customers gathered around a horribly tacky red bar, and the rest were crowded around tables in the middle of the room, or similarly red booths lining the walls. In the centre was an empty dance floor, with the only takers a set of multicoloured lights swirling around each other.

Shirley walked up to the bar, finding a spot between two men, trying to ignore the bizarre looks she was getting. She sat on a stool and patiently waited until the bartender saw her.

The bartender was a woman maybe twenty years younger than her – but still old enough to stand out in a place like this. 'Hey,' she said, coming up to Shirley. Shirley was grateful she didn't say anything about how out of place she was.

'Hi,' Shirley had to raise her voice and repeat it multiple times before she could even hear herself. What kind of music was this anyway? It just sounded like the twenty-first-century version of white noise – a club's version of 'let's listen to anything except each other'.

'Hey,' the bartender repeated, barely hiding a little amusement. She'd obviously got the 'Hi' the first time – used to reading lips. 'What do you want?'

'I'm looking for someone,' Shirley said.

The bartender laughed, 'Aren't we all?'

Shirley ignored that – she had no idea what that meant. 'I'm looking for Colm MacArthur.'

The bartender seemed a little taken aback. 'Are you the reason he's all shaken up? Usually he's here – you're sitting in his spot. But lately he's taken to sitting in the

304

booth at the back.' She pointed to the furthest booth – so far away in the dark that Shirley could barely see it. 'He's been in here since opening, so he might not be entirely coherent.'

'Thanks,' Shirley said, getting off the stool, but the bartender touched her arm to tell her to wait. She'd probably said something too, but there was no way Shirley had heard.

'One second,' the bartender said, holding up a finger. She pulled a pint and handed it to Shirley. 'He'll need one of these.'

Shirley nodded her thanks, picked up the pint and made her way across the expansive room. She felt incredibly exposed cutting across the dance floor with, no doubt, every single eye on her. As she got further back in the bar, the booths became totally empty – until she got to the last one, tucked away in the corner. At least the music was slightly quieter back here.

A man was sitting there, but in the darkness she couldn't see his features. He had a long, unkempt beard, and shoulder-length hair that glistened in the multicoloured lights. On the table, there were five empty pint glasses – one on its side with a puddle of liquid framing it.

The man looked up at her – she couldn't see his eyes under all the hair.

There had to be some kind of a mistake.

Shirley just stood there, holding the pint. 'I'm sorry, I'm looking for Colm MacArthur.'

The man grunted almost in laughter. 'Don't worry,

Mrs S. I wouldn't recognise me either.' And then she realised it wasn't laughter, the man was sobbing through that undeniable blend of Irish and Geordie.

'Colm?' she said, sitting down.

'Aye – that for me by any chance?'

Shirley slid over the beer and Colm snatched it greedily.

'Colm, what happened to you?'

Colm took a long drink, and when he righted the glass again, she saw that the pint was almost half gone. 'What, you mean why am I like this? Hah, well, after I got discharged from the Navy for letting my friend top himsel', I didn't have much else to become. This seemed like the easiest option.'

'But what happened wasn't your fault,' Shirley said. *It was Bob's. And Gabe's* . . . She was about to tell him, to alleviate all that pain, but she had to know if he was the killer first. And Colm might be more receptive in this state.

Atta girl. Bob's voice in her head. Was this all worth it if she was edging closer to becoming him?

'Why did you call me?' Shirley asked. 'After all this time. Why didn't you reach out before? I could have helped you get back on your feet.'

'Don't like to impose,' Colm grunted. And that was true. Even growing up, he had been the sweetest boy. Whenever he had come around after school, or at the weekends, he had always asked if he could do anything to help out and cleaned up after himself and made sure to be polite. Whatever he looked like now, he was still that kid underneath. 'But right now, I need your help.'

'What do you need?' Shirley said, not knowing what she could provide after all these years, and not knowing if she wanted to after what had been happening lately.

Even though Colm was still the boy she knew, there were echoes of something else. It was clear he had lost his way. He reeked of a combination of body odour and booze, and his eyes didn't hold the same life they once did. 'You've always been good to me, Mrs S. Like a mum really. And I don't have anywhere else to turn. And I know we haven't really talked since your . . . since Gabe . . . but I still think of you as someone I can trust.' He was still pretty eloquent for a day of drinking, even though his speech was wavy and inconsistent like an untuned radio station. It showed he was used to consuming large amounts of alcohol. 'You see, I'm too far gone, Mrs S.'

What did he mean? Shirley wanted to look around. Suddenly all the other patrons of the bar seemed very far away.

'I have these blackouts,' Colm continued, 'and I think I have hallucinations too.' He grunted in pain and clutched his chest. 'The only thing that helps is the drink. But I think that's probably the cause too. Funny how that always happens, huh?'

'So you want me to take you to the hospital?' Shirley said, still uncertain where he was going with this.

Colm laughed – a real laugh. 'Nah. Not quite. I ain't going there. Inoperable. No cure for what I got, what I've done.'

'What you've done?'

''Fraid so, Mrs S,' Colm said sadly. 'The other day I was drinkin' at me mate's. In the mornin'. Before this place opened. I had a little too much, blacked out, woke up in my mate's bathroom, blood on my hands. I think I killed him, Mrs S. Went downstairs and he was lying there. I killed him.'

Shirley tried to remain calm. He was talking about Frank Peterson. She just knew. He was in the house when . . . He had been in the house. Upstairs. That's why the police already had him down as a suspect. She was sitting across from a killer. But also it was still Colm. Those two factors crashed up against each other in her mind.

What he was saying though . . . he didn't kill Frank Peterson because of Mallet AM. So what did this mean for Gabe and the station? Was there still any possibility that Gabe did it?

Colm's next sentence erased any doubt in her mind. 'And you know what was weird. When I went downstairs, I was hallucinating something wild. Because for some reason, I thought I saw you standing there. But you couldn't have been there, could you?'

He didn't really seem to be asking, but Shirley heard herself quickly say, 'No, of course not.'

Making the kid think he's even more crazy than he is, eh?

Shut up, she thought. She couldn't admit she was there – Colm might want to get rid of her as a witness.

But once again the conversation took an unpredictable

turn when Colm took another drink and then said, 'So I need you to call the police for me.'

'What?' Shirley exclaimed.

'I can't do it myself. I tried, but I'm just too weak. I need to pay for this. I'm unhinged, Mrs S. And when you're off the hinges, you can't get back on. So please, can you do this for me? For old times' sake?'

Shirley didn't know what to say. And then she realised she needed to know something. 'Did you black out today?'

It seemed Colm didn't even think about why she wanted to know that. He just said, 'The first thing I remember was being right 'ere 'bout an hour ago.'

Colm could have killed Marsha Thompson. And he probably did kill Frank Peterson. Shirley was having a conversation with a killer. It just so happened that this killer had once been a sweet boy, who was her son's best friend. 'OK,' she said. 'I'll do it.' She felt sick.

It looked like Colm did too. 'Could I have another one?'

And Shirley somehow got to the bar on legs that were carrying the weight of the world and got Colm his beer. She sat back in the booth and tried to start saying something else, anything else.

But Colm was having none of it – he saw how uncomfortable she was and, even now, he was pushing her away to make her feel better.

Was this real? Could this really be happening?

'Just leave me to it, yeah,' Colm said. 'Nice to see you, Mrs S.'

Shirley blinked away tears, sniffing, and attempting to smile. What had he become? What had the domino effect from Bob's tyrannical regime done to him? 'Goodbye, Colm.' And Shirley left him to his beer and his booth. And when she was outside, she called the police.

02.08

Shirley spent most of Thursday with Colleen. It was horrible but the fact she could deal with someone else's emotions for once, instead of her own, was almost soothing. She could forget about Colm, and Gabe, and everyone else, and just focus on helping her friend.

Colleen was absolutely devastated still, and needed help packing up a suitcase. She was going to stay with Edna, which Shirley was happy about, as her good nature usually would have led to her offering a room herself, and she really couldn't have Colleen around at the moment. She felt she'd already involved the woman too much in this already, although Colleen didn't really know it.

Shirley offered to go upstairs, to get some of Colleen's clothes, but as soon as she crested the landing, she felt sick. There were two scarlet stains on the cream-coloured carpet, looking like two stark blotches of watercolour. Callie's stain, near the stairs, was small. Marsha's stain, near the bedroom door, was vast and deep as an ocean.

As Shirley stepped over the last remains of Marsha's life, her stomach turned and she felt the urge to be sick. She had to reach out to the wall to steady herself, as she tried to keep the contents of her stomach down. She rushed into Colleen's bedroom, and slammed the door – the feeling subsiding now there was a layer of wood between her and the horrific sight on the landing. It took her just five minutes to pack Colleen's case, but a full half an hour to psych herself up to go back out onto the landing.

Shirley stayed as long as Colleen needed her and then went with Colleen to take the bus down to Front Street, grateful for an excuse not to have to walk all the way home. She bid Colleen goodbye at the top of the street, leaving her with her suitcase as she awaited another bus out to Edna's house in Sacriston.

As the sun set, and the night began, Shirley finally found her way home. She knew something was wrong as soon as she opened the door. The bungalow was dark, as it should be, but there was something in the air. Something bad. She propped her cane against the wall next to the door and travelled up the hallway alone.

Moggins was sitting by the kitchen door – his eyes glinting every time he moved his head to look in the open kitchen door. In the moonlight, Shirley could see that his tail was three times the size that it usually was, and as she got closer, she heard him hissing.

Someone was here. No, why did she think 'someone'? She knew exactly who it was.

She got to the kitchen door and looked inside, without turning the light on. She didn't need to.

There was a figure sitting at the kitchen table. He looked incredibly menacing, sitting there in the half-light from the window, not moving – just waiting.

She walked into the room and sat down opposite him. She had her phone in her handbag, still on her shoulder. It would be relatively easy to get it – even though it would take her longer than the usual person. But she wasn't thinking about that, right now she was just concentrated on the person in front of her. It was so dark, she still couldn't see clearly – but did she really need confirmation?

Shirley had been thinking about Colm on the way home. She had been thinking about how pathetic he had looked. Could he really have killed anyone in the state he was in? Was Gabe just using him to his advantage? Was she sitting across from yet another killer?

'You didn't grace us with the news last night,' Shirley said, whispering for some reason. 'So if you've come to kill me, I'm afraid you'll have to do it without the pomp and circumstance. It's almost not even worth it.'

Gabe didn't move. For a second, it seemed he wasn't even going to respond. Shirley was starting to wonder if she had got it wrong and this was actually just a lifelike mannequin. But then, there was a long, drawn-out sigh from the other side of the table. 'You're still thinking . . . two dimensional. You need to start . . . belief-ing . . . me. I'm telling you the truth. Haven't I shown you enough?'

'You've shown me too much, Gabe,' Shirley said sadly, 'you overstepped. And you know it.'

Gabe was quiet. She actually thought that she might

have got through to him, that he was finally listening. But eventually he said dejectedly, 'You just don't understand . . .' in a manner that reminded her of when he was a child and he would do something naughty. He sat back in a flump so his face was shrouded in darkness again.

'Myself and Callie went to see this man. Arnie Enigma. A strange little man. But he knew about you. We know you've been trying this radio station thing – this prediction and foresight. You've been all over the North trying it. Different name but always 66.40 AM. But you were wrong every single time, every single prediction was wrong. So what happened? You came here and decided you just needed to be right.'

'Can you . . .' he started and then struggled to find the words. 'Can you please just try . . . try to imagine a world where all of this is possible? Where I can do what I say I can do?'

'That is so hard for me, Gabe,' Shirley said, wanting nothing more than to disappear into that world with her son. 'Every time I think I might be there, something just snaps me back to reality. Because things like this just can't happen.'

'Hmmm . . .' said Gabe, making an almost imperceptible movement. A flick of the wrist, a dip of the head. He was looking at his watch.

'Were you there . . . at Colleen Adams' house?'

'What?'

'Did you know I'd be there?'

'Yes.'

'Did you kill Marsha Thompson?'

314

Gabe scoffed. 'What . . . what . . . what kinda question is that?'

'The only one a sane person can ask,' Shirley said, 'and it's most definitely the only one a police officer would ask. They'd ask how did you know of the events that would lead to Peterson's death, and then they wouldn't even bother asking about Marsha, they'd just lock you away.'

'Shirley, I'm meant . . . to be your son,' Gabe said, in the closest his new stumbling voice could get to old Gabe. 'You can't just try to believe me?'

She couldn't really believe his audacity. 'You sat there for a year and didn't tell me you were still alive. You took advantage of me, you violated me by being in my house. You're lucky I'm not throwing you on the street, and you still want to be believed?' She was shouting now. 'Believed? Is that so important to you? You've given up the right to be believed. I should just call the police right now, I don't know why I'm even talking to you.' She got out her phone and was about to press the green button. But she couldn't. She looked at Gabe.

Gabe looked at his watch again. Why did he keep doing that? Was something going to happen? Had he really come to kill her and was just waiting for the exact time? No, Gabe may now be a lot of things, but she still couldn't bring herself to think that he would harm her. There was still enough Gabe in him for her to believe that.

'I just wish . . .' and she had no idea how that sentence was going to end. She put the phone down on the table

315

in front of her, defeated, knowing she wouldn't use it – no matter what happened.

Gabe, her one and only son, her firstborn, long thought dead, sat in front of her and all she could feel was an infinite sadness and a booming loss for what could have been. Bob moved about behind the two of them, just as he always did, creeping in his own destructive way. If she'd only put a stop to it. If only she'd run away as fast as she could, packing the kids up in the car, and driving across the country, the world, the universe. Somewhere he couldn't get to them. But she hadn't. She'd sat there and taken it, and she watched as the children took it too. The symphony of Bob every second of every day. She'd known they were unhappy. She was unhappy. But he loved so much to illustrate that there was no way out. And the thing was, there probably had been – she just hadn't been able to see it, from the emotional well she had been thrown down.

And what made it worse was that it was all below the surface, all behind closed doors. He'd never hit her, not once. And she wished, beyond wishes, that he had. That would have been something real, something tangible, something to hold up to people and say 'Look what is happening behind this closed door.' But he didn't. He hid behind a mask, and in their own ways, Shirley and Deena and Gabe did too. But Shirley could kid herself that she'd earned hers. The children were given theirs by him, and in turn by her.

Was this her penance? Seeing the obliterated, illogical mind of this new Gabe, one of the only people who

316

provided her escape in that dark time of her life. They had had Gabe back when Bob was kind and loving and paternal. Back when she shrugged off the warnings that her parents gave her. The little bundle of life in her arms was meant to be a new chapter, and it was, for the worse.

She wouldn't change having him though. Not for one second.

Not even now.

Gabe made a little movement of his head again.

'What are you doing?' Shirley asked through tears. How long had she been trapped in her memories, how long had she been here blubbering while Gabe sat idly watching.

'It should be coming . . . any time now.'

'What's coming?' Shirley said, altogether done with this. 'For once just talk some sense.'

'The chance to reconfigure your view, Shirley.'

Shirley huffed. 'Great. That's just great. Thanks a fucking lot, son.' Shirley's phone suddenly rang, the screen lighting up the darkness and the vibration pulsing strong enough to move the whole table. She recoiled. Gabe did not. She stared at him with wide eyes. 'Who is that?'

Gabe smiled, a little too smugly. 'I couldn't possibly know.'

Shirley gritted her teeth, wanting to ignore the call just to spite him. But she looked down at the screen and saw who it was. She asked Gabe a silent question as she picked up the phone and answered. 'Hello?'

The familiar and, right now, infinitely warm voice of DI Fletchinder came through the phone. 'Shirley, hi.

It's DI Fletchinder here. I thought I should update you on the situation surrounding your son, and his possible connection to the murders of Frank Peterson and Marsha Thompson.'

'Yes. Thank you, DI Fletchinder.'

'Again, please, Fletch. Anyway, the more basic stuff first. We've looked into all of Gabe's electronics, done a sweep of all of them. What we found is . . . well . . . it'd be more accurate to say what we didn't find . . . There's nothing really of any note. The only thing on the laptop was that Gabe had started to digitise some of his notebooks. The laptop and phone didn't show any correspondence at all – it is almost impossible that Gabe has any kind of accomplice or friend, as though they could communicate other ways, with Mallet AM they would have to almost stay in constant communication for everything to work out as intended.'

'What are you saying?' Shirley asked, knowing that Fletchinder was alluding to something and wishing he'd just get to the point.

Fletchinder was quiet for a moment, like he was steeling himself for what was to come. 'OK. We started with the murder of Marsha Thompson and we started circulating Gabe's picture. We got a hit on the town's CCTV network, and then we asked around. Since he left your house, he has been sleeping rough in the alleyway behind the bargain shop. When the murder was committed, we have a clear shot of him sleeping. It's high quality, and without fault. We are satisfied beyond reasonable doubt that it is your son.'

Shirley was confused. No, how could that be? It didn't make sense.

'Then, we looked into Frank Peterson's murder. That was easier. At the time of the murder, your son was in the local library reading an encyclopaedia. He must have snuck out of your house for a change of scene. Multiple witnesses, plus CCTV, for that one. There is no doubt to be 'beyond reasonable' about.'

'Wait, what?' Shirley said harshly. Her thoughts were coming thick and fast, a tremendous crashing waterfall of *What the fucks!*

'Neither of the murders could have been committed by Gabriel Steadman. We've eliminated him from the investigation. Entirely.'

'Then . . . But . . .' Shirley was struggling just as much for words as the figure sitting across from her. 'I don't understand. If he's not involved, if he doesn't have an accomplice . . .' Shirley looked at Gabe, stared at him. He was just sitting there motionless. 'What does this mean, DI Fletchinder?'

'For us, it means the investigation continues. We have another suspect who just got brought in in fact . . .'

Shirley almost said *Colm MacArthur* on impulse and then realised that would just lead to another long drawn-out conversation.

'. . . And we are still looking into this Arnie Enigma guy you mentioned. I'll keep you posted. For you . . . I'm not sure what this means. You'll have to work that out for yourselves. But your son is still very much of interest to us. Because . . . uh . . .'

'He can see the future,' Shirley said, and she thought she saw the edge of Gabe's mouth twitch upwards.

'I didn't say that. But . . . Look, I'll be in touch.'

'Thank you, DI Fletchinder,' she said, and hung up the phone, before he could say anything else. She placed it back on the table. 'It wasn't you.'

'No,' Gabe said simply. Because it really was that simple. It wasn't him. Never had been. And maybe he'd deserved to be smug.

Maybe she should have trusted her son.

The final block fell and the wall crumbled – the wall called 'This is the Real World'. If what DI Fletchinder said was true then . . . And Gabe couldn't have . . . Because it was impossible that . . . So many strands, so many crosses, crisscrosses and overlaps, but all led back to what was slowly becoming her cast-iron and impenetrable fort of truth. A fort her son had occupied for a while now.

'Do you need me to . . . know . . . no, to explain, yes . . . again?' he said.

'No,' she replied firmly. 'You never ever need to explain to me ever again. Because I am going to do what I should have done in the first place. You are my son. And this is your home. Because I believe you.' Gabe didn't move. He didn't even blink. Because to him, believing was the simplest thing in the world. Because it was actually happening to him. Somehow, some way, Gabe Steadman could see the future. 'I believe all of it.'

And she, Shirley Steadman, seventy years of age, couldn't believe that she actually meant it.

320

03.00

The Final Future

00.00 (Reprise)

Gabriel Steadman
Royal Navy – Operation Kingmaker
  (*Mine Countermeasures*)
50 miles off the Persian Gulf
Friday 12 October 2012
1.12 a.m.

Volunteering for night duty was the riskiest part of this whole plan. Who the fuck would, in their sound mind, volunteer for the most boring thing in the world? Honestly, most of the guys wanted another war to break out just to have something to do. But the top brass didn't bat an eye. Gabe just hadn't reckoned on Colm volunteering with him. Sometimes he was too good of a friend.

Gabe had had the dream a few days ago – or was it a vision? He had seen it all – how he was going to get out of here, how he was going to reclaim his life. It was so vivid that when he woke up, he felt an incredible sadness that it wasn't actually happening. That was until things started to fall into place just the way he had fore-seen. That vision was what led him to steal the supplies from the closet – the respirator, the waders, the warmth packs. The Persian Gulf definitely wasn't the coldest – and it would definitely warm up with the sun, but right now it was cooling, and Gabe would be in there for a while.

He had toiled over the problem of whether to tell Colm. Colm was his oldest friend, second only to Callie probably, and he would keep Gabe's secret. Also he thought, on the other side of tonight, he might need some help. Gabe Steadman was going to die and he was going to be free from this stupid existence. He could forge ahead on his own – but there were areas where he might need a helping hand. If he was legally dead, or at least legally missing, he wouldn't be able to do anything without a microscope on him. Colm could help, but eventually he decided against telling him.

Gabe knew from growing up with Colm that he was an awful liar. He remembered playing Nicky Nocky Nine Door as children, a game which was really just about being a nuisance to everyone involved. You ran up to a front door, knocked nine times, or rang the doorbell if you were feeling like a particular arsehole, and then ran off. You'd hide nearby to watch the utter confusion of the person answering the door and seeing no one there. Looking back, it was incredibly stupid and facile, but Gabe loved it as a kid. The one time he played it with Colm, Colm didn't run away fast enough and was reprimanded by the person at the door. While Gabe would have lied his way out of the situation as expertly as a cheeky little shit, Colm didn't end the conversation before giving the homeowner his full name, phone number and address. So, no, maybe he wouldn't be the best to tell about this.

They started the night shift, going their separate ways – Gabe patrolling one side and Colm the other. He would see him one more time before the end. But the last thing he actually truthfully said to him was, 'See you later.' And the last thing Colm said to him was, 'Yeah. Whatever,' still annoyed Gabe had saddled them with the job. Gabe could remind him that he had actually volunteered, but he didn't want to ruin the moment. This would be one of the last moments of Gabriel Adam Steadman's life, and he wanted to savour it. He had no doubt he'd be looking back at it for the rest of his existence.

Gabe did his job for a while, knowing that Colm would be slacking off like he always did. He'd be listening to Gabe's footfalls, sitting or standing by the captain's cabin on the other side. Gabe had to work quickly. He took a breeze-block from the on-deck storage at the bottom of the ship. He'd never really known the reason for having them in the storage until now – they were incredibly useful if one decided to end his own life – or at least pretend to. He hoisted it onto his shoulder and made his way as quickly as he could back to the deck. When back under cover near the cabin, he put the block down and retrieved the chains he'd hidden under a pile of ropes during the day. He worked as quickly as he could, tying the chains around the breeze-block, securing them and then shackling himself to it. He pulled himself up, sitting on the railing, legs over the side of the ship dangling there. He picked up the shower bag that he had inflated with air so it floated. Inside was the respirator, the waders and warmth packs, two bottles of water, five packs of dry astronaut food and a set of credit cards. He dropped it over the side and it gave a great splash.

Colm would have heard that. And, sure enough, 'Gabe?' from the other side of the ship. After no response, there was another 'Gabe?' He would know something was wrong, and he would be making his way over to where the sound came from. Gabe was sorry, he was so very sorry to Colm, but the plan hinged on him seeing. Seeing Gabe go into the water. Seeing him with the breeze-block, connected to him with chains. He had a shackle around his ankle.

Gabe had spent about a week, in his free time, trying various combinations of getting the shackle off his ankle. He lay on his bed and pretended he'd just willingly dropped into icy water with a breeze-block pulling him down into the deep. The obvious solution would be not to lock the shackle, but that had its own set of problems. What if the shackle fell off his ankle before he hit the water? It would ruin the entire illusion if Colm saw the chains independent of Gabe. So he secured them and hid the Allen key to unlock them in his waistband. He worked at unlocking the shackle, trying to imagine the sensation of plunging into the water, having to reach down in unbelievable pressure and unlock it. He tipped himself over the side of the bed so his legs were in the air, and his head and shoulders were almost on the floor, and then he used his upper body strength to pull himself

326

up to his legs and unlock the shackle. He did it again and again and again, until he was confident he could do it in under ten seconds. And then he practised some more. He knew it would still be a totally different job at the time.

He felt the key in his waistband now. He looked into the water and saw the faint light that he had put on the baggie of essentials. He had to catch it on the way down, or this plan might actually really kill him. If something went wrong, he was a goner.

It was almost time for . . .

Colm appeared around the captain's cabin. *What was he thinking?* Gabe wondered. If he knew Colm, the young man would have already concocted a radical plot in his mind, including boarding pirates or wading sharks or boarding sharks and wading pirates. Colm was looking the other way, down the length of the ship. Made sense – that's where Gabe was meant to be on his rounds.

Then Colm turned and his face instantly snapped to one of intense shock. Seeing Gabe in his full Navy uniform sitting there, suspended above darkness. 'Gabe – what . . .?' Gabe looked at him – his best friend. They had been through so much. But now it was the end. Gabe just hoped that Colm wouldn't blame himself. And maybe, somehow, he'd know in his heart that Gabe was still out there.

He wished there was another way. But there wasn't. This was the only way he could escape his past. This was the only way he could escape the shadow of his father. Gabriel Steadman. He gave him a shot. But . . . 'Wasn't meant to be,' he said aloud. And he saw Colm's eyes widen as he dropped the breeze-block over the side of the ship.

Gabe experienced the next few moments in slow-motion. The chains started to clink-clink over the side, rapidly disappearing. And then his leg was almost yanked out of his hip as he was pulled down the side of the ship. He took a deep breath in and grabbed the safety baggie as he crashed into the water.

It was colder than he thought. But not massively. He had been training for this. He was getting pulled down, down, down. All of his movements were harder in the water, but he wrenched his hand into his waistband and pulled out the Allen key. He was so happy he looked upwards, smiling, and thought – although he might have imagined it – he saw a head looking over the side of the ship.

He didn't have time to think about it though. He pushed his torso down, blinking away the salty water as he found the shackle around his ankle. He tried to put the Allen key in, missed, missed again and then missed again. He was running out of air, and couldn't get the respirator until he'd done this. If he got too deep, he was dead, with or without the respirator.

He was sinking too fast – faster than he'd taken into account. It was getting darker and darker. He almost couldn't see the hole to put the key in. He tried one last time – would hold his breath if he wasn't already – and then finally got it. He turned it and the shackle came off.

The relief was more intense than anything he'd ever experienced.

The weight pulling him down was free and it, and the chains, sank even more. But he was not sinking. He opened the baggie, took the respirator out, shoving it in his mouth, finally feeling air.

It had worked, and he was free. In more ways than one.

He swam upwards, leaving the thought of Gabriel Steadman to sink below.

03.01

'You believe me?' said Gabe, still monotone. If Shirley could glean anything from him, it was probably an air of disbelief. And then something happened that caught her off guard. He started to cry. He broke down in a split second and became a big blubbering mess in front of her. 'Thank you,' he whispered harshly. Tears gushed down his cheeks, so much so that she could see the salty tears reflecting in the moonlight. 'Thank you, thank you, thank you!' he kept saying as he became entirely deconstructed in front of her.

Shirley rushed over to the light switch and turned it on. Gabe immediately shrank away from the light, holding his arms up to shield his face. Shirley went back to him and touched his arm, lowering it. Gabe's face was a myriad of bumps, cuts and bruises.

Shirley had to stop herself from gasping. 'What happened?' she asked.

Gabe looked up at her sadly and shrugged — an act

330

that caused a flash of pain across his face. 'Sleeping . . . r-r-r . . . rough,' he rasped through the pain.

Shirley's heart broke. She knew two things as he broke down – that this was her son, her own flesh and blood, and whatever had happened, it was in the past and now he needed his mother.

And she also knew that there was no way this man in front of her had killed anyone. She was disgusted with herself for that notion ever entering her head. She believed that Gabe was somehow seeing these murders before they happened, however crazy that sounded, but there was categorically no chance in her mind that he had carried them out. Ever since she started down the road of trying to stop Mallet AM's predictions, she had forgotten one simple thing – she knew Gabriel Steadman. He was the boy who wouldn't sleep with the light off, the boy who wouldn't watch scary movies until he was fifteen, the boy who released spiders outside rather than killing them. He was still that little boy.

'Who did this to you?' Shirley said.

And Gabe looked at her like this was the stupidest question in the world. 'I don't . . . I don't know. They jumper . . . jumped me in the middle of the night. All they wanted was my cup . . . my liquid . . . my COFFEE. Wasn't even warm.' Gabe spluttered again into inconsolable sobs.

And Shirley pulled him up into a hug. 'Shh, shh, shh, it's OK, it's OK. You're all right.' She should have accepted him with open arms, she shouldn't have let the Mallet AM situation take over her thinking. This was

Gabe, and he was hurting. 'OK, let's go into the lounge, and I'll make you a hot chocolate. Do you want a hot chocolate?'

'Yes please,' uttered Gabe, reverting to his childhood in just two words.

Shirley guided him into the lounge and sat him down on the settee before making him a hot chocolate. She had always kept his favourite hot chocolate in the back of the cupboard — firstly it was for when he came home, and then it was because she couldn't part with it. And then she guessed it was for when he came home again. She reached into the cupboard and brought it out — he was home now, and Shirley would be damned if he would ever leave it again. She had her son back.

Shirley warmed the milk in the microwave, and made the hot drink before taking it back to Gabe. He was sitting up on the settee, having calmed down somewhat, and he was in a staring match with Moggins, who had misguidedly jumped up on Bob's chair. The cat was staring at her son, with a big bushy tail and hissing intermittently.

'I don't think it . . . likes . . . me,' Gabe said, still pushing through sobs as he was handed the hot chocolate.

Shirley shooed Moggins off and sat on the chair, checking her watch. Something was coming over her that she hadn't felt in a long time — she was feeling tired, actually tired. And what was more, she felt like she could sleep. Moggins jumped on the coffee table, stuck his arse in the air, gave one last long hiss and legged it out of the room. Shirley couldn't help but chuckle. 'He just needs some time to get used to you. You were an intruder in his house for quite some time.'

'Yes,' Gabe said, 'I'm sorry . . . for that.'

'It's OK,' accepted Shirley, surprised that it actually was.

Gabe sipped his drink. 'I'm tired.'

'Me too.' Shirley had so many questions for Gabe, she could compile them into a book. Questions about his time since he 'died', questions about his 'suicide', questions about his precognition – the sight – but they could all wait till morning. She just let one slip out. 'How did you know it was Colm that killed Frank and Marsha?'

Gabe took a long sip of the hot chocolate, seemingly stalling for time. He said eventually, 'It can't be Colm. Colm died.'

'What?'

'Colm died,' he said, thinking. 'Died on October fifteenth last year – 10.20 a.m. I saw it.'

Then you were wrong, Shirley thought. *Because I sat across from Colm just yesterday*. And although Shirley hadn't recognised him at first, it was definitely him. But that knowledge wouldn't help Gabe now, especially as he didn't seem particularly upset by it, so she asked, 'So how did you know they were going to die?'

Gabe looked at her; from his look, she obviously still didn't understand. 'It was written,' he said clearly, in his old voice. He totally and wholly believed it. And she did too, although she didn't know if she believed more in the actual notion itself, or the man saying it.

'OK,' Shirley said, nodding. 'I'm going to make up the

spare room. It's pretty much done anyway. We'll have a good sleep and then we'll start fixing things in the morning. I want to know all about this "sight". You might have to talk about some things you're uncomfortable with, but I need to know. I need to understand. OK?'

Gabe nodded. 'Yes,' he said, so quietly, she almost didn't hear it.

'But for now, for tonight, let's just sleep. And wake up in the morning with fresh heads. We can deal with this together, OK? And for now, you are absolutely one hundred per cent safe. The only person in this house bearing you ill will is maybe that bastard cat Moggins.'

Gabe couldn't help but laugh.

'So, rest up, and tomorrow is another day.'

Gabe looked around, lost. 'Why . . . why are you . . . being so nice to me?'

Shirley smiled sadly. 'Because you're my son.'

Gabe smiled too.

Gabe wouldn't go in the spare room, he said it was too much. So he rested on the settee in the living room while Shirley pottered around and got him a blanket and a pillow and some water. She made up a hot-water bottle for him, but when she handed it to him, he just grimaced and put it on the coffee table. He had never liked hot-water bottles as a child – they made him too hot, he said, and if he had a choice, he would always prefer to be too cold than too hot. She gave him the blanket and plumped the pillow up and put it under his head. It reminded her of when she would look after him when he was sick.

And maybe that analogy was more accurate than she

thought. Gabe was sick. Not only was his brain not working like it was supposed to, but he was horrendously beaten, with cuts plugged up by dried blood, and she could have been mistaken, but he seemed to be walking with a slight limp. If she thought too much about it, she wouldn't sleep. She had to take her own advice and just go to bed.

She plumped up his pillow again, even though he was already resting his head on it. She readjusted his blanket and tucked him in, even though he could almost certainly do it himself. Then she opened the window to make sure he had some fresh air, even though he didn't ask. As she fussed over him, she started to notice a smell that she hadn't before – something rotten and putrid coming from him. She would have to put him in the shower in the morning.

'Goodnight, son,' Shirley said, thinking how weird it was to say something she never thought she'd have the privilege to say again. It was almost worth all those years of grief and mourning to feel the elation she felt at being able to utter the words again. She kissed his forehead, trying not to recoil when she found it slick with stale sweat. She didn't care – all that mattered was that he was here and he was home.

Gabe looked up at her and smiled, 'Goodnight, Shirley.'

Shirley smiled back, slightly tinged by sadness. She turned off the main light, leaving the reading light by Bob's chair on, because Gabe needed some light to sleep, although she didn't know if that had changed now.

He wouldn't have had any light out on the streets. She couldn't bear to think of Gabe out there on his own, and she could bear even less the fact that she had driven him out of her home. The first thing she had done when finding out he was alive was get the police? She should have stopped Deena.

She left Gabe alone, trying not to feel upset that he still wasn't calling her 'Mum'. She didn't deserve it – now more than ever. Bob leered at her in the edge of her own cognition, telling her that she never deserved it, that her son would die before calling her that again. Bob, in her mind, was more self-aware, telling her that she should have saved Gabe from him. She shut him out. She promised she would do everything she could to earn the title back.

She went into the bathroom, washing and getting ready for bed, before she went into her bedroom and turned on the nightlight. Moggins was curled up at the end of the bed and opened his large eyes accusingly as she got in. She wondered if the cat would ever warm to Gabe after he had spent so long sneaking around. Back then – which felt like such a long time ago – Moggins was probably the only one who knew what was going on, had the full picture. Shirley laughed – Moggins had been trying to tell her. It must have been so annoying.

When Shirley lay down, her aching body finally finding some rest, Moggins came and snuggled with her, to show her there were no hard feelings. He sat by her head and purred loudly in her ear, making a therapeutic rhythm that soothed her. He started snoring, and Shirley felt an overwhelming contentment. For the first time, she felt that maybe – just maybe – everything would be all right.

She found herself falling down and down and down into the best sleep she had had for years – an all-encompassing sleep, which she hoped was a sign of things to come.

Unfortunately, it would be the last good sleep she had for quite some time.

03.02

Shirley's eyes opened naturally, as the morning sun seeped through her net curtains. It was early – as usual. But she felt immensely well rested. Moggins seemed to be too, as he was still asleep. He usually woke her up demanding food, but as she got up this morning, he stretched out and merely offered his belly up for a tickle.

As Shirley left her room, she had the overwhelming feeling that maybe she had imagined the previous night. Maybe she had been propelled by desire for everything to be OK, conjuring up the image of Gabe, just like she'd believed she had for the previous year. Maybe she would walk into the lounge and see a pillow and blanket arranged on the settee for no one at all. Maybe she had finally lost it – old age had claimed her like it had claimed so many before her. She would be shipped off to a home where endless bingo nights and conversations about the olden days beckoned. Deena and Tom would accompany

338

her to a doctor's appointments where the word 'senile' was never said but always implied.

But no. When she quietly and slowly opened the living-room door, Gabe was there, lying on the settee just as before, with one leg in and one leg out of the blanket. He was real, he was alive, and he was here. The numerous old people's homes would have to wait another day, because old Shirley Steadman wasn't done yet. He was stirring and, to her amazement, as she watched, Moggins trotted in and leapt up on him, purring on his chest. She didn't know why, but that solidified the scene for her. It was one of the happiest she'd ever seen in the little bungalow, and something she knew she would remember forever.

She felt so happy that even the sight of Gabe's leg almost didn't jostle her from her high horse of joy. Gabe's right leg – the exposed one, and the one he wasn't favouring last night – was an odd colour. It had a strange kind of moss-green tinge, but still pink enough for her to wonder if she was imagining it

'Good morning,' Shirley said, as Gabe's eyes fluttered open.

'Good . . . day . . . morning,' Gabe replied, looking down at his chest to see the fat cat presiding on it. Gabe jumped up and Moggins went flying, catching the end of the settee with his claws and steadying himself. The movement made Gabe's leg rub against the fabric of the settee and he let out a crisp yelp. Something was seriously wrong with that leg, and she saw just what as Gabe pulled up his boxer leg slightly to reveal what could only be described as a festering wound. A gash in the side of his upper leg, a mound of dead black skin and scabbed rotting flesh. He touched it tentatively and yelped again.

Shirley quickly moved, trying not to reveal how panicked she was at the sight. 'No, no,' she said, 'I'll get some water and we can clean it.' She rushed around and got a bowl of warm water, some cotton pads and a soft flannel.

'Thank you,' said Gabe, as she sat on the coffee table and took a better look at what she was dealing with.

It was putrid — the source of the smell, no doubt. With such close proximity to the wound, she almost couldn't breathe. She had no idea how Gabe could live with it, and that was without factoring in how it must have felt. She wet a cotton bud and started dabbing the horizontal slice, which had obviously caught and ripped open at some point. At every dab, Gabe let out another yelp, and Shirley offered slowly decreasing words of encouragement.

It took her fifteen long minutes to clean the area, and the outcome was almost worse than when she started. The water in the bowl was now a sickly pink, and the wound was free of most of the dried blood, exposing the real horrors within. The skin around the gash was blackened at the ends, and in the centre, where it had been pulled apart, the exposed flesh was a deeper green and purple than the rest of his leg.

'You need to get this looked at,' Shirley said, thinking

340

she had never said a truer sentence, and probably wouldn't again.

Gabe just grunted, pushing himself into a seated position, and concealing his horrific injury again. 'Thank you for doing that.'

'Did someone do that to you? When did it happen?'

Gabe looked down at his leg, as though he were recalling an awful memory. But instead he said, 'I can't remember. It feels like I've had it all my life.'

'Well you definitely haven't,' said Shirley, getting up. She had to call Callie, but she knew Gabe would protest. She decided to soften the blow by preparing him a bowl of cornflakes and a cup of tea in his TARDIS mug, on a tray with two rich tea biscuits.

Gabe took the tray patiently, his eyes betraying how ravenously hungry he was.

'Will you let me get you help?' Shirley asked. 'Even if you don't like it?'

Gabe waved away the notion, giving a sort of half-hearted consent while greedily chomping on his cornflakes like they were the most delicious delicacy in the world. It was as though his mind could not focus on two things at once anymore. A one-track mind that couldn't possibly conceive another way. It scared her.

She took out her phone, and dialled Callie's number. Luckily, she wasn't at work and picked up.

'Hello?' Callie yawned.

Shirley made some pleasantries, but couldn't for long, then told Callie what was wrong. 'Can you come over?' Shirley asked, while Gabe picked up the television

341

remote like it was a foreign object that he had never seen before. As the telly blared on, she went into the kitchen, ignoring Gabe realising who it was and mouthing 'No.' It was clear he didn't want to see Callie, didn't want to see anyone other than her. But he had to start meeting other people – he was going to have to restart life after all, get used to officially existing again. Once she shut the door, she explained to Callie about Gabe's injuries as best as she could, ending with the wound on his leg.

Callie was silent for a moment, and Shirley thought it was because of what she had just said. But in the expanse of nothingness from the other end, she realised that Callie was probably worrying about something else entirely. She hadn't seen Gabe yet. It was easy for Shirley to forget this fact, as she had been seeing Gabe for over a year. Granted, most of that time she thought he was a figment of her imagination, but still she had had adequate time to digest the fact that Gabe was now around again. Callie was new to this – she hadn't been able to sort through her emotions, reconfigure a designation for Gabe that countered the absolute – the dead usually stayed dead. It was completely natural for Callie to have a few misgivings.

But instead, 'Of course I'll come over,' Callie said, if a little apprehensively. 'Don't be worried, I'm sure it's nothing.' But she didn't even sound like she believed that. Shirley had been around enough sick people, through gathering requests for the hospital radio, to know that one, it wasn't nothing, and two, nurses always had to say that. 'I'll jump in the car now and I'll be there in . . .' Callie stopped.

Shirley waited a second, until she knew that she wasn't going to say anything else. 'Callie?'

'Shit,' Callie hissed through the phone.

'What is it?'

'Turn on the TV now,' Callie said quickly and harshly.

'What?'

'Turn on the TV now. Channel 3. *Morning Coffee*.'

'What's happening?' asked Shirley, going into the living room and grabbing the remote from Gabe, who was now half-watching a repeat of *Homes Under the Hammer*.

'He fucked us,' Callie said. 'That's what.'

Shirley switched the channel to see that it was currently on an advert break. They were just coming back, two hosts sitting on a bright sofa, in front of a breezy set and a large window displaying the River Thames.

The female host, a glamorous older woman, looked at the camera and smiled. 'Hello, and welcome back to your daily *Morning Coffee* with Ferrow and Alma. Now . . .' A tag flashed up at the bottom of the screen. It instantly made Shirley break out in shivers.

BACK FROM THE DEAD AND SEEING THE FUTURE?

And in smaller text – 'Gabriel Steadman said to be alive and well and reporting tomorrow.'

'Oh God,' Shirley said into the phone, and she looked down at Gabe. Gabe was just sitting there watching blankly, like he knew this was coming. Maybe he did.

Callie was making her way through her book of expletives in Shirley's ear. 'Arnie fucking Enigma.'

343

On the television, the presenters looked into a closer camera. The woman continued, 'What if your friend or a family member, who committed suicide almost a decade ago, turned up completely alive? And not only that, but he said he had started to see the future? Well, this is what happened to a family in Newcastle-Upon-Tyne and we have the whole story from a source who goes by the moniker Arnie Enigma. Arnie has claimed to have met this man named Gabriel Steadman . . .'

Shirley looked down at Gabe, who was shaking his head, with a blank look on his face. He looked like he had no idea what an Arnie Enigma was. 'He's lying,' Shirley said to Callie.

And Callie laughed drily on the other end. 'Of course he fucking is.'

'. . . Now, Enigma actually runs a conspiracy website called The Enigma Files and decided to send us an email with this bizarre tale.'

The later-middle-aged male presenter, Ferrow, which was a really dumb name, cleared his throat and looked morosely at the camera, his eyes telling a tale of a dream job that had degraded to this. '*Morning Coffee* received this startling email late yesterday, and it seems almost ridiculous really. Obviously good enough for this show though,' the portly Ferrow said, as his female co-host recoiled and shook her head. 'So this Gabriel Steadman was an officer in the Royal Navy, who was said to have killed himself by jumping off a ship into the Persian Gulf. But due to this email and report that we have received from The Enigma Files, which I'm told is a "faintly popular" conspiracy website, Gabriel, or Gabe, is actually alive and well and now living in Chester-Le-Street in the North East of England. Not only that, but he appears to have gained, what I can only describe as, super-powers . . . and he can now see the future. He reports the future on a pirate radio station that he operated out of his mother's home – where he was squatting, and – get this – pretending to be a ghost. We have reached out to his friends for comment, not his family, because if this is wrong, obviously it is a sensitive issue.'

The camera cut to a long shot. A woman was sitting opposite the hosts in a long purple dress and much jewellery wrapped around her arms.

The man continued reluctantly, just reading the autocue, along for the ride, 'To talk about this item further, we have, if you can believe it, Mystic Meg. Meg, hi . . . I must admit, I'd thought you'd died.'

'Everything will be different now,' Gabe said and Shirley turned the volume down. She'd heard all she needed to anyway, and her son was right. Everything would be different.

'Hang on,' Callie said in her ear, 'I'm coming over right now.' And she hung up.

'Can I . . . switch back to . . . *Homes Under the Hammer* . . . now? There was a run-down . . . semi . . . HOUSE . . . in Hull and . . .'

'Are you not slightly concerned about this?' Shirley said. 'This fucking idiot has revealed you to the world.'

Gabe shrugged and just went back to his cornflakes.

'Gabe, you said it yourself . . . this changes everything,'

Shirley continued, pacing slightly. 'People are going to know you're alive. Not only that, though, they know what you say you can do. People don't respond well to stuff like that. They'll hound you for this. And that's just the fucking normal people. The crazies, like that bastard Enigma, won't leave you alone.'

Gabe looked up at her, and his hesitance went away, as he assumed the voice of the Mallet AM presenter, which was just his voice, his old voice. 'They will come, I know. They'll come to see their ends. They'll come to see the freak of nature I have become, and try to profit from the future . . .'

Shirley almost wanted to back away from him when he talked like this. It was like something overtook him. It was like he was merely a conduit for something else to speak.

Gabe paused, mulling over something, before ending with: 'Because it was seen.'

03.03

Chester-Le-Street
Friday 19 February 2021
8.13 a.m.

Shirley just sat there with Gabe in the lounge, and watched him as he watched *Homes Under the Hammer*, showing more emotion on learning the outcome of the semi-detached in Hull at auction than when he was outed by Arnie Enigma on national television. She watched him like he was an unknown element – wondering what he would do next – and not her son. But, in reality, he was somewhere in between.

What did Enigma's move mean? Maybe he was muddying the waters – making even more of a mess for Shirley to clean up because she knew that Enigma had been at both scenes. Did that mean he was more involved than just being a casual observer?

She was out of her depth. She wasn't used to this kind of stuff. Gabe was now infamous. How many people watched *Morning Coffee*? It was probably in the millions, it had gone out before everyone went to work – to their normal jobs, continuing their normal lives. And they

347

were offered a window into Shirley's fucked-up, fantastical existence.

A few weeks ago, she would have been one of the people watching something like that on *Morning Coffee* and laughing about how dumb it sounded. It was almost impossible to believe that this was now her life.

She needed Callie.

Homes Under the Hammer went on to *Bargain Hunt* and then *Eat Well for Less* and Gabe still watched like nothing was going on at all. Shirley was about to say something when there was a harsh knocking at the front door – as if someone was forcibly trying to gain entry to her home, and using a battering ram to do it.

Shirley looked towards the door, cross. Callie could just come straight in. But the hammering continued. So she left the lounge and went to the front door and opened it.

It wasn't Callie. And she wished she hadn't opened the door. She wished she'd bolted it and got some comical wooden planks and barricaded it up instead.

The tall yet thickly set man standing on her doorstep was halfway to hammering on the door again, and the fact it suddenly got replaced by an old woman's face made him draw back, off balance. He remained upright, but it seemed to take a considerable effort.

His face was so utterly familiar that it hurt. His fat features and portly frame on her doorstep was almost a clash of her two worlds. 'Hello, I'm Ken Vox for Metro Radio,' Ken Vox said, his chins wobbling as he talked. His face had been plastered all over billboards in Newcastle. She saw it every time she took the bus to the library and came off the A1 just to meet his digitally enhanced white gleaming grin.

'I know who you are, Ken. We did a radio show together for three years,' Shirley said, looking behind Ken to see a young girl holding up an iPhone, what passed for a cameraman in this day and age. Ken was holding a small microphone that seemed to be connected to nothing and looked to be more for show.

'And here I am reporting for duty,' Ken Vox said, slapping her on the side of the arm a little too enthusiastically. She might even get a bruise from it.

'Why are you here? You're fast, even for a vulture,' Shirley spat.

'Oh,' Ken Vox chuckled, 'there's that sharp wit. I received an email from our mutual friend Arnie Enigma and he told me you wanted me reporting on your story personally.'

Arnie fucking Enigma. He must have researched Shirley. Known that she knew Vox, and probably – because everyone who knew him did – hated him. Putting Vox on her tail would surely slow her down. What was Enigma up to?

'So here I am, your ever dutiful Ken Vox.' He had the intensely annoying trait of always saying his full name. It was like a massive ego trip. Even on the radio, his guests called him his full name every single time. It was like he'd forget it if someone, or himself, didn't remind him of it constantly. 'How are you doing anyhow? You look a lot older. Feels like a decade since the 'ospital radio.'

349

Shirley snarled, 'It was only two years actually.'

'Oh, ar . . .' He cleared his throat and glanced behind him at his camerawoman. 'Anyhoo, to business, I'm here to possibly get an interview with Gabriel Steadman, the man of the moment, so to speak. I want to get to the bottom of this whole seeing the future schtick.'

'So Metro has you doing house calls now?' Shirley seethed. 'And what the fuck is she doing?' She pointed to the iPhone with legs.

'Oh,' Ken Vox said, pointing a finger back at his worker dismissively, 'pretend she's not even here. We'll record this, with your agreement of course. I think we have some contracts somewhere we'll ask you to sign – everything above board and all that. I'm trying to start up a Ken Vox YouTube channel. I'm gonna call it Ken's Vox Pops. Because it's gonna be me hitting the streets asking the hard questions, you know.'

'Great,' Shirley said, 'good luck with that. But I'm afraid we're not your first episode. Bye.' She tried to shut the door, but Vox slammed his hand on the wood.

'Look,' he said, smiling. 'There's lots of outlets that are going to cover this story, but I thought that I should come personally, you know, seeing as we're such good friends.' Shirley had no idea what he was getting at. She could have said something, but there'd be no point. Rule One of Ken Vox Interaction was to not believe a fucking word that came out of his mouth. 'I thought your story should be told by someone you can trust, someone who knows your . . . hmm . . . sensitivities. You know?'

'Like you?' Shirley spat, the daggers in her eyes not enough to strike down the mighty Ken Vox.

And, of course, as always, he was either painfully oblivious or painfully uncaring. 'Yes, I was sitting in my studio thinking that this would make a great first episode of Ken's Vox Pops and I thought you would really appreciate the opportunity to get your story out there to such a massive audience. I mean, the show goes out to hundreds of thousands of listeners, we're the biggest morning show in the North East! And there's no reason to think they won't transfer over to YouTube. So what'd ya say?'

Shirley looked him up and down. 'You really are a fucking snake, you know that?'

Ken Vox blinked – it was pretty much the only thing he did that proved he was human. 'Excuse me?' He looked back at his camerawoman, as though he were checking if he misheard. She just bobbed the camera in his face.

Shirley started to advance. 'You think I would "appreciate the opportunity"? Fuck you, Ken, fuck your fucking face, and especially fuck your fucking voice!'

Ken started to back away, down the garden path. His camerawoman followed suit. 'I'm going to have to ask you to stop swearing so much or the videos will get demonetised.'

'There are no fucking videos, Ken. You are going to stay away from me, and you are going to stay away from my son, or I am going to call the fucking police.' She had never felt such a fiery anger, and Ken and his camerawoman knew it – they had almost reached the garden gate. Shirley, somewhere in all her vitriol, registered a car drawing up outside her house. 'If there was one person I would trust with me and my son, and this story, Ken Vox would be the last fucking person. No, in fact, if there was no one else in the whole shitty world, I wouldn't even come to you. So why don't you take your little Vox Pops, and take your work-experience jail bait and fuck out of my life, you painful, disgusting, fat, little fucking weasel.'

'Hey!' a voice called from behind the scene. It was Callie at the gate. 'What's going on?'

They all turned to see her. Shirley was thankful, if apologetic, that Ken Vox started advancing on her friend. 'Ah hello, pet, we're just having a friendly conversation, hoping to talk with Ms Steadman here a bit about current events.'

'I think you should stop bothering my friend now,' Callie said definitively.

Ken Vox stumbled. 'There's no bothering happening here, pet. No bothering at all. We're just looking to have a nice chat. You may know me, I'm Ken Vox, I'm working with Metro Radio.'

Callie looked blank. 'Who?'

Vox looked perturbed. 'Ken Vox, Metro Radio.'

Callie shook her head. 'Nope, never heard of you.'

Ken looked like he'd just heard he'd been cancelled. 'I . . . What . . . I . . .' He looked at his camerawoman, then to Shirley, then to Callie. He threw his hands up in the air – he had no idea what to do.

'Can you leave now?' Callie said, and held the gate open for them.

With one final look, Ken Vox nodded his head to their van, and the camerawoman and himself filed out, passing Callie and walking down the street. They got in the van and drove away, Callie making sure to watch them all the way.

When they were finally gone, Callie turned to Shirley, smiling, and came through the gate, walking up to her. Shirley was so thankful to Callie.

'Do you really not know who he is?' Shirley asked.

Callie snorted. 'Of course I know who he is. Everyone in the North East knows him.'

Shirley laughed. 'I think you may have psychologically destroyed him.'

'Only what he deserves,' Callie said. 'I assume he was here to talk about Gabe.'

Shirley nodded.

'So he's really here?' Callie asked.

'Yes, come in,' Shirley said and led her inside. Callie was tentative at first, and then she overtook Shirley. Shirley followed her to the closed lounge door. She paused, her hand outstretched to open it. Shirley could hear the television on the other side of the door and could almost hear Gabe muttering something to himself. Seeing Callie's face, she obviously heard it too.

'What's wrong with him?' Callie said, obviously stalling.

Shirley quickly went through exactly the same things she had told Callie on the phone, ending with his leg injury. But she also wanted to prepare Callie for the feeling of him, as well as the sight. 'But it's not just the physical things. He's a different person. He's got something wrong with his . . . his mind. He gets stuck on words, and he has muddled thoughts. I don't know what has happened to him, but beneath it all, he's still Gabe.'

Callie nodded, took a deep breath in and out. 'OK, you can do this. You can do this,' she muttered to herself and then looked at Shirley. 'I think I have to do this alone.'

Shirley hugged her. 'I'll be right out here, and you won't be alone. You'll have him.'

Callie smiled through misty eyes. 'Yes.'

And she went through the door, closing it behind her, Shirley unable to do anything but wish her all the best in the world.

03.04

Shirley stayed outside the door until it became uncomfortable to do so. She couldn't hear anything going on in the room, except some almost inaudible muttering. At times like this, she often wished she was in a house and not a bungalow, if only so she could sit on the stairs. She paced the hallway and then went into her room for a while. She didn't know why she was so unreasonably nervous. Was it nerves for Callie? Or was it nerves for what the young woman might say when she came out? She couldn't help but want to know what was happening behind that door, be a fly on the wall so to speak. It wasn't because she was nosy – well, it wasn't just because of that – it was because she was worried. Maybe Callie would take to the new Gabe differently to herself. After all, the two of them had been thick as thieves even after they had broken up, before Bob and the Navy and the pseudocide. What if Callie rejected what Gabe had become? She thought that

355

would just about kill her son, for real this time.

Shirley couldn't focus on anything. She went in the kitchen to make a cup of tea and then decided against it, choosing to do some tidying instead, and then realised most of the clutter was in the lounge. In the end, she just cleaned the bathroom and before she knew it almost two hours had gone by.

She had just made her way back into the hallway when Callie came out of the room. She had just stopped outside the lounge door, so to Callie it must have looked like she had been listening in. It didn't seem to faze Callie though.

Callie led Shirley into the kitchen without a word, looking apprehensive. Shirley knew it was bad, but wasn't she more excited to see Gabe for the first time in God knew how many years.

'What is it?' Shirley asked, growing more and more apprehensive herself.

Callie sighed. 'That gash on his leg is infected. It must hurt like a bitch, and he should have had it dressed and been put on antibiotics when he first got it. I'd say he's had it a long time. It's bad.'

Shirley plunged into a pool of worry. 'How bad is it?'

Callie said nothing, just avoided her gaze.

Shirley followed her eyes, not allowing her to look away. 'How bad, Callie?'

Callie thought for a moment, and then apparently decided on the truth. 'As bad as bad can be. I've never seen anything like it. I'm surprised his leg hasn't fallen off. That bad.'

Shirley was taken aback. She almost wished Callie had lied. Gabe was ill, really, really ill. What if he had got that slice on his leg when he was in the water? That was so long ago, it couldn't possibly be true. But what if it was? Was Gabe's condition life-threatening? She didn't have to answer that – she only had to look into Callie's petrified face to know.

Callie got her phone out of her handbag, and started dialling. 'I'm going to call in some favours, see if we can get him admitted to hospital today.' Callie kept her phone held to her ear with her shoulder, as she went to get a glass of water – the question remaining unanswered. 'Hi, Jordan, yeah it's Callie . . .'

Shirley didn't know what to do. Her mind was racing and none of the avenues it was going down were good. She started to go into the lounge, to see Gabe, but she realised she couldn't bring herself to do it – not until they had a plan in place, until she had confirmation that this problem was going to be solved.

So she just sat down at the kitchen table and listened to Callie talking extremely fast into the phone. She lost track of what Callie was saying, and instead fell into a deep rabbit hole of 'What ifs'. What if Gabe had to have his leg amputated? What if Gabe was hospitalised for a long time? What if – and this was the big one – what if her son was too sick? What if he had left it too long untreated? What if Gabe was going to ripped from her arms once again? She didn't know if she was strong enough to endure that – once more knowing that she would never see her son again. But this would be different – because

357

this time she would know it would be for the last time.

Callie got off the phone, hanging up and finally getting the glass of water she had been struggling to get throughout the conversation, before sitting opposite Shirley. 'OK, we can take him in. He'll get an examination, but I'm telling you now, he's going to need some treatment and fast. I also told them about his brain issues, and hopefully if there's an opening in the schedule, we can get him a scan to see what's going on in there. You were right, he's muddled – wrong. His manner is almost more shocking to me than his leg.'

'I hope I prepared you enough,' Shirley said, but she didn't think any amount of preparation could have adequately braced her for the changes in Gabe.

Callie nodded. 'It's like he's wading through a fog – he doesn't really know what he's going to say until he says it, and when he can't think of the word, he stumbles over something.'

She was right. 'He said that pretending to perform a role helps him. He can focus on something else so he doesn't have to focus on the words. Like when he was pretending to be ghost Gabe or the presenter on Mallet AM.'

'I'm not used to neurology stuff, but that tracks with some kind of brain injury. If the brain was distracted by something, he wouldn't focus on his forced limitations. It would be like listening to music when you have a stammer.'

Shirley frowned. 'That doesn't begin to explain how he believes he has precognition though. And it wouldn't explain everything that's been happening around us that confirms he does.'

'That brings me to something else. There was something that Gabe said to me, did he say this to you? He said that that gash was the "source", or something. Do you think he thinks that that injury is the source of his – I almost don't want to say it because of how stupid it is – powers.'

'I don't know,' Shirley said.

Callie drank the glass of water in one go. 'If he thinks it's the source of his bogus power, then I really hope he's not going to mind when we try to mend it.'

Shirley remained silent. 'Hmmm . . .'

Callie put the glass down, and seized upon something. 'Wait, did you just say "confirms"? You can't possibly be starting to believe in this stuff,' Callie said. 'Shirley, don't you go nuts on me too.'

'DI Fletchinder called me. Gabe had a solid alibi when both murders happened. It couldn't have been him.'

Shirley expected Callie to refute the claim, seeing as she had come in contact with the murderer and still had the injury to prove it, but instead she said, 'I've already been wondering something else. Something that's been niggling at me. Now I've seen Gabe again. I think the man I saw was shorter than Gabe, slightly fatter too.'

'You're talking like you have someone in mind?' Shirley said, willing her to just get to the point.

'Well, don't you?' Callie said. 'I can only think of one person who might be against Gabe, against us? Maybe someone masquerading as a friend but who just dropped

359

Gabe in the shit? Someone who could easily be framing Gabe for all of this, whilst also cashing in on it.'

'Oh,' Shirley said, getting what Callie was saying.

'Yes,' Callie said, 'I think we should get Gabe sorted at the hospital, make sure he's OK and then we should pay another visit to Mr Arnie Enigma.'

03.05

Chester-Le-Street
Friday 19 February 2021
1.30 p.m.

Shirley sat in the hospital room, watching as Gabe, in his hospital gown, tried to work out the television and radio set system. She set it up for him, doing the usual thing of calling up the operator and registering him – she'd never done it for her immediate family before and she'd done it twice in the space of a few days. Once for Gabe and once for herself . . .

It felt so long ago that she herself had been lying where Gabe was now, in a hospital gown of her own. It seemed so inconsequential, now even less important than it had at the time. Why should she care about herself, when her son was back – and seeming to be increasingly un-well? A heart attack wasn't really big news – she almost morosely laughed when thinking that a heart attack was actually probably the bottom of the pile when it came to the severity of things that had been happening around her recently.

But, as she reflected on it, everything was connected

– a string of unfortunate events that all led here. She had a heart attack, and that caused Deena to be so angry she stormed in the house and caught Gabe out. And she'd had the heart attack because Marsha Thompson had got in her head about taking the stairs, an Amazonian warlord of a woman who was now dead. It all looped around, doubling back on itself – a tawdry tale, a tale with no end – not yet. But it all seemed to revolve around the hospital.

Gabe had taken a lot of convincing to even come to hospital. Callie and Shirley had gone into the lounge presenting a united front, but still they had almost failed. He kept saying there was nothing wrong with him, and that they would try to fix him but they would only fuck everything up. Shirley didn't really know what to say to that, just kept reassuring Gabe that anything that was broken desperately needed fixing – it was called broken for a reason. Callie had a different approach that showed that she was Gabe's peer and not his mother. She sat with him and whispered to him, in a small voice that Shirley couldn't even hear, then gave Shirley a look that said she had this, and instead of trying to cajole her son, Shirley instead packed him a bag with a change of clothes and one of his books. When she went back into the lounge, Callie and Gabe were standing up and Callie was sorting out Gabe's shabby look. He was all ready to go.

'What did you say to him?' Shirley had whispered to her, as the three of them went out to Callie's car.

'I just appealed to his current feelings,' Callie had

replied, letting Gabe into the back seat, and talking louder when she shut the door.

'What does that mean?'

Callie had sighed, not looking happy with herself. 'I asked him if he'd considered the fact that maybe getting help, getting better, wouldn't lessen his powers but maybe . . . enhance them.' It looked like it pained her to say. Shirley couldn't quite believe Callie would let herself say that. She seemed so opposed to the mere idea of Gabe's powers that it physically affected her to say that.

Callie had remained disgruntledly silent for the whole short journey to the hospital. Once there, she'd showed them to the ward, even though Shirley knew it well. Ward 11, the misfits ward. Gabe had his own room, almost identical to the one Shirley had been in.

A young nurse had come in to just fill out his chart and say that the doctor would be along shortly. Shirley had spent enough time around hospitals to know that shortly could mean anywhere from five minutes to five hours, so she was prepared to wait for the long haul. She hoped Gabe was too. The nurse and Callie talked for a long time outside the room, and then the nurse came back in and took a look at Gabe's leg. She didn't betray anything, but Shirley thought she saw some worry flash through her eyes. The nurse just wrote something more and left.

Her son had been very quiet since getting into the room. Gabe had never liked hospitals – he had always shied away from them, making every excuse not to go. He had only ever been in hospital to see his grandparents dying – all four of them in quick succession, all to cancer. To him, hospitals were a promise of death and sadness. Shirley hoped to God that this visit would change this bad streak.

The doctor came in, a middle-aged man with a neat brown goatee, and introduced himself as Dr Gimble, which seemed a humorous name for how dour he was. He examined Gabe thoroughly, paying special attention to his leg, and then asked him some innocuous questions to test his mental state.

Dr Gimble thought for a long while, once he was done. 'OK,' he said finally, 'first, what we're going to do is get a swab from the wound on that leg and some blood tests. From those, we'll see how serious the infection is. But you are going to need IV antibiotics. Second, I'll book you in for an MRI scan as soon as possible. Luckily enough, I believe there's an opening tomorrow morning. That'll show us exactly what's going on in your head, Gabe. And that'll give us a better idea of how to move forward, OK. Right now, we don't know. So let's get that sorted, and then regroup.'

Gabe seemed to like him. 'Thank you . . . doctor.' Shirley had been expecting her son to push back, but instead he smiled.

Shirley couldn't bring herself to be able to do that yet. 'How bad could it be, doctor?'

The doctor referred to Gabe even though it was Shirley's question. 'I'm not going to lie,' Dr Gimble said, 'it's bad. We need to start treatment straight away to stop the infection spreading. It seems to be localised to the leg right now. The good news is, it looks like it hasn't spread yet, which is incredibly lucky.

'In terms of your mental state, it is just a case of getting in there and looking at what we've got, what we can do. But often these things are just about adapting and learning to move forward. You seem to be a very capable young man, and you seem to have already adapted in many ways. Now it's a case of trying to find out exactly what happened and why you have to adapt.'

Gabe just nodded, seeming to take the news well. Shirley couldn't help but feel amazed how well he was taking it. Her son, who had done this to himself. Her son, who had been put on a path that was . . . actually, no, not entirely his own.

This was someone else's fault.

Hers. And Bob's.

Callie looked worried too, but she also still looked angry. Was it at Shirley? Was she seeing the same connections that Shirley was seeing?

Dr Gimble left, and they had a little time alone. Shirley held Gabe's hand, and finally forced herself to smile, even though inside she was screaming. Callie didn't meet her eyes, instead just checking her phone.

Soon, the same young nurse came in and dressed Gabe's leg, taking a swab and cutting off some of the dead skin and putting it in what looked like an evidence bag. Gabe didn't even flinch when she cut the black rotting skin off – it was dead after all. Shirley couldn't help but recoil at it, but, to her credit, the nurse just acted like she'd seen it all before, because she probably had. After the nurse left, another nurse popped in to say that Gabe's MRI was confirmed for 10 a.m. the following morning, and that visiting hours were now over and Shirley and Callie would have to leave. They could come back in the morning to accompany him to the MRI.

Shirley put up a little bit of a fight – she wanted to stay with Gabe, she would sleep at his bedside if necessary. But Callie told the nurse they would leave. Shirley was a little angry at that, but Gabe said he would be fine and would rather be alone anyway. Silently, Shirley gathered up her things, said goodbye to Gabe, kissing him on the forehead and leaving with Callie.

As they left the ward, Shirley felt an overwhelming sense of the future being totally out of her control. She couldn't do anything but sit back and see what happened, and that scared the hell out of her. Callie still wasn't talking. 'Do you blame me too?' Shirley couldn't stop herself saying.

Callie looked at her, confused. 'What?'

'Do you blame me too?' Shirley repeated.

Callie stopped Shirley in her tracks, holding her by her arms. 'Shirley, listen to me. Nobody blames you. Not me. Not Gabe. Not the doctors. Not the nurses. You shouldn't blame yourself either. Nobody blames anyone. All we can do right now is deal with the hand we're dealt. OK?'

'OK,' Shirley said, not knowing if she really believed it. 'So what now?'

Callie sighed, went into her pocket and pulled out her phone. She held it up to Shirley. She had been on the

Maps app, plotting a trip. 'We can be in Newcastle in twenty-three minutes. Pay an old friend a visit.' Callie tipped her head.

Shirley nodded. 'Yeah, let's go. I've got a few things to say to Arnie Enigma.'

Callie smiled. 'Let's see if he sees us coming.'

03.06

Callie didn't park at The Gate this time. She went around Newcastle, navigating the complicated city roads to get to Arnie Enigma's house. She drove with the fearlessness of one of the boy racers she often heard tearing around the Avenues in the middle of the night. She took the motorway at at least twenty miles over the speed limit, staying in the right-hand lane exclusively, leaving all the trucks and vans behind them. Shirley had never seen her act so recklessly, and she couldn't help clutching the handle of the passenger door in panic. Callie was obviously pissed off – and Shirley noted that she might have to keep her from Enigma when they finally got there.

Callie silently navigated the city with the confidence of someone who'd driven there thousands of times. Shirley didn't even want to look, but when she finally did, they were travelling up a familiar street. The street where Arnie Enigma lived.

She parked a little way away from the house, and got

out quickly, forcing Shirley to hurry to keep up. Callie was down the street, and going up Enigma's path, before Shirley even shut the car door. She hurried to join her friend, as Callie harshly knocked on the door, three swift pounds that seemed to echo up and down the street.

'What is our plan here?' Shirley asked, as she got to the door, out of breath.

'Talk to him,' Callie said, harshly, 'question him and try not to beat the living daylights out of him.'

Shirley was going to say something, but didn't. Callie was showcasing all the emotions one should expect from a situation like this. Arnie Enigma had gone after Gabe after all, selling him out. And Shirley would probably have matched her in emotional intensity if she wasn't just so damn exhausted of everything. But she had never seen Callie like this, jostled and disrupted from her normal temperament. It was a little startling.

She knocked again, so hard it sounded like she was pounding on the doors of a castle.

There was the sound of movement on the other side. And, slowly, the door opened a crack and the tired-looking woman from before was staring at them. Her hair was even more of a mess and the dark bags under her eyes had turned into puddles

Callie's anger faded, like it was masked by a friendly face. It was impressive to see. Shirley wondered if that was what she did in her job. 'We're here to see Arnie. Is he in?'

The woman laughed, coldly, and this time actually said something. 'Of course he's in. He's down in his basement. He'll be down there working on his fucking website.'

'Could we go down and see him?' Callie interrupted.

'Only if you remind him that we all still fucking exist up here. Haven't seen him since yesterday. You know where you're going.' And with that, she was gone, up the stairs like her life depended on it. But this time, she left the door open for them

Shirley and Callie stayed on the doorstep for a moment, non-plussed. Callie went inside first, with Shirley hobbling along afterwards. She felt very uncomfortable with this whole situation, being in Arnie Enigma's house. This person could be dangerous, and she didn't share Callie's intense anger. She was worried, deeply worried. Maybe it was because she knew she couldn't defend herself as well. That even a strong breeze could knock her down. She couldn't go up against a murderer – not like Callie could and had.

She had wanted to call DI Fletchinder straight away, but Callie wouldn't hear it. It would have taken too long.

Callie went to the stairs and the door embedded in them. She tried it and had it open before Shirley got there. She listened, and Shirley did too. There was no sound at all – apart from that of the woman humming a fractured song to herself. All that was coming from down the basement stairs was a steady thrum of electricity.

'Is he down there?' Shirley said. 'It doesn't sound like he is.'

'He is according to his . . . wife.'

Shirley sighed, 'OK, let's go.'

They both crept down the stairs, Callie one ahead of Shirley. At the bottom, they looked around to see Arnie Enigma's headquarters – the computer humming with life, the sign atop the whiteboard, as always, proclaiming THE ENIGMA FILES, the room lit by the lone naked bulb. It all looked exactly as it had a few days ago, when Arnie Enigma had summoned them. There was only one notable difference – there was no Arnie Enigma.

'Arnie?' Shirley said, almost immediately regretting it. She pictured Arnie leaping out of the shadows behind her and strangling her to death before she could even draw another breath. But that didn't happen.

Nothing happened. He wasn't there.

Callie started picking her way through the jumble of a room, going for the computer. 'Well, if he isn't around . . .' She started tapping on the computer, looking through the website. Shirley didn't know what had got into her, but she also made her way to the desk, noting that Arnie's scrapbook about those who could see the future was out and open.

Shirley looked down at it, to see it was turned to an unfinished page, currently being worked on. Another slice of Gabe's history still unfolding presented itself to her, but she didn't need to read it. She was living it after all. Arnie Enigma had stuck in a picture of Gabe, taken from a long way away and zoomed in, so it was all grainy. It was of him on the streets. Underneath, Arnie had written 'New Sighting. Feb 21.'

What was Arnie up to? Why was he so obsessed with Gabe? Why was he going after her son? Was he disgruntled by Gabe going around proclaiming to have 'the sight' – maybe Arnie had enough and decided to frame Gabe for these abhorrent crimes, while also directing attention towards himself. Maybe Arnie was nothing but a sad little boy who just wanted everyone to look at him. But was that enough to kill for?

'What the hell?' said Callie, looking at the computer.

Shirley tore her attention from the scrapbook. 'What is it?'

'Look at this,' Callie said, stepping aside to let Shirley see the computer screen. 'The article at the top. It hasn't been published.'

Shirley stepped forward, looking at a website management screen with a list of articles, viewing numbers and comments. There were hundreds of articles here, with impressive viewing figures – so much so that Shirley was surprised she'd never heard of The Enigma Files before. Shirley looked at the list, until her eyes fell on the title of the latest post – as Callie said, it had unpublished in brackets.

The title of the post was – 'I can't do this anymore. I'm sorry.'

With a glance at Callie, she grasped the mouse and clicked on the title. The post came up, or more accurately, the lack of a post. Below the title, there was nothing. A blank screen. The post was empty.

'What is this?' Shirley asked.

'I don't know,' Callie said, 'maybe he's shutting down the site? We should look around more.'

Shirley stayed at the computer, clicking on the next

372

post. It was posted a few days ago. It was entitled 'Terror At North Fern' and had nothing to do with her or Gabe. The next one was entitled 'The Red String Hotel'. Again, nothing to do with them. In fact, scanning down the list of articles, it seemed that, actually, none of them concerned her son, or even the act of seeing the future. She clicked away from the site, on an open tab saying Inbox. After a few clicks, she got to sent emails and there was the email Enigma sent to *Morning Coffee*.

Why had Enigma gone straight to the television when he had an adequate platform to report it himself? Maybe because he wanted to make a bigger splash. Maybe because he wanted to take the heat off himself and put the attention solely on Gabe. It made sense, she guessed.

She was acutely aware of Callie next to her, opening the cupboard door next to the desk. Callie yelped and fell back, loudly connecting with the floor with a THWUMP. She used her hands to get her as far from the cupboard as possible. 'Jesus fucking Christ.'

Shirley looked down at her from the computer. 'What?'

And Callie looked at her with wide eyes, before bringing up an uncertain hand and pointing towards the cupboard.

Shirley looked. And almost felt like yelping herself. In the cupboard, almost larger than life, was Arnie Enigma. He was hanging about a foot off the ground, suspended by a home-made noose wrapped around a clothes rack line. He was dead, his body jostled by the movement of Callie opening the door, and rocking slightly. Arnie's cold dead eyes looked at her as his body revolved round – the only motion he could ever hope for anymore. His limbs were limp against his padded frame, the last kinetic movement no doubt being trying to stop himself from suffocating.

Callie gave out another hoarse cry and scrabbled to her feet, trying to use the desk chair to get up but it launched itself away from her. She got up on her own and made a cold rasping sound. But nothing came out.

Shirley just looked at her. She didn't even really feel anything anymore. Why did this feel so normal? Why did this feel so obvious?

Of course, this had happened.

Of course, the bloodshed continued.

03.07

Shirley and Callie sat on the garden wall in silence, as Arnie Enigma's body was brought out in a black bag on a stretcher and put into an ambulance. The street was framed by the cries and wails of Mrs Enigma, who was standing by the ambulance, being interviewed by DI Fletchinder. The woman, who introduced herself to the paramedics as Mabel, was inconsolable and, what was worse, she had a podgy young baby in her arms – looking less than a year old. That was why she had always looked so fraught – she was looking after a baby. Was this Arnie's child?

Mabel was crying uncontrollably. Shirley couldn't blame her – it was such an awful feeling knowing that someone you loved had decided to end their own life. You went through such amplified emotions – a crushing sadness gave way to a fiery anger. You started to question why they would do that to you, why they would leave you behind, why everything was so bad when you were right there. Shirley had felt like that for almost ten years. She got a second chance. But she had seen Arnie Enigma hanging there. Mabel would not get the same luxury.

Callie seemed to be taking it well. She had initially been beside herself – even after seeing Marsha's body, which was unfathomably worse. But it was still a dead body, and Shirley felt sick to her stomach that she could now rank the dead bodies she'd seen by how much they affected her and others

Fletchinder finished talking to Mabel and handed her off to paramedics, who wrapped her in a blanket and started treating her for shock. The blanket wouldn't help, neither would the myriad cups of tea she would be made in the coming days. Mabel needed nothing now but time. The baby, though, would be fine, at least until he could understand just what he had lost today.

Fletchinder came up to them and sighed. 'Getting used to seeing you two.'

'We'll try to not make a habit of it,' Callie said, shaken. She thoroughly recalled her theory to Fletchinder – that Enigma was the one to blame for all this bloodshed.

And Fletchinder just sighed again, scratched his nose and nodded almost imperceptibly. 'Makes a lot of sense. Well, of course, we're going to have to thoroughly investigate all this mess, but it would track along with what we know now. Keith Smalls, or Arnie Enigma, tries to validate this precognition idea by murdering whoever Gabriel says dies, with the contingency that if it all takes a wrong turn he can pin it all on Gabe.'

'Then why kill himself?' asked Shirley. 'That's what I come back to.'

Fletchinder shook his head. 'That's what we need to find out. It's possible that he just couldn't stomach it. It happens sometimes. People don't understand the unbearable crushing weight of murdering someone – living with yourself after having extinguished someone's life. It's not for everyone – thank God. That's why hardly anyone does it.

'So maybe Smalls does Frank Peterson in just as Gabe instructed him to over the radio. Relatively clean way to kill someone. It just needs a lot of strength – strangulation. But your hands don't get too dirty. Then comes Marsha Thompson – he has to slash an old woman's throat, and of course, there was the added complication of Callie here. Compared to Peterson, it was a big fucking mess. Lots of blood – buckets. He had to feel what it was like drawing a knife through Thompson's throat. Changes someone, that.'

Shirley glanced at Callie. She looked incredibly unsettled at the thought.

Fletchinder continued, 'The realisation hits and it hits big. So Enigma changes tack, knows someone is going to go down for these murders. Sends a message to *Morning Coffee*. Puts all the attention on Gabe Steadman, and the fact that he reported the murders a day before they happened. It all fits nicely – Enigma probably thinks the police will just charge Gabe straight off the bat, not look too finely at the details.

'There's one thing he didn't count on though – you

two. He invited you into his home, and maybe he was going to kill you. Maybe you had a lucky escape.'

Shirley baulked at the thought.

'It's not a bad timeline, but it's still only a theory,' Fletchinder said, looking around as if surveying the whole sorry mess. 'And we still have another suspect in custody. Although that is turning up a lot of dead ends. I think we're just going to have to cut him loose.'

Colm might be innocent. That was a good thing, right?

'Have you found anything in Colleen Adams' house yet?' Shirley asked. 'Anything that could point to anyone?'

Fletchinder shook his head. 'No, nothing. The killer – Enigma or whoever it was – was very careful not to leave a trace. We didn't even find anything outside of the window – just the glass from the shatter. This one's a difficult one, but I'll keep you posted. And I'll still need to talk to Gabriel about his involvement in all this. The jacket that Callie grabbed from the killer is a key piece of evidence – and so far we have found DNA from Gabriel and Colm MacArthur. Of course, there's also DNA from Callie, but that's circumstantial. That's the only thing that doesn't fit the Enigma narrative.'

Fletchinder dismissed them, and Callie and Shirley got back in the car and started making their way back to Chester-Le-Street. They were both silent as they left Newcastle and got on the A1, both in their own heads.

Shirley couldn't stop thinking about Mabel Smalls. She should have said something to her – something about how it felt to be alone, something about how it would get better in time, and you could do nothing but hold on to that thought.

'I'm so done with this,' Shirley muttered.

Callie looked at her. 'What?'

Shirley didn't even really know what she meant, so the ramble she commenced was almost more for her than for Callie. 'The bodies, the death, the stupid theories about everything that's happened, is happening, is going to happen. My life used to be so simple – wake up, cup of tea, some telly, some embroidery, a light lunch, a cup of tea, some telly, some embroidery, maybe a sudoku, hospital radio, washing up, a few more cups of tea. I can't keep going on wondering when I'm going to see a dead person next. I'm not a police officer. I'm a fucking retired school teacher, for fuck's sake.' She paused. 'The only good thing to come out of this is Gabe.'

Callie took the next exit, and found the nearest place to stop. She switched on her hazard lights and turned to Shirley. 'I know this has all been crazy, but you have to focus on that. Gabe. Gabe is back – he's here and he's alive. He's lying in a hospital bed right now, but he's going to get better. You have your son back. And you have me back. Don't forget we weren't talking before this all started. Yes, we've been through some horrible shitty stuff – you even more than me – but there's good things that's come out of all this too.' She smiled and held Shirley's hand lightly.

Shirley gripped it hard. 'You're right. I have got you both back.' She realised she had tears in her eyes and Callie fished around in the glove compartment and handed her a tissue.

'Let's go and see someone we both love very much, yes?' Callie said. 'No more darkness, I promise.'

And Callie turned off her hazards. And pulled out, venturing back onto the A1.

Shirley dried her eyes, scrunching up the tissue and putting it in her pocket. She looked out the window, watching the cars go by. Was it all really over? Could it truly possibly be done? The story at an end. That sounded too good to be true.

There was still something niggling at the back of her mind. This puzzle fit together wrong. It made the picture on the box, but it wasn't the way it was intended. She would bet money on the fact this was not over. There was still darkness encroaching.

But Shirley felt blinded by the light.

03.08

They came for Gabe around half nine. Shirley had just got to the hospital after a very polarising night's sleep. She had pockets where she could sleep well and deep, but then she would wake with a start, and without even opening her eyes, she knew that when she opened them, she would see Arnie Enigma hanging over her bed.

Gabe looked like he hadn't had a wink of sleep. When she got in the room, he looked up from the television set and smiled sadly. 'Good . . .. Good . . . Good . . . Hi.'

Shirley sat down in the chair next to the bed and mirrored his smile. 'Hey.'

It felt like he'd got worse. The words were leaving him, fleeing from his brain, and he couldn't do anything to stop them. He desperately tried to recount a dream that persisted into waking, but Shirley couldn't make anything out. 'I . . . need . . .' Gabe mumbled, knowing that it wouldn't come out. 'There was a . . . I need to . . . tell you . . . There was a . . . a . . . Chester . . . kids . . . the

381

Baths . . . and happy. Until . . . Do you understand me?'

Shirley didn't know how to answer that question. She couldn't understand, of course, and Gabe was looking like he knew it. So she asked a question of her own, 'Is this a dream or is this you seeing the future?'

Gabe couldn't answer that. The dark bags under his eyes and the slick sweat coating his face seemed to answer for him. Shirley just held his hand, and told him they were going to find out what was happening to him, today. And, sure enough, when it came to the time, a nurse popped her head around the door, and said it was time to go to the MRI.

Now, Gabe lay down on a short and narrow bed, looking apprehensive. He was in the centre of a room – the bed sliding out from a large MRI machine. Shirley looked at it, perturbed. It was a lot bigger than she expected and it was giving out a steady thrum, like the growling of a monster. Gabe was right to look scared of it – she would be too, if she knew she was going to be offered up to this behemoth.

'OK,' the radiographer said, 'so we're going to put you in the machine – this bed gets pushed into the centre of the MRI where the magnets are. It's going to get very loud in there, so we're going to give you these noise-cancelling headphones. We're going to run multiple sets of scans, OK. The whole set should only take thirty or so minutes. Please don't try to move or we might have to start a particular run of the scans again. We'll lock your head in to this cage,' she gestured to a plastic cage at the top of the small bed – it looked like a torture device, 'just to help you not to move. Myself and your mum will be in the next room, behind that window. If you need to stop for any reason, I'm going to give you a little button – put it in your hand – and all you have to do is press it, OK?'

Gabe looked around at the mouth of the tunnel that he was about to be slowly moved in to. 'OK,' he said.

The radiographer smiled. 'Great, so last thing is – do you want any music in your headphones? We have classic rock mix, pop mix, a Ken Vox talk show, I think.'

Gabe went for the classic rock, and when he had lain back and been strapped in to the helmet device, the radiographer left the room. As Shirley went to leave, Gabe grabbed her hand, 'I need to tell you . . . I need to . . . Leisure . . . Chester . . .' Shirley reassured him that they could talk after the scans, and kissed him lightly through the helmet.

The radiographer sat behind a myriad of computer monitors with multiple programs open, and strings of numbers and formulas. One monitor was blank, and Shirley didn't have to ask to know that that would be where the scans came up.

The radiographer pressed a button, and through the window, Shirley could see Gabe getting moved into the machine. 'Don't worry,' the radiographer said to Shirley. 'We're going to get to the bottom of this. This is the big step.'

Shirley nodded, and the radiographer talked into a small microphone – to Gabe – to say they were ready. Gabe didn't respond – he couldn't. So the scans started.

Throughout, the blank monitor flashed up with black

and white scans of Gabe's brain. Shirley couldn't make head nor tail of it – it just looked like a normal scan of a brain, like something you would see in the movies or on a hospital television programme. But there was definitely something wrong, and if Shirley was correct, it was getting worse. This was the big step to seeing what was wrong with her son. And as the images flashed up, one after the other, she felt a little bit of hope.

After the MRI, Shirley and Gabe were taken to a waiting room in the neurology department and told to wait for Dr Gimble. They sat on small plastic chairs, with other families and young children running around. There was a play area in the waiting room, with a little playhouse that multiple children were climbing over. Next to it was a small CRT television on a trolley, hooked up to an N64, showing *Mario 64*. Gabe used to play that as a child, spending hours bouncing around and doing tricks. Gabe watched all the children with an impenetrable and constant stare that freaked out many of them. One went running to a young mother crying and she shot a disgusted look at Shirley. Gabe hadn't tried to tell Shirley what he needed to tell her. He had hardly spoken since the MRI. She just held his hand, and let him have his space.

They were called into Dr Gimble's office an hour later. Gabe limped into the room, and Shirley scuttled in behind. They were a perfect pair. Dr Gimble held the door open for them, waiting patiently as they sat down at the desk.

Dr Gimble smiled at them, as he sat down with a pleasant sigh. 'OK, let's see what we have here,' he said, although he had obviously been poring over the scans for the last hour. 'The good news is we now have a better idea about what is happening to you, Gabe.' He got up again, picking up a file and going over to a lightbox on the wall and turning it on. He put up a scan of Gabe's brain. 'So, this is your brain.'

Shirley looked at Gabe, who was staring at the scan. Shirley had seen this particular one flash up on screen. It looked OK to her – but then she wasn't a doctor. She expected Gimble was going to say a whole lot was wrong.

And unfortunately she wasn't wrong.

'So here,' said Dr Gimble, prodding the scan with a pen, 'we see the brain. There are areas, many areas in fact, that are absolutely untouched and fine, better than fine. What we need to concern ourselves with, however, are these patches.' He pointed the pen at multiple parts that were darker than the rest. There were actually more darker parts than light. 'These patches on the brain show damaged tissue.'

'But there's so much of it,' Shirley said. She glanced at Gabe. He was just staring at the scan with the intensity that had scared the children in the waiting room.

'Unfortunately yes,' Dr Gimble said. 'These patches show a trauma on the brain that has affected Gabe's cognition. This is why he has trouble speaking, trouble finding words that are practically on the tip of his tongue. The scan shows that although he has the word in his brain, he doesn't have the ability to move it to his mouth. If he keeps trying, he can do it eventually, but for most of us, obviously, the act of thinking of a word, constructing a sentence, or providing a rebuttal, is instantaneous. Gabe needs to work at it – maybe five times more than the rest of us.'

'So what happened to him?' Shirley asked.

Gabe said nothing at all, as Dr Gimble came and sat back down. 'From what I know about Gabe's history and what has happened in the past, I can really only theorise . . . But what I would say is it all links back to Gabe's fake suicide attempt.'

Gabe gave a grunt, but she couldn't tell if it was one of approval, disapproval, or something else.

'What do you mean?' Shirley pressed, looking from Gabe to the doctor.

'Due to the obvious lesions on the brain, and looking at the scans, everything is running in line with one particular theory. Are you familiar with the nautical concept of "the bends"?'

'The bends?' Shirley said, knowing what it kind of meant but wanting it explained anyway.

'Yes. The bends, or decompression sickness. It is a problem that occurs in scuba divers mainly. It happens when divers descend so far down into the water that rapidly ascending again can cause major issues with just about any part of the body. When there are rapid pressure changes, nitrogen comes out of the solution in the bloodstream and forms gas bubbles in the circulation. It can cause confusion, coma, even death – but it can also cause long-term issues with the body or the brain.

'My guess, looking at Gabe's case, is that he was in the water for longer than his muddled brain perceived. The

386

bends has been reported in cases where the diver was only ten feet down. I think Gabe was probably much lower, pushed down by the weight he had attached himself to. When he was finally free, and he began to panic, he ascended incredibly rapidly – of course he did, he was hypervigilant, his senses going crazy, probably thinking he was going to drown for real. He was caught between having to go down far enough to make it look like he'd disappeared and being pulled further down by the breeze-block than he ever intended.'

'Is there anything we can do for him?' Shirley said, acutely aware they were both talking like the man in question wasn't here. But it was hard when Gabe wasn't speaking at all – just staring. 'Is there something he can take, or some therapy he can undertake?'

Dr Gimble sadly shook his head. 'I'm afraid the damage is permanent. At this moment, it's about learning to live with Gabe's new mentality, rather than treating it.'

Shirley almost cried out, but she suppressed it. The doctor had tried to prepare her for this exact outcome. And she had tried to prepare herself too. But it was still another matter to hear it all laid out for her like this. Her son would never be the same again.

Gabe either didn't understand what this meant or simply thought it was of no importance.

Shirley held his hand. 'What do you think?'

Gabe, who'd merely been listening intently to the entire theory and diagnosis, opened his mouth for the first time since coming into the office. He held up a hand, like he was in school. 'Would . . . the beans . . . the beans . . . the BENDS . . . would that account for me . . . me . . . being able to . . . see . . . things before they happen? Would it . . . acclimb . . . account for . . . me being able . . . to see . . . the future?'

Shirley looked from him to the slightly baffled doctor, wondering why that was the only thing he needed to know and then realising that of course that was the only thing he'd be interested in.

Dr Gimble digested the question, and thought for a long time – most likely contemplating how to possibly attempt to answer. He sighed. 'Look, I can't pretend I don't know your case, Gabe. I know what you claim to be able to do. I can't and I won't tell you that you can't do what you claim. The brain is highly complex and there is still much we don't understand about it. I'm just a neurologist in a small town in a small country. My professional opinion is not necessarily – highly unlikely, in fact – the end of the conversation. But I feel it is my duty, my job, to tell you that I have never met anyone who can do what you claim. I have never seen any shred of scientific proof that what you claim could even be possible. Do you understand, Gabe?'

Shirley looked at her son.

'Yes,' Gabe said, clearly and succinctly. 'I understand.'

03.09

Dr Gimble accompanied Shirley and Gabe back to his room, adjusting his pace to fit theirs, without making it obvious. When they got onto the ward, Gimble hung back and quietly asked if he could have a word with Shirley. He didn't need to be quiet – Gabe didn't seem to mind, he merely looked at them both and went into his room without saying goodbye, shutting the door behind him.

The doctor smiled after him, and then turned to Shirley. 'It's important to keep him comfortable. You both have to adjust to the new Gabriel Steadman now. And I know just saying that doesn't take into account how hard it's going to be. There'll be times when you think you're living with a completely different person, times where you feel like you've hit a wall and nothing helps. There may even be times when you wish your son hadn't come back at all. But we're here. And if you run into any issues, or have any questions – and you're

389

probably going to have so many you'll have to write them down – we are here. I want you to call me,' he said, getting out a card and writing his number on it. He handed it to Shirley. 'If I'm not available, you can talk to someone else or leave me a message. Now, we have to get your son physically fit again. And I'll leave you in the capable hands of the ward doctors to do that.'

'Thank you, Dr Gimble,' Shirley said, pocketing the card. She didn't know if she would call him, but he seemed genuinely concerned and she was eternally grateful for that.

Dr Gimble gave her a compassionate touch on the arm, and then he left her. He probably had dozens of other patients to see, dozens of other stories, dozens of other lives to peer in on and then slink away. She was almost jealous of his detachment, his ability to step between worlds, being a major player in none. But she was here, and her son was waiting – and however much he'd changed, he was just that. Her son. So she went into his room and joined him.

Gabe was quiet and detached for the rest of the day. When she entered the room, he had already put his headphones on and was watching BBC One, ignoring Shirley as she sat down. But that didn't last long – he seemed to grow bored very quickly and threw off the headphones in frustration. He read for a bit, and then he tried to sleep but couldn't. Then the cycle continued.

Throughout these activities and the ensuing hours, Shirley sat, doing embroidery and reading, but actually covertly studying Gabe who was quietly muttering inaudible words, that were perhaps even nonsense. Sometimes Gabe looked directly at Shirley and said, 'I have to . . . tell you . . . some . . . mat . . . THING!'

'Tell me,' Shirley said, 'I'm here, no matter how long it takes.'

But Gabe would stutter and stammer, growing increasingly annoyed with himself. 'I . . . The . . . Baths . . . Playing . . . They go . . . To . . .' He just went around and around in circles, and he became so angry with his brain that he started slapping his forehead with his palm, just as he had at their kitchen table what felt like years ago. 'I . . . Their . . . Dangle . . . Dafter . . . Lesser . . . Leisure.'

Shirley wanted desperately to understand, to know what he was trying to convey, but she didn't. It was all just incoherent. And Gabe knew it. So he would stop trying and just attempt to engage with something else until trying again. This happened four times.

Shirley was so worried about Gabe – she had to distract him somehow. She didn't have to think long until the perfect activity came to her mind. The next time a nurse came around, she asked if it was OK to take Gabe out of the ward for a short time.

Gabe just looked confused, but he followed his mother regardless. Shirley led him down the many corridors to the hospital radio. Inside the small, cramped studio, Gabe's face lit up like he had just been dropped off at Disneyland. He darted around looking at all manner of different things – the equipment, the decks, the computer software. He gasped in amazement at the systems in play and the cable management. He pored over the myriad of records, until his eyes fell on one in particular. He pulled it out.

Half-Past Tomorrow.

Shirley watched him in the doorway, as he took out the record and smiled. 'You want to play it on the radio?'

Gabe looked confused. 'Wha . . . what?'

'You can play it on the Chester-Le-Street Hospital Radio if you like.'

'Re . . . Really?'

Shirley guided him into Studio One. As usual, a Ken Vox show was playing on repeat. She turned it off, switching to LIVE, cueing up a few music tracks while she got Gabe ready. She sat Gabe down in the chair and put the canned headphones on him. He looked like a little child at Christmas. She showed him how to turn the microphone on, and cue up the record player, but he already knew how to do most of it after running Mallet AM. Shirley watched him as he skilfully navigated the computer program that took new volunteers weeks to learn. Of course he already knew it, was self-taught. And sometimes that was better.

Gabe's mood was so unbelievably different, it was almost like he had shed the skin of the fumbling, un-confident man back in his hospital room. Gabe turned on the microphone as a music track started to fade out, and, with a glance at Shirley for approval, he began to talk. And what came out was complete, and strong, and the old Gabe.

'That was Taylor Swift and I'm Gabe Steadman, guest host of Chester-Le-Street Hospital Radio. I'm here to play one very special music track. It's a track that means a lot to me – my favourite song of all time. I first heard it at a very uncertain time in my life, and it reassured me that whatever the future held, I could be happy. This is the 1984 cult classic "Half-Past Tomorrow" by Chutney and the Boys. Hope you enjoy it.' Gabe turned the microphone off, cued up the record, started it and faded it up all in the space of a second. He was a natural.

He turned to Shirley, beaming, as Chutney started singing about a joker's dream. In his smiling face, Shirley saw the young Gabe – the funny, confident child that had been lost to the years. She knew in that moment that she would do everything to stand by her son, no matter how bad his cognitive illness became, no matter how difficult it was. Because he was still in there.

Shirley turned the radio back to automatic mode, while Gabe pored over the CD collection. When she was done, she just sat and watched him, grateful that he had finally got off his roundabout of trying to tell her something and getting angry at himself. He asked so many questions, it was unreal, although his questions were still marred in confusion and stuttering.

'What is this?' said Gabe.

'That is the amplifier for the entire station. It monitors the levels of bass, voice and rhythm that we can change so we don't blow out the listeners' eardrums,' laughed Shirley.

'So can the saloon . . . station . . . YES . . . can it broadcast on different freq . . . frequencies, or is it just hospital . . . radio?' Gabe asked.

'The main studio can only go out to the hospital, but Studio Two can be configured to be an outside radio station – meaning reachable on a frequency, yes,' Shirley said, a little proud that she could speak so knowledgeably about this.

'And . . . what . . . is this?' Gabe said, his voice full of wonder.

'That's a filing cabinet. Just an ordinary, run-of-the-mill filing cabinet,' Shirley replied.

'Oh yeah . . .' said Gabe.

The best part came when Gabe, like a child who clearly didn't want to go home and sleep, dove back into Studio One. He just went to the computer again and started looking through it. 'Maybe I . . . could come to hospital . . . radio with you from now on?' Gabe said, as he happily clicked through music tracks, to the hospital radio jingles.

Nothing would make me happier, Shirley thought as her heart soared. 'Of course you can,' she said, barely able to hide her excitement.

Watching him, she felt an overwhelming feeling of contentment. Maybe this really was all over. Maybe from now on she could just focus on rebuilding her relationship with her son, getting back to a semblance of normal life.

Maybe, just maybe, everything would be OK.

03.10

Shirley

Chester-Le-Street
Saturday 20 February 2021
5.22 p.m.

'Shirley.'

She didn't know where she was, but she knew she had a smile on her face. Her eyes were shut, but she could feel Gabe's hand in hers. That's where she was – the hospital. They knew what was wrong with Gabe, and although they couldn't really do anything, it was good to know. They had the building blocks to create a future, and maybe this future could be happy.

'Shirley.'

All they needed was each other. Gabe could move in – have his own room. The spare room was practically his anyway. They could clear out the attic – turn it into something else. Gabe could be enrolled in hospital radio. Usually it took about a month to go through all the paperwork and the inductions and the shadowing, but she could rush Gabe through it. He could be doing shows by as early as next week. She could just hope he wanted to do shows with her – Gabe and Shirley's Request Shows, Gabe and Shirley's Classic Rock, Gabe and Shirley's Jazz Hour, the possibilities were endless . . .

'SHIRLEY.'

Her eyes opened. She was sitting in the chair beside Gabe's bed. She had fallen into a contented sleep. Just like she thought she had. But there was something different, something wrong. Callie was standing by the bed, looming over her.

'Callie?' Shirley said confused. 'What's wrong?'

Callie looked white, like she was intensely worried about something – something Shirley wasn't sure she wanted to know. She wanted to stay living in her happy future for just a moment longer. But Callie denied her that, as she replied, in a voice drenched in apprehension, 'Shirley, where's Gabe?'

Shirley was wide awake then. She looked to the bed and found she wasn't gripping Gabe's hand but rather the remote control for the bed. The bed itself was empty – the covers pulled back to reveal the lonely white sheet. She looked at Callie with eyes filled with panic. 'I don't know.'

'Shit,' said Callie, fumbling for her phone.

Shirley shot up, grasping for her words. She felt like she had to justify herself . . . 'We were, we just had a nap, both of us, and he was right here. We'd just got back from . . .' she trailed off, a thought seizing her.

Callie was busy on the phone. She held it to her ear and a loud dial tone came from it.

Shirley didn't notice. She looked around. For any sign as to where Gabe had gone. But she didn't need clues. She knew, she just knew. But how could he get in . . .? Her hand moved to her neck, but she knew before she felt her bare skin. Her volunteer's lanyard was gone.

'Callie . . .'

'Why won't anyone pick up the fucking phone?'

'CALLIE,' Shirley said so viciously that Callie put down the phone. 'I know where he is.'

'Where?'

'He was trying to tell me something,' Shirley said. 'He was trying to tell me a . . . a future. So he's gone to report it.'

'What do you mean?' Callie asked.

Shirley explained as they made their way quickly down the hospital corridors. Nothing had ever been clearer in her mind. Gabe was going to broadcast Mallet AM from the hospital radio. That was why he was asking about outside broadcasting. Fuck, it was so obvious. But she had just been so happy.

They got to the corridor and Shirley realised she couldn't get in without her lanyard. But Callie held up hers and scanned it. Shirley flew through the door and down the corridor faster than she had even when she was a teenager doing track and field at school. Her joints sang with pain but she didn't care.

She got to the door, quickly inputting the code and turning the latch. She pushed – the door didn't give. Callie caught up with her. Shirley tried the code again – nothing. 'SHIT.'

'What's happening?' Callie said.

Shirley thought for a second. She had been hoping to find Gabe at the door trying to get in, but she underestimated him. Gabe must have looked at the code when she'd let them in the station. And he'd drawn the bolt on the other side.

'It's locked,' Shirley said, 'we can't get in.'

'What?' Callie exclaimed.

'They added a bolt when a patient decided to go walkies one night and crashed the radio station. Since then, volunteers have been able to lock themselves in.'

'Are we sure he's in there?' Callie asked.

'Wait.' Shirley pressed her ear to the door. The sound-proofing in the room was terrible, and if you listened closely you could hear what was going on inside. 'The auto-play's not on. I can't hear Ken Vox.'

'I'm sorry what?' Callie said.

Shirley had to think – what to do, what to do? How the hell were they going to get in the room and stop Gabe? But then another reality dawned on her. Maybe they shouldn't be trying to get in at all. 'Gabe was trying to tell me something,' she muttered almost to herself.

'I'm sorry?'

'Gabe, he was really trying to tell me something. He couldn't get the words out, he couldn't find the right—'

'Yes, you've said.'

'NO, he was *really* trying to tell me something,' Shirley stated, only half understanding what she was getting at herself. 'So . . . we should listen to him.' Shirley nodded, finally getting it. 'We should listen to him.'

'What do you mean?' asked Callie.

Shirley ignored her question. 'We have to get back to the room. We have to get back to the room. Right now.'

03.11

Shirley got into the room first and almost threw herself on the bed, pulling the patient television/radio set towards her. Callie came in behind her, bewildered and only half understanding what was happening. She just stood there and watched Shirley, throwing her hands up.

Shirley prodded at the touchscreen and got the radio up. She pulled out the headphones, so the sound of the hospital radio filled the room. There was Ken Vox talking about some music track or other. The reason she couldn't hear him outside the station though was because the main volume – that box in the foyer Gabe had asked about was on another frequency. And she knew exactly which one it was on.

She went through the radio stations, changing the cumbersome touchscreen program to manual frequency. 'For fuck's sake,' she said, as she had to prod every single time she moved it 00.01 frequency. It took her what felt like an age to get to the 60s. Static filled the room, and Shirley found herself holding her breath as she got to the correct frequency. She almost hoped to hear nothing – nothing at all – but as she clicked over to 66.40AM, the static gave way to music.

Mallet AM was broadcasting.

Shirley felt sick as the music started to fade out. They had got here just in time. Gabe had obviously waited until the half-hour to report the news. Being professional.

Gabe started to talk, clear and concise, but also less confident. His voice was hesitant, like he didn't want to say what he knew he had to say. Shirley and Callie looked at each other and Callie stepped closer. 'That was . . . you know what, I'm not sure what that was . . . you'll have to forgive me, I'm working from a new studio. And this will be the one and only time I broadcast from here. In fact, it's . . .

'Look, before we get to the last item on today's news, we here at Mallet AM have a very unfortunate announcement. Today is Mallet AM's final broadcast. After the news, the radio station will shut down permanently. We are proud of what we have done here at this station, but sometimes you just have to move on. Sometimes your future is written. We . . . I will always be out there, letting people know what is in store. You just need to look in the right place.'

There was something in Gabe's voice that Shirley hadn't heard on the radio before. Was he crying? Something was wrong. And she really didn't want to hear what he had to say next. But she had to.

'This is it. The final ever item of news. The final item of the future. Eagle-eared listeners will of course know that I usually report the news just under a day before it happens. I'm afraid I was . . . waylaid for this item. And it's going to happen in a mere few hours at 7 p.m., today, Saturday the twentieth of February 2021.' Gabe broke down crying for a second, before fighting through the tears. 'I am so deeply saddened to say that the bodies of two young children will be found lying in the deep end of the large swimming pool in the abandoned Chester-Le-Street Leisure Centre.' Shirley gasped, her hand shooting to her mouth. 'It looks like the children were playing in the derelict building when they slipped and fell three metres into the drained pool. Neither of them survived.'

'Oh my God,' Shirley said, and Callie gasped. Shirley looked at her to see she had started crying. 'Holy shit.'

Gabe had broken down again. And suddenly she saw the future herself – the very close future. Shirley suddenly knew why Gabe was crying. She knew what was happening. And she willed it not to happen. She willed Gabe not to say it because then it would be true. Gabe cried and cried, gasping for air, then: 'The children have been identified as Maisie and Kenneth Wright-Steadman.'

Shirley felt dizzy. She staggered off the bed and doubled over, retching. Everything Gabe had said, everything he'd reported, had come true. Shirley and Callie hadn't been able to stop any of them. Their best efforts had proved totally pointless. Arnie Enigma, the man who was supposed to be the catalyst to all this, was gone. So why did she still feel sick?

Because Gabe can see the future, her inner voice offered. Because, however hard she tried, Deena and Tom's children were going to end up dead at the bottom of that pool.

No. No. No.

Gabe was openly weeping now. 'That is it. That is all I have. Sometimes, maybe, you shouldn't know what lies ahead. I am cursed with the knowledge of tomorrow. But you don't have to be. Live for now. Death is for another day.' Gabe became distraught — he continued talking. 'So I'm signing off now. Goodbye, and good luck.'

Silence. No line, no frequency, nothing. Gabe had shut it down.

A wail from Callie — she was going through the exact same set of emotions. 'Why them?' she was muttering. 'Why'd he have to say it? Why'd it have to be them?'

Shirley tensed — she had absolutely no idea what to do. The entire world was wrong.

But as she looked around at Callie's white face, and listened to the absolute absence of anything from 66.40 AM, she saw that she was the one who had to have the answers. She had to take charge.

She got out her phone — tried Deena's number. Nothing. She tried Tom's number. Nothing. Why didn't anyone ever pick up the bloody phone when it was an emergency?

'Callie,' she said, in a shaky voice — one that didn't even sound like her own. 'How fast can you get to Deena's?'

Callie was crumpling up, shutting down. She was almost on the floor. Shirley had to grab her and pull her up, their eyes meeting.

'CALLIE. How fast can you get to Deena's?'

Callie finally got a grip. She wiped her eyes, and said, in a manner that would appear cold if she didn't know they had a job to do, 'I can get there . . . I . . . Once I'm out of here, ten minutes.'

'Good,' Shirley said. 'Go.'

'I can wait for you,' Callie offered.

'No,' Shirley said, shaking her head. 'I'll only slow you down. Get there as fast as you can, and protect those children with your life.'

Callie nodded through her tears. 'What are you going to do?'

Shirley sniffed harshly and said through gritted teeth. 'I'll be right behind you. But first I'm going to go and find my son.'

03.12

Chester-Le-Street
Saturday 20 February 2021
5.50 p.m.

The hospital radio was empty. Shirley slammed through the door, ready to confront Gabe. But there was nothing, no one. The studio doors stood open, and a pile of CDs had been knocked over, but apart from that there was no sign that anyone had ever intruded at all.

'Shit,' Shirley shouted loudly, almost hoping Gabe would hear it. Where the hell was he? There was no way he could have anything to do with this, was there? He had solid alibis for the last two murders, Frank Peterson and Marsha Thompson, he was cleared. But if he could tell the future, could he fake it too? Was he going to make sure his niece and nephew died?

No, she couldn't bring herself to believe that. The pain in Gabe's voice when he said it over the radio, that was real. Unless it wasn't only pain for his niece and nephew's death, but pain that he would have to kill them.

Shirley got her phone out, almost dropping it when

405

her hands started shaking. She dialled DI Fletchinder's number as quickly as she could.

'Hello?' Fletchinder said.

And Shirley told him as quickly and concisely as possible what was happening. 'Gabe is gone, I don't know where,' she finished. 'My grandchildren are in danger. We don't have much time. Callie's gone over there.'

'What?'

'There's been another broadcast. You said you released Colm?'

'No,' Fletchinder said, 'the paperwork hasn't come through. And we found a loophole to keep him for a few more days.'

'So if it was Colm or Enigma . . .'

'You said Callie's already gone?'

'Yes,' Shirley said.

'OK, I'll come and pick you up. We'll go over to Deena's and lock those children down. Don't worry. They are *not* going to die today. Whether it's Gabe or someone else, I promise you, they are NOT going to die. Get outside, I'll be five minutes.'

'Thank you, DI Fletchinder.'

'Please, Fletch.'

Shirley got outside the hospital in record time. Her entire body was screaming at her to slow down, take a break, but she couldn't. At one point, she got a familiar and horrifying feeling – a pulsing near her heart. She pushed the feeling away, she didn't have time for a heart attack. She didn't have time to die.

Fletchinder pulled up fast next to her, and without

being invited, she got in. The only thing she said to Fletchinder was Deena's address. And they were both silent as Fletchinder drove to the alleyway behind Front Street.

As they pulled up to Deena's house in her quiet cul-de-sac, it was almost possible to believe that it was a normal day. There was a man wheeling a bin outside his house. Two boys were kicking a football about, as their mum was trying to get them in. A woman was taking shopping bags out of her car boot. Life was slow and quiet.

Fletchinder parked behind Tom's van and Shirley got out before the car had even totally stopped. She quickly hobbled up the garden path and hammered on the front door.

A few seconds later, Tom opened the door, in his work clothes and tool belt. 'Hey, Shirl pet, you all right?'

'Tom,' Shirley said, 'is everything OK?'

Tom looked confused. 'Aye, it's all good. Who's this?'

Shirley didn't understand, until she remembered DI Fletchinder. He came up next to her and stuck out his hand. 'Hello, my name is Detective Inspector Fred Fletchinder. Please call me Fletch.'

Tom shook his hand, with raised eyebrows. 'A Detective Inspec'or?'

'Yes,' said Shirley, with absolutely no time to explain. 'Is Deena in?'

'Aye,' Tom said, pointing behind him. 'She's in the ki'chen.'

Shirley passed him without another word, as Deena poked her head out of the kitchen door. 'Mum?'

'Where are the kids?' Shirley asked, looking around the house, in the kitchen past Deena and then in the garden, through the kitchen window. They were nowhere to be seen. A splinter of worry ran through her, before she remembered that Callie was here and everything was going to be fine. But where was Callie? She hadn't seen her car outside.

Deena wiped her forehead with the heel of her wrist. 'Oh, the kids. Callie's been a godsend. She just took them out for ice cream down at that new place. What was it called – Creamy Creamy Ice Cream. They were really excited.'

Shirley breathed out. They were safe. They were with Callie. It was all right. It was, what . . . She looked at her watch . . . it was 6.15. Callie had them, and there was no way they could get to Chester Baths and in danger in forty-five minutes. Gabe's future was not going to come true.

But something was still gnawing at her. Why would Callie take them out of the house? Why would she take them closer to the Baths? Surely she would wait for Shirley, wait for Fletchinder, who she must have known Shirley would call.

Unless . . .

'Mum,' Deena said, 'what is it?'

Fletchinder was checking upstairs, Tom talking to him already like he was an old friend. Fletchinder came back down and made his way into the kitchen, but Shirley hardly noticed. She wasn't here, in this room. She was in her head, refuting.

No. No. That was fucking stupid. No. No. She was seeing shadows everywhere. She was second-guessing everything – everyone. No, that just wasn't . . .

But the more she thought about it, the more the pieces fit together. And a horrible, horrible puzzle took shape. She finally understood what had been happening the last few weeks. She felt disgusted, mortified and deeply, deeply sad.

Because who could have killed all three people exactly as Gabe had described. To justify Gabe's wild delusion.

Why hadn't she seen it before? It was right there.

The one person who would do anything for Gabe. Even make him believe he could see the future.

'We have to get to Chester Baths RIGHT NOW.'

Fletchinder looked confused. 'Wait, why?'

Shirley looked up at him, her eyes streaming with tears, not even believing what she was going to say.

'Callie's going to hurt the children.'

03.13

DI Fletchinder drove through the town well over the national speed limit, taking every turn with the abrupt skill of a race car driver. Shirley held her breath the entire way, and it wasn't even because of the driving. Deena was in the back seat sobbing – she didn't understand any of this, and she wasn't listening. She wouldn't have wanted to hear what Shirley was saying anyway.

'It's Callie. It's always been Callie,' Shirley was saying, as Fletchinder swerved tightly onto the road that went away from the town centre and snaked up to the Baths. 'She wasn't with me when Frank Peterson died, and she was the only one there when Marsha Thompson died. You haven't found evidence of anyone else being there because no one was. She must have sliced her own forehead open. And now she's going after Maisie and Kenneth, because she thinks she has to justify Gabe. When we were listening to the news broadcast, listening to Gabe, she said "Why the children?" or "Why does it

410

have to be them?" or something like that. And she was crying. I thought it was because she was worried for them, but it was because she knew what she had to do. I should have seen it, I could have stopped her before she took them.'

'Don't do that,' Fletchinder said, 'don't blame yourself. I was the officer, and if what you're saying is true, I didn't spot any of this either . . . Ah shit.'

Shirley looked up to see that the Leisure Centre had been completely cordoned off with high metal fences. What Gabe had been reporting all this time was true – the Leisure Centre was getting ready to be demolished. Was he hinting at this all along?

'Hold on,' Fletchinder said.

They were speeding up to the fences, across the road, and Shirley realised a little too late that Fletchinder wasn't going to stop. She clutched the door as the car crashed into the fence and it gave way. The car flew through the air as it was propelled by the fence, and slammed back down.

Shirley's heart hurt. The beating was getting faster. But she couldn't think about that now.

The Leisure Centre was up ahead, abandoned, on a slight hill. Fletchinder swerved into the car park. There was a digger parked there, and a tractor-like machine. Nothing else. The place looked empty. Except Shirley knew it wasn't.

She looked at her watch as the car screeched to a halt – 6.40.

'OK,' Fletchinder said, looking inside. Shirley looked

411

too – there was no door, just an opening to the derelict, half-destroyed building. 'You should both stay in the car.'

'That's not going to happen,' Shirley said, and Deena spoke up for the first time too.

'I need to go in there and get my babies!' Deena shrieked.

Fletchinder sighed. 'Yeah, I was expecting that. OK, but you both have to stay back.'

Shirley agreed, although she wasn't going to do any such thing. She followed Fletchinder as he got out of the car. She held Deena's door open, as she got out slowly. She would have preferred Deena to stay in the car – hell, she would have preferred Deena to stay home – but she had a right to be here. Shirley didn't know how much use she was going to be, if any at all, but she would stick with her.

As Fletchinder walked towards the place where the entrance used to be, he reached into his waistband and brought out a pistol. Shirley had never seen a gun before, and very much thought she would die without ever seeing one, but it stood to reason Fletchinder had one. And it stood to reason this situation was adequate need for one.

Deena looked up and saw the gun, and gave out a fresh wail, and Fletchinder stepped back towards them, angrily. 'She has to be quiet, or she can't come in. Her children's lives depend on it.'

Shirley put an arm around Deena, and her daughter caught her breath, quietened down and nodded. There was an unspoken agreement that she wouldn't make another sound.

Fletchinder made his way towards the entrance, gun at his side, and Shirley and Deena followed behind. They were fast but quiet – trying to cover as much ground as possible without raising a peep.

They all went inside the building – the hole where the doors used to be opening in on a dilapidated reception area. Shirley remembered bringing Gabe and Deena here for swimming lessons, and Deena took Maisie and Kenneth in turn. They would know where they were going, they would be confused and scared. God only knew what was happening. She just hoped it wasn't too late.

She looked at her watch. It was 6.43 p.m.

If there was one thing she knew, it was that Callie would follow the instructions to a T, to make it look like Gabe could tell the future. The children were safe for now – they just had to find them, quick.

Fletchinder turned on a torch, as the natural light failed to come in. It was like walking through a building that had been decimated by an earthquake. There was rubble and work equipment everywhere. Walls were half-knocked down, floors had patches in them that showed whatever was beneath, wind whipped through the place from somewhere, almost trying to push the intruders out. Shirley shivered as one gust threatened to knock her back as she got out her phone and turned on the torch.

They were in the vast expanse behind the reception.

413

There were two options of where to go next, but both led to the same place. The changing rooms all went to the pools – the kiddie pool and the adult pool.

They all rushed through the women's changing rooms – a depressing collection of open lockers, wooden benches and changing quarters. It was an area that no longer served its purpose – a black hole of a thing that just stood in their way.

As the odd trio got to the showers, they started to hear noises. Voices. Two of them. One male. One female. Neither of them children.

They got to the pool area. Fletchinder looked around the corner and so did Shirley, into the adult pool area, where the voices were coming from. The large windows in the pool room doused everything in a faint reflected street light.

The female voice was Callie, there was no doubt about it. 'Don't you see, don't you understand??'

It was so echoey that Shirley couldn't make out who the male was. Until she heard the voice stutter on a word.

Gabe.

'Please just . . . don't . . . don't . . . you don't have to.'

'It's Gabe,' Shirley hissed.

Fletchinder looked around to the ladies. 'Is there any way to get closer?'

Deena perked up. 'There's a seating area this way.' She pointed down a little corridor that ran parallel to the pool. 'We can get closer to them, without them seeing.'

414

Fletchinder nodded and led the way. They all inched closer as Callie and Gabe talked.

'I don't understand,' Callie was saying, her voice echoing around the massive room. 'You knew this was going to happen. You foresaw it. I'm only here to make sure that happens. I'm a casual observer too.'

'You . . . you're . . . not . . . you're causing this. Pleats . . . please, Callie.'

They reached the seating area as quickly as possible, without alerting Callie or Gabe. Shirley's heart was pounding, and it had nothing to do with the fact she'd recently had a heart attack. The children were in danger, and now Gabe was too.

'How can you not understand?' Callie said. 'How can you have these visions and not understand what they are? This isn't just the future, it's the final future. This has to happen, Gabe. And you are special, you are the chosen one. You are the prophet − our Nostradamus.'

Callie sounded insane, and what was even scarier was the fact that she had hidden it so well. Gabe's predictions had changed her, Gabe coming back from the dead had broken her, her dedication to Gabriel Steadman was just too great.

Shirley ignored Fletchinder and peeked around the corner. They were so close to them. Gabe was standing with his back to her, looking at Callie, who was standing with her hands around the mouths of the children. Maisie and Kenneth were silently weeping. And it was easy to see why − Callie was holding them next to the deep end of the drained pool, over the edge was an three-metre drop. If Callie took one small step back-wards, they would all free fall down and slam into the ceramic tiles below.

There would be no saving them.

'Callie . . . please . . .' Gabe was saying, trying to inch closer. ' . . .Please, you don't . . . we can change it . . . we can change it . . . we can change it together . . . please . . . please . . .' He was openly weeping, and Callie was too.

'No, Gabe,' Callie said, the children remaining still at her hip, 'you may not understand the importance of your visions, but I do. I don't want to do this, do you honestly think I do? I'm not a child killer. But I need to stand by you, and your power. That's why I've been there from the start. I was your first listener, even before your mother. That's why I distracted Sebastian Starith and made him fall, that's why I walked out in front of the milk truck and made it crash, that was why I stran-gled Frank Peterson and cut Marsha Thompson's throat. I even got rid of Arnie Enigma because he was trying to meddle with you – the one true prophet. I am the con-duit to your visions, Gabe. I am the one to carry them out. And these children have to die, here and now.'

Deena let out a small squeak behind Shirley, but the room was so vast, it didn't carry anywhere near the demonic woman in front of them all. It was Callie all along – none of it was real, none of it. Gabe didn't have any powers – never had. He had had some odd dreams about real people that had come true thanks to a demented, fanatical woman.

Gabe was making a sound, digesting what he'd just heard. This was going to break him. 'I'm . . . I'm not . . . I can't see . . . the future.'

Callie shifted slightly, her grip on the children softening. 'No, Gabe, you're still not understanding. You can. You're special, Gabe. You always have been. You've always been special. Special to your mother, special to the world — special to me. Everyone deserves to know how special you are. And they will. With you and me together, we will show them how special you are.'

'I . . . I . . .' Gabe seemed to be actually considering it, and then, clearly and in his old voice, 'No. I'm not special. And my niece and nephew will not die today.' He quickly rushed at Callie, and Shirley gripped the side of the wall, to keep from crying out.

What happened next happened so fast, but also so slowly, that she saw everything even though it was over in a blink. Callie saw Gabe coming, understood he was going to try to stop her, so she retaliated instinctively. She shifted the children over to one hand and reached back, behind her, with her other hand. What she brought out turned Shirley's stomach, as it glinted in the moonlight.

A large kitchen knife.

Gabe was rushing at her so fast, he wasn't able to stop. Callie's face looked as shocked and sad as Shirley felt when Gabe got to her. She would replay the entire scene in her mind over and over again for the rest of her life.

Callie's knife slipped into Gabe.

And that was that.

03.14

'Nooo!' screamed Shirley and stepped out from behind the seating. She rushed to Gabe as he shrieked and staggered back, dropping to the floor. Shirley caught him as he fell.

'Let the children go!' Fletchinder shouted, his gun raised, as he stepped out too. He slowly advanced until he was standing over Shirley. Deena stayed back, looking inconsolable.

'Oh,' Callie said, 'this wasn't foreseen.'

'You've killed him!' Shirley shouted at Callie, her voice harsh and thunderous.

Gabe was spluttering, his mouth spewing blood. 'Mum, Mum.'

'I'm here,' Shirley whispered to him, 'I'm here, you're going to be OK.'

'I don't think so,' Gabe said, his mouth becoming an explosion of blood and mucus. Shirley was covered in her son's blood. And slowly, Gabe's eyes started to close.

'No, no, no, no,' Shirley wailed.

But it was too much. His eyes closed. And they weren't going to open again. He was gone.

Shirley erupted in tears, cradling her son. She had lost him again. And it was all her fault. She looked around at Callie, her eyes as dead as Gabe's. And she lay her son on the floor – his stomach still steadily spurting blood. 'You killed him,' she said flatly. 'Was that part of your future? Was that foreseen?'

'No,' Callie said. For the first time she seemed to be doubting herself. 'He's not dead. He can't be.' She still had the knife in her hand, waving it in front of the children's faces. 'He is the prophet. He is the one who will tell us . . . tell me . . . tell me what to do.'

'Put the knife down,' Fletchinder instructed.

Both women ignored him.

'So what do you do, Callie? What do you do now? Your prophet is dead. You killed him.'

'I . . .' Callie said, 'I don't . . . I don't know.'

'You're about to kill two beautiful children, Callie. And it doesn't sound like you're sure why you're doing it. There's no reason to do it anymore,' Shirley said. 'So don't.'

Callie looked around at the whole scene. 'I . . .' And she trailed off, never to finish that thought.

'There's only one person here that can see the future right now, Callie, and it's you,' Shirley continued, putting her hands up in surrender. 'You are the only one who has the power to know how this is going to go. You have the power to do the right thing.'

Callie frowned, and Shirley thought she had said something wrong. That Callie would take a step back and Deena's children would be gone. And Shirley would never forgive herself. But instead, Callie nodded, and then looked upwards. 'I see it. I see the future. The future is filled with . . . love.' Callie looked back at her and smiled, a warm and genuine smile.

She let the kids go.

Shirley quickly beckoned them over, and Maisie and Kenneth ran into her arms, wailing. She hugged them tight, so hard they could burst. She pointed behind her and the children looked, their faces lighting up when they saw their mother. They ran to her and Shirley heard the family reuniting behind her, happy. Unfortunately, she couldn't join them – not yet, maybe not ever.

Her son was dead, her greatest friend, at least recently, had killed him.

'Put the knife down, and slowly come over to me with your hands up,' said Fletchinder.

Callie looked at him, like he was of no consequence to her – he wasn't even in her world. She took a tiny step backwards. 'I see the future. But I'm not there.' Shirley couldn't stop her. She wouldn't have been able to. She locked eyes with Shirley and shrugged. 'Wasn't meant to be.' Callie started to fall backwards, and Fletchinder rushed to her, barely grasping her before she fell into the pool. 'Nooo,' Callie screamed, as Fletchinder pulled her up.

Shirley screamed again, the emotions overwhelming her. Deena grasped her and hugged her as she cried more than she'd ever cried before. She could stay in her daughter's arms forever, but Gabe's body was on the floor, alone, so she pushed her away. And she held her son. She held him as Deena and the children left, as Fletchinder called the scene in and police officers flooded the vast hall. She held him until the paramedics came and put Gabe on a stretcher. She stayed at his side as he was wheeled out of the ruins. Walking out in to an uncertain future.

Epilogue

Chester-Le-Street
Monday 15 March 2021
6.55 p.m.

'Eeee, pet, nice to see ah familiar face. And ooh, ain't you a sight faa soore eyes?' old Harold said, as Shirley walked up to his bed with her badge and her clipboard. He was still here – or maybe he had left and come back. One thing was for certain though, he was in exactly the same place as before, with the same arm elevated in a sling. 'Seems you've been a bit busy since we last met.'

Shirley smiled. 'So have you, it looks like.'

'Ah,' he said, looking at his arm, 'this thing breaks more than a Maccy's ice cream machine. I'm starting to think there may be sommat wrong with it. Meebee I ought to trade it in for a new one.'

'Good luck with that,' Shirley laughed, resting on her cane. She'd become more comfortable remembering to use it, and even more comfortable with not caring what anyone else thought about it. 'Can I interest you in a request today, Harold?'

'Hmmm . . .' Harold pretended to muse. He would probably have been comically scratching his chin if his arm wasn't stuck in a sling. 'Wey a bit o' Bowie, o' course. Giss a the one 'bout the spacemen.' His memory also wasn't the best. But Shirley couldn't really hold that against him — neither was hers. 'How's it go agen?'

Shirley felt an intense feeling of déjà vu as she wrote down 'A Space Oddity'. 'Done. And who's it to?'

'Wey you of course,' Harold said, predictably.

And Shirley laughed. 'I'll make it out to your wife, how about that?'

'Aye I guess you better had,' Harold said. 'It true you're getting ya owwn show on Metro? Leavin' all of us here in tha dust?'

'No, that's a filthy rumour,' Shirley replied, although she had been approached. She had turned it down of course. She wasn't in this to be a star, this wasn't an ego trip like it was for Ken Vox. She just liked talking to people, brightening up their day, and that was what she got here. When she'd turned them down, she'd felt a sudden rush of energy — she was doing what she was supposed to do, being where she was supposed to be. That feeling, right there, maybe that's what Gabe was chasing — the warmth and comfort of knowing everything was on the right path.

'Well, I'm glad ya still ganna be coming round,' Harold said.

'You're planning on continuing to break your arm?' Shirley asked, putting her requests clipboard under her arm. This was the last stop.

423

'If it means we keep meeting like this, aye,' smiled Harold.

Shirley sighed but smiled as she said her goodbyes.

Before she left the ward, she asked the nurses whether they wanted anything dedicated to them. They talked amongst themselves for a moment, before one nurse came forward and said 'I Want To Break Free' by Queen. They all sniggered and Shirley dutifully laughed, noting it down.

Some things never changed. And she found some solace in that. It was like nothing had ever happened. And that was how things should be.

The ward as a whole had some good choices. And it was shaping up to be a good show. She sanitised her hands and left, going down the corridor. She paused in front of the lifts, her finger halfway to the button. The stairs crossed her mind, but she denied them. She pushed the button.

Back in the studio, she had to go into the record room to find one of the older patient's requests. She found it and her eyes fell on the old radio still pulled out from the rest of the equipment pile in the corner. It looked a little sad just sitting there and Shirley had the compulsion to take it out, hook it up to Studio Two's deck and check 66.40 AM. But she didn't. Because she'd already done that – every single night she had come here since the swimming pool night. Of course she never heard anything on 66.40 AM – Mallet AM was shut down forever, closed for business. But something about the static on that frequency was familiar, homely. It made her feel a little closer to her son. Obviously that was just her, and she had to work at stopping – which is why she didn't take out the radio, even when she finished her request gathering and had time for a cup of tea in the foyer, having nothing to do but listen to Ken Vox regaling his audience with a tale of when he walked into a bar and there was actually a priest, a vicar and a rabbi there.

When he was done with the depressingly serious story, she went into the studio, clicked the recording off and started the show. 'Hello everyone out there, this is Shirley Steadman, and here we are with the requests show this beautiful Monday, the fifteenth of March.' The actual date, not tomorrow's date or yesterday's date. Today. Living in the now.

The show went well, and when Shirley was done, she cued up all the recordings for the next twenty-three hours. Ken Vox's shows were due to run all day and all night, God bless the listeners. She shut down the computer monitor, turned off the lights in the studios, and stood in the foyer. She breathed in and out. And she went into the cupboard – she found the old record player in the equipment pile and pulled out the one record that she always passed every night at the radio.

With the record under her arm and the record player in her hands, she put on her coat, got her bag and left the radio studio, walking down the corridors going to Ward 11. As she walked, she felt the weight of everything that had happened – that she allowed herself to forget while she was focused on her volunteer job. So much was different now, but, like the nurses' constant requesting, so much stayed the same. Life went on, with nary a blip. Mallet AM and Gabe were nothing to the future, the real future.

The timelines realigned themselves, and everything was OK.

Seb Starith had finally got his new sign up over his bakery. When the news came out about Mallet AM and Starith's involvement, he decided to make a show of putting the sign up. He had a little gaggle of people outside and he was offering free samples of his Stollen Slices. When he started to ascend the ladder, he played a drumroll over loudspeaker, and when he finally secured the sign above his store, the crowd cheered and whooped.

Roy Farrow was the talk of the town when *The Advertiser* ran a front-page story about him receiving a new state-of-the-art milk truck to replace the one he crashed. Compared to the old model, it looked like the car from *Knight Rider* and if Farrow was to be believed, it had an automated voice to match. 'This thing has motion sensors, a reverse camera and it beeps if it looks like I'm gonna hit summat!' Farrow could be heard saying all over town. Shirley was happy for him, even though she did question the lesson learnt when he got rewarded for almost causing an accident.

Shirley's home life was pretty much the same as it always had been, like it was before Gabe. The bungalow was as quiet as ever with her just pottering around, cleaning, doing laundry, watching TV and doing embroidery, with the occasional visits from Deena, Tom and the children. Deena had conceded that she needed to take a step back from constantly hounding her mother, if said mother promised to call her if something was wrong. Shirley gladly agreed.

Gabe's room had remained untouched, with the boxes from the attic staying unpacked. It didn't feel right for her to unpack them without him. Any secrets there were within those boxes were Gabe's secrets and his alone. Sometimes she went into the guest room and just sat on the bed, and grew misty-eyed. She never outright cried.

Moggins and Big Mac weren't getting on in the slightest. Moggins still hadn't forgiven Shirley entirely for bringing another cat home, but when she had seen the fostering advertisement on Facebook, she had taken responsibility for Big Mac straight away, as if she owed it to Frank Peterson, and maybe she did. Moggins tended to hang around upstairs and in the living room, arching his back and hissing whenever Big Mac decided to try his luck at socialising. It didn't happen often however. Big Mac laid claim to the kitchen, constantly wanting to get inside, most likely to get a cold beer. He'd have to go cold turkey though as Big Mac had just got his one-month chip from feline AA.

Marsha Thompson's funeral was in a week's time, delayed because of the investigation. Shirley had been asked to say a few words, seeing as she was the new local celebrity, and the others from the embroidery group couldn't summon up enough nice words about her. Shirley accepted and had already written a few things and had decided on a short Robert Frost poem to read out. It wouldn't blow anyone's mind, but it didn't need to. They were saying goodbye to Marsha Thompson yes, but her legacy would loom large for years to come. And Shirley guessed, if the old battleaxe had had to choose a way to go out, being part of a fantastical future-past murder conspiracy would probably have been her first choice.

Deena had finally recovered from the scare she had had with Callie and the kids. She was afraid of the toll that Callie's trial would have on her mother, and had fallen back into her loving but daughterly ways. Deena had struggled for a long time with the fact that she had shared so much with Callie. That she had let Callie into her home, hundreds of times. She had let Callie play with the kids. She had let Callie share parts of her life. Shirley didn't know how to explain to her daughter, but she didn't blame Deena in the slightest, and what was more she didn't blame Callie. In her mind, Callie hadn't always been a bad person. She definitely hadn't been when she knew the young woman before – when she was Gabe's girlfriend and life had been more simple. And she didn't think Callie was wholly bad at the end either. Even when she was holding Maisie and Kenneth over the abyss, threatening to let go. She was just in love, genuinely and resolutely – a person who would move heaven and Earth for Shirley's son. Gabe had always had that effect on her.

Maisie and Kenneth were enduring the tyranny of a freshly paranoid and justified mother. They could barely be out of Deena's sight for ten seconds before she started worrying. In the early days after the incident, they all came round for a Sunday lunch, and Maisie and Kenneth immediately started their usual racing around. Deena had got incredibly distraught when Kenneth was on a particularly long lap around the bungalow, and became emotional when he didn't appear for a minute or two. The children didn't know what was going on – would probably never understand exactly what happened until they were older. Even Maisie, who was old enough to comprehend it, was already showing signs that her mind was healing around the event, trying to cover it up. Tom was trying to fight their corner against Deena's tyranny – allowing them pretty much the same level of freedom as ever, when he was allowed to decide. Shirley just watched the family from afar, not butting in with an opinion or recommendation, mainly because she didn't have one, couldn't possibly begin to unravel the complex and difficult situation the two parents must be in. So she didn't blame Deena or Tom or the kids. They were just trying their best, and they would just have to try to get by until time began to heal them.

Callie's crimes were all laid out for Shirley – DI Fletchinder came to the bungalow to tell her about everything that had actually been going on. It made her feel sick to her stomach. She re-enacted Gabe's truth, convinced herself she was helping him, helping her one true love. To Callie, what she was doing was noble. She'd brainwashed herself into thinking that Gabe needed to be protected, he needed to be right. Shirley supposed that that was partly her fault – Gabe needed a win because he hadn't got one at home.

Shirley finally got to Ward 11. With the help of her new cane, it was much easier navigating the glossy clean corridors. When she was inside, she put down the record player and the record, sanitised her hands and picked her quarry up again.

The nurses said hello as she passed the nurses' station. They always wanted to talk – talk to the woman of the moment, the soothsayer's mam, but she never did unless she was scheduled to do requests. They always wanted the same old stuff, really just wanting to chat to her. They skirted around the subject of Callie, someone that they must have known, if only in passing. No, they really wanted to hear all the juicy details – the death and the blood, the precognition and the fantasy, the mother and the son. If she was in a good mood, she would humour them – telling them grand tales like a seasoned storyteller. For she had now become part of the gossip that was peddled around the town – so she thought she may as well tell it herself.

There was one part of the story she would never tell though. Gabe – lying there, with so much blood gushing from him, it seemed endless. She always had nightmares of that moment and probably always would; every time, the panicked look in his eyes getting more so, the amount of blood becoming an ocean. She would wake up in her cold, dead bungalow and cry until sun-up. She had to keep reminding herself that, in reality, the actual moment was not some horrific grindhouse film, it was actually rather poignant. And that final look he gave his mother and those final words he said to her? They were hers, and hers alone. And that was what got her through the sleepless nights and the therapy sessions and the constant questions. That look, and those words.

There was something she never finished the story without though. The fact that Gabe was the hero in the end. The fact that Gabe was cut down saving the lives of his niece and nephew – a valiant and noble act that was steeped in the desire to make up for everything that had happened. Shirley couldn't explain to everyone just what this meant – she didn't have the words or the knowledge to properly explain it, but she tried the best she could.

When Gabe had done what he did, he still believed that he could see the future. He believed that what he saw was what was going to come to pass, and by extension, would come to pass. When he decided to try to save his niece and nephew, he was going against what was written, what was seen. In his mind, Gabe was going up against time itself. And yes, there was no truth to it, and yes, having some distance from the event, it was almost a silly notion, but the fact that he believed it and was willing to fracture time itself meant the world to Shirley. Science fiction, yes – and Shirley always emphasised the fiction part in her stories – but it was what he believed. In the books and TV shows Gabe had consumed so voraciously as a child, changing time meant he could possibly break the entire universe. All for the life of his family.

She got to the room she wanted without even thinking. She had spent hours every day here for over a month now, and wasn't going to stop any time soon.

Why would she? Deena tried to tell her it was unhealthy, but by the time she had laid out her argument, even her daughter would see the heart of it. So she would be quiet and try to change the subject – Deena was not coping with it well, but thankfully would concede that this was Shirley's way.

She knocked on the door, knowing that no one would answer. Shirley went into the room. It was dark, and dingy – like there was no life here. Except there was. There was a steady beeping, and some hope.

And there was a figure in the corner of the room. A man standing there paused in mid-conversation. It was Colm – freshly shaven but still weary and tired. He also looked a little thinner. He smiled at Shirley with an old soul. 'Hey, Mrs S.'

Shirley smiled too. 'Hey, Colm.'

'I was just thinking about going. You can take over.' Colm started out of the room.

'Wait . . . you can stay,' Shirley said.

'No, Mrs S. It's fine. I just had a question to ask that's all. Thought I might find you here.'

'Any way I can help,' Shirley replied. It was really the least she could do.

'You mentioned that Gabe said I was dead. He said he knew the date and time that I supposedly died. Do you remember when that was?'

Shirley searched her mind and, for some reason, realised she could indeed remember. Maybe because it was so specific not to be important. 'I think he said October the fifteenth, 10.20 a.m.'

Colm nodded. He knew that was what she was going to say. 'That was the exact date and time of my hospital appointment. When I found out.'

'Found what?' Shirley whispered.

'Lung cancer. Inoperable,' he said it like he'd come to terms with it. Like the world had been forgiven. 'I'm living on borrowed time. It's spread, you see. Procedures'd be pointless. I barely heard anything that doctor said when he told me. And I got out that office, and remember going to meself "I'm dead now. The rest is just overtime." And don't go crying over it. That isn't what's important here. What is, is how do you suppose Gabe knew that?'

Colm had . . . Wait – how *did* Gabe know that?

'Because, Mrs S, I've been thinking . . . What if all this . . .everything that happened . . .what if all this happened exactly as he saw it? What if he knew about Callie, and the deaths, and the damn pool? What if he can see . . .?'

'I guess we'll have to ask him when he wakes up,' Shirley interrupted. She knew the roads Colm's mind was taking him down, she'd been there herself. She didn't want to revisit them.

Colm looked like he had more to say, but merely smiled at this, took his coat from a chair and turned to leave, but not before saying, 'Yeah. When he wakes up.'

Shirley watched the closed door for a long time, mirrored only by the beeps and sounds of machines. And then cried a little.

When she was done, she took the record out of its

sleeve – Chutney and the Boys still rocking out on top of the Sphinx. She plugged in the record player and put it on the dresser by the window, putting the record on top like a seasoned veteran. She turned it on and placed the arm over it. The crackling silence. And then 'Half-Past Tomorrow' began, and she finally let herself look to the bed.

Gabe was lying there, bundled up, a mass of protruding tubes. He hadn't been dead. But he almost was. The doctors put him in a coma, said he may never wake up again. He'd lost so much blood, and his brain had already endured so much trauma. He was responding to medication and his body was fighting the infection from his leg. Some good news at least.

But whatever happened, Shirley would be here by his side. Now and forever.

She sat down in the chair beside his bed, and held his warm but lifeless hand.

And she wished for tomorrow. With all her heart.

Acknowledgements

Thank you to my partner, Aimy, my two dogs, Winnie and Roo, my cat, Toony, and a whole plethora of small animals. I love you all for providing constant support to me, and my writing. Roo actually loves my books so much that he ate my only German copy of *Guess Who* . . . which had a really cool cover and I cherished . . .

To my agent, Hannah Sheppard, my editor, Francesca Pathak, and the teams at Orion and DHH Literary Agency. I am privileged to have an amazing team behind me and my ideas. I always feel like I have somewhere to turn if I have an issue, and it's been really fantastic for a still relatively new writer like myself.

To my alpha and beta readers, Daniel Stubbings and Sarah McGeorge. Dan was the first person to read *HPT* and always tells it like it is, so when he said it wasn't bad I was thrilled. And Sarah McGeorge was one of the last to read, and particularly helped with the medical details.

To the other members of the Northern Crime Syndicate — Trevor Wood (whose help with the Navy section was invaluable), Robert Parker, Robert Scragg, Judith O'Reilly, Fiona Erskine and Adam Peacock. It's great to have a support network of writers, as well as having loads of fun in online panels. 2020 would have been very lonely without these guys.

And lastly, as always, to the #SauvLife crew – Jenny Lewin, Lizzie Curle and Francesca Dorricott. Love you guys.

Credits

Chris McGeorge and Orion Fiction would like to thank everyone at Orion who worked on the publication of *Half-Past Tomorrow* in the UK.

Editorial
Francesca Pathak
Lucy Frederick

Copy editor
Jade Craddock

Proof reader
Linda Joyce

Audio
Paul Stark
Amber Bates

Design
Debbie Holmes
Joanna Ridley
Nick May

Editorial Management
Charlie Panayiotou
Jane Hughes
Alice Davis

Operations
Jo Jacobs
Sharon Willis
Lisa Pryde
Lucy Brem

Finance
Jasdip Nandra
Afeera Ahmed
Elizabeth Beaumont
Sue Baker

Contracts
Anne Goddard
Jake Alderson

Production
Ruth Sharvell

Marketing
Tanjiah Islam

Publicity
Alainna Hadjigeorgiou

Rights
Susan Howe
Krystyna Kujawinska
Jessica Purdue
Louise Henderson

Sales
Jennifer Wilson
Esther Waters
Victoria Laws
Frances Doyle
Georgina Cutler

If you loved *Half-Past Tomorrow*, don't miss
Chris McGeorge's epic locked-room mystery:

ONE ROOM. FIVE SUSPECTS.
THREE HOURS TO FIND A KILLER.

*'An inventive, entertaining locked room mystery that kept
me utterly hooked'*
ADAM HAMDY

'An ingenious twisty mystery'
CLAIRE McGOWAN

Then jump into this enthralling,
fiendishly clever puzzle…

Six people went in.
Only one came out . . .

FROM THE
AUTHOR OF
GUESS
WHO

NOW
YOU
SEE ME

CHRIS McGEORGE

**SIX PEOPLE WENT IN.
ONLY ONE CAME OUT . . .**

Or *Inside Out* – a claustrophobic locked-room
thriller like no other…

SHE WAS SENT DOWN . . .

SHE WAS SET UP . . .

BUT THAT WAS ONLY THE BEGINNING.

*How do you find a murderer in the place
where everyone is one?*